. . . e turn the page
. . . ore reviews . . .

D1016860

"A REAL PAGE-TURNER . . .

Perry showed me something new and wonderful with this book. Not content to write another garden variety thriller, he has produced a masterpiece that goes far beyond the 'novel of suspense' designation on its cover. All an awestruck reader can do is sit back and wait to see what he comes up with next."
—*Wichita Eagle*

"Thomas Perry has fashioned a unique and fascinating heroine for this, his sixth novel. . . . Original and intriguing . . . There's plenty of thrills and taut suspense. . . . [A] compelling adventure-thriller with a fiercely savvy heroine equally capable amid dark city streets or a primordial forest."
—*Blade–Citizen Preview*

"Laced with icy humor, VANISHING ACT offers a rich look into the mores and philosophy of the Seneca Nation—and beats Tony Hillerman at his own game."
—*The Hartford Courant*

"With a strong heroine and . . . [an] engaging story line, VANISHING ACT deserves to be read."
—*South Bend Tribune*

"Gratifying . . . Jane knows an impressive amount about a lot of things and is entertainingly resourceful."
—*The New York Times*

"RARE AND WONDERFUL . . .

Perry outdoes himself. . . . Jane Whitefield is the most exciting and welcome female character to appear in a long time. There is not a more completely realized woman protagonist in all of today's crime fiction. . . . VANISHING ACT has the intelligent and thoughtfully developed exploration of being and becoming, using ancestry and survival as the vehicle."
—*Mostly Murder*

"Edgar winner Thomas Perry is a character-driven writer. . . . Perry knows New York State well, and his descriptions resonate with that knowledge. . . . Moreover, his blending of the natural and the spirit worlds within the mind of his unusual heroine make VANISHING ACT a memorable novel."
—*Nashville Book Page*

"The most intriguing aspect is the lead character, Jane. She is an original and truly fascinating because the author weaves her mixed heritage so well, making her a woman of character and highly distinctive. This novel is not just a character study . . . [it] moves swiftly along, taking the reader with it."
—*The Ellenville Press*

"A unique novel of suspense and thrills . . . This is a novel of love, betrayal, mystery, and vengeance. . . . Perry's historical background is fascinating, his characters are originals, his dialogue is sharp; and VANISHING ACT is an engrossing thriller."
—*New Smyrna Beach Observer*

"OUTSTANDING . . .

[VANISHING ACT] is so good that the clichés that normally appear in reviews—and on book covers—can't do it justice. It's that good because Perry is an excellent writer. It's that good because he introduces the reader to an unusual, and highly likable, heroine who's a mix of modern womanhood and ancient Native American spirituality. Most of all, it's that good because Perry abandons all formulas and offers the reader a completely original plot."
—*Lexington Herald-Leader*

"Mystery/suspense novels have had American Indian heroes and they've had female heroines—but few of them have displayed the combination of raw courage and compassion as does Jane Whitefield, a Seneca Indian who helps hunted people 'disappear.' . . . Although many male authors have attempted to write from the female point of view, few actually succeed with the easy grace as does author Perry. . . . In Whitefield, he has crafted a sensitive, loving woman who also happens to have the courage of a Roman gladiator."

—*Mesa Tribune*

"[Thomas Perry] has demonstrated an ability to be fast-paced and clever, amusing and erudite. . . . Perry has done a lot of homework for this book, and the historical fabric is rich with tidbits of our shared past. . . . [He is] a spellbinding storyteller."
—*Winston-Salem Journal*

"A taut thriller . . . [An] unusually intriguing heroine."
—*Publishers Weekly*

By Thomas Perry:

THE BUTCHER'S BOY
METZGER'S DOG
BIG FISH
ISLAND
SLEEPING DOGS*
VANISHING ACT*
DANCE FOR THE DEAD*
SHADOW WOMAN*

*Published by Ballantine Books

Congratulations Cynthia!

VANISHING ACT

Thomas Perry

IVY BOOKS • NEW YORK

This book contains an excerpt from the hardcover edition of *Dance for the Dead* by Thomas Perry. This excerpt has been set for this edition only and may not reflect the final content of the hardcover edition.

Ivy Books
Published by Ballantine Books
Copyright © 1995 by Thomas Perry
Excerpt from *Dance for the Dead* copyright © 1995 by Thomas Perry

http://www.randomhouse.com

Library of Congress Catalog Card Number: 95-95082

ISBN 0-8041-1387-4

This edition published by arrangement with Random House, Inc.

Manufactured in the United States of America

First Ballantine Books Edition: April 1996

10

For Isabel

With love to Alix and Jo

There is nothing in which these barbarians carry their superstition to a more extravagant length, than in what regards dreams; . . . in whatever manner the dream is conceived, it is always looked upon as a thing sacred, and as the most ordinary way in which the gods make known their will to men.

For the most part, they look upon them either as a desire of the soul inspired by some genius, or an order from him; and in consequence of this principle, they hold it a religious duty to obey them; and an Indian having dreamed of having a finger cut off, had it really cut off as soon as he awoke, after having prepared himself for this important action by a feast . . .

The affair becomes still more serious, should any one take it into his head to dream that he cuts the throat of another, for he will certainly accomplish it if he can; but woe to him, in his turn, should a third person dream that he revenges the dead.

Pierre de Charlevoix,
Journal of a Voyage to North-America,
1761

Jack Killigan used the reflections in the dark windows to watch the woman walk quickly up the long concourse, look at her high heels so she could take a few extra steps while the escalator was carrying her down, and then hurry around the curve so she could step onto the conveyor. She didn't even know he was shadowing her. They always looked behind them every few seconds, but they never looked in front—didn't really look.

Here she was getting off an airplane, so how could anybody not know where she was heading now? He could have just strolled straight to the baggage-claim area and waited for her there, but this one was worth serious money, so he had decided not to be lazy about it. He was a hundred feet ahead of her on the moving walkway, so he felt confident enough to look back.

She looked like a French model—or maybe Italian—chestnut hair, tall and slender, with legs that seemed longer than they really were because the leather skirt was shorter than it should have been. A lot of times they were like this. They didn't have any idea of how to be inconspicuous. He only did rich women. Their husbands or whatever they called themselves were the only ones who had Killigan's fee. The average guy who had this kind of problem would try to take care of it himself, but not just because of the number of dollars. He would do it because he couldn't conceive of hiring somebody else to bring his woman back for him. He wouldn't want anybody to know about it. But these rich guys were brought up with it. People washed their underwear for them and emptied the wastebasket where they threw their used rubbers. A lot of times the men were older—too old to do what had to be done.

Killigan's peripheral vision caught the woman turning away from him again to look back for her imaginary pursuers. He turned his head to watch. She had to bend a little at the hips to lean over the railing and stretch her neck to see around the bunch of Wichita Chamber of Commerce types who had stopped behind her. He couldn't help noticing the skirt again. That was typical. They would run away from home dressed like they wanted to be noticed, either because they didn't own a dress that cost less than a used car or because they didn't know there was such a thing. His eyes lingered on the shiny leather stretched across her buttocks. It was a long time on the road from Los Angeles to Indiana. Once he had her in the van, anything might happen. Women sometimes considered all kinds of options if they wanted out bad enough.

As though she had somehow heard what he was thinking, her back seemed to give a shiver, and he barely managed to turn his head away from her in time.

Killigan stepped off the conveyor and headed for the row of public telephones along the wall, to give her time to get past him. She came within four or five feet of him as she passed the telephones, and he caught a scent of her perfume, a slight change that made the air taste like a spice. He was busy wondering what that stuff cost when she turned the wrong way. "Oh shit," he said into the telephone. "Coitus interruptus." He was getting all geared up for it, and she was . . . of course. He caught sight of her walking into the ladies' room.

Killigan hung the telephone on its hook and walked

to the other side of the terminal so he would be behind her when she got around to coming out.

The woman emerged after a few minutes, and he almost felt sorry for her. She had put on sunglasses and a short jacket and a long blond wig to cover the dark hair, but she was carrying the same handmade leather flight bag that matched the leather skirt. He could even detect a fresh drop or two of perfume. The only person who wouldn't recognize her was somebody who wasn't looking for her at all. Those long legs in those dark stockings: If she'd had any sense at all, that was what she would have covered.

Killigan waited while she put a good two hundred feet between them before he started toward the baggage area. He could feel the universe rolling along smoothly now, the way it was supposed to. That had just been a little bump in the pavement. She was watching for her luggage, staring down at the metal track that wound around the waiting area. It was all a question of timing now.

He saw her spot her suitcase. She watched it all the way from the moment it brushed in through the weather flaps and went around the track; then he saw her lean forward and strain to drag and bump it over the rim onto the floor. It made her seem more vulnerable and ripe to watch her balance on the toes of those high-heeled shoes and do that. There wasn't a lot of strength in those arms.

Killigan waited until she had hauled it to the door and shown the security woman her ticket with the stub stapled to it that matched the one on the suitcase. Then the door opened and she stepped out onto the sidewalk with Killigan at her elbow. At the curb she stopped and looked to the left to find a taxi, and Killigan moved in.

He flashed his identification wallet in her face as he said, "Come with me, please, Mrs. Eckerly," clutched her arm, and pulled her along with him, so there was never a second for her to think.

She tried to dig in her heels, but he knew exactly the way they reacted, so he gave her a first taste of it. He bent her wrist down enough so she knew it would break if she didn't come, and jerked her along more quickly. It wasn't just the pain that worked on them, it was the fact that he knew how to inflict it so easily. It proved to something deep inside them that he represented genuine authority—cops and law and government and, even more, all the massed force that made people do what they were supposed to do.

He hustled her across the street in the crosswalk, not even waiting for the light to change, just holding up a hand and counting on the drivers' reflexes. He knew that, too, would help. And then he had her inside the big concrete parking structure and he was already feeling relief, because he was through the hard part, where real airport cops might be loitering and where, if she screamed and ran, it might be hard to subdue her without attracting some man he couldn't scare off by flashing an imitation-leather wallet with his license on one side and a business card with a picture of an eagle on the other.

He had parked the van on the first floor, just about twenty feet from the exit. To get that space he'd had to be here early and hang around all evening, but it was paying off now. She was already to the back door before she said, "Wait, you're making a mistake. Don't do this." She never pulled herself together enough to look up at him.

It was exactly what they always said, but it was a little disconcerting, because usually they tried to use their faces—the tiny quiver in the lips, the big wet eyes. And there wasn't that little sob in her voice. It was like a whisper in the big concrete place, and it went right through him. He couldn't let up for a second, he knew.

"No mistake, Mrs. Eckerly. There's a legal complaint, and you'll have to go back and clear that up. Face the van, please." He had hoped to do this after she was inside, because the sight of the handcuffs sometimes made them panicky, but he had a feeling about this one. He slipped the cuffs off his belt and turned her away from him. As he pulled her left arm around behind her, it came too quickly.

He pulled harder, but that didn't seem to help. He had been keeping her off balance, trying not to give her a chance to think, but she had been waiting for him to have to use one hand to get the cuffs. She stomped on his instep, turned with him, and brought her elbow up against the bridge of his nose. He heard the bone break and felt the warm blood streaming out of his nostrils into his mouth. He knew he was in trouble, because of the pain and the slowness. And something bad had happened to the bones in his foot. He stepped back to try to get time working with him again, but his toes didn't want to hold him, so he had to rock back on his heel and use his other foot for balance. He was angry, maddened with pain. He was going to make her hurt just as much. In a second she would turn to run, and he would be on her. He pushed off to get started.

The woman didn't turn, and she didn't run. She drifted toward him, and he sensed what she had in mind. She was winding up for a kick in the groin. They always taught women that in those self-defense classes. He bent his body and held his hands low to grip her leg when she did it.

As he watched her legs, she leapt forward and butted her forehead into his face. The blow to his nose had been painful, but this time the world exploded. She had pushed off the ground with both legs, and knocked him backward with all her strength.

Killigan let out a howl as he hit the pavement. It was a screech of hurt and shock and, for the first time, fear.

Killigan was desperately injured now, and he was down, where he couldn't defend himself. She would go for his eyes in a second. He clapped his hands over his bloody face and rolled onto his belly on the concrete and shouted, "Help! Help me!"

His ears told him she was hovering somewhere nearby, dancing around, circling to look for a chance to do whatever they had taught her to do. He tried to see between his fingers and keep his face down, and then he felt it. The handcuffs went around both of his wrists at once. He was outraged, scandalized.

He scrambled to his knees and tried to stand, but her voice came again. This time it was louder, but still calm: "Stay down on the ground." He put his fists on the pavement and pushed himself up, but the patch of concrete in front of his eyes seemed to flash as though it were electrified, and then he found himself on his side, his legs spasmodically working, trying to run. It had been a kick to the kidney. It occurred to him he could be dying. He lay there and screamed again. "Help!" he shrieked. "Help me!"

Suddenly, he saw lights that didn't go away: bright, blinding and steady, and his sluggish consciousness tried to decide if she had gotten his eyes after all. That didn't make sense, because he could see his hands. And then he heard it. "Police officers! Don't move!"

He tried to smile, but it hurt. His top front teeth felt loose, and his upper lip was swollen to a tight, hard lump that didn't seem to belong to him. Then there were footsteps, and they got louder, and he could see one pair of cops' black shoes and black pants, and he knew it would be all right. Then big, hard hands rolled him over onto his back, and the pain surprised him so much that he didn't see anything anymore.

When Killigan awoke he was in a hospital room. He had no idea how long he had been there, but he knew he had not been wrong about the damage he had sustained. His whole head had a tender, fragile feeling, as though moving it would cause something to come loose and bleed. He heard a rustling noise, and then the cop was standing in front of him.

"Mr. Killigan?" He was the kind of cop that Killigan liked the least. He was trim and neat, with a short, carefully combed haircut that made him look like an army lieutenant. He pulled a little notebook out of the inner pocket of a gray tweed coat, letting Killigan see the strap of the shoulder holster.

"Yeah," he rasped. He wasn't sure why his voice sounded like that, and then he tasted that he was swallowing blood.

"I'm Detective Sergeant Coleman, L.A. Police Department. I need to ask you some questions about what happened. Your I.D. says you're a private investigator."

"Right."

"Were you working?"

"Yeah."

"What were you doing at the airport?"

"Picking up a woman named Rhonda Eckerly. Citizen's arrest. There's a complaint. She's wanted in Indiana."

"What charge?"

"Grand larceny."

"So you're a bounty hunter?"

Killigan heard something he didn't like in the sound. It was a careful modulation of tone, as though the cop were trying to keep contempt out of his voice. Well, Killigan would make enough on this job to pay his salary for a year. Maybe he would find a way to mention the number and let this guy chew on it for the next few days. "The victim retained me to locate the suspect and bring her back."

The cop squinted and tilted his head a little. "Who's the victim?"

"Mr. Robert Eckerly."

"I see," said Sergeant Coleman. He stared at Killigan for a long time without letting his face reveal anything. Finally, he said, "I'd like to bring in the woman who was arrested when the officers found you. Are you up to that?"

"Yeah. I want her held. I'll press charges."

The detective's tongue made a quick search of his teeth as he headed for the door, but then he turned around again. "How did she come to assault you?"

So that was it. The little bastard was so sure Killigan was weak—that it couldn't happen to him. "I was escorting her to the van, and she surprised me. She must have taken one of those courses."

"Were the handcuffs yours?"

"Yes."

The detective pulled a chair close to the bed and sat on the edge of it. "Mr. Killigan," he said. "You're in a dangerous business. You must have some idea of how to pull this kind of thing off without getting yourself in trouble. I think you made a mistake."

"It would seem so," said Killigan. "Now, where the fuck is Rhonda Eckerly?"

The detective stood up, walked to the door, and opened it. A uniformed cop came in with his hand on the arm of a woman. She was about thirty. She was tall and slender and olive-skinned, with large eyes and black hair. Then Killigan realized that she was wearing Rhonda Eckerly's clothes. "No," he said. "No. That's not the one."

"This isn't Rhonda Eckerly?"

"No!" he shouted. A pain gripped him from his hairline to his jaw. It was as though his whole face had been peeled and a cold wind blew on it. "You got the wrong one!"

"No," said Detective Coleman evenly. "You did."

The sanctimonious little cop hadn't needed to say that

because, even distracted by pain and half paralyzed by the dope they'd shot into him to make him lie here, Killigan had been able to figure out that much. She was a ringer. The clothes, the amateurish way Rhonda Eckerly had tried to do things—it had all been planned so they could change in the bathroom.

The woman said, "Can I talk to him?"

"I guess so," said the cop.

"Alone?"

"No," said the detective. "Not a chance."

She didn't look surprised. She walked a little closer to the foot of the bed, and the uniformed officer stayed at her elbow. "Do you know anything about Rhonda Eckerly?"

"Enough," said Killigan. "She's a fugitive. Fair game."

The woman turned to the cop. "Thank you." She took a step toward the door.

"That's it?" Killigan asked. "Aren't you going to laugh at me and tell me how easy it was?"

"No."

"Why not?"

"I understand you now. Telling you anything would be a waste of time. You're the walking dead."

"You both heard it," Killigan said with glee. "She threatened to kill me."

The detective stared at him again, his head tilted to the side a little. "We'll discuss that later." He took the woman by the arm and ushered her out the door.

When the door closed behind them, Coleman walked Jane Whitefield down the hall, past the emergency room desk and the waiting area, across the black rubber mat. The doors huffed open and outside, in the hot night air, he led her past a couple of ambulances to his plain blue car.

"You got into this intentionally?" he asked.

"Yes," she said.

"Why?"

Jane Whitefield took a deep breath and let it out, then said, "Robert Eckerly married a girl. She was about twenty, he was about fifty. He's a rich man in a small town. He's charming. He's also a sexual sadist."

"Whose diagnosis?"

"She ran away once before, and he managed to have her caught, like this. I don't know if he thought of the theft charge by himself or if he called somebody like Killigan and that person told him that was how it was done. She was released into his custody. He didn't just beat her up. He chained her by the neck in a room and invited a few like-minded friends to come and help." She looked at Detective Coleman.

He nodded. "Go on."

"Nothing shocks a cop? This would have. When they got too drunk and tired to just keep raping her in some ordinary way, they started trying to think up ways to make her beg them to stop hurting her, because that turned them on." She looked up at him. "What are you thinking? That you don't want to hear the rest?"

"Will it do her any good?"

"No."

"Where is she now?"

"If I told you I don't know, you wouldn't believe me."

"No."

"Then I'll just say she's far away."

Coleman leaned on the hood of his car, folded his arms, and stared at her for a moment. "So what are you going to do?"

"I've done it. She's gone."

"About Mr. Killigan. He went up to a strange woman in an airport and attempted to handcuff her and stuff her into a van. You could file a pretty impressive array of charges. Are you going to?"

"There's no point."

"Are you afraid?"

"No. Rhonda Eckerly isn't coming back to testify to anything. And Killigan wasn't attacking an innocent woman minding her own business. I stalked him and trapped him."

He stared at her thoughtfully. "Then there's still the issue of what to do with you."

"Nothing. I'm going home."

"I didn't say you could. You just told me you trapped him and beat him up on purpose."

"You can delay me for two or three hours. If you write up a charge, the D.A. won't file it. I told you I cooked this up myself, so there aren't any loopholes. He attacked. I resisted. In this state I could have killed him if I wanted."

"You're pretty sure of that, are you?"

"I have an attorney waiting for me at the station. He can explain it to you if you want. When that's over, you can drive me back to the airport and put me on my plane."

"What are you, anyway—a detective? A lawyer?"

"A guide."

"Guide? That's a new one on me."

"Sometimes people need help. I sometimes give it to them."

"Me too."

"I know, and I'm not trying to give you a hard time. I admire you. I would like to shake your hand and go catch an airplane." She grabbed his right hand and gave it a shake, then started to walk out of the parking lot.

Coleman stared at her, but he made no move to stop her. As he watched her walking away, he tried to explain why he was doing it, but there were too many reasons to pick just one. If he wrote down her name, Killigan was the sort of man who would try to find her. And she was right about the legal outcome. No judge in

California would let this one come to trial. Finally, he called out to her, "Is this a woman thing?"

She stopped and looked at him. "No. Sometimes the victim is a man. Sometimes the guide is too." She smiled at him. "Or an animal, or just a figment of somebody's imagination."

2

Jane Whitefield stepped off the airplane in Rochester, New York, wearing a pair of jeans and a dark blue silk blouse with a Japanese-print pattern of trees and flowers on it. She carried the suitcase that Rhonda Eckerly had checked on to her flight in Indianapolis, but there was no longer any resemblance between them.

She carried the suitcase to the car-rental lot and picked up the keys to the car she had reserved during her layover in New York City. Then she drove up South Plymouth Avenue into the city, inside the nest of freeways the local planners had named the Inner Loop, and onto West Main. She turned into the underground parking lot of the Presidential Hotel and let the valet take the car out of sight.

Upstairs in the enormous old lobby, decorated in green-veined marble and dark hardwood, she walked past the reservations desk and the portals that led to bars and restaurants and entered the small shop beside the newsstand. There were four women in chairs already, getting their hair done in a respectful silence. People in hotels were all strangers, and they seemed to talk only to the hairdressers and to watch the mirrors carefully to be sure nothing unauthorized was being done to them. When the slim, dark woman entered, two of the women used the mirrors to glance at her without seeming to, but the manicurist, a plump woman in her fifties, stood up and said, "Mrs. Foley, so nice to see you again."

Jane said, "Hi, Dorothy. Slow day?"

"Too early to tell," she answered. Dorothy was already moving her to her cluttered worktable. She sat down across from her and examined her fingers. "These two are really something," said Dorothy as she carefully pared the nails.

"I broke a couple playing tennis," said Jane.

"And those scratches on your knuckles," said Dorothy. "You should stand farther away from each other when you play."

Jane shrugged to signal that the conversation was over, and Dorothy worked in silence. When she had finished her cutting and filing and buffing and soaking and enameling, Jane followed her to the cash register and handed her a folded bill. The manicurist handed her a small plastic bag.

When Jane Whitefield had walked out of the shop, one of the customers leaned forward in her chair and said to the manicurist, "Was that what I think it was?"

Dorothy turned her business smile on the woman. It was attentive, cheerful, and utterly impenetrable. "Would you like a manicure?"

Jane Whitefield walked out of the lobby and down Main Street for two blocks to the tobacco shop. When she entered, the studious-looking young man with the pipe looked up from the book he was reading and went to turn the knob on the sound system to make Mozart's Third Horn Concerto recede to a safe distance. "What can I do for you today?" said the young man.

"I'd like a bag of the best grade of pipe tobacco," she said. She held up her hands in a bowl shape. "About this much."

He put his pipe under her nose and waved it back and forth. "What do you think of this?" he said. "I make it for myself. A little Latakia, some prime Virginia, and a little secret I happen to know about."

She dodged the blue-gray smoke and wrinkled her nose. "You cut it with sumac to take the bite out of it?"

The young man looked genuinely injured. "Are you in the business?"

"Just a guess," she said. "I heard you were the best tobacconist in town." This seemed to make up for her knowing.

He led her beyond the glass door into the humidified room, reached to the top shelf, and took down a cannister. He weighed some of his precious mixture and put it into a plastic bag for her. "I hate to part with this stuff," he said. "But for you—" he flipped his wrist to pour another stream of shreds into the bag—"anything. I assume you don't smoke it yourself, so I guess this isn't the beginning of a beautiful friendship."

She paid him in cash and put the bag into her purse. "No, I don't smoke," she said, "but if it's good I'll be back."

Jane Whitefield parked her rented car by the curb on Maplewood Avenue and walked up the sidewalk. It was a quiet street full of three-story nineteenth-century houses shaped like plump boxes, built close together near the curb. This part of Rochester had a lot of placid old neighborhoods like this, left from a time when people who had money wanted to live on streets that seemed urban, where a carriage could pull up to the front door and lawns weren't of much interest because people were only a mile and a generation from the farm. Most of the houses had been partitioned into apartments now, but there were probably fewer people living in them than in the old days, when a family included eight children and two servants. She came to the end of the street and crossed over into the little park.

The grass here was the bright, luminous green that seemed to come in early April and last only until the new blades grew tall in the warm weather. When she stopped to pluck a blade, it was swollen and crisp, and when she split it, her hand was wet with chlorophyll. The trees were old, much older than the houses. They had long ago grown to their full height, and now some of the trunks were four feet in diameter. She could see the buds on the lower branches already, waiting for this part of the earth to tilt a little closer to the sun before they were ready to unfurl into leaves.

Jane Whitefield passed to the left of the big Romanesque structure of the Christian Science church. It looked old and white and heavy, like a mausoleum now that the central part of the city had changed. Then she walked on to the edge of the grass, leaned over the thick iron railing, and looked down into the gorge.

Fifty feet below her, the dark ribbon of the Genesee River moved along sedately to the north, far from its source in Pennsylvania and still a day's walk from Lake Ontario. Genesee meant "pleasant banks."

Down in the gorge, the river was maybe forty feet across at its widest point, and beside it, up a pebbly bank, was about a hundred feet of flat, weedy ground. As she stared at the flat place below her, it wasn't spring anymore. The leaves were thick and dry on the trees, and the air was hot. It was late in the summer.

The village of Gaskosago had been on that spot along the water, the elm-bark longhouses all oriented east to west, the smoke that rose from the chimney hole in the center of each roof going up in a straight line, only to be dispersed by the steady breeze from this side when it rose to the top of the chasm. On a quiet afternoon, the small children would play down there in the cool, clear water. Mothers never did much watching of children after they could walk, because the people believed it would stifle the self-reliance they would need later.

The women were up here on the level ground, working with hoes and digging sticks to chop the weeds and turn the soil around the roots of the cornstalks. The plants were almost ready for harvest, so the women gossiped and laughed as they worked, invisible to each other through the tall stalks. In the early spring they had planted the corn, and then after it had sprouted, they had planted the beans and the squash so the vines could grow up the cornstalks to keep the vegetables off the ground. They called the plants the three sisters. Only the women were up here, because crops not tended by women would not grow. The men were out hunting or fighting.

Then, down in the village below, a couple of the dogs that had been splashing in the water with the children started barking and growling. Jane watched as a young woman stopped and listened to it. When it didn't stop, she looked up from her work and walked to the edge of the field. She could see that women were running out of the cornfield to the low limbs of the trees where they had hung their babies in cradleboards.

One of the older women hurried to the edge of the gorge and shouted "Go-weh! Go-weh!" at the children below. She waved her arms up and down frantically and screamed at them to run. Suddenly, the older woman's body gave a spasmodic jerk, and a big red blotch exploded out of her back as she fell backward. There was the loud report of the rifle, echoing back and forth among the rocky cliffs above the village for a second. Jane watched the young woman turn her head to try to see where it had come from.

What she saw were the first of the four thousand soldiers streaming out of the woods from the east. They were already on the flats, setting fire to the cornfields and the orchards. The young woman threw down her digging stick and began to run. There were more rifle shots now, first a loud, long barrage of many guns fired at once and then a ragged, uneven patter as single soldiers leveled their sights on someone running. The young woman sprinted, dashing among the tall corn-stalks, making sharp turns and zigzags until she was in the woods. She ran to the north and west. Before long there were more women, a few slipping between the trees with cradleboards on their backs, others with bigger children they had scooped up in their arms, all of them trying to fade into the deep forest and away from that awful place.

Jane closed her eyes and took a couple of deep breaths to erase the feeling of panic, and when she opened them, she stared up and away, at the quiet Victorian houses across the street from the park. All of that had happened long ago. The man who had ordered the attacks was named George Washington. From that day in 1779 until now, the only way of referring to any American president in the Seneca language was Destroyer of Villages.

The people who had lived here didn't call themselves Seneca. They were the Nundawaono, the People of the Hill. The name came from their having come into the world on a hill at the head of Canandaigua Lake, about thirty miles south of here. But everybody had been gone from this place for a long time. The only ones left here were the Jo-Ge-Oh—the Little People.

Jane Whitefield opened her purse and pulled out the pouch of pipe tobacco. She tossed a pinch down into the gorge. "This is for you, Stone Throwers," she said quietly. "Thank you for the luck with Rhonda. She's safe now." The Stone Throwers were one of the three tribes of Jo-Ge-Oh. They were only about as tall as a person's hand, but they were very strong in spite of their size, and they looked very much like the Nundawaono who had lived here once. They made a practice of saving people from the horrible things that could happen, taking victims out of the world and hiding them.

The second tribe of Jo-Ge-Oh was responsible for

making sure the plants of the western part of New York State came up on time and flourished, and the third for guarding the several entrances of the underworld around here, to keep the supernatural beings down where they belonged. The Stone Throwers lived only in the rocks of the Genesee. They were hopelessly addicted to tobacco and had no supplier except the Nundawaono. Jane held the pouch at arm's length and poured the rest of the tobacco down into the gorge, watching the brown shreds sprinkle and spread out in the breeze to become invisible. "There you go, little guys. Don't let it stunt your growth. This is for Rhonda."

The Little People had, in their occasional discussions with the Nundawaono, specifically requested fingernail clippings. It was their hope that the large animals that were a nuisance to little people everywhere would smell the clippings and think there were full-sized human beings around. Jane Whitefield glanced over her shoulder to see if anyone was looking, took out a small plastic bag and undid the seal, then poured her fingernail collection down to them. "Take these, and keep the luck coming."

Jane Whitefield walked back across the green grass to Maplewood Avenue, got back into her rented car, and drove out toward Mt. Read Boulevard. She could pick up the Thruway and be home in Deganawida in a couple of hours.

3

As Jane drove to the west along the New York State Thruway toward Deganawida, it didn't bother her that in the cars she passed, few of the drivers had any idea where they were or where they were going. If that little girl in the next car said, "Were there Indians here?" the daddy, the serious-looking guy with the glasses, would say, "Sure, and before them, mammoths, and before that, dinosaurs." He looked like a kind, patient father who had answered a lot of questions on this long drive. It didn't matter if he didn't know that the flat, grassy country from Sodus Bay to the Niagara River was part of Nundawaonoga. He couldn't see it any more than he could see who Jane was. It looked different from the way it really was.

Jane drove until she saw the sign that said DEGANA-WIDA, veered off the Thruway at Delaware Avenue, and turned up the long block to Main Street, then turned again off Main at Campbell Street, near the old cemetery. The cemetery had run out of vacancies sometime around the Civil War, and most of the graves in it were those of soldiers. The houses in this part of town were all two stories high, built before the turn of the century, when the lumber business was thriving.

She pulled into the driveway, and old Jake Reinert stopped painting the white trim on his porch next door, carefully laid his brush down, picked up a clean rag to wipe the nonexistent drops of paint from his square, pink hands, and walked to the edge of his lawn to watch her. She opened the car door and got out. "Hi, Jake."

"Hello, Janie," he said. "Can I help you haul your bags in?"

"No, thank you," she said with a smile. "It doesn't take two." She swung out Mrs. Eckerly's suitcase. A day ago Jack Killigan would have been surprised to see her pluck it off the car seat and set it down. She had told Rhonda Eckerly to put it on the bathroom scale to be sure it weighed no more than ten pounds before she left her house in Indiana. A fifty-pound suitcase was a burden; a ten-pound suitcase was a weapon.

Jake stepped inside his front door, then came back and walked around the privet hedge. She saw he was holding something in his hand besides the rag. "Here's your mail," he said.

In the winter, if Jane didn't get up in time to shovel her snow, she would wake up and see Jake give his bright red snowblower a pull and happily run it up her driveway and sidewalks before he did his own. She was always loudly grateful, not because she needed an old man to move the snow, but because the circumstances of the universe had given her the gift of a neighbor who would want to do it, and given Jake the pleasure of being able to do such things in his old age.

She glanced at the little pile of envelopes, her eyebrows raised. "Did I get anything interesting?"

He shook his head. "You know I just look for the magazines, but it looks like old Barney got to them first this time." Jake was the chief perpetuator of the myth that magazines in Deganawida arrived later than they did in other towns because Barney Schwick, the mailman, read them before he delivered them. "Oh, I forgot," he said. "There was a fellow here to see you yesterday. Tall, fit, dark hair, dark eyes."

"An Indian?" She felt a slight alarm, although she couldn't imagine why it felt like bad news.

"Well now, I couldn't say," said Jake.

Yesterday was too soon for anybody Eckerly might have sent after her. She had taken a taxi to Burbank to fly back to New York City under the name Helen Freeman. She had used Lila Warren to fly to Rochester, then rented the car under her own name. "Did he say anything?"

"Not to me," said Reinert. "I didn't talk to him."

"Well, thanks," she said. "I'm tired. I just spent the morning staring at the white line on the Thruway." She walked up the steps and unlocked her door, then rushed to punch in the code on her alarm system before the bell went off. People in Deganawida didn't believe in alarm systems, but they respected personal eccentricity. They didn't mind their own business, exactly, but they pretended to, and that was just as good. An unmarried woman who lived alone like Jane Whitefield was expected to be fearful, and could do what she wanted to preserve the calm that was the only defensible reason for living in Deganawida.

She walked into the living room and sniffed the air. She had been gone for two days and the house had been sealed to keep out the wet, cold winds of spring. The air in the house should have been dead and stale, but it wasn't. It was fresh and clean and alive.

Jane stayed where she was and listened. She had opened the front door to come in, so in a few seconds the first cool air would reach the thermostat in the hallway by the bedroom and the oil furnace in the basement would kick on. She glanced again at the keypad of her alarm system on the wall. The little red letters said RDY: ready.

She decided she must have left something open. No, if she had, the furnace would have been churning away down there, trying valiantly to heat up the whole outside world to sixty-eight. It must be a crack somewhere, a tiny one that she wouldn't have noticed if she had been here.

It was an old house, and twenty or thirty layers of paint had a way of making things fit too snugly to let air in. She felt a little tightness on the sides of her face as a chill passed on its way to the back of her neck. What was she thinking of excuses for? Somebody had been in here.

She backed to the umbrella stand and picked up her black umbrella with the metal tip on the end. She was prepared to admit that there were people on the planet who were capable of fooling any alarm system, but hers was a pretty good one. Had the power been turned off? The digital clock on the kitchen counter would have flashed twelve o'clock if the power was off. But he would have seen that too, and reset it. She quietly moved to the television table in the corner and opened the cabinet to look at the VCR. That too was glowing steadily with the almost-correct time. By her watch it was 3:47, and the display said 3:45. It had always been two minutes off. This should have reassured her, she knew, because he might have been alert enough to reset it, but he wouldn't do it wrong. But she only wondered how he had thought of it.

The rational thing to do right now was to step back out the front door and walk around the outside of the house to look for the broken window or the scarred doorjamb, and when she found it, she could wait for the police at Jake's house. That was what she would have told someone else to do, so why wasn't she doing it?

It was because he was still here. He was hiding in a closet or behind a door or in the basement, or maybe just beyond a doorway. She stepped around the corner of the dining room, keeping her back to the wall, but her mind kept sending her bulletins of alarm. He had to be waiting for some reason, and the only part of the establishment that hadn't been laid out in plain sight for his leisurely inspection was the woman who lived here.

She stepped into the kitchen and saw the gun on the table. It was wide and black and squat and ugly, with crosshatched grips that looked too big for a human hand. The cylinder was open and she could see five fat bullets inside like hornets in a nest. She froze for a second. Why would he leave it there? He was a psychopath. As she stepped closer, she could see the little colt etched on the blue metal above the handgrips. It was either a Diamondback or a Trooper. It was not a good sign when they spontaneously chose standard-issue cop equipment. It was a hint that their confusion had reached the who's-who? stage. Maybe he was crazy enough to be the kind that took possession—ate all the food in the refrigerator, went to sleep upstairs on her bed, and forgot about the gun. That wasn't something she felt like betting anything important on, and it set off another little alarm in her brain. If he wanted to put his mark on everything, there was one thing left that he would be waiting for. He wanted her to rush in, try to take the four steps to grasp it, and that would be when he jumped on her from behind.

If he had spent this much time looking around, he would have at least glanced into a closet and seen that she was tall or found a photograph of her. And if he was that sure he could instantly subdue a five-foot-ten woman without her making a sound, he was going to be big and strong. Maybe he had a kitchen knife and was ready to bring it across her throat while she was inhaling for the scream.

In order to do that, he had to be on the other side of the refrigerator. There was no other place. Okay, she thought. Time for a surprise. She took a deep breath and let it out to calm her nerves. When she moved, it was fast. She threw her shoulder into the side of the refrigerator and kept digging in with her feet. It rolled an inch on its casters, hit a crack in the tile, and tipped.

As it toppled, she swept the gun toward her across the table with the crook of the umbrella, snatched it up, flicked her wrist to snap the cylinder into place, ducked down, and aimed.

To her surprise, the refrigerator fell only as far as the counter and caught with a thump and a muffled sound of breaking glass. To her greater surprise, the man wasn't crouching on the other side of it.

The voice came from the living room. "Do you have the gun?" He must have come down from upstairs.

She couldn't think of a reason to deny it. "Yes," she said.

"I left it there."

"I know that."

"I mean, I did this so you wouldn't be afraid."

A part of her mind wanted to call out, "It didn't work," but she controlled it and said, "What do you want here?"

This time his voice was nearly at the kitchen door. "I need your help." Why had she assumed there was only one? Maybe he had let Jake see him just to give that impression. He was coming closer. This was her last chance to look behind her, so she took it. She swirled her head, her eyes searching hungrily for the shape of a man, but there was none.

"Can I come in?" he asked quietly.

She hesitated, slipped to the side of the door by the tilted refrigerator as quietly as she could, and turned her head to the side to let her voice come to him from the center of the room. She cocked the hammer and said, "Come in."

4

J ake Reinert applied the paint in long, even brush-strokes. He was not the sort of man who put too much paint on a brush and hoped that would keep him from having to do a second coat. Foolproof nondrip paint was still in the realm of the perpetual-motion machine and the philosopher's stone. In fact, paint was one of many things that had actually gotten perceptibly worse in his lifetime. They had taken the lead out so the whole country didn't get retarded at once, but whatever they had put in there to replace it was as good as money, because it meant you had to buy paint twice as often, and sometimes it seemed as though the whole world had gotten mentally damaged anyway. The only thing to be said for painting was that it helped a man keep his mind off things that worried him and that were none of his business. If Jane Whitefield wanted to tell him something, she knew where to find him.

Jane Whitefield had taken up a lot of watching time, because he had begun early and kept up with it. He had started worrying about her before she was born. He had felt a little trepidation about it. The old folks had been pretty reasonable about Henry Whitefield's marrying an American woman, as near as Jake could tell. But he had seen situations before where everybody pretty much minded their own business until the babies started coming. Then there would be a lot of arguments that were deep and nasty about whether the kid was going to be

Protestant or Catholic, who it looked like, who it would
be named after, and all that. But with the Whitefields it
hadn't been like that. They didn't seem to notice.

Her hair was as black and shiny as the lapel of a tux-
edo, and it hung so straight it sometimes looked as
though it were made of something heavier than hair.
But Jake had seen at about six months that the eyes
weren't turning brown, not even darkening a little, and
he had mentioned it to Henry.

Henry had laughed about it. He said the Seneca had
captured so many white women over the years that the
blue eyes might have come from him. Then he reminded Jake of something he hadn't thought about
since high school: that the last great Iroquois chiefs, Joseph Brant and Cornplanter, both had had white fathers.
He said he had read somewhere that the more mongrel-
ized a person was, the better the chance that he would
be healthy and intelligent. *Mongrels* wasn't a word Jake
would have used, and it had shocked him, but he
guessed Henry had a better opinion of dogs than he did.

Henry lived long enough to see that Jane had turned
out all right: nice-looking, smart in school, fine athlete.
Jake's own girls, Amanda and Mary Ellen, who were a
few years older, had doted on Jane until they had gone
away to college. He had assumed that these were going
to be lifelong friendships, but history had fooled him
and made lifelong friendships obsolete. By the time all
those kids had come back from school, there wasn't
really a whole lot that the town could offer them to do
for a living. His had moved on; Jane had stayed.

There was a natural question in Jake's mind as to
how she was accomplishing that. Her mail was always
full of stuff from stock brokers and banks and mutual
funds, so she must have a little money from her folks.
But that couldn't be what she lived on. Henry had been
shrewd, but he had never concentrated on getting rich.
He had worked construction jobs for thirty years. A few

years ago, when Jake had pried out of Jane what she was doing, it had sounded like a puff of air in his face. She had a research and consulting business. What the hell was that?

She went off a lot on sudden trips, sometimes for a day or two, sometimes for sixty days. And now and then there would be strange people coming to her door. He had seen how she had looked when he had told her about the man. She didn't even know who he was, but it didn't strike her as a pleasant surprise. Jake didn't know everything, but in his experience, people who had nothing to hide didn't cringe when they heard somebody had come to see them.

His stomach felt hollow and queasy when he looked at the pure arithmetic of the situation. You had a very attractive young woman who spent a lot of money. When you asked her where it came from, she named a profession that didn't involve making, buying, or selling anything and didn't require her to leave the house on a regular basis. He had never met anybody who could be described as a call girl, so he didn't really know how that business worked from the inside, but he suspected that from the outside it would look quiet and respectable and too good to be true, a lot like the way Jane Whitefield lived.

As he scrutinized his work and set aside his brushes, Jake felt a little sad. His generation—his wife, Margaret, his closest friends—were all gone. Amanda and Mary Ellen were grown-up and raising their own kids a thousand miles away. Here he was spending his time worrying about Jane Whitefield's personal life. In his younger days Jake Reinert would have disdained the idea of being the next-to-last live person in a dying place. He would rather have put a gun to his head. But life had a way of presenting you with a dogshit sandwich and tailoring events perfectly so that you just had to hang around and eat it.

5

Jane Whitefield aimed the gun at the doorway and quietly stepped to the other end of the kitchen. She held the big pistol in both hands to ride out the recoil without allowing it to kick upward and deprive her of the second round. She aimed ten inches to the left of the doorjamb and three feet above the ground. If he was honest, he would walk in slowly and upright. The gun would look to him as though it weren't being poked into his face. If he was dishonest, he would charge in low and the muzzle would be at the level of his chest. She would spend the evening cleaning the floor and spackling the hole in the wall.

He walked into the kitchen with his hands held out wide and the fingers spread, as though he were offering to hug somebody. His voice had sounded as though it was coming from above her, so she wasn't surprised that he was tall. He was slim but muscular, and that wasn't a good sign. He had short, dark-brown hair and brown eyes, so he was probably the one Jake had seen. His face looked as though he was in his late thirties or early forties, too old to be a sneak-thief. He had about three days' worth of dark beard on his face, and he looked tired. That part was good.

"My name is John Felker, and—"

"How did you get in here?" she asked.

"You weren't home, and I couldn't find a safe place.

The motels . . ." He seemed to see that he wasn't answering the question. "You mean the alarm system?"

"You know I do," she said evenly. "How?"

He gave a small, apologetic shrug. "They always wire the windows and doors and things. You can't get past them. But on the attic of every house there's a vent at the peak, just under the roof. If you take off the grille, a man can sometimes fit."

"If he happens to be up there."

"Your neighbor is painting his house. He has an extension ladder."

Jane resolved to have the alarm company come back if she survived this. "Then what?"

"Once you're in the attic, there's a trapdoor to come down. I cut off the alarm."

She worked her jaw and lifted the pistol a few degrees to aim at his belly. "The alarm has a battery for backup in case the power is shut off."

His eyes settled on the gun. "The terminal box for your system is in your bedroom closet. I couldn't find the battery, so I connected the battery circuit to your hair dryer until the battery was drained before I shut off the main circuit breaker for the house. They were smart enough to wire your phone-junction box, so I had to be sure it wasn't hot before I disconnected the phone wires."

"You shouldn't have done it," she said.

"I'm sorry," he said, "but I had to. Once the phone was off, I turned the power on again so the alarm would still sound inside the house if somebody broke in. I just couldn't have the alarm going off at the police station. The battery is charged up again. No harm done."

"If you get shot, I won't be able to call an ambulance."

"If you shoot me from there, I won't need one." He looked a little hopeful, his eyes now fixing on hers. "If you don't, I can hook up the phone wires again as soon as you turn off the alarm."

"That was a lot of work. What did you do it for?"

"I need to disappear."

"And you're afraid of the police."

"Yes."

"Then you're a criminal."

"So are you."

She caught herself liking him a little for that. He was straightforward and quick, not watching her for a reaction and then changing his story. But nobody knew that much about how alarm systems worked unless he had some very good reason ... or some very bad reason. "Tell me what happened."

He looked down at his feet, then at her. "Like this?"

"You can sit. If you like, you can lie down."

"Where?"

"Right there," she said, almost smiling at his befuddlement. "On the floor."

He sat down on the floor and she watched him as she moved across the room, until she was eight feet away and could be sure nothing he did would neutralize the advantage of the gun. He sat absolutely still on the bare, shiny floor with his knees pulled up, held by his arms. He was lean and athletic and wore a clean pair of blue jeans, a black T-shirt, and a pair of good sneakers. The signs were ambiguous. Since he was clean, he probably wasn't crazy. But men his age tended to let their bellies go a little bit unless what they did for a living involved fighting or they had some kind of sexual problem or they had spent a lot of time in prison, and there was a lot of overlap among those three. She decided he did look a little bit like a prisoner as he sat there on the floor, not at ease but motionless—maybe a captured soldier.

"Who told you to come here?" she asked.

"Harry Kemple."

Hearing the name was like feeling an injection of tranquilizer stab into her arm. The effect should have been calming, but the first impression was of the sharp, silvery needle sliding directly into the vein. Her impulse was to fight it. "Where did you meet Harry Kemple?"

"I used to be a cop."

She felt the ground under her begin to crumble. That was one of the few good explanations for the way he looked. Maybe it would even explain why he knew so much about breaking into a house and why he had a gun. But Harry Kemple would not have told a cop anything about her. So this one must be lying, and Harry Kemple had probably never made it home free.

Thinking of that term caught her by surprise. It was from the game that she and the Reinerts and the other neighborhood kids had played most summer evenings. When grown-ups noticed, they would ask, "Are you playing hide-and-seek?" but its only name here was chase. That reflected its seriousness and scope. It was played with competitiveness and cunning, and there were no boundaries at all. Combatants could and did climb trees to the roofs of houses or run a quarter mile to the river to crouch among the rotted pilings and mossy rocks from the old ferry landing.

Each person who was caught would become one of the chasers, until at last, one person, the best, would be pursued relentlessly by all of the others, sometimes in a roving pack and sometimes spread out to sweep the neighborhood like tiger hunters. It wasn't enough to be the last one left. To win, you still had to make it back alone to touch the big tree where everyone had started. Hot and dry-tongued and panting, you would make the final dash from the last bit of cover, across the open space, arm out to slap the tree, and yell, "Home free!"

She felt sad. Harry had lasted long enough to be the last one out, but still out. "Did you take him in? Arrest him?"

"No," said Felker. "He got in touch with me to tell me."

"Why would he do that?"

"Because I helped him once. It was maybe five, six years ago. You know about Harry?"

"Something. Tell me how you helped him."

"I was a sergeant in St. Louis. Harry got picked up in one of those group arrests that sometimes happen. You've got three or four guys on a dark street and they've all got blood on them, and their clothes are all messed up and each one says he was minding his own business when somebody hit him."

"So you arrest all of them?"

Felker's eyebrows went up and he gave a sad chuckle. "See, when you get there, you're alone. You call for another car and get out on the pavement and what you think about is that there is no way in the world one man can control four except to shoot them. Usually, they know that as well as you do. You try to talk, you try to scare them with the lights and the baton and all that to get them to separate. When you do, they're all yelling at once about who did what. If you get one aside to give you a clue, the others either run or attack him. It's ugly. So what you do is survive on bluster until more cars get there, then sit them down and sort it out."

"And Harry was the victim?"

"I don't think Harry was ever exactly a victim. He was just the worst fighter. You know Harry."

"I knew Harry."

"What do you mean?"

"I haven't seen him in a long time."

Felker looked at her for a moment without speaking, then said, "Anyway, when they brought him in he was acting strange. If there was a fine he wanted to pay it, if there were charges he could file against anybody he wanted to forgive and forget. This is from a guy with a split lip, a black eye, and a nose that was probably broken. At first I figured, Okay. This guy is wanted. But when I checked ... nothing. So I sat him down and talked to him."

"What did he tell you?"

"He had been running a floating poker game in Chicago for over a year. It seemed like it was a great idea. Harry wasn't betting anything, and he got to take a rake off every pot. He would recruit the players and bring them in and introduce them to each other. He had a couple of very rich guys who liked the danger of it: sort of an anonymous, low-life way to gamble for big stakes. The higher the pots, the bigger the rake, and Harry was also getting a chair fee and catering it like a party."

"What did Harry say went wrong?" She was listening for anything that would tell her that this was a lie.

"Like everything else that's supposed to be the most exclusive thing in town, this game started to get famous. So the inevitable happened. A man came to him and demanded to get in. The problem with that is there's no way out. You say yes or the next guy in the door might be wearing a badge or he might not, but either way he's going to have a gun, and the nice little business is history. The man who wanted a seat at the table was used to getting in where he wasn't wanted. I forget his name ..."

"Jerry Cappadocia."

"That's it. If you know the story, why are you making me repeat it?"

"So I can decide whether to shoot you."

"Oh." He stared at the floor for a moment. "What if Harry told it two different ways?"

"You can take it up with him in the afterlife," she said. "So what happened?"

"He let Cappadocia into the game. Harry never knew if what he had in mind was to take over the game or cheat the rich suckers or if he just wanted to play poker with people who had the kind of money he had but didn't know enough about him to let him win. About the third week, two guys kick in the door and shoot Cappadocia. Whether they were just trying to do a holdup and recognized him, or he resisted, or if they were after him to begin with, nobody knows. But the minute the door hits the floor, the guy who organized the game is in trouble. The rich guys know he put a mobster in their game. The friends of Jerry Cappadocia think he sold their buddy. The police want to talk to him. The people who shot Cappadocia also have to be interested, because the others are, and even if he didn't see anything, if the inducements were right, he might make a plausible guess. Jerry Cappadocia's father is semi-retired, but the people who know him say he could make Harry want very much to come up with a name. So suddenly Harry has enemies."

"What did you do for Harry?"

"I asked some more questions. He didn't think the three men arrested with him were trying to kill him for the Cappadocia thing, because they weren't armed. He admitted he had also given them fresh personal reasons to hit him. He had been picking up traveling money by doing card tricks without saying 'Abracadabra.' I thought about it for a while. It seemed to me that what he had been doing wasn't nice, but it wasn't a capital offense, so I held the others overnight, put down a name for Harry that he was too scared to make up for himself, and let him go."

"Where did he go then?"

"I don't know. Maybe here. I didn't hear from him again until a few days ago."

If this one was a liar, he was good at it. He had the facts, or some of them, right, and they were the ones he could be expected to know. But he was also telling her something she wanted to hear. She wanted to believe that Harry was still all right, that someone had seen him alive a few days ago. "Where did you run into him after all that time?"

"I didn't. He called me."

"Why?"

"He knew I was in trouble. He told me that if I needed to disappear, there was a door out of the world. He told me that this was where it was."

"And you believed him?"

Felker looked at her, his eyes unblinking but showing puzzlement. "He had no reason to lie to me."

"You didn't know him very well, and what you knew wasn't very good. Why trust him?"

Felker seemed to look back on it with the kind of incredulity that people feel when they try to figure out the reasons for the decisions they have made. "Maybe it was the story. It was so . . . odd. He said that years ago he had met an old guy on a cruise ship. Gambling is legal on the sea. They have pools on things and slot machines, and on some of them even a couple of tables. Cruises are expensive, so the long ones have mostly people with money."

So he knows that too, she thought. Was there any way to know that besides having Harry tell him? She listened for a mistake.

"So Harry bought a ticket and posed as an amateur who was bored with slot machines and went to find more amateurs. Only there's an old guy in the game that Harry just can't beat. No matter how long he waited, all his practice never swung the odds over to his side. The old guy is a South American industrialist. From Venezuela or someplace. One night they're playing in the old man's suite and it comes down to where everybody else goes back to his own cabin broke except Harry. They're playing one-on-one now, and Harry is still losing. Finally, Harry is in for the price of his return ticket, and they show their cards. Harry loses."

He was watching her now too, probably thinking he must be doing all right because she hadn't shot him yet.

"The old man stands up to rake in the money, and he gets a funny look on his face. His eyes bulge out and he freezes like a statue and starts to topple over. Harry makes a grab for him and gets one hand on his arm, but the other one kind of brushes his face. The guy's mustache comes off."

She listened, and she began to hear what she had been listening for—not mistakes, but evidence. He was beginning to sound more and more like Harry as he told the story. The voice, the cadence of his speech were the same. He wasn't exactly mimicking Harry, because it wasn't conscious. But he had heard Harry tell this story.

"This is not enough to think about, but the man is having a heart attack. Now Harry's got a decision to make. When the old guy fell across the table, what he landed on was, among other things, all of Harry's money and a whole lot more. And he knows that unless they do things a lot differently in South America, a man with a false mustache is not called an industrialist. But Harry did the right thing. He got on the phone, called the doctor, and then bagged all the money and locked it in the little safe in the cabin. The man recovered. Before they took him off in a helicopter, he gave Harry two things—the forty thousand in cash that was in the safe and your address. You see, he knew what Harry would need most . . . had known from the beginning, because he was no more an amateur than Harry was."

As Jane listened to Felker's story, the events in her memory rose up to fill in the empty spaces. She could almost feel the hot, humid air that night in late June at the Big Wind Reservation of the Shoshone and Northern Arapaho in Wyoming. It was the summer of her last year at college, and she had joined the Tecumseh Society, a student group formed on the theory that the Shawnee leader who traveled from tribe to tribe in the early 1800s to unite the Indians might not have been entirely misguided.

Jane's assignment that summer was to travel with a Jicarilla Apache named Ilona Tazeh through the northern plains to establish voter-registration programs on the festival circuit: the Northern Cheyenne Fourth of July Powwow and the Crow Fair in Montana, the Oglala Nation Powwow and the Standing Rock Powwow in South Dakota. That night after the celebrations, she had lured a few young recruits into the air-conditioning of her tiny motel room. The theme of her pitch was that attempting to deal with the society at large only as Senecas or Commanches or Navajos was tantamount to suicide.

What she talked about were the abrogations of law and decency the state and federal governments had committed against the Iroquois in the preceding twenty years: confiscating all of the Cornplanter Reservation in Pennsylvania and much of the Allegany Reservation in New York for the Kinzua Dam; taking a large part of the Tuscarora Reservation for a reservoir; and Canada and the United States conspiring to slice off sections of the Mohawks' St. Regis and Caughnawaga reservations to widen the St. Lawrence Seaway. She was already getting good at this speech, which she always delivered like a messenger from a distant front arriving breathless and weary to warn soldiers who were already fighting similar battles on their own doorsteps.

Ten minutes after they had left, while she was wondering whether she had inspired or bored them, she heard a knock on the door. She opened it to find four old men. At first she thought they had come to look for their sons or daughters, but they told her they were a delegation of elders from different nations. It seemed that earlier in the day, Ilona had tried to impress a tall, handsome Shoshone student with the group's daring by casually mentioning that her friend Jane had the knack for hiding fugitives from injustice. The elders had come to commend Alfred Strongbear to her care.

She found Alfred Strongbear to be a special problem. At the time she met him he had just finished pretending to be a Greek. He had found it necessary to finish because he had decided not to be just an ordinary Greek. He had been an exceptional Greek, a relative of both Aristotle Onassis and Stavros Niarchos who had enormous projects in the works. He had pillaged various parts of the country on the strength of these schemes—using his cousins' discarded oil tankers as floats to harness the sea tides to produce electricity, assembling a group of American investors to buy one of the television networks because he, as a foreigner, was prohibited from buying it in his own name. There was even one that Jane had never quite understood, about using airport-security fluoroscopes to produce involuntary more-than-nude photographs of famous passengers and publishing them for pornographic purposes under cover of a Belgian shell corporation. By now he had collected a great deal of money from investors who should have known better, and there were a great many policemen looking for him who did.

Jane had summoned her courage, glanced at Alfred Strongbear, and said, "You want me to risk my future, maybe even my life, to save a man like that?"

The leader of the delegation of elders was a Southern Brule named Joseph Seven Bulls. He said quietly, "The man is a piece of scum. But he is also probably the last Beothuk Indian left on earth."

Jane asked, "Beothuk? Did you say *Beothuk*?" It was commonly believed that the last Beothuk on earth had left it in the 1820s. The one issue the French and English who settled Newfoundland agreed on was the extermination of the Beothuk. The Beothuk had never grasped the European concept of private property, so they were deemed to be a nation of thieves.

An Arapaho man of a scholarly demeanor named Ronald Kills on Horseback said, "Look at California. They had a dedication ceremony for Point Reyes Park and who shows up but the first Wappo and Coastal Miwok anybody's seen in a hundred years. Same thing happened up along the Oregon border. Half the people that showed up for the memorial to the exterminated Modoc were Modoc."

Jane said, "But Newfoundland isn't northern California, and we're talking about a hundred and sixty years."

Seven Bulls said, "He knows some stories, and he knows the language. He's a disgrace, but letting them take him at his age and put him in prison is a death sentence. You want everybody to get together to further the cause of the Indian. Well, here's an Indian. He's carrying what's left of his people in his head."

Seven Bulls had her and he knew it. She had driven Alfred Strongbear aka Alfred Strong aka Demosthenes Patrakos off the reservation in the trunk of her car past a roadblock of state cops who had traced him that far and figured he would try to hide in the crowd.

She had been the one who made Alfred Strongbear a Venezuelan. She had been new at the craft in those days, but she had an aptitude for it. In the early part of the century, people used to take a name off a gravestone and get a copy of the dead person's birth certificate, which they used to start collecting other documents in that name. By the eighties that method wasn't working in the United States anymore, because it had been done too often. But Jane gambled that it might still work in a country where there wasn't much demand for false identities and the records weren't all computerized. Jane had a college friend named Manuela Corridos who was spending her summer vacation at home learning her parents' sugar business in Merida, Venezuela. Manuela had found it exciting to collect the names and file the papers.

The bargain the elders had made with Alfred Strongbear was that within one year he would make one thousand hours of videotape recordings of the stories his parents and grandparents had told him—Beothuk mythology and cosmology, anecdotes about the old times, and whatever else they had managed to retain over five or six generations—and one thousand hours of videotapes in the lost language of the Beothuk. When Jane had seen him off in New York on what must have been the first of many cruises, he had given her a blessing in a language she didn't know, winked, walked up the gangplank, and said something to the purser in Spanish. She had felt relieved to see the last of him.

A year later she received an envelope with the return address "Kills on Horseback, Big Wind Reservation, Wyoming." Inside was a photocopy of a letter from a professor in the anthropology department of the University of California at Berkeley. It said that the first five hundred hours of the tapes had been copied, circulated to experts, and analyzed. They were in an unaffiliated language that showed many similarities with what had been pieced together of the Beothuk Language Isolate. He needed to know more about Alfred Strongbear. Jane had sent the letter on to the mysterious Venezuelan in care of the shipping line.

Four years later, Alfred had sent her Harry Kemple. It had been the middle of a cold winter night, with the wind blowing hard across the river from Canada, and she was wearing thick wool socks and a flannel bathrobe. She had just come in from a trip to Chicago to transplant a teenaged boy named Raul. She had done this to hide him from a Los Angeles street gang who would only temporarily remain under the impression that they had succeeded in beating him to death for quitting. When Harry had said, "My name's Harry Kemple and I'm from Chicago," her first thought was that he had something to do with Raul. He had said it apologetically, as people spoke when they came to announce that somebody had died.

Somebody had. Harry told her the story of meeting Alfred Strongbear first as a kind of credential, but he got around to the part about Jerry Cappadocia soon enough.

Harry told it to her differently. She could see him telling it now. "So Jerry Cappadocia walks up to me in the middle of the lunch hour at Mom's. Hell, it was worse than that. What walks up to me is not a guy but a couple. What I see first is the girl. She looks like a cheerleader in one of those movies about cheerleaders where the whole thing is a waste of time until they end up in the shower, you know?" Jane didn't, so he explained. "She's very blond, very smooth, very young. Now, Mom's has not seen a girl like this for some time. Mom's is not in the guidebooks. Mom's is what the polite would call a hole. It's likely that this is the only female in the place who still has all her own teeth. So every head in the room turns to stare at her and each of her components. And to make matters worse, her name is Lenore. Not Eleanor, not Lena. Lenore. It actually occurred to me after I knew Jerry Cappadocia that having her was some kind of security measure—like in a war, they send in a big artillery barrage and aerial bombardment and flares to dazzle the enemy before a few little guys in olive-drab suits slip out of their foxholes and attack. But he seemed to really like her. I actually heard that she wasn't even his full-time. He had to compete, because she couldn't decide if she liked him or somebody else better.

"Anyway, now that he's got the attention of half of Cook County, he makes his announcement. He likes to play poker, and he is interested in an invitation to my game."

Felker hadn't mentioned any of this. Maybe Harry had told him an abbreviated version. Harry had been talking to a cop, and when someone talked to a cop, he tried to say the things that mattered. What mattered would have been the murder.

She tried to bring back what Harry had told her about the murder. "So Jerry Cappadocia is a bit ahead. I've been watching his hands like I'm considering putting mustard on them and eating them. It had occurred to me that a man like Jerry might very well be waiting for a chance to palm cards or even slip in some readers. Not that he needed the money, but because it was a reflex. This was not a sportsman; this was a thief. So far I hadn't caught him at it, but tonight he was getting a little ahead, and that could mean he was doing it or it could mean nothing. But when amateurs start to see those chips piling up in front of them, even the best of them get some kind of euphoria, and they take chances.

"I had been drinking club soda all night to keep my head clear, but by now it has to go somewhere. I'm a little nervous about leaving the room to go to the can at this time, but I convince myself that this may be the best thing to do. If Jerry is going to cheat, he'll pick the time when I'm gone to do it. That night the game was in an old-fashioned motel with eight little cabins. The bathroom is right behind Jerry, who always liked to face the front door, for obvious reasons.

"So I go into the bathroom and find that five or six bottles of club soda take a long time to drain out of a person. This gives me lots of time to stand there looking around. I notice that there's a vent over the door. If I put one foot on the bathtub and hold on to the towel rack on the door, I can actually see down into the room. Better than that, I can see it from above, the way the bosses watch the dealers in Las Vegas. There's only one thing I haven't figured out, and that's what I'm going to do if I catch Jerry cheating.

"Next thing I know, there's something going on at the front door. I didn't hear anybody knock, but I guess somebody did. This guy Milhaven, who is a very rich guy who probably never got a door in his life, says, 'Must be more drinks. Harry, get that, will you?' He sees I don't hop to it, so he goes to the door.

"He gets his hand on the knob and turns it, and that's about all he gets to do. The door is kicked in, and it hits him. He's on the ground. The two guys who kicked it in are already inside. One of them holds his gun in two hands to aim and pumps two rounds into Jerry Cappadocia's chest, while the other bends over Milhaven and puts one into his forehead. There are four more guys in the game, and they go crazy. Nadler the lawyer charges toward the door, but the guy who shot Jerry stands his ground and drops him, then steps aside to let Nadler fall while he aims again. Somebody kicks over the table, and Villard the grocery king and Smith the broker duck behind it. I could have told them this was going to turn out to be a bad idea. They each get hit three or four times through the green felt. Hallman, who owns a bunch of sporting-goods stores, decides to go acrobatic and dive through the closed window. He gets two steps before they clip him, so what hits the window is a dead Hallman. About this time I hear another shot, and I'm ready to faint. I mean, there's nobody left to shoot at but me.

"I'm still in the bathroom watching this, too scared to move. These two either don't know about me or they heard somebody say I wasn't around to get the door. They start stealing things—taking wallets and watches and stuff. Now, these particular six players represent a pretty impressive chunk of money. Each time they arrived to play, I would sell each of them ten grand in chips. It was a kind of assurance that everybody was serious. But each of them brought a lot more, so they could buy more chips if they had a setback. Gentlemen don't ask each other to take checks for gambling debts. So right now these two shooters are doing pretty well pocket-mining. They get the money, walk out the door, and close it behind them.

"I'm still clinging to the bathroom door like a kitten that climbed up a tree that was bigger than it looked. I'm shaking. To tell you the truth, I'm glad they didn't break in until my bladder was empty. After about a minute, I can't think of a reason not to let myself down. I go and look at the six guys on the floor and see there's no chance anybody is going to make a quick trip to the emergency room and make a dramatic recovery.

"I think maybe I'll call the cops. I mean, I'm an innocent bystander, right? I actually reach for the phone, but I stop. There's nothing I can do for these six guys, but there's a lot I can do for me. See, what happened is strange. Maybe it's just a robbery. They got maybe a hundred thousand and change. But what happened when they kicked in the door wasn't that somebody said, 'Give me your money.' The first one in found Jerry Cappadocia and put two holes in him. I went to look at Jerry's body, and sure enough, while they were robbing the corpses, one of them had put another shot through his left temple. That was what I heard.

"It's possible that these two robbers were good judges of character and realized in a tenth of a second that if anybody was going to give them trouble it was Jerry C., or maybe he made a move I didn't catch and the robber panicked. I don't know. But it looked to me like one of those situations where somebody wanted to kill one particular man and everything else was just to cover that. At this point I start thinking about how this affects my future. I can be excused for that because I've just established that I'm the only guy in the room who has one. The room, in fact, is my first problem. It would not take the C.I.A. to figure out who rented the room for the game. There's also the fact that Jerry C. heard about the game a month before. If he had, just about anybody else could have too. And even if for some reason he didn't tell his buddies about it, there was his girl."

"Lenore?" asked Jane.

"Yeah, Lenore," he said. "Her last name was Sanders."

"She would go to the police?"

"The police were my primary concern," said Harry. "But they were not my ultimate concern. One way or another the police were going to find out it was my game. They were also capable of counting the bodies and noticing that mine wasn't one of them. Would this cause me harm? Some inconvenience, certainly. They would try to find me and hold me for questioning. But there were other considerations. I start thinking about the five original gentlemen I recruited for my game: Villard, Milhaven, Nadler, Hallman, and Smith. I realize I don't really know much about them. If I get picked up and questioned and let go, are their families and friends going to forget it? Maybe. But in my experience, nobody in this country gets rich by accident. A lot of people who haven't gotten caught at anything are pretty ruthless. The heirs and colleagues of men like that can be pretty ruthless too. And speaking of heirs and colleagues—"

"—Jerry Cappadocia," she said.

"Yes," said Harry. "Him I don't have to wonder about. I know about his colleagues. A couple of them used to show up once a week in the attic of a furniture store where Handy Andy Gurlich ran his bookie operation to collect the Cappadocia family's license fees. Any two of them together were evidence that human evolution is not a straight line. There are lots of dead ends and throwbacks.

"Then there's the question of heirs. Jerry Cappadocia's father has a certain renown. He had announced a couple of years back that he was retiring and Jerry would run the family businesses. This is a man who spent forty years building those businesses with his hands, and what they consist of is killing people who don't give him money. He's healthy, no more than sixty-some years old. I've heard he speaks English like a native, except there are a few words he never learned, like *mercy*. What is this man going to do when he learns his only child has been killed? It's true I was a little worried about getting picked up by the police for questioning, but it was only because they're the ones people call when they hear shots, and they drive through red lights to get there quickly. What was really on my mind was getting picked up later for questioning by Jerry Cappadocia's father.

"And that brought to mind another problem. I really didn't know anything. I saw two men kick in the door and murder six men and then spend five minutes kneeling on the floor to search them. I had never seen either of them before. I didn't see their car, if they had one. They both wore white coats they stole out of the motel's linen cart. I saw them through a vent, so most of what I saw was backs and the tops of heads covered with navy watch caps. But if these two shooters read in the papers that there was a guy who was watching them, what were they going to do? I mean, if the first order of business when they kicked in the door was shooting Jerry Cappadocia, they must have known who he was, right? They had to know what would happen to them if Mr. Cappadocia found out who it was that killed his son."

"Are you sure they'd know about Jerry's father?" she asked.

"I know you're not from Chicago, but trust me," Harry said. "Not knowing about Mr. Cappadocia is like saying, 'You mean Nancy Sinatra has a father?' "

"So they're probably looking for you too."

"As soon as they reload."

"What do you want to do?"

"I want to disappear for a little while," he said. "I don't know who these two guys are, so I can't get the police off my back by telling them, and I certainly can't get Mr. C. off my back. And if I'm right, these two guys were not working on their own. Somebody hired them to kill Jerry C. In fact, this is the only bright spot."

"This is a bright spot?" she asked.

"For me it is. These days my standards are lower than other people's. I figure the reason to hit Jerry is somebody wants to take over the Cappadocia operations. If that somebody now makes a move on Jerry's father or goes around trying to slide Cappadocia businesses onto their own inventory, the somebody gets a name. Then I got nothing to tell anybody that they don't know already. There's no reason to put my feet in a meat grinder to ask me questions, and no reason to cut my head off to keep me from answering them."

As Jane brought it all back, this was the part that came back to her most vividly. Harry was only going to have to disappear for a little while. She could see him saying it, his face haggard and hopeful, like the face of a flood victim saying the rain had to stop soon. It was Harry at his most basic.

Harry had shown up at her door with nothing to offer except the story about Alfred Strongbear. The two robbers had left no money for him, not even the table stakes for the final poker game. He had tried to make up for it with expert advice. He once asked if she liked horses, and she had answered, "Yes," before she realized that he had said "*the* horses." "Never bet on anything less than a twenty-to-one shot," he advised. "It's not worth your time. You can't make anything. The secret is, the numbers fool people into thinking that handicapping is an exact science. No expert can figure it that close. When a horse opens at twenty-to-one, all they're saying is that it's a long shot. Fact is, it's probably ten-to-one, or even eight-to-one unless it's got three legs. One race in ten or fifteen, the others all go out and trip over their shoelaces." Harry had spent his life convincing himself that the long shots were going to come in. After she had studied him for a time, she understood that this was because he identified with them. If people had been assigned odds the way racehorses were, Harry would have been a twenty-to-one shot. She had an intuition that Harry was going to have to stay under longer than a little while, so she had given him a cover that would hold up. That had been five years ago.

Felker had gotten the essential parts of the story right, the ones Harry would have told a cop to get him to help. There was an account of the murder vague enough to reassure the cop that Harry didn't know the kinds of details that would make it worth the cop's while to put him in a cell, but vivid enough to convince him of what would happen to Harry if he did.

She was feeling a very strong impulse to believe Felker. It was just like Harry to have said Alfred Strongbear had given him forty thousand dollars instead of five thousand, and where would any of the story have come from if Harry hadn't told him? And then there was the way he told it. He had listened to Harry's voice, and she could tell that he liked Harry, thought he was funny. Maybe Harry was safe. Maybe this one was another like Harry, a man nobody was willing to take in and protect because he wasn't exactly an innocent but who wasn't a monster, either. The missing parts, the ones Felker didn't know or didn't remember, made it seem more likely. Harry had asked Alfred Strongbear, "If you want a mustache, why don't you just grow one?" The old man had told him, "It comes in too thin. People would know I'm an Indian."

Jane said, "All right. You can get up now." She relaxed her arm to let the gun muzzle point down at the floor and walked into the living room.

"You'll help me?" he asked.

"I didn't say that," she said. "I'm just not afraid enough of you to shoot you. Go connect my phone."

6

She waited in the living room and watched John Felker come in and sit in the chair across the room. She picked up her telephone, listened to the dial tone, then put it back in the cradle. "You were a policeman." The light was behind her, so it shone over her shoulder to illuminate him and remind her that there wasn't much time left before dark.

"Eight years. You want to know why I'm not now."

"Yes."

"It's a long story."

"What else have we got to do?" It sounded wrong, even to her. It was almost flirtatious. She tried to be businesslike. "I've got time."

"It came to me that the job just wasn't what I pretended it was."

"What was it?"

"You take a long, close look at all the people you've arrested, sometimes the easy way, sometimes the hard, with broken bones and blood and abrasions. They're mostly the kind of person who, when you talk to him, just hasn't got a clue."

"A clue about what?"

"It isn't just that they don't know there's a law about resisting arrest. They're not too clear on laws like cause-and-effect and gravity. The world goes on around them and steps on them all their lives, but they don't have any idea why, and it drives them half crazy. They

51

don't know why the guy next door has a new television set and they don't. Later on in prison they get tested and they can barely read, and they're addicted to everything, and their future is nothing."

"You felt sorry for them?"

"Not sorry enough to stop arresting them. What happened to me was that I could see that my own future was the same as theirs. I was going to have to spend twelve more years with these people—dragging them in, because they don't even know that much, that when they're driving at a hundred and ten, the helicopter over their heads isn't going to lose sight of them if they go a hundred and twenty, or that fifteen cops at their door aren't going to give up and leave them alone, no matter how hard they fight. If you spend all your time with them, you're just living the other half of their lives."

"Twelve more years—that was until retirement?"

"Yeah."

"So you quit?"

"I quit. I drew my credit-union balance and went to school. I got a C.P.A. license and went to work as an accountant at Smithson-Brownlow."

"What's that?"

"It's the twelfth biggest accounting company in the country. The St. Louis office is one of seventeen."

"Sorry, I count my own money. What happened?"

"I lasted almost five years. Then one day I was at work and I ran across a problem. I think it was an accident, but I can't even be sure of that. Somebody may have been setting me up to see it."

"See what?"

"One day a guy I didn't even know, on a different floor of the building, comes in, turns on his computer, and a message on the screen says, 'Bang. You're dead.' Then everything that was in his hard disk rolls across the screen and disappears forever. It's a computer virus. You know how they work, right?"

"Sure," she said. "You lost everything."

"No," he said. "They lost everything on his machine and five or six others and the mainframe. But one of the bosses was in early, kept his head and stopped the rest of us from turning ours on. The computer company sent over a program doctor, like a detective. He managed to find out how the virus worked, and delete it from the program. It took him about two weeks. He also searched every floppy in the office and found out the virus came from a disk somebody had brought in with a computer game on it. Every disk he used that went into another computer got that computer too, and so on. Of course nobody admitted to the computer game, and they couldn't tell whose machine was first. But mine was clean."

"Why did yours miss out?"

"I was handling a lot of single-client personal accounts. I would enter what I was doing and pass the disk on to the woman who oversaw the mainframe, and she would feed it to the machine for the company records. She kept the disk for backup and I got a new one." He looked tired now, his brow wrinkling a little as he remembered. "So I took a chance. I spent the first two days of the quarantine printing out everything in my files. Every word came out. For the next day or two I looked it over for signs of the virus."

"What did you find?"

"A lot of transactions I didn't know about."

"Stealing?"

"Yes. There was a pattern. There were lots of accounts where somebody had money in a portfolio—retirement funds, mostly. There would be dividends that were supposed to go for reinvestment, but instead they went to money-market accounts inside the portfolio. Then there would be a withdrawal from that account marked as an internal transfer to another account. The problem was, that one wasn't part of the portfolio. It didn't belong to the customer. I checked the number and it wasn't even an account that was under the company's control."

"It doesn't sound complicated enough to be the perfect crime."

"It wasn't. But the customer wouldn't notice right away. His balance wouldn't go down, it just wouldn't go up as much as it was supposed to. If he saw a report of the transfers, he would see that dividends received were being moved from one of his own accounts to his holding account and then to another account. He would assume that was his, too. Finally, I called the money-market fund's customer service number to get the name of the owner."

"Wait. They'll tell you that over the phone?"

"I was just trying to find out if it was legitimate. If it was one of our accounts, they'd tell me what I wanted to know. If they wouldn't, I'd know it was trouble. I said, 'I'm John Felker, from Smithson-Brownlow. Can you fax me a copy of the last statement for account number 12345678?' "

"And they did it?"

"Yes. Only not for the reason I thought. They did it because it was mine. There was almost half a million dollars in the account."

"It was in your name?"

"Yeah. At first I was furious. It took me maybe an hour to get scared."

"What did you have to be afraid of?"

"I started thinking. The computer virus had nothing to do with the company. It's a random act, like a drunk throwing a beer bottle into a crowd at a ball game. This was different. Somebody who had studied the operation—my part of it, specifically—had gone through and carefully moved things around. Whoever did it had access, knew the names of clients, that kind of thing. They were doing it to *me*."

"Did you go to your boss?"

"I was going to, but you have to imagine what the atmosphere was around there. They were losing money, probably clients. We were all suspects for bringing the virus in, so they were looking at us like the enemy anyway."

"So what? They already knew about the virus. This might have been part of it—some angry ex-employee or something."

"Right. But what if I had been stealing money? All of a sudden the virus hits and everybody in the firm starts scrutinizing all of the old records. All I could do was go to the boss and tell him the transfers on the computer were part of the joke. Only they weren't in the computer, like the virus. The money had really been moved and deposited in my name. I decided that before I brought this up, I had better keep looking until I found out enough to prove I wasn't a thief."

"Why would anybody do this, anyway? If they put it in your name, it wasn't for the money."

"That was what my boss would have said. Then it occurred to me that the half million could have been only part of it, or it could have all been done to set me up."

"Did it occur to you to transfer it all back where it belonged?"

"I told you what I found. I can't tell what I didn't find. For one thing, I didn't find anything like a half million in transfers. They could have been from accounts I never saw, didn't know about. And if these people could put money in, maybe they could get it out, too. There could be another half million already gone."

"You were an ex-cop. Why didn't you go to the police?"

"Believe me, I thought about it. But being an ex-cop made me more worried. I thought about what had happened in cases like this when I was a cop. You get a guy—a banker or accountant or lawyer—we got lots of lawyers. Some company blows the whistle. There's an account in his name with half a million in it. What does the D.A. do? He puts him in custody, quick. The judge doesn't grant bail, because if he's got one account with that much in it, he might have five more, and finding them takes months. He's a sure thing for jumping bail. While I was sitting in jail, anything could be happening with those records, and none of it was going to help me."

"So what did you do?"

"Here's where Harry comes in. After all this time he called me."

"Where?"

"I don't know where he was. I was at home."

"What did he say?"

"Two things. One was to stay out of jail. He had heard that some guys had been shopping a contract on me inside the prison system."

"Shopping?"

"Yeah. It was open. Anybody who got me was going to collect."

"Is that normal?"

"It hardly ever happens. It's too risky. There are so many people who would hear about it who need something to tell the police more than they need money."

"How did Harry hear about it?"

"He wouldn't say. Not in prison, and not in St. Louis. He was calling long-distance from a pay phone, and he kept pumping money into it and I kept hearing cars go by."

"What did you do?"

"I thought it through eighty different ways. No matter what I did, I couldn't imagine a way things could work out that didn't include my spending a lot of time in a prison waiting for an investigation. Harry said the contract was for a hundred thousand. That meant somebody must have stolen a lot. He might have taken ten million, left a half million lying around to get me arrested, and gotten me killed before my trial."

"Would that put an end to it?"

"Sure. He keeps the nine million or so, and everybody figures I took anything that's missing in the whole company."

"So it was somebody in the company."

"It might have been, even somebody in one of the other branches, but I couldn't be sure. It might have been somebody I arrested when I was a cop. For a long time now, they've been giving inmates computer lessons as part of the job-training program. It beats lathes and drill presses for getting a job afterward, and they can't use them to make a knife. You can learn a lot about computers in a five-to-ten sentence. Or it could be something bigger. If you can steal money by phone, then anybody anywhere could be doing it, and I just happened to be the victim."

"What did you do?"

"Any way you looked at it, the minute the computer man got the company's machines up and running and they took a close look at what was in there, I was going to jail. Within two or three days after that I would have to sleep, and then I would be dead."

She looked at him closely. "You stole it, didn't you?"

"What else could I do?" he asked. "I was an honest man. I didn't have the kind of money it takes to go on the run."

She seemed to be staring through his eyes into the back of his head. "Did it occur to you that this might have been what they wanted you to do?"

"Of course it did," he said. "If they were capable of thinking up the rest of it, they could think of that, too. But if I did nothing, each day the prisons were going to graduate maybe a hundred guys whose only offer of employment on the outside was killing me. If I brought it to the police, I was going inside, where the rest of them were. Even if I didn't, the company was going to find the pattern soon, just as I had."

"So you took the money."

"Some of it. So now I'm not just being set up. I really did what they're going to kill me for. I'm guilty."

"If you get to be safe and secure, will you give it back?"

He stared into the distance, toward the window behind her, for four or five breaths. "I'd like to. I doubt it."

"Why not?"

"We were all bonded. When they find out, the customers will get their money back. The insurance company will raise its premium, and life will go on. I'd like to be honest again, but embezzlers always say that, and I don't have any reason to believe I'm any better than the rest of them. I don't know if I'm ever in my life going to be in a position where I can bring myself to give it back. I'm going to be scared."

She kept the gun in her right hand while she picked up the telephone and cradled it under her chin. "What was the phone number of your station when you were a cop?"

"555-9292." He said it quickly, as though it had worn a groove into his brain and would never go away. "314 area code. But police stations won't tell you anything about an officer."

"I know," she said, and then somebody answered. She said, "Hello. This is Rachel Stanley from Deterrent Health Plans." She listened for a moment, then cut in and talked fast. "I'm calling because I'd like to set up a seminar for any police officers who might be interested in an exciting new plan for supplementing the coverage of law enforcement professionals." She stopped, as though she had run into a wall. "Oh?" she said. "What sort of plan do you have now?" She listened again. "Well, it's very good, but if anyone there is—I understand. Goodbye."

She dialed another long-distance number on the telephone and said, "I'd like the number of Missouri Casualty," listened for a moment, then dialed again, her eyes on him all the time. He could tell she was listening to a recording, and when she heard the right choice, she punched a number. After a pause, she said in a voice that was something between a purr and a threat, "Yes. This is Monica Briggs in admitting at U.C.L.A. Hospital in Los Angeles. We have a patient here named John Felker who is a retired St. Louis policeman."

She listened for a sentence or two, then sounded preoccupied as she repeated, "Social Security number . . . let's see . . ."

Felker handed her his wallet with the card showing and she read it off. Then she punched the speaker button so Felker could hear it too, and put down the receiver to hold the gun in both hands, aimed at his chest. The woman's voice on the other end echoed through the living room. "Oh, that's too bad. At the time when Mr. Felker left the police force, he had only been employed for seven years, nine months. His benefits weren't vested. I'm afraid he has no coverage with us."

Jane lowered the pistol and said into the speaker, "Oh, he has primary coverage. This would have been secondary. He'll be fine." She punched the button and put down the gun. "I'll help you."

7

Jake Reinert cleaned his brushes on his father's old workbench in the cellar. In a way he felt unworthy using it. His father had been a real craftsman. His own father, Jake's grandfather, had been a cavalryman in the royal hussars of the Austro-Hungarian empire and he hadn't wanted his son to be a soldier. He had sent the boy to school, but when he was about to be beaten for some infraction or other, the boy had either punched or pushed the teacher, depending on how much of his wine he had swallowed when he later told the story, jumped out the school window, and run. Then the soldier had sent his son to be apprenticed to a cabinet-maker, but he had gotten kicked out of there, too. The cavalryman foresaw that like him, the boy was left with nothing but the military to keep bread in his mouth. So he did what tens of thousands of fathers all over Europe had been doing with boys like that since 1492, and got him on a ship to America.

Now that Jake had grown up, he suspected there had probably been a bit of self-interest in the decision, since there were advantages to being able to ship a juvenile delinquent to the other side of the world. But Jake knew there was sincerity, too. It was just about at the point in history when men riding full-speed on horseback waving swords were pretty sure to run into artillery and machine guns, even in that part of the world. No man would want his son in on that.

Jake's father must have learned a lot in his apprenticeship. He had come over at sixteen and never had much trouble finding work. He had made fine furniture, done the interior woodwork of the fancy cabin cruisers they built down at the boatworks, even carved some of the beautiful, fanciful animals they mounted on the merry-go-rounds at the Mitchell-Bauer carousel plant.

Jake was at the stage of life where he had come down here enough times to find his brushes hardened into paddles, so he soaked them for an hour or two in fresh turpentine after the visual evidence said they were clean. He also could look out the cellar window from here and see the light in the side window of Jane Whitefield's house. The lights would come on shortly, and then he would be able to see shadows on the ceiling and, sometimes, silhouettes in the window.

The world was old now. Most of the unexplored territory left was in the space between people's ears. Jane Whitefield's mother had comported herself with dignity and modesty during her marriage to Henry Whitefield. But Jake's wife, Margaret, had once regretfully implied that she had quite a past. Jake had asked a few questions, to see if he had glimpsed a side of Margaret that he hadn't suspected—jealousy or some need to put any strange woman who showed up in her bailiwick under suspicion—but he hadn't.

Her hint had been based on certain knowledge, some woman-to-woman confidence, and it was what it had sounded like. Jane's mother had been left without resources in New York City at the age of twenty. There was a myth that said that there was a time in our society when a twenty-year-old girl could not be left without resources, even in a big city. Somebody would pick her up and let her belong, just as a lost fingerling swims into a school of fish and disappears. Jake was always willing to admit the possibility that such a thing might once have been real, but even in those days it wasn't true to the experience of anyone then living. He supposed that was what small towns were for. Jane's mother hadn't been in a small town. Instead, she found herself a succession of boyfriends who periodically vacationed in places like Elmira and Attica.

Margaret had never been one to be critical of anyone for having had a lot of sex. That would have been completely alien to her nature. The way she always said it was "People have a right to try to be happy. It's in the Declaration of Independence." But she implied that Jane's mother had tried harder than most before she was finally able to bring it off. Margaret had a genuine sympathy for that, because sympathy was the thing that came easiest to her.

On the whole, Jake was a nurture-over-nature man, but he could not rule out any possibility that science hadn't ruled out first. When Jane was younger, he had sometimes watched her behavior for the sort of sweet tooth that her mother had. Whatever else had been true of Jane's mother, she had never turned it into a business.

Young women, even young women of considerable intelligence and self-reliance, had been known to get themselves into trouble with this sort of activity. They had even been known to be found dead. Because no matter what sort of caution a young woman had, once she was in a private place, out of earshot of trusted friends and in any of the positions necessary for what the polite called consummation, there wasn't much she could do to alter the course of events. It was best to accomplish whatever checking of credentials needed to be done well before that stage.

He glanced over at the cellar window and past his rosebush at Jane's side window. He had been right. There was a second silhouette. It looked to be about the size of the young man who had been knocking on her door yesterday.

* * *

Jane opened the cylinder of the pistol and emptied the bullets into the palm of her hand, then handed the gun back to Felker. She hesitated a second, then held out the five bullets too. He looked puzzled, and she said, "If you didn't ask, they're not the only ones you have."

He took the five rounds and put them in his pants pocket. "What do we do now?"

"We figure out what I can do for you," she said. "Are you married?"

"I used to be. After about three years of being a cop's wife, she saw the future before I did."

"That would be—what—ten years ago. What about girlfriends?"

"Why are you asking these things?"

"Is there anybody in St. Louis who will already have called the cops and reported you missing?"

"No. I told my boss I couldn't do much while the computers were down, so I would take some vacation time. I told him to leave a message on my machine when things were normal again. My family consists of my sister, Linda, who is married and has four kids and talks to me once a year on the phone, and about thirty cousins I haven't seen in twenty years. When I told Linda about this, she said I was right to run, and good luck."

"Did she know where you were going?"

"No."

She thought hard for a minute. "I don't suppose you speak any foreign languages well enough to fool anybody?"

"No. A little Spanish."

"Do you have anything else that would help you hide in another country?"

"The money. That's not mine, but the passport is."

She studied him with a hint of sadness. "I know all this has happened fast, but you have to think a little bit ahead. A passport with John Felker on it isn't going to help. You aren't going to be able to sit at a café table in Rio reading American newspapers until you see that they've cleared your name. You're not innocent."

"No," he said. "I didn't think . . ."

"Where do you want to go?"

"I don't know. They can't be looking for me harder than people have looked for Harry. Where did you send him?"

She sat in silence for a time, then said, "I guess it'll have to be somewhere inside the country. That's easier, but it takes more discipline."

"What kind of discipline?"

"You might have special problems." Then she brightened. "Were you ever an undercover cop, with a different identity?"

"No," he said. "I was the regular kind. What's the problem?"

"Unlearning old habits," she said. "If somebody hits a cop, he hits back, harder."

"I haven't been a cop for a long time," he said.

"Some people can live with the idea that they have enemies and never try to find out who they are. Can you?"

"Why are you asking these things?"

"I need to know who you are, and I want you to know who I am. Who I am to you, anyway. If you want peace, I'll risk my life to give you that. If you want revenge, take your gun and go back."

"I gave that up when I decided to come here."

"I'm just telling you that I don't waste myself. Nobody finds his way to me until his old life is used up. If you come with me, John Felker is dead. You're somebody else, who doesn't have any enemies."

He thought for a long time. "I can do it."

"How did you get here?"

"I took a Greyhound from St. Louis to Buffalo, then a cab."

"Buses are slow and have regular schedules. Anybody who wants a copy can pick one up and read it. Did anybody follow you?"

"I don't think so." Then he admitted, "I never looked."

"Did anybody see you come into my house?"

"Your neighbor. The old guy."

"Where's your suitcase?"

"In your closet upstairs."

"Go get it."

Jake Reinert heard the sound of the car starting in the driveway next door. It was nearly dark already, but he couldn't help going to the corner window to take a peek at what he could already see without using his eyes at all.

It was Jane Whitefield's rental car, and the man was in the driver's seat. Jake Reinert watched the man adjust the seat and the mirrors. As the car slowly moved past his window, he stared at the man hard, with the knowledge that in a week or so he might very well have to describe the face to Dave Dormont down at the police station.

8

J ane pretended to look down into her leather bag, but her eyes slipped to the side to confirm that Jake Reinert was where she had thought he would be, in his corner window.

"Where am I supposed to drive?" Felker asked.

"Go north along River Road while we talk."

"All right."

"While I was packing I noticed that you had searched my room. You went through the papers in my desk. Why?"

"I wanted to be sure that you were the woman Harry said you were. Even if you were, people move."

"What did you find?"

"You have some credit cards that aren't in your name. Finding your bills was a big relief." He watched her closely for a moment, and she seemed satisfied. He asked, "Where are we going?"

"We're going to change cars."

"Before we start?"

"This is a rented car. If somebody saw the company name on it already, then they're not looking for one out of sixty million cars anymore, it's one out of ten thousand or so. Say ten percent have New York plates. Now it's down to one thousand. Half are this model? Five hundred. Half are this color? Two-fifty. If they have the company's records, they'll know where it gets turned in."

66

He drove in silence a couple of blocks west before he reached the river. It looked big and dark in the early evening. Across the channel, the shore of Grand Island was dark except for the bright grid of windows on a hotel. He turned right and followed the road. "Do you really think they could get the car company's records? It used to take us a couple of days to do that, and we needed a court order."

"If they can get into your company's records, why not any company?"

"Yeah," he said glumly. "Why not?"

"I'm not trying to ruin your morale. I'm just being as careful as I can. We don't know who they are or why they did it to you. But we do know they probably got, or are getting, a lot of money, and they think if you die, they can keep it. So they'll spend as much as they have to."

Felker sighed. Then he seemed to remember something. He turned toward her. "Money," he said. "It's funny how when your life is in danger you stop thinking about it. What do you charge for this? What's your fee?"

She looked out the side window and watched the familiar buildings going by: the pizza parlor where she and her friends used to spend about half their evenings. It was Jimmy Connolly's skinny ankles that had made her fall in love with him. She could see them now, but somehow she had lost the ability to bring back why they had seemed so attractive. A few doors down was the big old movie house that was called the Berliner until the First World War and the Tivoli for sixty years after that. It had closed twenty years ago and been broken up into little stores. The upper stories of the building still had the elaborate scrollwork because it was carved in the stone, and she could still remember the smell of ancient popcorn and the feel of the worn velvet seats. They used to show Tarzan movies on Saturdays for a quarter, so children had watched them without complaint. She had sensed that it was always a big moment when Jane got wet, but at the time the significance was lost on her. "I don't have a fee," she said. "Sometimes people send me presents."

"You mean you live off presents?"

"I didn't say they were small presents." She smiled slyly.

He frowned. "Just give me some idea. I want to be fair."

He was such a ... man. Things had to be decided, nailed down and certified. He probably wanted to have each of them say it and then shake on it, give her hand one of those single, hard shakes. She turned toward him and said, "Okay, I'll tell you how it's going to work. When this is over, you're going to sleep for a day or so, and then you'll take a week or two getting used to a new place, and then a month getting used to being somebody different. One day—maybe then, maybe a year from then—you'll sit down and think about how it happened, and you'll send me a present."

She let him think about that, and stared past him at the river. The road was good and fast, through the quiet old towns that had grown up along the Niagara in the 1790s, after the Revolutionary War. From the beginning of time, all of this land had been a place where people lived. As a little girl she had walked along the river and found arrowheads, and they were still finding them, three hundred years after the metal brought in by the fur trade had replaced them.

As they crossed city lines, a stranger like Felker probably didn't even know he wasn't in Deganawida anymore, because the distinctions between these little towns were subtle and had to do with things that had happened through time. They weren't boundaries, they were stories.

As they passed the long grassy strip on the way out

of North Tonawanda and the brush began again, she caught herself watching for the marker along the river, where the river widened and she could see past the tip of Grand Island. The marker was old, almost invisible thirty feet from the road in the grove of trees that had grown up around it, so she tried to look fast, but it was too dark to spot it. That didn't matter, because what was worth looking at was something that couldn't be seen with the eyes anymore.

On this spot one summer in the 1670s the Frenchman La Salle had built the *Griffon*, the first ship to sail the Great Lakes. It must have looked strange to the Seneca staring at it from the dense forest beyond the stumps of the trees the Frenchmen had cut for lumber. The keel and ribs of the half-finished hull would have loomed just at the shore like the skeleton of an enormous fish, and the Seneca, who were still invincible in this part of the world, must have been more curious than threatened.

Beyond the town named after La Salle, the road grew into a parkway that took them past the congestion that had grown up around the Falls. Hennepin, the Jesuit priest on La Salle's expedition, had been the first white man to blunder out of the woods and lay eyes on them, so people remembered his name. That had always struck her as funny. Here were these falls, well over a half mile wide and 180 feet high, so loud you could barely hear anything else and throwing big clouds of mist far into the sky that you could see for miles. In the 1670s every Indian from Minnesota to the Atlantic knew all about them, because they were the only serious interruption in the ancient trade routes. And those were the days when gods still had addresses. Heno the Thunderer lived in a cave right behind that wall of water.

As they continued on up the parkway, she glanced at Felker again. He was doing pretty well, considering the fact that his whole life had been destroyed in a couple of days and he had been on the run ever since. There was no whining, no questions she couldn't answer. She supposed that if he had lasted eight years as a cop, the least he could be was tough. She had felt a little alarm when she had seen that he had searched her room, but he was a cop and that was the way cops were trained to find out who they were dealing with. And he had, at least once, been in the position she was in. He had seen a harmless little guy like Harry, with enemies closing in on him, and he had thought about it and decided to save him. She would do her best for him.

She tried to prepare herself. This was one of the hard ones, and she was tired. It was one thing when two so-cial workers were at a convention and they were sitting at a bar in a city strange to both of them and confiding in each other, and one of them said she had a case that was horrible and the system just couldn't be made to work, and the other one looked down into the bottom of her glass and said, "I know a woman . . ." But it had long ago grown into something else. She had been out six times in the past year. She forced herself to forget what had gone before. She needed to keep thinking ahead.

She could see they were only a couple of miles from Ridge Road, where the Tuscarora Reservation started. She looked at the signs, watching for the garage, built outside the border of the reservation so people couldn't watch its proprietor too closely. Finally, she saw it and said, "Pull in up here, away from the gas pumps." Fel-ker drove the car up onto the cracked blacktop and kept the engine running.

"Want me to fill the tank?" he asked.

"No," she said. "Just wait for me." Jane walked to the little lighted building beside the garage and went in-side, away from the sounds of the cars flashing by on the road.

The man sitting on the stool behind the counter was

watching a small television set next to the cash register. He smiled when he looked up to acknowledge that he had seen her, and his eyes returned to the television set. He said to it, "Hi, Janie."

"Hello, Cliff," she answered. "Nice night."

"You come to watch the game with me?" Clifford Tarkington smiled his special smile, and his broad Tuscarora face seemed to widen and his dark eyes narrowed, but his mouth didn't move. "Big night. The Indians are playing the Yankees."

The Tuscarora all had names like Wallace or Clifford or Clinton, just the way the Seneca did. The Seneca had never given children the names of Christian saints. The Mohawk at Caughnawaga, on the Canadian side of the St. Lawrence, had been called the Praying Indians. There had never been any praying Seneca, and if there had been any praying Tuscarora, they would have gotten cured of it in 1712. That was the year when a Swiss mercenary had led an army of South Carolina colonists and enemy tribes to take their homeland in North Carolina. The winners had feasted on the body of a dead Tuscarora and then sold their prisoners at the slave markets. The survivors had been taken in by the Seneca and given the village of Ga-a-noga to live in.

"I came to relieve you of one of those old junkers you keep around here," said Jane. "I can see you need the space."

"I might be able to part with something elegant yet understated," said Clifford. "What kind?"

"Mid-size," she said. "Nothing eye-catching, not just out of the box."

"But not too old either?" he guessed. "I got a 'ninety-two Ford. Cherry, runs good, low miles."

"What color? I don't want one of those cars put together in the Ford plant in Hamilton with Canadian two-tone colors on it so everybody thinks I just came out of the woods."

"Pearl-gray. Hell, they're all gray now, or white. Five a week if it comes back the same color."

Two years ago, she had been taking a twelve-year-old boy out of Ohio where two sets of cousins who had let him stay in foster homes all his life had learned he had an inheritance coming. They had put a description of the car on television. She had run the car through a one-hour painting shop and had them put the two-hundred-dollar special on it. Clifford had sometimes thought to mention it during subsequent negotiations.

"Five hundred?" she exclaimed. "You misunderstood. I don't want to own it. How about two hundred?"

"Four-fifty," he muttered at the television. "It's a T-bird. It's loaded."

"Two and a half, and I won't play with the power seats."

"Hasn't got them."

"And you said it was loaded?"

"Three-fifty, and I throw in a full tank."

"It's already on full if it's sitting back there. You're afraid it'll get water vapor in the tank. Three hundred, and I'll forget about what you owe me for the paint job on the other one."

"Three twenty-five and I'll take back the rental you got parked out there."

"Done," she said, and handed him a check she had already written.

He looked at the amount and said, "It's always an education to do business with you, Janie."

"Yeah," she said. "Except I always pay the tuition."

He handed her a ring with two keys on it. "Later, Janie."

"Later," she said, and walked out onto the pavement. She kept going around to the back of the building and found the car sitting on the cracked cement foundation of an old, vanished building that Cliff used as a parking lot. The Ford wasn't bad to begin with, and when she started it she could hear and feel that he must have just tuned the engine. She let it idle and walked back around to find Felker standing beside the rented car, leaning on the door.

As they got in, she said quietly, "It's better at this stage of the trip not to stand around under a light unless you have to."

"Why? Did you see somebody?" He checked his impulse to whirl and look behind him.

"I don't know," she said. "At least fifty cars have gone by here since we stopped, but I don't know who I'm looking for. They do."

She drove around to the back of the building, where the other car sat running. "Pull that one out so I can put this one in its place."

He got in behind the wheel of the Ford and pulled it out, waited for Jane to stop, and lifted their two bags out of her car, then opened the door of the Ford to set them in.

Jane said, "It's cash, isn't it?"

He shrugged. "Well, yeah. I didn't think I'd be in a position to cash a check or something."

"Put it in the trunk. It won't be any safer two feet closer to you on the back seat."

He opened the trunk and put the two bags inside, then started to close it, but hesitated. "I don't want to keep guessing wrong. Is it all right to keep the gun up front with us?"

She was at the rear of the rented car, opening the trunk. She said, "It's fine with me. Keep the trunk open." When she slammed the trunk and came around to the new car, she was carrying a backpack and a short-barreled shotgun. She put them in beside the bags.

"You still want me to drive?" he asked.

"If you don't mind. People always take a second look if the woman is driving. It looks like the man is drunk or something." She set the keys on the hood of the rented car and got in beside Felker.

"Drive straight north again. When you come to the intersection with Ridge Road, take a right."

He bumped the car slowly around Clifford's building and glanced past it to gauge the speed and distance of the next set of headlights coming toward them. She saw that his eyes focused on her for a second before he stepped on the gas.

"What's wrong?" she said.

"It's typical Harry. He didn't bother to tell me what you looked like."

"Why? What do I look like?"

He shrugged. "Well, you don't look like a body-guard."

She regretted having asked that way, as though she wanted him to tell her she was pretty. She regretted saying anything at all. She should have ignored it. She hadn't been given enough time to prepare for that too, the special strain of traveling with a man who wasn't too old and wasn't too young and had gotten used to the fact that most of the attention he had given women was welcome. She had to keep him thinking in another way, so she pretended to misunderstand, as though the whole idea had never entered her head. "That's the way it's done," she said. "You've got to get used to thinking one way and looking another way. Turn right at that light up there."

He made the turn and accelerated onto the eastbound highway. Then he looked at her again. "It's a beautiful disguise." He seemed to realize he had gone too far. "Very smart."

"Yours has got to be better. It has to come from inside your head. When was the last time you were afraid for your life?"

"That's easy," he said. "When I was a cop."

"Cops are dogs. Try to think in rabbit."

"What?"

She said it carefully, so he would understand. "This is like dogs chasing a rabbit. When the rabbit wins, he doesn't get to kill the dogs and eat them. He doesn't get to be a dog. He just gets to keep being a rabbit."

He opened his shirt and held out the pistol. "You mean rabbits don't need one of these."

"It's an asset if you think of it as a last resort. Just don't imagine that a shoot-out with the people who are looking for us is going to help you. Once anybody has discharged a firearm, sooner or later everybody left standing has to talk to the police."

"And we can't talk to the police."

"A few days in a jail cell won't hurt me. I've done it before. But if these people are any of the things you think they are, then *you* can't." She paused for a moment, then said, "Or any of the people you haven't thought of yet."

"What people?"

"I don't know."

"Why aren't you saying it straight out? What is it?"

"Whoever it is wants you killed in jail before a trial. Doesn't that have a familiar ring to it?"

He answered too quickly: "No."

"So you have thought of it."

"I've thought of everything. I've heard those stories too, but not from anybody who would know. And not in St. Louis."

"The contract on you is being circulated in prisons. Money doesn't do a lifer much good. Other things do."

"It's not cops."

"Nobody seems to be afraid that a prisoner who hears about it will take it to the authorities. It does make you wonder."

He was irritated now. "I wasn't a dirty cop who knew things about other dirty cops. I did my job until the day I quit, and when I left, as far as I know, everybody else

did his job too." He simmered for a few minutes while
she waited in silence. Then he said quietly, "I'm sorry.
I just . . . my life just kind of blew up. It's taken a few
days to get used to the idea that the last five years,
when I was an accountant, were a waste. I was probably
just being set up. I'm ready to give up everything I ever
was, but I'm not ready to decide that everything I've
ever done was worthless. Does that make sense?"

"Of course it does," she said. She had gone as far as
she could for the moment. Some of the rabbits took to
it instantly because they had been hiding and ducking
all of their lives. Some took longer.

As they drove along Ridge Road, the dense thickets
of bright electric lights along the river faded and threw
no illumination in front of them. Ridge Road had been
laid out on the northern branch of the Waagwenneyu,
the great central trail of the Iroquois that ran from the
Hudson to the Niagara. The north branch had been
placed just below Lake Ontario on the long, flat escarp-
ment that was the prehistoric edge of the lake.

As she looked out into the darkness past the little
pool of light that the headlamps threw, she could feel
the Waagwenneyu under them, just below the pavement.
In the dark, the road sliced through the middle of the
property of some rich guy who thought of himself as a
country gentleman. Her view was blocked by a dense
second-growth of trees that the owner's farmer ancestor
must have left there to protect his crops from the wind.
The thick trunks presented themselves one after the
other and swept by, and the overarching branches fifty
feet above nearly touched each other in the middle, and
looking up at them put Jane a few inches lower, below
the pavement on the Waagwenneyu. The path was
mostly straight, winding here and there to avoid a thick
tree or a muddy depression. It was narrow, only eighteen inches wide, but deep—sometimes worn a foot below the surface by hundreds of years of moccasins. This

was the branch of the trail that took the Seneca from the Genesee valley and the Finger Lakes northwest into Canada. The other branch was now Main Street in Buffalo, and it ran to the shore of Lake Erie and continued along it into Ohio and beyond. Those were the paths to war.

In the direction they were traveling now, it was the trail home, to the soft, rolling country where the Seneca felt most safe. The world then was all tall forests that had never been cut, oak and maple and elm and hickory and hemlock and pine, alternating in stands and mixed together. Sometimes runners would move along this trail eastward to tell something urgent—alarms or councils. They ran day and night, naked except for a breechcloth and belt, their war clubs stuck in the belt at the back and their bows strung across their chests. They always ran in pairs, one behind the other, silent, never speaking. They could cover a hundred miles a day, so the trip from Neahga, the mouth of the Niagara, to Albany, in the country of the Mohawk, took three days. In all that distance there was no point where the trail emerged from the forest. It was marked at intervals by hatchet gouges on the biggest trees, but the runners didn't need to look. Sometimes they would glance up and to the left to navigate by the constellation of the loon, but most of the time they could feel the trail with the balls of their feet.

When the trees had thinned out again, Jane replaced them with ghost trees beyond the range of the headlights, so that what was beyond eyesight could be the great forest again, deep and thick and shadowy. The secret was that the forest was still here, the descendants standing tall in parks and groves and windbreaks. The Seneca were still here too, driving this road to jobs in Lockport or Niagara Falls, dreaming Seneca dreams.

There was a disturbance coming from outside her, a light that rushed up from behind and pushed the forest back on both sides, where she couldn't feel it around her anymore. She sat up. "How long has that car been behind us?" she asked.

"I don't know," said Felker. "He just switched his brights on."

"Think for a second," she said. "Was it there when we made the turn?" She knew the answer. It wouldn't have been so dark if the other car had been behind them. It must be all right. They hadn't been followed.

"I don't think so," he said.

The car came closer and closer, catching up quickly, but the driver didn't dim his lights. Felker reached up and moved the rearview mirror to cut the glare of the rectangle of light that it threw across his eyes.

"There's a long, straight stretch in a minute," said Jane. "When we get there, let him pass."

"I'd be delighted." He reached the section where the road straightened. On both sides were low, crooked fieldstone walls and houses built far back from the road, as houses had been when these were still farms. Felker slowed to forty, then thirty, but the car slowed too and stayed behind. Finally, he coasted off onto the shoulder and the car came up behind. When he had nearly stopped, the other car pulled to the left, its glaring headlights merging now with his to illuminate the slight decline ahead and then halfway up the compensating slope. The car slowly slid past and gained speed.

Jane stared at the back window while it was still in the beam of the headlights. There were four heads in it. That usually meant it was kids, probably farm kids who had spent the day in the city. Her eyes moved downward. It had New York plates, and that was a relief. But there was a license-plate holder around it with the name of a dealer.

"Does Star-Greendale mean anything to you?" she asked.

"Where did you see that?"

"People from around here buy their cars around here. I never heard of it."

"St. Louis," he said, frowning. "Greendale is a town outside St. Louis. But it's not Star, it's Starleson Chevrolet."

"Stop," she said. "Leave the lights on, but give me the keys. Somebody saw you get on the bus in St. Louis."

She slipped out and closed the door, then ran to the trunk. She pulled everything out and tossed it into the back seat, then climbed over it. He watched her in the back seat as she opened the backpack. "What are you doing?"

"The car has New York plates. They must have damaged them prying them off somebody else's, so they left their holder on to cover it." She was busy pushing shells into the long tubular magazine of the shotgun. "They're waiting for us up there somewhere. If we go back the way we came, we're a half hour from anywhere crowded enough to lose them."

He checked the load of his pistol and then snapped the cylinder back into place. "There's a box of ammo in my suitcase," he said. "I'd like to have that where I can reach it before we go ahead."

"We're not going ahead. We're not dogs, remember?"

"What, then?"

"Take the backpack. Put your money in it, or whatever else you think is worth saving. Don't leave anything here that will tell who you are—I mean tell anybody, even the police. Wipe off everything you touched."

"We're going to walk?"

She didn't answer, so he quickly did what she had told him to. The money wouldn't all fit in the knapsack, so he put some of it in his pockets. Jane put her leather bag over her shoulder and held her shotgun in her right hand. "Time to go," she said, and walked across the road. She swung her legs over the stone fence and into the empty cornfield beside it, then stood still as he hurried to catch up.

"All right," she said. "Walk only on the trenches between the rows. That's the way the farmers do it because the corn is planted in the raised places."

"You care about their corn?"

"No, I care about leaving footprints you can see with a flashlight."

She started off across the cornfield, taking two rows at a step, and Felker followed. She could hear him coming along behind her, and it made her comfortable, because if he had stepped on the soft ridges of dirt, it would have been silent. Now and then he stopped to glance up the highway, and that put him behind, but she didn't care. He was tall and strong, and he wouldn't have any trouble keeping up.

She angled away from the barnyard, where there would be animals to smell them and bring the farmer out. When they reached the windbreak of trees at the north end of the field, she stopped and touched Felker. He leaned down and she put her lips to his ear. "We'll watch from here."

She set down her bag and sat on it, leaning against a tree trunk, the shotgun butt on the ground and the barrel upward. Felker slipped the backpack off his shoulders and sat by the next tree. It took five minutes. The Chevrolet's headlights came over the horizon, aimed first up into the sky and then dipping at the crest of the hill. The car was moving fast, at least seventy, judging from the way it gobbled up the space between the telephone poles.

When the driver saw the car parked by the side of the road, he slowed down. There were no heads visible in the borrowed Ford, so the driver had a decision to make. The Chevrolet veered to the center of the road and passed the parked car at about the speed of a walking man. It proceeded a hundred yards farther, and then its lights went out before it stopped. The doors opened and three of the four men got out and started to walk back along the road.

Jane didn't see the dome light go on, and she didn't hear any door slam. None of this was reassuring. The one in the car left the lights off and kept going down the road, then stopped and turned around. It was too far from the parked car for Jane and Felker to have heard it if they were hiding on the floor. The three men on foot spread out when they were still a hundred feet behind the parked car. Two of them went into the fields behind the stone fences on either side of the road, and all three slowly approached the car. When one was in front of it and one on each side, they stopped, pulled guns out of their coats, and aimed them at the Ford.

Felker leaned close to Jane's ear and whispered, "If we're going, shouldn't we get started?"

She shook her head. "I want to see one more thing."

The Chevrolet began to move slowly up the road toward the parked car, its lights still off. When it was almost bumper to bumper with the Ford, it suddenly shot forward and rammed the back bumper to knock whoever was inside out of their crouch. The man on the road flung the back door open and aimed his gun. After a second he slammed the door in frustration, and the light went out before he turned his head.

"Now," Jane said. She turned and crawled a few feet deeper into the windbreak and then stood up.

9

She went off at a slow jog, going due north, first among the trees and then across a second field. This one was unplowed and full of short weeds that whipped against the stiff denim of her jeans. When they reached the far side of the second field, she stopped and looked back. The headlights came on suddenly and bathed the Ford in a pool of whiteness.

Then she was running through the night across the fields, the bag over her left shoulder and the shotgun balanced in her right hand. She could hear Felker's breathing behind her, and she judged that he had the stamina to keep running.

It was going to be possible if she could keep her vision clear. Everything about modern life made people think of the world as a network of roads. But in country like this, the roads were just the narrow borders of broad expanses of rolling, fertile farmland. The four men weren't about to abandon their car in the dark and take off on foot across the fields after them. If they were like most people, they wouldn't even think of it. They would already be searching a map for the place where Jane and Felker would come out on a road. The obvious thing to do was to take a loop, come out behind the men on Ridge Road, and hope to make it eastward into Lockport, where there would be lights and police. But what if she and Felker didn't double back? If she remembered, if her vision was clear, there were no more big east-west roads between here and Route 18, just on the outskirts of Olcott.

Felker moved abreast of her and said between deep breaths, "Where are we running to?"

She said, "Olcott."

"What's Olcott?"

"About seven or eight miles."

"What's in Olcott?"

"Save your strength," she said, then regulated her breathing again to bring in oxygen to keep her head clear. "Don't talk."

They ran in silence then, and she lengthened her strides to match his, so the sounds of their feet struck her ear at the same time, a strong, rhythmic cadence, not a ragged pitter-patter pitter-patter that drained strength and wore out the runner. She kept her head up and tried to relax her shoulder muscles, but it was difficult carrying the shotgun and the leather bag that bounced against her hip at each stride.

She pulled the strap of the bag over her head so it went across her chest between her breasts and the bag was on her back. Then she slipped off her belt as she ran, and threaded it through the swivel on the end of the shotgun magazine, then through the trigger guard, and slung it tightly over her back so it was held against the leather bag. When she had done that, the running went faster.

It was a clear, cool April night, so the sweat formed and dried almost instantly, and the air came into her lungs like a cold intoxicant and came out in steamy huffs. She thought about Felker and listened to his breathing. He was disturbing. Jane had never taken a fugitive out of the world who had had this much trouble this early. Yet he seemed to be accepting it. She could hear him breathing deep, steady breaths, not short irregular gasps. He didn't seem to be afraid. He had more to be afraid of than some of the people she had protected, less than others, but they had all been afraid. They had come to her because they had already tried all of the forms of shelter that people believed in: laws, blood relations, friends, even society's capacity for simple outrage and disgust that a lone, powerless person had been laid open to evil. He had come that way too, but he wasn't one of them. He wasn't afraid.

They ran through the fields and pastures, thickets of small bushes and groves of old trees, once coming so near to a house that they had to duck a clothesline before they slipped along beside the white clapboards. There was a dark window in the back where she could see the ghostly blue glow from a television set on the ceiling, but no people. The night was empty now. They were all penned inside houses and cars, separated from the night by plates of glass and the electricity they immersed themselves in, thick blankets of sound and light and warmth.

Jane felt strangely elated. She could feel the air and the trees around her, and because she could feel them and because she was running, she was part of it too. She was straining, exerting her legs and arms and her eyes and ears to move across the land in a way that people didn't do often anymore, without some machine or a pavement to keep the land away from them.

She never glanced at her watch, because time had a different pace now. She couldn't measure mechanical time against a distance she had only guessed was seven or eight miles but might be five or ten, and wasn't uniform and smooth and level like a track at the university. The pace of her feet was the only time that mattered, and she kept it steady and even, like the beat of a song without any tune and without any words.

She saw Route 18 coming from a long way off. There were three streetlamps somewhere off to her right and, far beyond the road, the glow of more lights in the sky. The houses were coming more often now, and they were harder to avoid because they weren't farms but suburban houses on smaller plots of land. Now was the time when she had to decide about the shotgun. Even when most people were asleep, she couldn't take the risk of walking down a village street carrying a weapon. She said to Felker, "Stop here."

He came closer. "What is it?" His breathing was hard and fast, and his voice was a little hoarse, like hers.

"Let's catch our breath."

They walked along the fence of a big pasture, and she waited to let her heart stop pounding and her slower, deeper breathing come. She kept moving to fight off the cramps that were waiting to grip her calves and hamstrings. Felker swung his arms and walked along, trying to recover from the long run, but she could feel his eyes on her. She reached up behind her head and held up the long hair to cool the nape of her neck in the night air. Finally, she said quietly, "That road up there is Route 18. It's the last big highway."

He said, "What's beyond that?"

"A quiet little town."

Jane decided she couldn't get close enough to the highway to detect a parked car without its occupants seeing her too. The two shoulders would be at least ten feet each, and forty for the pavement itself. Then, after they were across that, the other side might not be the houses she was hoping for. It might be more open land. She said aloud, "How does the chicken cross the road?"

"That's it?" he said.

"If they guessed right, they'll be waiting for us here. They'll take us in the open."

"I guess I walk across and you cover me with the shotgun until something happens or I'm behind something. Then it's your turn," he said.

She looked at him for a minute. "Not very good, but I suppose it's the only way."

He shrugged. "It's the only way they ever taught me."

They walked along the field until they could see the road ahead of them. On the other side there was an open field, but the trees beyond it gave her some hope. At least there weren't a lot of lights on this stretch. They crept closer and closer to the road until they reached an empty lot overgrown with tall weeds that ran up to the shoulder.

She crawled forward in the weeds until she reached a shallow drainage ditch at the edge of the road, and looked hard to her right toward the lights, then down into the darkness to her left. There was nothing on the pavement in either direction, but she still didn't feel right. Maybe it was just that the long run had made her light-headed. There never had been much chance that any four strangers would realize that she was heading north for Olcott.

She had been driving eastward when they had caught up. When that had failed, it would have made most sense either to walk around their ambush and keep going east or try to go back the other way, toward Niagara Falls. Olcott was a tiny community on the shore of Lake Ontario, at least half of it summer cottages closed from October until May, when the wind off the lake lost some of its cruelty. Besides, Olcott was too far. Nobody would try to run eight miles across country at night, through cornfields and woods and over barbed-wire fences.

She knew Felker was getting impatient. She looked in both directions again, letting her eyes stare at each tree, each distant building, each mailbox along the shoulder, then just looking, letting her eyes go unfocused to detect movement. It was foolish. The barrier was imaginary.

Jane rolled onto her side to nod at Felker, then watched him take a step before she rolled back onto her belly to watch the road. She heard Felker coming through the weeds, then heard his feet hit faster, and then he was stepping onto the open pavement.

Somewhere in the distance she heard the familiar sound of a car starting. She turned her head from side to side quickly, trying to hear the exact direction. Felker had heard it too. He quickened his pace, running now to get across before the car—any car—caught him in its lights. Jane still couldn't see it, but now there was the sound of tires on gravel, and then the engine's whispery hum, getting louder and louder as it accelerated. She pumped the shotgun.

The car swung out of the dark driveway of a house a couple of hundred yards off. Its lights were still off, and the hum grew into a deeper roar. It was too dark to see clearly, so the car seemed not to be coming nearer as much as growing in intensity and anger.

She rested on her elbows and hugged the shotgun tightly to her shoulder. She could feel the smooth, familiar stock against her right cheek. She stared down the barrel past the groove cut into the top of the receiver, but she couldn't see the little ball that formed the front sight above the muzzle. Her finger pushed the safety. "Not yet," she whispered. "Not yet, not yet, not—" and she saw the dark shape of the car that seemed to materialize out of the darkness like something congealing.

She blew out a breath and held it, keeping her forefinger on the trigger just enough so she could feel it. She could sense Felker's progress without looking at him as she strained to judge the car's momentum. He was almost across the road now. She whispered, "Run, damn you."

The lights came on like a splash of caustic liquid thrown into her face. It was a flash that didn't go away but burned brighter as the car approached. Suddenly, the car swerved away from her to the left side of the road, trying to hit Felker, but she knew it was too late. There was no Felker. The wind from the car's backwash whipped the weeds around her as it passed, leaving the road in darkness again.

Jane was up and running now, sprinting for the other side in the dark. She watched the red taillights out of the corner of her eye as she ran. They seemed to expand when the brakes went on, like a pair of eyes widening. There was a squeal of tires, but the driver was good enough not to lock his brakes on a rural highway. As Jane left the pavement and felt the gravel under her feet, the car made a fast turn.

She made her legs pump hard, and slipped between the rails inside the fence, then lay there to look back at the road. The car started to accelerate again, then slowed and veered toward her. This is it, she thought. They were trying to get the lights onto her to pin her to the ground with them. She raised the shotgun again, and this time the front sight seemed to glow, then disappear as she pulled the trigger. There was a deafening *boom!* and the left headlight was gone.

As she pumped again and leveled the sight, she heard Felker's pistol. There were three shots, and the car skidded away from her and gained speed. She went to her knees and leveled the shotgun on it, but it kept going down the road, faster and faster.

Felker was at her elbow. "You okay?"

She stood up. "We've got to get out of here." She ran northward again, through the field. She could see a light go on in a window of a farmhouse on the other side of the intersection, but it was at least a quarter mile away. The shots had awakened somebody. If the farmer was turning on his light, at least he wasn't outside with a deer rifle. But he might very well be trying to see the dial of his telephone, and that was probably worse. She ran through a muddy slough that smelled like a chicken yard. She kept going, trying to outrun the police car that might be on its way to the first real street on the southern edge of Olcott.

Then it occurred to her that she had not been thinking clearly. It had been dark, and the house was too far away. People had probably heard the shots in the middle of town. But the farmer would have heard it best, looked out his window and seen—what? A car with one headlight squealing off down the highway. Felker had been hiding out of sight of the car, and Jane had been lying on her belly inside the wire fence in somebody's alfalfa. When the farmer called, he was going to report some drunks driving around and shooting road signs. She made it to the next fence and stopped. "Fence," she said, and heard Felker stop too.

The fence was a cordon of old wooden posts with little porcelain electrical insulators on them to hold the invisible wires. They had gone through a dozen like this in their eight-mile run. Jane had stopped at the first one and patted the wire, half expecting a jolt that would feel like a punch in the arm. It had been turned off, and so had all the others. Farmers in this part of the world didn't leave their cattle in the fields at night. She tested this one too, but felt only the cold strand of metal on the tips of her fingers. "Dead," she said.

They ducked to step between the strands of wire and then entered a big apple orchard. As she trotted through it with Felker at her heels, she wondered if she had stumbled on one of the old places. The trees weren't planted in the usual long, straight lines. They were just growing haphazardly at fairly regular intervals here and there. They were old. They couldn't be old enough, but they could have been descendants. The Seneca had planted orchards wherever they lived: apples, pears, plums.

When the white people had taken the land after the Revolution, they had cut the hardwood trees and burned the stumps so they could plow, but not the orchards.

She wished she had been here in daylight, so she could get a better look at the trees. Maybe she would come back when the fruit was on them and verify that they weren't Macintosh or Rome but the small, hard apples that the women had planted in patterns like this.

She didn't really need to, though, because she knew that this was a Seneca place. The lake was so close she could smell the change in the air and the Waagwenneyu was just a few miles to the south, down Black Creek or Eighteen-Mile Creek. The women who had planted the trees and tended them were asleep somewhere nearby. Maybe one of them had stirred as Jane Whitefield passed. "It's only me," she whispered.

"What?" said Felker.

"Just talking to myself."

She moved along in silence, trying to choose what was best to do. The police would come and they would be looking for the one-lighted car. If they didn't, the four men would at least have that to think about, and it would make them search for Felker on foot. She had to get him into town before the men got there.

They jogged between houses and through yards, listening for watchdogs and policemen more carefully than for the four men. At last they reached the lake road. There were arcades and small shops, all still boarded up from the winter, and little cottages built low and sturdy because the storms coming in off the lake could be fierce. She considered breaking into one of them and hiding until daylight came and the four men had to leave.

"That one," she whispered.

He said, "Let's take a look."

She watched him dart across the road, and then followed. He stepped to the side and looked into the window of the garage. "No car," he whispered.

Jane looked into the garage window. She cupped her hands against the glass to keep out the reflections and tried to make out shapes. It took her a few seconds to be sure, and then she spun around. Felker was gone.

Jane walked around to the back of the house and found him. He was standing with his face beside the electric meter, staring at it in the dim light. "What are you doing?" she asked.

"If anybody's here, the house uses electricity—refrigerator, furnace, clocks."

"No," she said. "Come back."

He followed her to the garage. There was a big, thick padlock that held a sliding bolt that went into the woods beside the door. She tugged on it. "Do you have a knife?"

He nodded and pulled a lock-blade pocketknife with a four-inch blade out of his pocket.

"Try to carve it out," she said. As he started to gouge the wood, Jane went to the front corner of the house to keep watch.

In thirty seconds he was beside her. He held up the bolt with the lock still attached. "The screws popped. It was old."

They dragged the aluminum boat out of the garage. Jane could tell that the owner had done this often, because as soon as they had cleared the noisy gravel of the driveway, the boat found its own keel mark worn into the ground. They pushed it down the sloping path to the edge of the water, climbed back up, and went into the garage.

It was dark and dusty. In the summer the owner probably kept his boat on the shore and parked his car in here, but now it was a storage shed for all the equipment that had to be protected from the weather.

Jane found the oars leaning upright in a corner, and a couple of life jackets hanging from a six-penny nail driven into a stud. There was a crude stand made of a two-by-ten nailed upright on a sawhorse for the ten-horsepower Evinrude outboard motor. Felker began to unscrew the clamps, but Jane stopped him. "Take this stuff down while I look for the gas can. If we don't find that, it won't be worth much."

Felker took the oars and life jackets and hurried down to the boat, then returned. She held up the red five-gallon can with the double hose attached and shook it. "Empty. I was afraid of that. Everything's too neat, too squared away. This guy wouldn't leave gas in a wooden garage for six months. If he had, we would have smelled it. Let me think for a minute."

Felker said, "We could row."

They went outside again and stared up and down the road. There were several buildings that weren't really cottages. They were houses, and they looked occupied. There were cars in some driveways, and big yards. "Somebody's cutting the lawns," she said. "Lawn-mowers."

"Do we have time?" he asked.

"Let's give it one try. If we don't find it right away, we leave."

They sneaked across the road to a house with a big, well-trimmed front lawn. The wide sliding garage door was closed, but the side door was unlocked. Jane slipped inside. There was a big car, an old Oldsmobile that took up most of the space, and there was a lawnmower against the wall. Jane moved closer to it and sniffed. There was no smell of gas. She touched it, and felt the long, coiled cord. Her luck tonight was un-believable. How many people had an electric lawn-mower? She stepped back and her bottom touched the side of the car. She turned and looked at it closely. It was at least twenty years old, and that was promising. Maybe it was old enough not to have a lock to protect the gas.

Jane opened the gas door and felt for the gas cap. It unscrewed. She hurried to the door of the garage and took the gas can from Felker. She found some duct tape on the shelf at the back wall of the garage and taped down the thumb release on the motor end of the hose, then draped it into the car's gas tank, unscrewed the cap on the five-gallon can, and started pumping the rubber bulb on the hose. As she pumped, she thought it through again. It should work. The mechanism was supposed to pump air into the gas tank from one hose to increase the pressure, so the gas would flow into the outboard motor through the other hose. With the cap off and the hoses in the car's gas tank, the gas should come through the air hose into the— It worked. She could hear a squishing sound and feel the change as the rubber bulb filled with gasoline. Then she was milking gasoline into the can. As she worked, she looked at the floor under the car. She could see a shine that indicated the Oldsmobile was also old enough to leak oil. It took her a moment to spot a yellow plastic pint bottle with the Pennzoil logo on the shelf above the car. She unscrewed it and poured that into the gas tank as she pumped. The oil might not be the right weight, but it would probably keep an outboard motor from seizing up for one night.

Suddenly, Felker was beside her again. "They're out there," he whispered. "In the street. Better get ready."

Jane stopped pumping, picked up her shotgun, and stepped to the side door of the garage. She opened it a crack and saw them. They had spread out, and two were walking on one side of the street and two on the other. Each time they passed an empty cottage, one of them would leave the road and walk around the back, only to emerge again and go on to the next one. She closed the door the rest of the way and smiled. They had the right street, but this was one of the few houses they would avoid, because it was occupied.

She waited a few minutes to let them get far enough away, then left Felker at the door and went back to pumping gasoline. When the can was full, she capped it and handed it to Felker. She went across the street first this time, then stopped by the corner of the cottage to stare in the direction the four men had taken. When Felker had loaded the can into the boat and carried the heavy outboard motor down the slope, she slowly backed around the cottage and went to the garage. She fitted the padlock and hasp to the door and pushed the screws back into the holes, took a last look, and hurried down to the lake.

She and Felker pushed the boat a few feet forward until the bow began to bob in the quiet waves. "Gentlemen first," she said.

Felker stepped into the boat and set the oars in the oarlocks. Jane handed him her shotgun and said, "Go up in the bow." When he did, his weight raised the stern of the boat off the shore. She gave the boat a hard push, scrambled past the motor over the transom, and they glided out a few feet, bobbing in the gentle waves.

Felker came aft to the oar seat, handed Jane her shotgun, and began to row. The aluminum boat was no more than fourteen feet long, and built to be light. Felker was not a great oarsman, but he was strong. A few powerful strokes propelled them past the hissing one-foot breakers out onto the long, rolling swells. She busied herself with the outboard motor, connecting the fuel hose to it, checking to be sure Felker had screwed it onto the transom tightly enough, and getting it ready to start. If the four men happened to be looking at the lake, then it wouldn't matter how loud the motor was. She was going to have to get them moving.

They pushed out into the darkness in silence. Jane faced the stern, her shotgun across her lap, staring back at the shore. All of the cottages along the waterline were dark. The only light came from farther back, where the streetlights were. The only noises now were an occasional squeak of the oars in the oarlocks and the quiet swish of the blades in the water. If they could just get out far enough onto the lake without the four men seeing or hearing them, this would work. The four men would lose them completely. They might go back and search her house in Deganawida. They might even get caught doing it.

It was cold on the water. Within a few minutes she was convinced that the northwest wind was proceeding unimpeded from some glacier in the center of Canada across the empty lakes to the sweat-soaked clothes of Jane Whitefield. She folded her arms, hugged the shotgun in them, and kept her eyes on the shore.

She waited until the lights of Olcott were almost invisible and she hadn't been able to detect the shapes of the low buildings for some time. Then she set the throttle on the outboard motor, pulled out the choke, and gave a pull on the starter. The motor coughed twice, then burbled and putted. She tapped the choke in, shifted to get the propeller turning, and headed out slowly.

She listened to the motor for ten minutes at slow speed as she moved them away from the shore. It was firing evenly and it was reasonably quiet, but there was no telling what sort of gas had been in the Oldsmobile or what it would do to the motor in the long run. She ran out a few miles from shore, then slowed down again and let the motor idle. "Give me your gun," she said.

"What?"

She said it louder, over the sound of the motor. "Your gun."

He pulled his pistol out of his shirt, and she took it by the handgrips and tossed it into the dark, deep water. Then she held her shotgun out with both hands and released it at water level beside the boat. "They won't do us any good now," she said.

10

The light aluminum boat slapped along at a good speed, the motor churning a white rooster tail on the black water and the hull pushing diagonal waves to the sides. The wind dried Jane's hair and then blew it out behind. She watched Felker settle into a comfortable position with his head resting on his forearm.

Jane kept the bow pointed west, trying not to get close enough to the shore to be noticed. That was the way the canoes used to travel this lake. If it had worked for them, it would work tonight. Whatever else had changed, the lake hadn't. The Seneca had made their canoes from the bark of a red elm or a bitternut hickory, stripped from the tree in one piece, stretched over a frame of white ash, and sewn at the bow and stern. Some of them had been forty feet long, much bigger and easier to see than this boat. All she had to worry about was keeping out far enough so that if any noise reached the shore, it was disembodied.

The incessant, unchanging drone of the motor pushing the boat through the dark made her eyes heavy. They were heading back toward the mouth of the Niagara now. Neahga. The land along the lake had changed, but from out here at night no eye could see it. The lake was the same. Jane could as easily have been wearing the gaka-ah, gise-ha, and ahdeadawesa: the skirt, leggings, and long shirt that her grandmother's grandmother wore. They made a lot more sense for this kind

96

of trip than a wet sweatshirt and jeans. Her clothes would have been embroidered in porcupine quills with patterns of flowers and trees, but even she would not have been able to see the colors in this darkness. She would have the gaaotages, a necklace woven of fragrant marsh grass, for perfume. Why was she thinking of perfume? It was probably the smell of the gasoline. The darkness and the persistent sound of the motor were making her drowsy, and there was something about being on the water out of sight of land. What was out of sight began to lose its reality after an hour or two.

It was easy to imagine why people would believe—no, not believe, exactly, just express the mystery of it this way—that the world was begun when Sky-Woman fell and was caught by the sea birds and placed on the shell of a gigantic turtle. Out here, where the dark sky and the dark water met with nothing in between and her mind was too tired to censor any thought that came into it, the turtle seemed no more unlikely than the Big Bang. He would be lying out here just under the surface, motionless and huge and prehistoric, like a sunken island. And for a second or two, it was possible to imagine the feeling of being the first woman, falling. Slowly, maybe because the noise of the sea birds had reached it under the water, the turtle would rise from the dark depths, at first the curved top of the shell emerging a little, the water streaming off the green moss growing on it, and then more and more of it, until—

There was a loud clunk, then a horrible scraping along the keel of the boat, and then the motor screamed as the propeller was pushed up out of the water and the intake sucked air, and then it stalled. Jane was thrown forward off the seat to the hull, and her mind shrieked, trying to break its fall. She had to fight the first, shocking feeling that somehow she had conjured the immense turtle, that because she had been thinking of it, the turtle had come. The part of her mind that worked all the time had known from the first instant that it wasn't an imaginary creature. It was a log or a rock or something.

Felker was crammed between the bow and the first seat with his feet in the air when she saw him. He said, "What happened?"

She snapped, "We hit something. Are we leaking up there?"

He pulled himself up and put his hands to the hull. "No. I don't think so."

"Thank you," she muttered.

"You're welcome." But she hadn't meant him to hear it. They were about five miles out. This was April and the water was like—

"—Ice!" he said. He was leaning over the gunwale and touching something beside the boat. "It's a big piece of ice. I can't believe it. You hit a damned iceberg, like the *Titanic*."

Jane laughed out loud, letting the tension go out of her.

"What did you think it was?" he asked.

"You wouldn't believe it." She laughed harder, and in a moment she heard him laugh too. "You sure we don't have any leaks?"

"Wait," he said. She held her breath. She could hear him running his fingers along the riveted seams near the bow. "I'm sure," he said.

She slumped in her seat. "What a relief. At least we don't have to worry about dying."

"Dying? Can't you swim?"

"Yes," she said, "but I don't know if I can do five miles in forty-degree water dragging a full-grown man in my teeth like a Labrador retriever."

"Hey," he protested. "I just ran ten miles through mud puddles and rowed a boat halfway across a lake. What do you have to do to impress girls around here?"

"We like it when men help us get our boats off ice cakes," she said. "Take an oar."

They each pulled an oar out of its oarlock, stood up, and stuck an oar into the frosty surface of the ice floe. When Jane said, "Heave," the other end of it rose above the surface six feet ahead of the bow, and the boat slipped backward a couple of feet. After two more tries, the boat slid free and glided a little.

Jane said, "I apologize," and sat down.

"I should think so," said Felker.

"I mean, I should have remembered about the ice when we saw there weren't any boats moored at docks."

"There weren't any docks."

"Right. People put them in each spring after the ice goes down."

"You mean melts?"

"Not exactly. Lake Ontario is too deep to freeze much, but Lake Erie isn't, and some of the other lakes go far enough north so that they freeze too. There's a boom at the mouth of the Niagara to keep the ice from flowing down the river and wrecking the machinery at the power project. They open it every spring to let the last of it go."

He shrugged. "I can see how people around here might want to circle that date on the calendar."

"It's a different day every year." She tipped the outboard motor back down into the water. "Let's hope we haven't sheared a pin. If we have, maybe we'll drift up to Montreal in a few weeks."

"A pin?"

"For a guy your size, you really aren't the outdoorsy type, are you?"

"I grew up in the city. When we want fish, we buy fish. What kind of pin?"

"A shear pin. If the prop hits something, there's a little pin that breaks, so even though the propeller is stopped, the drive shaft can keep turning."

"Why in the hell would anybody put a fiendish thing like that in a motor?"

"Just cross your fingers," she said. She set the controls, gave a pull on the lanyard, and the motor started. She listened for a second, and it sounded strange. She shifted to engage the propeller and nothing happened. She leaned over the stern and looked into the water, said something Felker couldn't hear, and turned off the motor.

Felker said, "Pin?"

Jane shrugged. "That's how they act when that's what's wrong. It doesn't mean there aren't other things, too."

Felker carefully made his way toward the stern. "Any chance it can be fixed by two rabbits?"

Jane smiled. "We forgot to steal the toolbox. People carry extra pins."

He thought for a second. "Describe the pin."

"It's a little peg of metal ... soft metal, I guess. About an inch long and an eighth of an inch thick."

"How is it held in place?" He sounded different now, and she wasn't sure whether it made her uncomfortable or if she was grateful for it. She supposed it was his serious, patient cop voice.

"It just sits in a little slot."

"Where?"

"Down next to the prop."

"Do we have anything to lose if we try to fix it?"

She shrugged. "Beats rowing, and there's no reason not to try," she said. "The pin will be in two pieces, but we might be able to use something else."

He unscrewed the clamps and lifted the motor into the boat. Jane touched the propellor. It didn't seem to be bent. It must have dug into the ice long enough to shear the pin before it had come loose.

He said, "I feel something sticking out—wire?"

"The cotter key," said Jane. She could tell without

being able to see that he was pinching the two legs inward. Then he took out his knife and put the point into the loop and extracted it.

"I wish we had some light," he muttered.

"Those four men wish we did, too. By now they're looking in our direction."

"I guess so. What's next?"

"Feel that part that's shaped like a big bullet?"

"Got it."

"Depending on the model, it either comes off in your hand or you have to turn it."

She heard him fiddling with it, and then he said, "It's off."

"Now feel for washers—almost paper-thin."

"Just one," he said. "Big one."

"Now it's my turn." She carefully lifted the propellor off and felt for the shear pin. "Here it is," she said. "Only now it's them."

He held out his hand and she placed the pieces in his palm. He pushed them together, felt them, then touched the slot in the motor. "How about a nail?" he asked.

"Great," she answered. "Got one?"

"No. I saw about ten of them in that garage."

"He pounded them in with the hammer from the toolbox."

"How about a piece of wood? We could cut one off an oar."

"Too soft. Go for too hard. At this point I don't care what happens to a stolen motor."

Felker said, "Do you have a piece of jewelry or something?"

"No," she answered. "I don't wear jewelry when I work unless it's a disguise." Then she said, "My belt."

"What about it?"

"The little piece of the buckle that goes through the holes is about the right size." She pulled off the belt and handed it to him. He felt it, held it up to the slot in the motor, then set the belt on the seat beside him and went to work prying it off the bar with his knife.

"Here it is," he said.

She placed it in the slot on the motor, sliced a little leather off the belt to pack it tight, and whistled with pleasure.

"What was that?" he said anxiously. "Did you hear it?"

"I was whistling. It fits. Or it feels like it fits."

"You know, I never heard a woman whistle before."

"You've lived a sheltered life." She started carefully replacing the parts on the motor. "Where's the washer?"

"Here. You mean you could all whistle all this time and you just didn't do it?"

"Yes, and do arithmetic and pee outdoors and smoke cigars." She reached for the next part, but found his hand was already on it in the dark. They touched hands for an instant, and she pulled hers away to let him put the bullet-shaped piece on. "I hope you still have the cotter pin."

"Yeah," he said. "It's a little bent up, but I can straighten it enough." She could hear him fiddling with it on the motor. "I think it's done."

"Let me feel it," she said, and then realized she was warning him to get his hand out of the way so they wouldn't touch again in the dark: the rules. "It feels as though everything is where it should be," she said. "If it only lasts a mile or two, we're still ahead."

He stood to lift the motor onto the transom again, then went to his knees beside her to tighten one side while she turned the other clamp. Then he made his way forward again.

Jane felt for the fuel hose, connected it, and said, "Keep your eyes open for ice. If you see anything, don't be shy. Sing out."

"You're assuming this will work."

"The lady in the store where I bought that belt said

it was timeless and perfect for all occasions." She gave the motor a pull.

He said something else, but his words were drowned out by the sound of the motor coughing. It gave its familiar sputter, then hummed with a louder, even sound. She was glad she hadn't heard him. There was something about their relationship that was getting too fluid. His good-natured words were like ambassadors sent out to penetrate her defenses. It was making her uncomfortable. He was changing things, moving the line back, closer and closer to her.

What he hadn't said was bothering her, too. He had been a cop. He must have thought of the shotgun right away. There were two parts on a shotgun—the pin that held the trigger assembly into the receiver, and the pin that locked the magazine plug—that would have been better than the belt buckle. Cops saw shotguns every day of their lives, rode with them upright in a rack in their patrol cars. You had to pop the pin out even to clean and oil the trigger mechanism. He would have been perfectly justified in saying, "Too bad you dropped the shotgun into two hundred feet of water."

Had he kept himself from saying it because he thought she wouldn't have known what he was talking about, or because he had known she would have thought of it already—how she had stupidly gotten rid of it when it was full of little pieces of metal in just about any shape you wanted? The answer was that he knew she would have thought of it and that she would feel guilty enough already and that she would be grateful to him for never mentioning it. Jane didn't feel like being grateful. She didn't want to have to give him credit for being considerate or calm or cheerful or for having big, strong hands that could bend a cotter key or for anything else. Everything he did was calculated to slip through her defenses, to decrease the distance that made her feel comfortable. But maybe it wasn't calculated, and her defenses just weren't what they ought to be.

She kept her ears tuned to the sound of the motor. It seemed to be all right. The minutes went by, and every one of them was a reprieve from rowing, and added to their chance of hopping out of reach of the men who had been chasing them.

Felker got up on the seat on his knees and pointed. He half-turned his face to her, so she twisted the handgrip on the throttle and slowed down to hear him. "Big one ahead," he called. "Go to the left a little."

She changed course a few degrees and kept the motor's revolutions low enough to let her hear the next sighting. She was being unfair to him, she knew. This had to be the worst week of his life, with the high probability that the next one wouldn't be as good. She wasn't used to making men like him disappear. Most victims weren't even men. They were women and children. For the children, the whole world seemed to be a dream, first the bad kind, and then the kind where they were compelled by her voice to keep moving, going through unfamiliar landscapes for no reason they could explain. The women stopped bristling at another woman's authority only when they were sure she was about to go away again. Most of the men had been thrown off balance by surprise and fear before she met them. They just wanted to know how to get out fast. That was his problem: He hadn't been thrown off balance. He hadn't just run; he had sat down and thought it through and decided to come to her, without relinquishing control.

She started to feel the proximity of the Niagara River long before she came close enough to make out lights along the shore. There was something different in the air, and in the water. Suddenly, the motor's pitch skipped up to a whine again and the boat glided to a stop. She cut the throttle and said, "Broken again. This time we'd better row to shore."

"Okay," said Felker.

"I'll help," she said. "We'd better get in quick." She tipped up the motor, moved forward to sit beside him, and took an oar.

"Why?" he said as they took their first stroke shoulder to shoulder.

"Why what?"

"Why quick?"

"The river is an international boundary. Over there is Canada. They're not especially hard-nosed about it, but both sides probably have somebody watching. If you saw a man and a woman rowing a fourteen-foot boat in off Lake Ontario on a cold night with the motor out of the water, what would you do?"

He looked up to his right above the water. "Is that them up there? It looks like a fort."

"It is," she said. "Fort Niagara. It's old. Ignore it."

They rowed hard. He provided most of the forward movement, and Jane concentrated on keeping the boat straight against his size and strength. Felker had a good eye for strategic places. This was the narrowest part of the river. The name for it was O-ne-ah, the Neck, and at one time it had been one of the prizes of the earth, the strangle point in the North American fur trade. The portage around the Falls, the Carrying Place of Niagara, was the one big obstacle in the route from the center of the continent to the sea. The French, the British, the Americans, and all of the Indian tribes allied with each of them had fought for control of that fort from the 1680s to the 1780s. Now it was empty, a museum. It was one of the quiet places where all the old human blood had made the grass grow green.

They rowed on, and crossed the border a mile or two out from shore. When they had rowed in silence for a long time, Felker said, "Somehow I can't picture Harry doing this."

"No." She chuckled. "Not Harry. Harry got to ride in a car."

Jane let Felker's stronger strokes push them toward shore just before dawn. They could already begin to make out shapes in the little Canadian town. There were beautiful old houses and perversely neat lawns and tightly planted beds of flowers everywhere. It looked more like England than the American towns a half mile across the river.

Jane guided the boat up to a concrete jetty and tied it between two cabin cruisers so that it was hard to see. Then they took their bags and walked up the dock into Canada.

"What is this place?" asked Felker.

"Niagara-on-the-Lake," she said.

"It must save them a lot of time giving directions," he said. "Where to now?"

"To find a phone."

The police car seemed to come from nowhere. It appeared on the street ahead and two cops got out. "Let me handle this," she whispered. She watched the two men come toward them. They looked like policemen from another time, tall and Irish or Scottish, one of them with bristly blond eyebrows and a pink face and opaque blue eyes. "Good morning," he said.

"Good morning," said Jane, but Felker had spoken too, in a little chorus. She hoped he wasn't going to get overconfident because he thought he knew more than she did about policemen.

"The two of you look a bit . . . lost. We wondered if there was some sort of assistance we could offer."

"No," said Jane, and forced a smile. "We're on vacation. We arrived in town a little early, so we're waiting for a decent hour for breakfast at the Oban Inn."

This seemed to please the cop. "Really." He glanced at his partner. "I believe they'll be serving at six or so." His partner nodded smartly.

"Good," said Jane. "Thank you very much." She started to walk past the two policemen, and Felker drifted along with her.

"Ah, one moment, please," said the cop.

Jane stopped.

"I believe you're Americans?"

"Yes."

"I'm sorry to trouble you, but it's rather unusual to see two Americans arrive with rucksacks at this hour. If I could see your identification . . ."

Jane took her wallet out of her leather bag and opened it. She did the sort of searching people did when policemen asked. It wasn't an accident. It allowed her to flash a thick sheaf of American money. Policemen were fairly predictable: seeing the money would reassure them that Jane and Felker weren't burglars.

Jane ended her search and handed the policeman a lot of little plastic windows. Felker could see credit cards and a driver's license. Then, to Felker's surprise, she reached into the bag again and pulled out a man's wallet.

"Ah," said the cop. "Mr. and Mrs. Whitefield. And where did you cross the border?"

"Niagara Falls," she said. Then she turned to Felker. "Da-gwa-ya-dan-nake ne-wa-ate-keh."

Felker nodded thoughtfully, but the policeman said, "I'm sorry, but I didn't catch that."

"I beg your pardon," said Jane. "It's a habit. We use the old language at home."

"I see." He handed the two sets of documents back to her. "Well, thank you very much. I hope you enjoy your holiday."

"Thank you."

The two cops got back into their car and smiled at them, then drove off. "I seem to be using my last resorts first," she said. "I couldn't let them ask to take a look inside the bags and find your money."

"How did you do it? What was that gibberish?"

"It wasn't gibberish," she said. "It's an Indian language. One of the old treaties gave Indians the right to go back and forth across the border. Anything that sounds like police harassment would be a lot of trouble."

"Where in the world did you learn that? Do you know some Indians?"

"Yeah. My family."

He looked at her closely. "What kind of Indian?"

"The usual kind," she said. "Feathers and beads."

He looked at her skeptically. "What tribe?"

"Seneca. Wolf Clan."

"You have blue eyes."

"Yes."

"Are they contact lenses?"

"No."

"Okay, then . . ." He seemed to expect her to supply his conclusion, but she only waited. "What did you say?"

"Just now?"

"In Seneca."

"Part of the Lord's Prayer: 'Deliver us from evil,' " Jane said.

"Do you pray?"

"No, I run," said Jane. "But things my mother taught me come out of my memory sometimes while I'm doing it. Let's go find a phone before we get into more trouble."

11

It was already eight o'clock. Jane and Felker were sitting on the edge of the dock, swinging their feet above the water. Felker had been silent for a long time. Jane watched him out of the corner of her eye. It was times like these, when he was stuck waiting and had time to think, that would wear him down. She knew she should do something to keep him from spiraling downward. "Tell me what you're thinking."

He smiled, but he kept his eyes on the water out beyond the harbor. "I was thinking about you."

She looked away from him. She had made another mistake. He was at the point now where he realized that he didn't know anybody anymore. Except the nearest woman.

"I was thinking I should apologize," he said. "I mean, it doesn't matter to me whether you're a full-blooded Indian or one ninetieth, does it? I guess I should say Native American."

It wasn't what she had been dreading, and she was relieved. "Not to me," she said. "I'm as Indian as I can be."

"Then where did the blue eyes come from?"

"My father looked pretty much the way you would have wanted him to. He had a face like a tomahawk and skin the color of a penny. He was a Heron."

"A what?"

"A Heron. The bird, you know? Big long legs? That was his clan."

"Oh," he said. "So why are you a Wolf—a blue-eyed Wolf?"

"Blue-eyed because my mother didn't start out as a Seneca. She looked like a negative of one. Very blond and white and Irish." She smiled as she remembered. "When I was really little they started making Barbie dolls, and the first time I saw one I thought it was supposed to be my mother. I called them Mama dolls. There weren't a lot of people in Deganawida who looked like that."

"Or anywhere else. If your mother was a Barbie and your father was a Heron, why aren't you a Heron?"

"It wouldn't make sense to you."

"We don't have much to talk about except my troubles, and those make me nervous."

"Okay," she said. "The first thing you have to know is that all family relationships go only through the mother. Your father is still your father, but he's not a relative. The kids live at the mother's house and belong to her clan—her family."

"That's simple enough."

"It is, really. Only it carries through to all relatives. Your father's brothers, sisters, sister's kids are in his clan, so they're not related to you. You with me?"

"I think so. If I could work it out on paper."

"Okay. Then there's marriage. The nation is divided into two halves."

"That much I know. Men and women."

"Not those two. Half the clans are on one side, and half on the other. Anthropologists call them moieties. You can only marry somebody who is in the other half. My father was a Heron, so he couldn't marry a Deer, Snipe, Hawk, or another Heron. She had to be a Turtle, Wolf, Bear, or Beaver."

"Hey, I just realized where you're going," he said.

"If your mother was a Barbie and you can't be related to your father, it kind of leaves you out in the cold, right? You aren't related to anybody."

"Very good," she said. "Except that in the old days they ran into this problem early on. See, all of the Iroquois tribes were always at war."

"Always?"

She shrugged. "As far as we know. The first ones to see them who could write were the French, in the 1530s. There was a war with the Algonquins that had been going on for as long as anybody alive remembered. The next time there was peace was 1783, when the Revolutionary War ended."

"Two hundred and fifty years . . ." He seemed to be thinking about it, but then he frowned. "But how did that get you to be a blue-eyed Wolf?"

"If you fight all the time, two things happen. You lose a lot of people, and you take a lot of prisoners. They used the prisoners to make up for the casualties. There had to be a provision for that—adoption."

She watched him for a moment to see whether he understood. Incredible acts of savagery made necessary equal acts of mercy. Hawenneyu the Creator and Hanegoategeh the Evil-Minded were twin brothers.

"So you were adopted."

"No. My mother was. My father took her to visit his reservation on Tonawanda Creek—probably to show her what she was getting into. She hit it off with a couple of the ladies in the Wolf clan, and they got together before the wedding and did some lobbying with the old women, who made it official in open council." Saying this brought her mother back. Mentioning her like that, casually to a stranger, was like lying, because it didn't say who she had been.

Jane could see her now—not dying of cancer, but the way she was when Jane was a child. Probably, the picture came from the sixties. She was so tall and thin, with all that blond hair, breezing into every unfamiliar situation as though she had arranged it herself, not brash, exactly, but determined. And not fearless, but showing no fear, or even any awareness that anyone could be less than delighted at that moment: Who could imagine anything more fascinating than taking her only night off to go to Jane's school and meet all of Jane's teachers? If someone spoke, she would turn it into a conversation; if someone smiled, she would hug; if someone hugged, she would kiss. The Wolf women would have been overwhelmed and hypnotized at the same time. It was only after Jane was older that she realized her mother had invented herself. "If your mother is a Wolf, you're a Wolf. Remember?"

"So you're fifty percent Seneca, and fifty percent adopted Seneca."

"No. I'm just Seneca. There's no such thing as half." She turned to stare past him along the dock toward the shore. Felker looked, too, and saw a battered pickup truck towing a trailer pull into the parking lot. Two men got out. They had dark skin, black hair, and Oriental eyes. The older one was dressed like a farmer, in overalls and a John Deere hat, but the younger one had an earring and a T-shirt that said OTTAWA ROUGHRIDERS.

"There's our ride," said Jane.

"More Seneca?"

"Mohawk." She stood up and walked down the dock, threw her arms around the younger man and hugged him, then planted a respectful kiss on the cheek of the older man. His eyes seemed to glitter with affection, but he pretended not to see Felker, who was just behind her.

Jane turned and pulled Felker a little closer and said, "This is John Felker." Felker stiffened a little at the mention of his name, but she went on. "This is Wendell Hill, and this is his son, Carlton." The men dutifully shook hands. Jane said, "Uncle Wendell, the boat's over here."

"Let's take a look," said the older man. He walked out along the dock and glanced at it, then announced, "We can do it."

Carlton jumped into the truck and backed the trailer into the water, while Wendell lowered himself into the boat and rowed it onto the first rollers of the trailer. Carlton handed him a rope and he snapped it onto the bow ring. Then he kept walking onto the narrow tongue of the trailer and up to the bed of the truck and cranked the boat up with a winch. No words were spoken. Wendell stepped up into the cab with Carlton, and Jane and Felker climbed into the flatbed.

"So you're part Mohawk, too?"

"Just Seneca," she said. "I told you before, you can't be two things."

"But you called him your uncle. He's your father's brother, right?"

"No," she said. "My mother."

"But your mother—"

"—was a member of the Wolf clan. Wendell is a member of the Wolf clan. Everybody in the same clan is a relative. It doesn't matter if you're Seneca, Cayuga, Onondaga, Oneida, Mohawk, or Tuscarora."

"So your father would be related to a Mohawk in the Heron clan."

"Theoretically, except there is no Mohawk Heron clan. They just have Turtle, Wolf, and Bear."

"And Carlton is your cousin."

"Please don't make me go through all this again," she said. "I'm tired."

"Come on."

"Carlton's mother is a Turtle, so he's a Turtle, and I'm not related to him at all. We're just friends. Give up. You're never going to get it."

Felker shook his head and laughed. "I don't give up. Let me try again. If you married me, I'd have to be one of the other half of the clans. The ones that are birds and things."

It was a jolt like a small electric shock. Her voice went flat. "Yes," she said, then added, "If you're good at sleeping in trucks, this is a great time." She laid her head on her leather bag, turned away, and closed her eyes. After ten minutes, she gave up the pretense and sat up. Even after the past twenty-four hours, she still couldn't lie motionless in the metal bed of the truck. Every bump seemed to be transferred in an amplified form to her left hip. They were heading west, so the morning sun was in her eyes.

"You can't sleep either?" he asked.

"I catnap," she lied.

The truck crossed the bridge over the Welland Canal, where two big freighters on their way to the St. Lawrence and the sea looked as though they were stuck. She stared at them and wondered what they were carrying. Half the time the flags had nothing to do with where they were from.

"Where are we going?"

"This is Saint Catharines. They'll probably get on the Queen Elizabeth Way in a minute. It's a freeway, so we'll get blown around for a while. Then around Hamilton they'll get off and take 53 the rest of the way."

He sighed. "All right. No more personal questions, and no asking where we are or where we're going. What else is there? Harry. We both know Harry. A mutual friend. Is this the way you took Harry out?"

Jane looked at him closely for a moment. He was beginning to feel the loneliness of it, and she wasn't helping. He was never going to have that kind of intimate, open talk again. Even if the other person spilled his guts over a dozen martinis, Felker was going to have to keep quiet. She was just being secretive because it was a habit. Or maybe she was using it to keep him disoriented and off balance so she could be in charge. "I'm sorry," she said. "We're going to the Six Nations Reserve on the Grand River."

"So his new life is on a Canadian Indian reservation?"

"Who?"

"Harry."

"I wasn't talking about Harry. I was talking about us." She didn't like the sound of this, either. "We're going this way because it was the safest place I could think of when I saw they were that close behind us." She shrugged. "Wherever they think we went, it's not here."

"Six Nations Reserve. So it's all of the Iroquois."

"Sort of," she said. "Remember the old fort we passed?"

"Sure."

"That was where the tribes ran to during the Revolutionary War. They had fought on the side of the British for a hundred years, but when the Americans won, the British forgot to put anything in the treaty to protect them. A British general named Haldimand felt guilty and got them this place."

"Is this your reservation?"

"I'm not sure how to answer that," she said. "I'm sort of a citizen because everybody is, but most of the Seneca are still in New York. My family. When the others left, they couldn't bear to do it. This isn't exactly a reservation. It's a sort of refuge. These people have been holding out since 1784."

12

The truck took them out into the country, where there were small farmhouses with lots of automobiles of about the same vintage as the pickup truck, in varying states of disrepair, parked in yards. One that looked as though it must have been left there for a long time had white chickens walking in and out of an open door.

"Is this the reservation?"

"Yes." She studied him for a moment. "What are you thinking—that the people look poor?"

He shrugged. "I wasn't thinking about them. I was wondering about what they're going to think of me. I'm wondering how I'm going to fit in."

"You don't. You just came with somebody who does. This isn't where I wanted to take you. When you're running from men with guns, you don't lead them back to your brother's house. What I'm doing is wrong, but I felt I had to."

"Are you telling me to behave?"

"I'm telling you *how* to behave. In some ways they're no different from the Canadians who live around here. They're sort of old-fashioned and conservative, but not isolated. They know what you know about the rest of the world. A lot of them work out there. But I don't want them to know why we're here. I'm probably the only criminal they know."

"Have you done this before?"

"Done what?"

"Brought people here?"

"Just be polite and friendly. These people are family."

The truck stopped at a farmhouse that wasn't easy to distinguish from any of the others. It had been painted dark red like a barn, but that appeared to have been a long time ago. In back of the house was a small field that had old corn stubble in it and a small orchard of about twenty leafless fruit trees. When Jane slipped her bag over her shoulder and jumped to the ground, Felker picked up his knapsack and joined her.

Wendell was out of the cab. He said to Felker, "Where do you want your boat?"

Jane smiled. "Please keep it, Wendell. It's a gift."

Wendell nodded. "Thank you, Janie."

Wendell and Carlton drove off in their pickup truck, and Jane turned to Felker. "Don't make me explain that."

He looked at the house a little uncomfortably. "Is this where we're going?"

"Janie!" It was a woman's voice, and in a moment Felker could see her coming around the house. She was dark brown and her skin had wrinkles at the eyes from smiling, and as she approached, Felker could see them deepen. "It's wonderful to see you. Come on in." Her voice sounded like the voice of any farm woman, but there was a subtle difference in inflection, and Felker detected a slight peculiarity. When she said "Come," her lips didn't quite touch. He had noticed the same thing with Wendell when he had said "me," so he supposed he must be noticing an Iroquois accent.

"This is John Felker," said Jane. "Mattie Wilson." Then she added a few Seneca words that seemed to be part of the same topic. When the older woman happily answered her, Felker listened. There were no enunciated b's, m's, or p's.

They entered the house and found themselves in a big farm kitchen. Jane sat down at the table without being asked, at least in English, so Felker did the same. He looked at her for clues, but all he got was a smile.

Mattie Wilson laid out cornbread, honey, and blueberries and poured strong coffee, but she didn't sit down with them. Instead she hovered, adding dishes of food as they talked. "Jimmy's off on a job in Brooklyn," she said. "You two should be reasonably comfortable over there."

Jane added commentary. "Jimmy is an ironworker. He and his brothers, George and Henry. They travel a lot."

"When they're working," said Mrs. Wilson cheerfully. "The rest of the time they eat and lie around like a pack of dogs."

Felker laughed. "I think I hear my mother talking. It makes me homesick."

This seemed to put Mrs. Wilson in an even better mood. "Well, if you're no better than the rest of the men, I ought to write your mother a letter. Because I know *you* won't."

"No," he said. "I don't think I want you two getting together. I'm no match for her as it is." He tasted the food again. "Just send her the recipe for this cornbread."

Jane watched him in nervous tension. Whenever he spoke he seemed to be teetering on a high place, but each time he went to the edge, he came back with more of Mattie Wilson's affection.

When she was satisfied that they had eaten enough, Mattie went to a drawer under the counter, found a keychain, and gave it to Jane. "You'd better get settled over there," she said. "Will you be around for o-ta-de-none-ne-o-na-wa-ta?"

Jane said, "Maybe," then got up and kissed Mattie Wilson. Felker said, "Thank you, Mrs. Wilson. If I had known how wonderful it is here, I wouldn't have waited for Jane to bring me. I'd have come alone."

As they left, Mattie said to Jane in Seneca, "Keep

one hand on that one. He's beautiful, but he didn't learn that much about women from his mother."

They walked among the dried husks in the cornfield, then between the trees of the orchard. "What did she say?" he asked.

Jane smiled. "She said you had a blueberry caught in your teeth."

He swept his tongue around in his mouth. "I do not."

She shrugged. "My Seneca must be getting rusty."

They made their way to a second farmhouse, this one a little better kept up but smaller. Jane walked up onto the front porch, opened the door with the key, and entered. Inside, the house looked like the home of a bachelor, but one who hadn't been here in some time.

"Is this Jimmy's farm?"

"Well, title is complicated here," she said. "It's Jimmy's house, but it really belongs to his mother because she's the senior woman of his clan. They don't divide land like, 'Here's the boundary; let's put a fence on it.' They use what they need until they don't need it. Jimmy doesn't have a wife. When he does, he might live here, or he might go live in a house that belongs to her."

"That doesn't sound too complicated."

"It isn't," she said. "But sometime in the twenties the Canadian government decided that all Canadian Indians had to be patrilineal. So legal ownership could be in the name of some man who isn't even related to Jimmy. It doesn't matter. Right now it's ours. I'm going to take a bath and go to sleep in it."

"I was hoping you'd say that," said Felker. "Is there a couch or something . . ."

"There are two bedrooms. Pick one."

He hesitated. "Jane . . . before I go to sleep I should say this. You saved my life maybe three times last night. I want to thank—"

"Save it," she interrupted. "We can talk later."

* * *

Jane soaked in Jimmy's bathtub for a long time, letting
the warm water soothe the muscles in her back and
arms and legs. On the wall above her, presumably for
Jimmy's contemplation, was a large poster of a blond
woman who for some reason had taken off all of her
clothes and sat straddling a big black motorcycle. Jane
viewed her critically. She wasn't really that attractive. It
was only a matter of attitude.

13

She woke up slowly, fighting off consciousness for a long time as she lay in the bed with the sun beginning to shine into the room. She had held herself in the dream, had explored it and found that it wasn't the kind of dream with boundaries but the kind that opened out before her in every direction she looked. She finally had relinquished it, like a swimmer giving in to the need to rise to the surface for air. When she opened her eyes she felt an instant when she couldn't remember where she was, and it was like coming up and gulping for air too soon and breathing water. She felt a sensation like drowning must be, a desperate reflex to get up and out of it.

She sat up and looked around her at Jimmy's room to make the dream go away. Then she listened for Felker. He was moving around in the living room. That was probably all it had been: She had heard him, and her mind had acted to absorb the noise into her dream so that it could get the sleep it needed. She stood up and went to the dresser to get her leather bag, and took it into the bathroom with her.

When she was dressed in clean blue jeans and a sweatshirt, she came out and bypassed the living room to get to the kitchen. When he came in to join her, she was making coffee. She didn't look at him as she said, "Sorry I slept so late."

"That's okay," he said. "I just got up myself." She

turned around and saw him run his hand over the thick whiskers that had grown in on his jaw. "Do you think I should grow a mustache?"

"A mustache is not a great disguise for you."

"What's a great disguise?"

"Great? Great is like you take female hormones for a year, get a sex-change operation that's so good that your reclusive billionaire husband never suspects that you weren't always a woman, and neither do any of his army of security people."

"I'd better settle for good. What's good?"

"I haven't decided yet." She frowned. "You're a big, muscular, hairy ex-cop. You add a mustache, it just makes you look more like what you were anyway. You'll need something that makes you look like a different kind of person who just happens to look like you."

"This is starting to sound like Zen."

"It's not, but it is an attitude. What we've got to do is think about you." She stared at him for a moment. "You know who looks most like cops?"

"Who?"

"Criminals. They walk the same and they have the same facial expressions. Criminals just have worse tattoos and better haircuts."

"Passing for a criminal doesn't sound like a step up."

"That was just an example," she said. "You could pass for an old soldier. Were you ever in the military?"

"Yeah. Army. I hated it."

"But you know the names of things and where the bases are and all that. If you just don't try to pass for a soldier in an army camp, you're okay."

"I also don't get paid. Say I'm a retired master sergeant. How does that help?"

"It gives people a box to put you in, so they don't have to spend any energy thinking about you. We do all the thinking ourselves now."

"But what's the smartest thing to be?"

"Just start thinking about who you really are. I mean, what would you have done if circumstances and accidents hadn't pushed you into all this? We can make up other circumstances to account for anything. It just has to be something you can keep being for a long, long time."

"How long? Forever?"

"Say, twenty years. I imagine you've noticed, but it's amazing how few people who carry guns for a living last that long."

"I noticed," he said. Then he added, "But there's an endless supply."

"But the replacements won't care about you, because John Felker is dead too and you're somebody else." She watched him for a moment. "So what do you want to be when you grow up?"

"I don't know."

"Then keep thinking about it."

They spent the day in the kitchen, sometimes sitting across the table from each other, sometimes up and walking around the room, now and then stopping to eat something, wash dishes, or make more coffee, but always talking.

"A lot of it is premeditation," Jane said. "You think ahead so that what you do doesn't cause somebody to ask questions you can't answer yourself."

"Like what?"

"Apply for a job where you need a security clearance or where they give employees lie-detector tests."

"That one I know. The first question they ask is your name, so they'll know what it looks like when you're not lying. What else?"

"You don't buy a house until you can survive a credit check. You rent. You think before you do anything."

"So I live like a rat in a hole forever."

"No, just the opposite. You look for ways to be average. You don't get a job as a dishwasher, for instance. It's perfectly honorable, but it's what people do who are convicts or something. It makes you as vulnerable as they are. You pick the best career you can handle. If you need references or papers, you call the number I'm going to give you. They'll come."

"You have people writing fake references?"

"Let's just say there are people who do it. Or fill out ten years of fake tax returns on the right obsolete forms. Whatever it takes."

"I've seen some forged papers in my time, but none of them were quite right."

"If you knew they were forged, then they weren't. It's like anything else you can buy."

"You make it sound like an industry."

"It is," she said. "I didn't invent it; I just found it. You're used to picking up some career criminal and seeing his papers have somebody else's name. It's much bigger than that."

"What do you mean?"

"Nobody has any idea how many people are living this way. There are divorced parents who take their own kids and run off, millions of illegal aliens, women hiding from some lunatic who's stalking them, people who made a bad start and don't have the right degree or the right discharge or good enough grades. Ones who just got fed up and wanted out. All of these people need the same things. Most of them come on paper or can be gotten by using paper. When there's a market, somebody will get into the business. It's a lot easier to counterfeit a driver's license than a twenty-dollar bill, and you can get more than twenty dollars for it."

"But won't these people know who I am and where I am?"

"That's a problem I solve. I don't help people who are running away from debts or paternity suits or something. I don't use shops that laminate I.D.'s so teenagers can buy a drink. I use the very best."

"But they're still criminals."

"So are we. The paper is the easy part. What we've got to work on is you."

By the time they quit, it was after midnight. The next morning when Jane came into the kitchen, he was smiling. "I think I figured it out."

"What did you figure out?" she asked. She was glad to see that he had made the coffee. She had been dreaming again, and it had left her feeling confused and irritable. The dreams were caused by anxiety, she knew, and the constant talk and concentration on every aspect of his past and future to the exclusion of everything else in the world, like air and sunshine. She poured a cup and turned to face him.

"The reason I decided to be an accountant was that I liked math. I was good at it, and accounting sounded like a sensible thing to do with as little math as I knew. But what I really would have liked to be was a teacher."

She looked at him judiciously. The most common reason police officers gave for getting into it was that they wanted to help people. When they found themselves dragging their hundredth bloody suspect into the emergency room, some of them decided that wasn't the way. "It's kind of a lousy time in history to become a teacher. Real ones are getting laid off all over the place. Of course, math teachers are always hard to come by."

"I thought about it a lot last night. I don't want to spend the rest of my life just hiding. If I live to be ninety, what do I say to myself—that I lived to be ninety?"

"Keep talking," she said. "I'm just thinking about it."

"It's average, right? A nice job, but not high-profile. The outsiders you meet are mostly parents." He looked at her hopefully for a moment.

"Maybe," she said. "What sort of education do you have?"

"That's a problem. I dropped out of college in my freshman year. The draft board was after me, so I figured I'd get the army out of the way. Then, after I quit the force, I got a B.S. in accounting at night."

Jane paced back and forth for a few minutes. "The more I think about it, the better I like it." She stopped and studied him. "You're sure about this?"

"Yes."

"All right, then. You're going to need to spend some more time in a college. That's fine, because colleges are a great place to get lost if you know what you're doing. You're too old to be anything else but a guy who's starting a second career, so we need an excuse."

"How about the truth? I was a cop who wanted to be a teacher."

"No. In that environment, the cop part would make people curious. You have to throw away something or be one of a kind. Losing your B.S. in accounting would cost you years. You were something else, and you were laid off. What kind of job could you have done with your credentials that wouldn't bring you into contact with companies like Smithson-Brownlow?"

"A lot of things. All big corporations have accounting departments. Aerospace?"

"No, not a big company. There are too many ways to approach a big company and ask about you. We need a small company, so if somebody wants to get in touch with them, there's only one number to call."

"Uhhh . . . stores, banks, insurance agencies . . ."

"Banks. You worked for a small bank and it went out of business. It's boring and there's nothing you have to explain. It happens all the time. You apply to get into a teacher-credential program. You have an accounting degree—not the real one, of course—and you want to major in math."

"Everything I do creates obstacles. A fake degree, fake jobs . . ."

"I told you to forget about the paper. That's the easy part."

They spent the day talking about his new career and developing memories for him to take with him into it. The next morning, when he got up and came into the kitchen, she was there waiting. "You're up early," he said.

"We have a lot of work to do." She had torn herself out of the dream this time and found it was five o'clock. She had decided it was better not to go back to sleep because the dream was waiting in the back of her mind.

She went to the counter and picked up a 35 millimeter camera. "I dug up Jimmy's camera. We're going to take your picture. That wall over there with the reflected light on it looks the best. We'll do the first few standing up."

He slowly walked to the wall. "Why?"

"Driver's license, et cetera." She aimed at him and said, "Smile," then lowered the camera. "That's a smile?"

"I don't know a whole lot about this, at least from the fugitive's point of view," he said. "But doesn't it strike you as a little dangerous to have pictures of me floating around?"

"Trust me," said Jane. "The people who will see the prints would die if any pictures got into the wrong hands."

"They would, eh?" He looked at her skeptically, his eyes half closed. She clicked the camera. "You took one already?"

"That was your driver's license. Everybody looks that way on their driver's license—like they just ate a worm."

He smiled and the camera clicked again. "Hey," he said. "What was that?"

"I don't know. Maybe the bank's Christmas party."

"I wasn't ready."

"Then they'll paste you in with your arm around the boss's wife, like you got caught." When he didn't smile, she said, "Stop worrying. They only need a couple of prints. You and I can burn the rest of them together."

"The negatives?"

"Those too. Now go find a nice shirt and tie in Jimmy's closet and put your coat on over it."

When she had taken all thirty-six exposures, Jane said, "I'll be back in a couple of hours with the prints. If anybody comes to the door, let him in and be nice."

She removed the roll of film, put on a jacket that belonged to Jimmy, and walked outside. He looked out the window and watched her making her way across the cornfield to Mattie's house.

She returned before the two hours were up. She had a blue envelope with the negatives and glossy prints inside. Felker spread them out on the table and looked at them one by one.

"Thirty-three," he said.

"I mailed three of them to the specialist. Next time you see them, they'll be glued to some official paper."

"Why three?"

"Have you ever seen anybody with the same picture on everything?"

He gathered the photographs and put the envelope into his pocket. "What now?"

"Now we wait, and we work to get you ready."

That day they walked along the banks of the Grand River and up country roads past small farms and through woods. Always they talked.

"It's time to use our imaginations," she said. "Think like a cop. The person you're looking for is you. The fugitive has a false name and false papers, and he's starting a new life. Where do you start?"

"Put out a circular with everything we know about him: his description, picture, habits."

"Very good," said Jane. "Who does it go to?"

"Everybody."

"Bad answer, but at least you're thinking like a cop again. It goes to police stations. That's not everybody. Nobody ever sees these things except other policemen. What's the moral of the story?"

"Stay away from cops?"

"Right. There are ways to do that. The obvious one is to watch out how you drive. You're never again going to be in enough of a hurry to speed or double-park. But you don't go where trouble is, either."

"That much I know," he said.

"What do you do if you're walking down the street and a man tries to pick a fight with you?"

"Walk away."

"What if he doesn't let you walk away?"

"Call for help?"

"Think harder. This shouldn't be news to you," she said. "You obviously haven't called for help much. Nobody jumps in, but sometimes they call the police. The safest thing for you to do is put him down fast, immobilize him, then get out. The people who couldn't pull themselves together enough to stop him won't be any better at stopping you."

"I guess that's true."

"Suppose you come home from work and find out you have a burglary?"

"That one I've thought about. I don't call the cops. The fingerprint people will take prints from all the surfaces, and they'll need to take mine to be sure which ones belong to the burglars."

"Very good. But what if you're home when it happens? You're asleep in bed and you hear them breaking in?"

"Same thing. Let them take what they want and go."

She shook her head. "No, I'm afraid that's the exception. There are very few burglars who don't case a place to see who lives there before they decide. There are almost none who can't tell if somebody's home before they break in. So what you'll have is an intruder who knows who you are and that you haven't gone out."

"You mean—"

"I'm afraid so. It would probably mean that it's not a burglar at all. One of the people who is after you has found you. The only thing you can do is get out."

"But if I could subdue him somehow, I might be able to find out—"

"Find out what? Who he is? I can answer that now. He's one of the hundreds of guys in jail who heard you were worth money, and he's the one who guessed right."

"What if there is no way out?"

"You'll have to decide for yourself," she said. "Nobody can tell anybody else what the circumstances are when they're justified in pulling the trigger. You're not a cop anymore, so there aren't any rules. Just make sure you do whatever thinking you have to do in advance."

"Okay, what if I did it?"

"Even if you have the best case of self-defense in history, they'll still find out who you are. You do whatever you can to hide the body and bail out. Come back to me and we try again."

Each day they walked the same route through the country, taking the roads that ran along the fields and away from the houses. Two days later Jane asked, "Remember the circular that John Felker the policeman was going to put out to catch John Felker the embezzler?"

"Sure," he said.

"What else was on it?"

"Age, height, weight—"

"Can't help you much there, but there are ways of thinking about it that are useful. What you have to think about isn't the way you look but what photographs of you exist. Only one in a thousand of the people who will be looking for you have seen you in person. The last picture the police have would be at least five years old, right?"

"Right."

"If there are any more recent ones—say your sister has some—try to get rid of them. Call her and tell her to burn them. Your ex-wife—"

"No problem there. If she has them, they'd be ten years old."

"Good. Then, when you work on your appearance, think of the photographs as though you were John Felker the cop. The best things to do are simple. You're tall, so you drive a small car. It has an unconscious effect. People just think: small. Wear a hat or sunglasses—anything that would keep John Felker the cop from making the connection at a glance. Unless you're in some other trouble, a glance is all the time they'll have. What else is on the circular?"

"Distinguishing marks or scars."

"Do you have any?"

"No." He smiled. "Should I get some?"

"Hardly. What else?"

"Distinctive personal habits."

"Okay," she said. "Go beyond the stuff that's on the circular because the cops aren't the only ones who will be looking. You don't seem to smoke. Do you drink?"

"Not heavily. I've been known to have one or two."

"One or two what?"

"Beers. Once in a while some scotch and water."

"Where? Bars?"

"No. We used to spend too much time going out on calls to bars to want to go back after a shift. There were a couple of places in St. Louis that a lot of cops went to—not many civilians, so some cops felt relaxed, but I didn't. It was the same faces I'd seen at work."

"Good. Stay out of bars. Things happen—fights inside and robberies in the parking lots. If you were in the habit, that's one of the first places they'd look. Besides, the strangest people get sanctimonious. When some guy goes out to get ripped, he doesn't want to rub elbows with his kids' math teacher. What about the rest of your social life?"

"What do you mean?"

She walked along for a step or two. "If you're uncomfortable about this, we'll close the topic. Just think about what I'm saying. You've been divorced for about ten years. You don't have any girlfriends at the moment. Are you gay?"

"No," he said.

"Are you celibate?"

He chuckled. "Not for long, and never by choice."

She seemed to choose her words carefully now. "Okay, I don't need to know anything about this. If you have some ... attitude about sex that's unusual, just take it into consideration in the future."

He looked at her closely. "Unusual?"

She walked along for a few steps in silence, and then said, "What I mean is predictable."

"There's nobody in my past that I can't resist getting in touch with."

She sighed in frustration. "Good. But there are other possibilities. Since you're single and you haven't been celibate, presumably there are a number of women around who could tell somebody things about you. Since we don't know who is trying to get you, it's not out of the question that a woman is involved. Women can sometimes get other women to discuss things that they wouldn't tell a man."

"I don't think there's anything they could say."

It came too quickly, so she realized she was going to have to be more specific. She looked ahead and made her voice sound impersonal and cheerful and clinical. "There are also things that can be unintentionally revealing. If your wife and all your girlfriends looked alike, you might want to widen your horizons a little. If you got into the habit of knowing all the prettiest prostitutes, as some cops do, that might be a good thing to change. If you can find the prostitutes in a new town, so can they, and they'll pay them just for talking. If you subscribed to a pornographic magazine for people who have some . . . special interest, it would be smart not to get another subscription in your new name. They make money by selling their mailing lists. That goes for other interests too, from coin collecting to motorcycles." She stopped abruptly. She knew where that had come from—Jimmy's stupid poster.

Jane walked along in silence for a long time. Finally, she glanced up at him and saw he was staring at her and grinning. He shrugged. "No hits so far. But go on. I like hearing women talk about sex."

"Forget it," she said. "Do you have any chronic physical conditions that would mean you have to see a specialist or take medicine?"

"Is this the same topic or a new one?"

"New one. And I'm trying to help you stay alive, so I'd appreciate it if you'd try too."

He was serious again. "No medical problems."

"All right," she said. "Let's go into buying habits. Go through your wardrobe in your mind. Picture your closet. Look at the ties, suits, jackets, shoes, and shirts. Men your size sometimes buy particular brands or even through mail order, to get a better fit. Even though you're gone, the catalogs and things will keep coming to your house. Your clothes are still there, and people will study them. Even if you're smart enough to buy the same kinds of clothes with different labels, the ones in the closet will give them a very accurate picture of how you'll look."

"Now you've got me," he said. "I'm one of those guys who found a few things he liked and stuck with them."

"Change," she said. "Don't buy anything you would have bought a month ago. It shouldn't be too hard. You're going from being an accountant to being a student."

"I hope I am, anyway," he said.

"You are," she said. "Be absolutely certain of that. You're only going to be running until we get you settled. Just keep that in mind. This is hard, but it's going to end."

When they walked back to the house on the fourth day, they didn't stop. Now there was a frantic quality to their conversations, as though Jane were trying to tell him everything she knew at once. While she made dinner, she had him pretend he was talking to his academic adviser at a college, telling her why he wanted to be a teacher, how he discovered he was interested in working with young people. Now and then she would ask him questions.

"Give me a list of the mathematics courses you had in your first degree program."

"Math 101–102, Math 363 and 4 . . ."

"Time out. Say, 'advanced calculus,' or 'probability theory.' Don't give them numbers, because the fake transcript might not have the same ones. The transcript will have to carry the same numbers as the catalog for the college you supposedly attended. Anytime somebody is writing down your answers, you have to think ahead."

They went on into the night, making pots of coffee and sitting in the kitchen again, staring at each other across Jimmy's table.

"What are you going to do with your money?"

"Bury it, I guess. I can't put it in a bank. There's a reporting requirement for cash deposits over ten thousand dollars."

"How much did you take?"

"Three hundred and fifty thousand."

"There are ways to hide it," Jane said. "You open seven or eight checking accounts in different banks: two in the town where you live, and the rest in other places."

"In my own name?"

"Yes. You put a few thousand dollars in each one—say, eight thousand. Make sure they don't pay any interest, because that gets reported to the IRS."

"Then what?"

"Then you get one of the local banks to think you're a businessman who leaves cash receipts in the night-deposit box, a few hundred dollars a night, to feed that checking account. You use that one to pay the others now and then."

"What does that accomplish?"

"It lets you start an investment account with one broker or mutual fund for each checking account except the one you're feeding. You set up automatic monthly withdrawals—a couple hundred a month. You can add a little cash once in a while, but most of the money comes in checks from your local bank. When you get behind, buy travelers' checks with cash and use them to make deposits in the checking accounts."

"Does that keep me from getting noticed?"

"If you pay taxes on the bogus business and on the investments, it does. You keep the cash deposits small but steady, so nobody thinks you're doing anything illegal. To the extent that you can, you live off the cash. That also gives you change, so it's not all hundreds or round-number deposits. When you need to write a check for something like tuition, do it from the second local account. After a few years, you end up with about

two thirds of your cash in seven or eight good investments you've built gradually. You stop the automatic
withdrawals, close all the checking accounts except
two—one local and one somewhere else, so you can
still pass a little money from one hand to the other
when you need to. By that time your teacher's salary
will have kicked in, and you can live like everybody
else."

"That leaves me with a third of the cash, less whatever it costs to live until I get a job. What's that for?"

"That's in case you make a mistake," she said. "That
gets you out."

"How did you learn all this?"

She shrugged. "It's what I do."

"Why do you do it?"

"Because I need to do something that makes sense."

"You know a lot about colleges, so you must have
gone to one. What were you studying to be?"

"Nothing, really," she said. "To tell you the truth, I
spent most of my time in the library. One of the great
ironies of being an Indian in the twentieth century is
that you have to do a lot of reading. I had a vague idea
I might go to law school, but I got distracted before I
made a decision."

"What distracted you?"

"I was a sophomore when somebody I knew got into
trouble. He was a little older. During the war, he had
been drafted and ducked out. He hadn't even changed
his name, just stopped answering their letters and went
to a different college. He wasn't exactly a problem for
the government. He just didn't want to kill anybody, but
his local board decided he wasn't a conscientious objec-
tor. They probably knew where he was all the time, but
they were too busy to go pick him up. After the war
ended, they found the time."

"How did you know him?"

"We took a class together. Sometimes we'd have cof-

fee after a seminar. It wasn't much of a relationship.
But one night he came to me in the dorm and told me
the F.B.I. had come to his apartment looking for him
while he was out. While he was talking, I could tell he
had decided that if he had to go to jail, he would kill
himself. He was saying goodbye. Not to me—we
weren't even involved, really, but I was the only girl he
could talk to right then, that night, and so he was saying
goodbye to all women through me—the ones he had
known but didn't anymore, and the ones he would have
known if he had lived."

"Did you talk him out of it?"

"No," she said. "I wanted to, but all of a sudden I realized I wasn't listening to his words. I was looking at
him and thinking how easy it would be to make him
disappear."

"As a sophomore? You must have been—what—
nineteen?"

"I had worked two summers as a skip-tracer for a
bill-collection agency in Buffalo, so I had a pretty good
idea of what worked and what didn't. I also got a feeling for how the dogs hunt. They're not all the same, and
they don't look equally hard for everybody who's on
the run. A young guy who's a student and isn't dangerous, sometimes they figure he'll just turn up sooner or
later. He'll pay taxes or apply for a marriage license or
a loan or something. Sometimes I think they got a special kick out of arresting draft-dodgers twenty years
later, so it would get into the papers to remind people
that they never stop looking."

"So you made him disappear?"

"Yes. Then a few people found out about it—friends
of his, friends of mine."

"And they told other people?"

"Not right away. But people grow up and the years
go by, and just about everybody meets someone at some
point who needs that kind of help."

He nodded. "So they made you do it again."

"No," she said. "It wasn't them, it was me. When I realized I could do it, there was a temptation to do it again. I was the one who decided."

When the sun started to fill the room they turned the lights off and made breakfast. As they washed and dried the dishes at Jimmy's sink, Felker said, "What's next?"

Jane pulled the plug in the sink and let the water go out. "We need to sleep." She had kept it up for almost twenty-four hours now. She wasn't sure she had burned the dream out of her mind, but she knew she hadn't been doing him any good for the past hour or two. "If you wake up before I do, spend the time thinking about the future. Try to pick out things you're not sure about. Forget the past. There's nothing deader than that."

14

Jane woke up in the dark room. She felt agitated, troubled. There was a throbbing of drums far off, and then the voices of the people singing the Ga-da-shote. The chorus of voices in the first column of dancers was singing, "Ga no oh he yo," and the other column of dancers would answer, "Wa ha ah he yo."

"Are you awake?" Felker was in the room.

"Yes," she said. She pulled the covers up to her neck and sat up. "What is it?"

"I was going to ask you the same thing."

She laughed. "I'm sorry. You startled me. Are you dressed?"

"Sure. As soon as I heard the war drums, I figured I'd better."

"Give me a minute."

She watched his shadow slip out and the door close. Then she got out of bed, turned on the light, and searched her bag for clean clothes while she tried to bring her mind back up from the panicky feeling she had gotten in the deep, restless sleep. She caught sight of herself in the mirror on Jimmy's dresser when she stepped into her jeans. She looked frightened.

She walked out into the living room, brushing her hair. "Mattie will be here in a few minutes to find out why we're not at the dance."

"Shouldn't we wait for her?"

"No. If we don't go now, we're being rude." They

walked out into the field and headed for a long, low building a distance off. There were lights, cars, and the sound of the drums and voices. "It's not a war dance, by the way. It's called the Trotting Dance. It's the first dance you do in a big celebration."

"What are we celebrating?"

"Thanks to the Maple."

"You mean the tree?"

"It's the first big party of the year, because the first good thing in the spring is that the maple sap starts running. Then there's the Green Corn Festival, Strawberry Festival, Harvest, New Year's. You know, the usual."

"New Year's I know about. What do they do on New Year's?"

"They used to strangle a white dog and hang it on a pole."

"The usual."

"And then they'd have the guessing of dreams."

"That sounds like fun. Did you just have a dream?"

"Yes."

"Can I guess it?"

"No."

As they walked through the cool night air toward the low building, the music seemed to grow louder. The doors, one on each end of the building, kept opening to let more people inside, and each time a light would shine out into the darkness and the sound of the singing would rise. The beat of the drums and the squash-shell rattles were amplified by the thumping of hundreds of feet.

When they reached the edge of the light shining from the doorway, Felker stood still and listened. "Getting shy?" Jane asked.

"A little." The music changed. It slowed down, and this time a lone male voice that reminded Felker of a zydeco singer, with breaks and falls in his clear baritone, sang, "Ya ha we ya ha!" and the two or three hundred voices, men and women and children, chanted, "Ha ha." "I've got to wonder what they're going to think of me."

She reached out and touched him. She put her arm through his and gently tugged him toward the building. "Think of it as a Polish wedding. Everybody is welcome and everybody is here."

He started to walk along with her again. "That I can understand. Just like in St. Louis."

"Not like St. Louis," she said. "This is Poland."

The door swung open and they were inside. The room was a big public meeting hall, with benches along one wall but bare otherwise. The people were in four giant moving circles, one inside the other. As the outer circle passed by them, here and there a brown face would grin at Jane or a head would toss its long black hair to reveal glittering almond eyes that focused on her and only passed shyly across Felker. But there were other faces he would not have expected to see here— people with white skin and light hair who didn't look any more like Indians than he did. He started to feel less conspicuous.

Jane tugged his arm again to pull his head closer and said into his ear, "Remember, Polish wedding. Join the fun and you're a guest. Stand around and you're a stranger."

Felker took a deep breath and stepped forward to enter the outer circle, but once again Jane held his arm. "Boys in front, girls in back." She pushed him into the line in the middle of a string of men. Three little girls who had seen him try to step in among them giggled, careful not to look at him. He saw Jane slip into an inner line between Mattie Wilson and a woman in her late twenties, who looked over her shoulder to clasp Jane's hand and then release it. They danced until people were hot and winded, and then the leader stopped singing.

Suddenly, Felker heard an unearthly noise, like a

dozen men growling and bellowing. The drums started again, and people grinned and backed off the floor. A strong hand gripped his arm. He turned to see an old man with skin like the brown leather on Jane's bag. He was grinning so his black eyes narrowed. "Come on," the old man said. "You'll get trampled."

Felker walked with the old man to the bench by the wall. "I'm Basil Henrick," said the old man.

"John Felker." He shook the old man's hand.

The door on the east end of the building flew open and ten men danced into the room wearing dark blue carved wooden masks with pointed leather ears and tufts of fur on top, huge eyes, and big teeth. They grumbled and grunted, bent over and glared at the people gathered around the walls. As he watched, he saw one of them pass Jane, who was on the other side of the building with about five young women. Some of the women wore Indian skirts with elaborate embroidered pictures on them and a loose red tunic above, dangling earrings, and big silver brooches like plates. Others were dressed like Midwestern farm girls after church, in modest dresses, skirts, and sweaters. They all seemed amused by the men in the masks, who were now roaring and grunting as they danced.

"This is the Buffalo Dance," said Basil Henrick.

"Buffalo Dance?" said Felker. "I didn't know there were buffalo around here."

This seemed to please Basil Henrick. "There weren't. War parties ran into herds of buffalo around the Kentucky salt lick." He stared at the dancers and nodded his head to the beat of the drums. "They said, 'What in the hell are those?' Couldn't get over it."

Felker found himself smiling. "What were they doing way down there?"

"Fighting Cherokees. They fought pretty regularly everywhere from Maine to South Carolina, and from the Atlantic to the Mississippi. Any place farther than that, I figure they just went once in a while to steal women." The old man looked at Felker. "You know Janie from college?"

"No," said Felker. "I met her through a mutual friend."

"Yeah," said Basil. "You look over there at Janie, the first thing you notice ain't her mind. You don't say, 'Now, there's a scholar.' " He gave a hoot, then said, "Her daddy used to bring her up here when she was little. They'd go up to Toronto and see a show or something and then come down here and put on the blanket and be Indians again. Fine man. When he fell, must have been five or six hundred people went to the mourning council down in Tonawanda."

"Fell? What do you mean?"

"He was working a construction job. Big bridge out west somewhere. A cable snapped and down he went."

"Terrible," said Felker.

"It's good money, and the Iroquois crews have always been able to get work because we're not afraid of heights, but people die."

"You're really not afraid of heights?"

Basil shrugged. "*I* sure as hell am. I was a railroad man myself. I got to see plenty, but I saw it from ground level. I think the part about not being afraid is bullshit. An Iroquois just trains himself to tolerate it. They used to say a warrior needed a skin seven thumbs thick." He pinched his arm. "Mine is maybe five thumbs thick."

The buffalo dancers danced out the door to cheers from the crowd.

"She putting you up at Jimmy's?"

"Yes," said Felker.

"I figured. Mattie loves to have young people around."

"Has she brought other people for visits? I mean, strangers?"

Basil looked at him slyly. "Can't say."

The drums grew louder, there were rattles and clicking sticks, and the door flew open again. This time it was twenty-five men, all in breechcloths and paint, wearing feathers and bells on their knees, ankles, and arms. The dance was quick with sharp, violent movements, and the music was different now.

"What's this one?" asked Felker.

"War Dance. The Wa-sa-seh, that's the real name. It means Sioux dance. I figure when Great-Great-Grandpa had fought his way past the Mississippi, that's who he ran into in the open country. It made an impression."

"They lost?"

"My guess is that's an understatement. A war party that far out was probably no more than thirty fellows. On the average day out there, it wouldn't have been too hard to run into a couple hundred Sioux warriors out for their morning pony ride, and those guys weren't about to take any shit from us. Grandpa probably beat it back to the woods as quick as he could."

"You sound like you wish you'd seen it."

"With binoculars," said Basil. "Not up close. In the good old days, sometime around 1650, they took a census. They put one kernel of corn in a big basket for each person. That would have been maybe seventeen or eighteen thousand people. Throw in the rest of the Iroquois tribes, it was maybe fifty thousand. That's not a lot to fight the whole world."

When the warriors disappeared, Felker looked for Jane, but he couldn't pick her out in the crowd. Two men walked to the middle of the floor and sat down face to face, with a drum and a pair of rattles. They sat quietly talking to each other for a few seconds, and nobody paid much attention to them beyond not stepping on them. Finally, the drum and the rattles started, the two men nodding their heads together to keep time, and at an invisible signal they began to sing.

"Fish Dance," said Basil. "Come on. I'll show you."

He waited for the column of dancers to pass, then stepped into its wake, dancing backward, and pulled Felker with him.

Felker's eye caught a movement to the side, and he turned to face Basil. As he did, Jane stepped between them and began to dance with Basil. Two young women Jane had been talking to across the room stepped in together and began to dance with Felker.

"Two partners, John," said Basil. "Only honored guests get two."

Felker grinned and gave a little bow to his two dancing partners. They were both dressed in Indian skirts, with elaborate embroidery at the hem and up the front to look like flowers. They had deerskin leggings with a slit in the front to show the beadwork on their moccasins, and they wore long silver earrings that glinted against their long black hair. All of their movements were precisely simultaneous. When they turned to dance forward, they spun like a pair of matched horses and took him by surprise so he had to glance over his shoulder to be sure he could change direction without stumbling.

The two singers in the middle picked up the pace gradually, and their volume went up with it. In the noise of the feet of so many dancers and the song of the two men, it was possible to forget that this was a world that was gone. The two young women were unmistakably a kind of offering to a warrior who had come in from some battle, and they were still that. They weren't some pale echo of an old tradition because here they still were, no less real than they had ever been. They were more than a ceremonial welcome, more than a symbol of abundance: They were the antidote to death. Their ornaments said so. It was written in all the colorful flowers embroidered on the clothes of these women from a nation that was always at war.

The dance ended and the two women shook his hand. One of them said, "I'm Emma. You're catching on very well."

Felker said, "Thank you. I appreciate your giving me a chance to learn." In his peripheral vision he was watching as the other girl whispered something to Jane, who made a wry face and pinched her so she had to retreat, laughing.

The music started again, and Jane stepped in front of Felker and began to dance. "Enjoying yourself?"

"I've been in tighter spots than this," he said. He glanced around. "Hey, my interpreter's gone. What's this one called?"

She said, "It's called Shaking the Bush."

The people regrouped as the clear, melodious voices of the singers cut through their murmuring. Emma stood before a young man who looked like an Indian warrior in a movie, and Felker recognized him as one of the war dancers. The warrior and Felker were shoulder to shoulder, dancing with Emma and Jane. All over the room these double pairs formed, the women choosing their partners and then all four dancing to the sound of the drums and rattles.

In the heat and the noise, Felker's mind began to lose the simple habit of insisting that it see only what was in front of his eyes. He looked across at Jane in her blue jeans and white blouse, and Emma in her costume of an ancient Seneca woman, and the two images began to merge and then to trade places. There was no difference at all. They could have been sisters—for all he knew, were sisters in the strange, ornate family system they had—or even the same girl seen at different times or in different aspects, like a ghost. Emma was smiling, but Jane was staring straight into his eyes, as though she was reading something there.

He studied her closely and then said, "Why is it called Shaking the Bush?"

"It just is."

He leaned closer and realized that her eyes were glistening, welling up. "What's the matter?"

"Nothing," she said, and quickly looked away. After a second she brushed her sleeve across her eyes and looked straight into his gaze again, unflinching.

After a time the music stopped. The man who had been singing stood up and gave a loud and apparently serious harangue in Seneca. Women went to the end of the room and collected covered dishes and put jackets on sleepy children. Young couples drifted out into the darkness with their arms around each other.

Felker and Jane walked in silence across the dark field. The night was still and cold now, and their breath puffed little clouds of steam into it. Jane said, "Well, what did you think?"

"I think the world got screwed up when we stopped living in villages. Having tribes, I guess. There were tribes in Scotland, where my family came from. They painted themselves blue and went out to throw stones at the Romans."

"Maybe we can find a village for you," she said. "One with a lot of nice stones."

He blew out a breath sadly. "You know, I actually forgot for a couple of hours."

She held his arm. "Good," she said. "That's the way it has to be." She looked up at him critically as they walked. "You know, I think you're going to be all right. Once we get you settled, you might actually be better off than you ever were."

"I don't know," he said.

"Happier, I mean." She squinted at him critically. "You're no accountant."

They walked up the steps to the front porch of the house and entered. She had not locked the door. She walked in without turning on the lights, and he didn't either. He went into his room, took off his shoes, and sat on the bed. He took a deep breath and blew it out in a sigh before he became aware that she was in the room with him.

She stood beside the bed, the moonlight through the curtain illuminating her as she unbuttoned her blouse. The light shone through it as she pulled it out of the top of her jeans and slipped it off her shoulders.

"I know your dream," he said quietly.

"Do you?" she said.

"You dreamed we were going to be lovers."

She stepped out of her jeans, then her panties, and began to unbutton his shirt carefully, one button after another, with a slow inevitability. When she reached his waist, she unbuckled his belt and waited for him to stand. Her hands were slow and soft and soothing as she stripped the last of his clothes off him, and then she ducked into his arms and her hair draped on his chest, still cold from the night air outside.

15

F elker awoke to the sound of a bird making its first quiet call, somewhere far off. He was alone in the bed, and there was no sound inside the house. He rolled to the side of the bed to look down at the floor and saw that her clothes weren't there.

He listened again, then sat up, swung his legs to the floor, and walked to the closet, where he had hung his backpack. It was still there, and the money was still inside. He found his clothes on the chair, where he would have put them. He was fighting the possibility that it hadn't happened. He went to the window and looked out into the gray light, but there were only the empty fields and a few acres of woods about a quarter mile off. He looked down at the bed, but her side showed no sign that anyone had slept on it. He bent down and put his face into the pillow. He could smell Jane's hair, a very light scent of flowers, but sweat too, a sweet, musky smell that made her real again and brought back the feel of her in the dark.

"What are you doing?" It was her voice.

He turned and straightened. "I was trying to identify the perfume."

"I'll have to ask Jimmy. It's his shampoo."

Felker shrugged. "There's more to Jimmy than meets the eye." He looked around him. "I guess there would have to be."

He followed her into the kitchen. She was wearing a

149

man's red plaid wool shirt that hung down over her jeans, and her hair was pulled back into a tight ponytail. "Where have you been?"

"I went out to get some eggs for breakfast," she said. She pointed to a basket on the counter beside the door.

"You walked to the store already? What's open at this hour?"

She laughed. "This is a farm. You just go out and lift up a couple of chickens." She started to slip out of the big hunting shirt, and glanced at him. She could see he was staring at the way her breasts stood out under her T-shirt. She raised an eyebrow.

"Come on." He took her hand and led her into the bedroom.

"I thought you'd be hungry," she said. Her voice was low and tense, almost a whisper. "I brought breakfast."

"This is more important," he said. "If I die today, I won't care if I had two more eggs."

Then his hands moved up under her T-shirt and were on her breasts, and then he was slipping the T-shirt up over her head, and he tossed it somewhere, and the jeans were coming down over her hips, and he seemed to be everywhere at once, touching her and kissing her in a way that made her ache until she kissed him back.

She had needed to hear him say he wanted to, so she could be sure that it wasn't just something people did because they had been to bed together once, and knew that if they let that cold-light-of-dawn feeling go on for any longer it would go on forever. Then she forgot all of that because none of it mattered at all. It hadn't happened. What was going on now was what she would have imagined while she was out walking in the dark morning, if she had let the longing take the form of a wish. He must have been thinking of it too, because there was nothing tentative, no hesitation. What they thought, they seemed to think at the same time, and the impulses were already movements before they knew.

They drew together to let their lips meet in slow, moist, leisurely kisses that neither of them started or stopped because it hadn't been an intention, just an attraction they hadn't resisted. Their bodies had learned to know each other in the course of the long night, while the things they said to each other were still the words of strangers. She accepted it because there was no other choice, and she began to let herself feel glad instead of ashamed that this had happened.

Later they ate breakfast. It was better with the sun up and light bouncing around the bright white kitchen, with the smells of fried eggs and hot coffee and the busy chirping of sparrows outside the window. "Want to have a picnic?" asked Jane.

"I'd like that," he answered.

Just as they were packing their lunch, they heard the first drops popping on the roof. It rained for three days. The cornfield outside turned to a rich, muddy soup and the grass in the fields turned an impossible emerald-green.

On the fourth day the rain stopped, and on the sixth they woke up to find that the world had changed again. It was the first week of May now, and the small half-inch buds that had been folded tightly on the branches of the trees exploded into luminous light-green leaves.

The letter came on the seventh day. Jane began to clean the house.

16

It was morning, and they sat at the kitchen table trying to keep their eyes from settling on the two suitcases Jane had bought in Brantford.

Felker broke the silence. "Should we leave some money to pay for all the food and stuff?"

"No," she said. "There are rules about hospitality. Some time I'll give Mattie a present."

"Like you did Wendell?"

"Yes."

"I know this is kind of an odd question, but what would happen if we just stayed here? Didn't go on to another place?"

"Eventually something would happen. You'd get sick and have to go to a hospital, or maybe the government agent here would notice you and start making quiet inquiries, or you'd get a speeding ticket." She smiled sadly. "We've got to get you settled."

There was a knock on the door. Jane went to open it, and she saw Carlton the Mohawk on the porch. Felker stood up and took their bags out to the truck. They drove to Mattie's farmhouse, and Jane ran inside.

Mattie was at her stove, and a soap opera was on the television set. "Hi, Janie," she said. "Leaving us so soon?"

"Yes."

Mattie came up and gave her a big hug. Jane could smell chicken feathers and flour and fresh air somehow caught in the big, soft apron during the early morning chores. When she held Jane out at arm's length to look at her, she said, "You've been crying."

"Don't be silly."

"Yes, you have. Not just now, maybe, but at night in the dark." She nodded at the door. "Did he see you cry?"

Jane shook her head.

"Smart girl," she said. "Keep it that way. Men don't like problems they can't solve. It just makes them mad."

Jane gave Mattie a kiss on the cheek, handed her Jimmy's keys, and said, "See you, Mattie."

Carlton drove them north through Galt and picked up the 401 above it, then rode into Toronto on a stream of thick, fast-moving traffic. As soon as he had made the turn into the airport loop, Carlton said, "What parking lot should I go to?"

"None of them," said Jane. "Drop us off in front of Air Canada." When he pulled up to the curb, Jane said, "Be good."

"We'll miss you," said Carlton.

As Jane and Felker approached the terminal doors, Jane spoke under her breath. "I'll do this."

She paid for the tickets with a credit card that said Janet Foley and specified that the other ticket was for Daniel Foley. She checked their two suitcases and then gave Felker his ticket as they walked across the lobby.

"Take this," she said. "The gate is 42 and the flight leaves in forty minutes. Go into a men's room and lock yourself in a cubicle until then. I'll see you on board."

"Is that necessary?"

"Do it," she said. "This is the last place where a sensible person would look for you. Once we're out of here, they've lost you forever."

He stepped into the first men's room they came to, and Jane walked on as though she had nothing to do with him. And so I don't, she thought. She bought a magazine in the gift shop and went to Gate 42. The magazine was just the right size to hold in front of her while she watched for the wrong sort of men to show up at the gate.

There were a couple of Canadian naval officers traveling in uniform. No matter how resourceful the ones chasing Felker were, they couldn't have anticipated far enough in advance for the uniforms. There were eight Pakistanis, three African-Americans, nine Chinese. The men she had seen that night had been light-skinned. The most suspicious people were a young couple who appeared to stare around them a lot, but then she saw that they were staring because their two children were being allowed to play on the seats a couple of rows away, supposedly by themselves. Two men appeared who were distinct possibilities, but then they sat down and she saw that one of them had a pair of leather-soled shoes with an imprint on the sole that said Eaton's. An American trying to look like a Canadian might buy something Canadian to wear, but not shoes. She calmed down. As a bonus, she noticed that on page 127 of the magazine there was a camel coat that an actual living woman might like to wear. She folded the corner of the page and went on with her vigil.

The airline functionaries arrived at the gate a few minutes before time, set up shop at the desk, and began to make announcements into the microphone, first in English, then in French. After the second one, Felker drifted in. She put down her magazine and scanned the faces. The only ones who stared at him and pretended not to were two teenaged girls by the window who had some sort of hormonal interest in men who looked like him but probably still had an inaccurate idea of why this should be so. There was something to be said for locking them up in convent schools until they knew how to conjugate lots of foreign verbs, she thought.

The next announcement came, and she felt reassured. "Now boarding." She waited until he was in line so she could watch his back, but she still saw nobody who had any interest in him.

She sidestepped along the aisle inside the plane, past people stowing things in the overhead compartments and taking off coats, and sat down beside him. When the plane had bumped along up the runway and taken off, he leaned close to her and said, "They have very clean restrooms in Canada."

"Lucky you," she said.

"Why Vancouver?"

"For the next few hours, we eat, sleep, watch a movie, read magazines, whatever. We don't talk."

"Not even about Vancouver?"

"No."

"Come on. Is there somebody on the plane who doesn't know where it's going?"

She smiled. "Please. Just do what I ask. It'll be better."

"Will you make it up to me?"

"No."

"How about a neutral topic? Is that where Harry is?"

"Harry's not a neutral topic."

Over the Great Plains she fell asleep. She slept without moving, simply fell into the darkness and stayed there until people started ignoring the pilot's recitation of the rules about not standing up until the plane had stopped at the terminal.

Jane opened her eyes to see Felker watching her.

In the terminal, she hurried him to the baggage area without speaking. She was still watchful, but things had changed. She was no longer expecting to see the four men. Whatever had been chasing Felker hadn't gotten big enough yet to send hundreds of watchers to all of the major airports on the continent, but soon it might. She just hoped that his boss hadn't gotten tired of calling his answering machine by now. When he did, Felker could be on the list of people that the F.B.I., Interpol, and lots of local police would be watching for. Accountants who embezzled money from clients traveled.

When they made it out of the baggage area, she took a deep breath. It was late afternoon here, and the air was damp and fresh and cool. The airport was on an island, clutched between the two arms of the Fraser River, with the Strait of Georgia to the west. The first taxi in line pulled to the curb and the driver got out while the trunk popped open.

"Going to town?" he asked. He was short and blond and red-faced.

"Yes," said Jane. "The Westin Hotel."

The man snatched up the bags and set them in the trunk while Jane and Felker climbed inside. The cab pulled into traffic and took the route north on Granville Street. Jane stared out the window at the city. She liked being in a car, away from the lighted glass enclosure of the terminal.

When the taxi stopped at the hotel, she handed the driver one of the Canadian twenties she had picked up in Brantford. They let the bellman scoop up their bags and lead them to the front desk.

"Dr. and Mrs. Wheaton," said Jane, obliterating Janet and Daniel Foley. Everything was little jumps to make breaks in the trail. Never use the same name on the airline ticket and the hotel register. Never miss a chance to mislead.

"Yes," said the desk clerk, plucking a white card out of a box behind the desk with her long, manicured fingers. "We have your reservation right here."

Felker signed the card, and the desk clerk handed the keys to the bellman, who pushed a tall cart ahead of them with their bags on it, using it like a moving barricade to shield them all the way to the elevator. He opened the door for them and bustled around, switching lights on and off just long enough for Jane to slip Felker some money and for Felker to pass it to the bellman.

Everything was quick, smooth, and private. That was another part of the method. You used the facilities that had been invented to insulate the people who had a little money from the rough edges and annoyances. The Dr. Wheatons of the world didn't have to wait for buses or stand in lines. They stepped out of one enclosure into another. For them waiting was irritating. For the John Felkers of the world it was dangerous.

Felker flopped backward onto the bed and stared up at the ceiling. "Now I can ask, can't I?"

"Ask what?" Jane crawled onto the bed next to him.

"Why Vancouver?"

"We're here because this is where a man named Lewis Feng is. He's the best."

"The best what?"

"He's the one I sent your pictures to."

"What's he doing here?"

She sat up and looked down at him. "The people who need the best American passports and licenses and things aren't in the United States. They're on the outside looking in."

"Who are they?"

"Right now what's driving this market is China," she said. "There are a lot of rich people in Hong Kong who don't think it's going to be a great place to be rich when the British lease runs out. Some are setting up to move to other places, maybe sending a couple of members of the family to establish residency, set up bank accounts, that sort of thing."

"So why do they need fake papers? A person with serious money can still buy a congressman and get real papers."

"Some of the richest probably do. A billionaire doesn't have any trouble getting in anywhere, but then there's family, retainers, friends, and if you've lived

through, say, sixty years of Chinese history, you get
used to the idea that governments change their minds
fast. So a lot of them are hedging their bets, setting up
a second place they can run to if the door closes, a second identity if the first one doesn't hold up. The same
thing is happening in Taiwan and Singapore. A lot of
people who have made a lot of money in the past
twenty years don't want to bet their lives that China is
always going to leave them alone, either."

"So all of a sudden Vancouver is the best place to get
forged American papers?"

She shook her head. "God, no. Just one of the places.
There's Miami, where you have refugees, drug runners,
and prospective revolutionaries, or ones who already
tried and blew it. L.A. is the big money-laundering center now, and that means bagmen have to bring it in, and
others have to get enough I.D. to do a lot of banking
and buying. And New York, just because it's New York
and it's still the best place to buy anything you want."

"That's where we were heading, wasn't it? New
York."

"Yes. That was before." She didn't say before what.

"Why didn't we just fly there?"

"This is safer for you."

"Why?"

"Because Lew Feng has a very specialized clientele.
A lot of them may be gangsters, but if they are, they're
from Shanghai or someplace, not St. Louis. That means
they aren't interested in you and they don't know anybody else who is. In New York I can't guarantee that."

"All right," said Felker. "What do we do now?"

"I go out and make some more arrangements, buy
you some clothes. You're going to stay here, out of
sight."

"How long?"

"We meet Lew Feng tomorrow night."

17

It was a small shop on a quiet block, the third in a row of seven narrow painted fronts, each with a single door and a small display case full of expensive knitted clothes, ivory carvings, furs, or leather. The sign over the door said WESTMINSTER STATIONERS. When Jane pushed the door open, a small bell attached to a spring on top tinkled for a few seconds, then rang again when Felker closed it. On all of the shelves were neat displays of boxed stationery, open stocks of vellum and linen, hand-pressed paper of silk threads and cotton, and colored inks and pens for calligraphers, artists, and architects.

Jane stood still in the middle of the room in front of the video camera so she could be recognized on the monitor, and in a moment Lewis Feng appeared. He was about six feet tall and very slim, dressed in a dark suit and a shirt so white and starched that it seemed to belong on the shelves with the paper. "Hello, Jane," he said.

"Hi, Lew," she answered.

"Come in." The way he said it told Felker that this was only an anteroom.

He led them into an office that looked like a doctor's consulting room. He went behind his desk while Jane and Felker waited, then opened a filing cabinet and pulled out a key. He used it to open another door, which led into a large workshop with dozens of pieces of equipment, a few of which Felker recognized. There were a light table, an enlarger, engraving machines, even an old-fashioned printing press. Felker understood. A stationer could have an incredible collection of printing equipment and special papers without anybody giving it a thought. Lew Feng noticed that Felker was looking around, and said, "The foundation of our relationship is our mutual lack of curiosity."

"Of course," said Felker. He glanced at Jane with a wince.

Feng went to a shelf where there were ream-size packages of paper with the wrappers still on them. He lifted one off the pile, tore it open on a workbench, pulled a piece of paper out, and set it in front of Felker.

"Here is your birth certificate. The form is genuine. The signature is forged, but the county clerk in question is both real and dead." He paused while Felker glanced at it, then reached into the package again. "Driver's license. This is genuine. The written examination and driving test were taken, and the license issued. The only thing on it that we've added is your photograph. The military discharge papers and the old tax returns are convincing but false. You can use them with anyone but the government. The Social Security card is genuine, but its value is limited. The only way to get one was to have an eighteen-year-old with a second birth certificate in your name apply for it. So you can safely use it and pay taxes into the account, but I'm afraid you would have to wait forty-seven years to collect the benefits."

"I'll just have to save my money," Felker said.

Lewis Feng betrayed no amusement. "I know this doesn't seem like a big penalty compared to your present problems, but you need to know. If you misuse these documents, you could be . . . embarrassed."

"I understand," he said. "Please, go on."

"This diploma is a Bachelor of Science from Devonshire-Greenleigh College, a reputable small college in

Pennsylvania that ran short of money about eight years ago and closed. We maintain the fiction that there is still a registrar's office that employers can write to for a transcript, funded by the alumni, so if you need academic records, just write to the address on the envelope."

Felker picked up the diploma and read, "John David Young."

Lew Feng said, "Many of our clients are Orientals, so we use Oriental names that don't attract attention in North America: Young, Lee, Shaw, and so on. Jane specified the first name John, and we had a John Young."

"Had one?"

"We had been building one. Jane asked for the deepest kind of cover, and that takes time. The credit cards are real. The car was bought from a dealer in John Young's name—"

"Car? I have a car?"

"It's the safest way to cross the border."

Felker looked at Jane, then at Feng. "What is all this going to cost?"

"We were paid in advance," said Lewis Feng.

"We'll talk about it," said Jane.

Lewis Feng went on. "This is the key to your apartment in Medford, Oregon. It was rented for you by a legitimate apartment-finding service, so nobody is going to be expecting you to look like the person who put down the deposit."

"This is all safe?" asked Felker.

"Nobody knows anything except members of my family, and I protect them by making sure they never see the customer or know anything more than a long list of new names we make up. I have to keep some record of the information that we've generated so that when you need additional documents, we won't create inconsistencies. But it's well hidden and it's never cross-referenced to your original identity, which I don't know. As I said, our mutual lack of curiosity is the foundation of our relationship."

He handed Felker a crisp manila envelope for his papers and keys and held out his hand. Felker shook it numbly. "Good luck in your new life, Mr. Young."

"Thank you."

They walked out of the shop in silence, then down the street for two blocks. "This is your car," said Jane. It was a gray Honda Accord, with Oregon license plates, parked by the curb. He stopped to look, but Jane pulled him along. "Leave it. I don't want them to see it at the hotel."

He stopped again. "Where did the money come from?"

"People give me presents. I gave you one."

"I have my present. I'd be dead if you hadn't—"

"Hold on to your cash. You'll need it until you're settled."

She flagged down a taxi, and they got into it. They didn't speak all the way back to the hotel. When it pulled up in front of the entrance to let them off, she said, "Wait for me." Felker pulled her aside. "What's going on?"

"You're alive," she said. "You're a new man, with a suitcase full of cash and a new car and a new apartment. You have a fresh start. See if you can do something with it."

"Let's talk about this inside."

Jane shook her head. "I've already checked us out of the hotel. The doorman has our bags, and my plane leaves in two hours."

"You mean it's over?"

"This is over. The old John is missing, presumed dead."

"You know what I mean."

"Maybe sometime you can get in touch with me, if

you live. If I live, I might meet you someplace." She looked up into his eyes, then threw her arms around his neck and hugged him hard. She whispered, "Happy birthday, John Young." Then she walked to the doorman's cubicle, handed him a receipt and a Canadian bill, and took her suitcase.

As she stepped into the taxi, she said, "Airport, please." As the cab pulled away from the curb, she didn't look out the window at John Young. She opened her purse and pulled out her wallet. She reached into the little pocket and pulled out the photograph. It was her favorite one. It was the one she had taken before he was ready. Telling him she had sent Lew Feng all three pictures was the only lie she had ever told him.

Twenty minutes later, John Young walked up to the Honda Accord. He put his suitcase into the trunk, hid all of the documents except his new driver's license in the wheel well, and closed the trunk. Then he got into the car, drove it around the block, and parked it again. From here he couldn't see the ocean, but he could see the fog coming in, the ocean's presence beginning to obscure everything else. He sat perfectly still and prepared his mind for what he now had to do.

18

J ane stepped off the airplane at five in the morning. While she went about picking up her suitcase and finding a taxi, the sun used the time to rise high enough to irritate her eyes. She had slept the last couple of hours on the plane, but it had only made her feel hollow and light-headed. The Buffalo airport was small and simple, but the emptiness and lack of distractions gave her time to succumb to the feeling that she didn't want to be in the flat landscape outside the windows. While she was still inside an airport, she was still in transit, in motion. She could turn back and choose a gate, and beyond it would be the world. But once outside the door, she was only in western New York again, back where she had started.

At other times when she had arrived here, the sensation had been relief that she was finally home. Even the grimy, wet pavement of Genesee Street used to feel friendly to her. Today she clenched her teeth until she was on the Thruway, and then the houses she could see beyond the fences were small, dirty, and depressing.

She had no trouble understanding it, because she had been trying to prepare herself for this morning from the second when she had walked out of the hotel in Vancouver. She shouldn't be here. She should be with him. She reminded herself that she had invented all of the rules, and what they said was that a guide was not in the business of transporting people with all their attachments to other addresses—a guide took them out of the world. When she set the rabbit free, he had to be a new rabbit. He could only be that if he was alone.

When he arrived unencumbered and uncomforted, he would be forced to form new relationships, to dig deeper into the new ground and quickly become indistinguishable from the people around him. People who had never had anything happen to them always seemed hard and unchanging, but they weren't. Human beings were vulnerable and malleable. Within a couple of years they picked up regional accents, walked differently, changed their preferences and habits without ever noticing it. They didn't do it to fool the chasers; they did it because it was the only way to touch the people around them, and touching them left an imprint, made them like the people they saw every day. People needed not to be alone.

The cab took only fifteen minutes to reach Degana-wida, and then Jane took over. "Turn left at the next light. Go straight for two lights. Turn right up here. It's the third house from the corner, the one with the green door."

The cab had just made it out of her driveway and Jane was picking up her suitcase when Jake Reinert came outside. It was only six-thirty in the morning, but there he was, all dressed and walking stiffly outside with shower-wet hair combed straight back on his head. She was too tired for Jake. "Hi, Jake," she said, and hurried toward her door.

The old man danced down his steps and, with a haste she couldn't remember seeing in years, stepped across both his lawn and hers, leaving deep, wet depressions in the saturated grass. "Hold up, Jane," he said. "Got to talk to you."

She set down her suitcase on the porch and got out her keys. "Sure," she said unenthusiastically. "Come on in."

She swung open the door and hurried to the keyboard on the wall to press in her code and turn off the alarm system. When she turned around, Jake was inside and shutting the door. "You had a burglary while you were gone."

"Oh?" she said. "Did they get caught?"

"Not exactly."

She had been expecting this, right up to the word *no*, and she assumed that she was going to have to face a big housecleaning because they would have vented a little of their rage on her belongings while they searched. It didn't matter. She never kept records of her clients. Her clothes were the only expensive things in the house, and it would probably make her feel better to spend the next few days buying new ones. "Why not exactly?"

Jake seemed to be shuffling his thoughts into logical order. "Here's how it happened. They broke your back window, here." He took a couple of steps toward it to show her the plywood nailed over the break. She could see the black fingerprint dust the police had used all over the glass, but he answered the question she hadn't asked. "That set off the alarm at the police station. They heard it ringing inside, so they started to run. But I woke up, and turned on my porch light just as they were coming around between the two houses. You know how bright that is. It's a two-fifty flood. Like daylight. It was so bright it startled them. They all turned to look right at it for a second, then covered their faces and ran to their car."

Jane was so exhausted that she felt giddy. She started to laugh. Jake's floodlight was so powerful that on the few occasions when he had turned it on, she had been furious. "You really did get your money's worth on that light, Jake."

"The hell I did. The damned hardware store sold Margaret the fixture years ago, and when I got a look at it and took it back, they wouldn't accept it. The bulbs cost five dollars even in those days. You could use it to jack-light deer."

"Well, for once I'm glad you had it. They didn't get inside at all?"

"No," he said. "Not with the light and all. And of course they knew an alarm must be connected to something, and how long could it take for the police to get here in a town this size?"

"How long?"

"Too long. Maybe four or five minutes. By then they were probably that many miles away."

"Well, if they didn't get in, then nothing's lost," she said, and lifted her suitcase to take it toward the bedroom.

Jake ignored the hint. "I saw them."

"Yes," she said noncommittally.

"Really saw them," he said. "Saw them so clearly it was like a flash picture. There were four of them, and not kids, either. Grown men. When I turned on the light, one of them started to pull out a gun. He couldn't see me, because the switch is inside by the front door."

"Did you describe them to the police?"

"Sure, but they're not from around here. The Deganawida police aren't going to pick them up and put them in a lineup for me."

"I don't think they could do a lineup for you, Jake. They have to put in extra people to fool you, and you know everybody," she said. "But if they were just passing through, at least they won't break into somebody else's house tomorrow."

"Jane . . ."

"What?"

"You know the chief, Dave Dormont, he's a good friend of mine. I pulled him out of Ellicott Crick one time when we were kids. The Rowland boys had tossed him in and I was ten years older, and . . . Anyway, he's a really good cop. Maybe it's because he got picked on when he was little, so he doesn't put up with the strong hurting the weak. He was an F.B.I. agent for years."

"I heard that," she said.

"That wasn't just gossip. I was saying he might be able to help."

"Oh," she said. "I don't think I need anything special. Look around. Unless they wanted some women's clothes . . ."

"They weren't after your stuff," he said quietly. "And you know it."

"I do?"

"I said your house was burglarized, and you didn't get scared or run around looking to see what they'd taken. I said 'they,' instead of 'he,' and you didn't say, 'How many?' When I said I saw them, you didn't ask what they looked like. You knew what they looked like because you've seen them too."

"Jake," she said carefully. "You know I love you and I value your friendship and I don't forget the things you did for all of us kids when we were little. It didn't matter whose kids were whose, we all piled into the car and fought for the window seats and lined up for Popsicles. But I don't need any help."

"You mean I'm wrong?"

"I mean this is a conversation we're not going to have all the way through."

He stared at the floor for a moment. "All right. I just want you to know that it won't matter if it turns out to be your own fault. I saw those four, and I know men like that don't just come out of the blue after a young woman in Deganawida. You have to go where they are to attract their attention. How it happened doesn't matter to me. I'm on your side." He started for the door, then stopped. "And thanks for not lying to me about it. You know I'd hate that."

"Yes, I do," said Jane.

Jake went out and closed the door, and she hurried to lock it behind him and activate the alarm system. She blew out a sigh of exhaustion, frustration, and despair. She decided she would face her life better after a bath and some sleep. As she walked into the bedroom upstairs, she saw that the light on her answering machine was blinking. Her heart stopped, and she actually heard herself gasp. Did he know her number? Why not? He'd been in here alone for days, and it was on the dial. Maybe something was wrong. She carefully pressed the button, superstitiously afraid that somehow she could press the wrong one and erase it.

"Jane?" It was a woman's voice. "You know who this is." There was a pause. "I wanted to let you know I made it. I'll never forget what you did for me. Never." There was some complicated clicking, and she heard two seconds of dial tone before the machine disconnected. It was Rhonda Eckerly, and the message was at least a week old. Jane released the breath she had been holding. She could hear the happiness in Rhonda's voice, her throat so tight she was almost choking on it. Jane tried to feel the happiness, but she couldn't. She had wanted it to be Felker. Even though it would have been a stupid thing for him to do, she wanted to hear his voice. She wanted him to be as stupid as she was.

Jane lay in the bathtub for nearly an hour, until the water was cold and her fingertips and toes were wrinkled and every molecule of dust from the road had been soaked off. Then she put on sweats and lay down to think. She awoke on top of the covers at four in the afternoon, already thinking about the police.

She sat up and dialed information to get the number they used for normal business. "Deganawida police," said the deep, resonant voice.

"Hello," she said. "This is Jane Whitefield. I just got back from out of town and I understand I had a burglary?"

There was a short pause. "Are you reporting it, or did you already?"

"The police were here already."

There was another short delay, and the voice came back sounding cheerful, so he must have found what he was looking for. "Yes, ma'am."

"I just wanted to know if there was anything I had to do. I was gone when they were here."

"Well, no," he said. "If you find anything missing, you should come fill out a report. Your insurance company will need a copy of that."

"Nothing's missing. They never got inside."

"Okay," he said. "I'll just make a note."

"Good," she said. "Thank you."

"Oh, and one more thing." Where did they all learn to say that? "If you see any suspicious activity, be sure to call and we'll check it out. Sometimes they come back."

"I sure will," she said, and hung up quickly. She sat cross-legged on the bed and considered. The fact that the four men had come here at all was an immense relief. It meant that they had completely lost the trail in Olcott, only a few miles from here. If they hadn't even gotten inside the house, they hadn't learned anything about her that would have helped. Whatever they learned from now on was useless. There was no logical way for them to piece together the trail from Olcott to John Young of 4350 Islington, Apartment B, Medford, Oregon.

She walked down the stairs and took his picture out of her purse. The best course of action would be to take it into the kitchen and burn it. Then it occurred to her that the picture didn't lead anywhere, either. If they had been following him, they didn't need a picture. And if they had seen him come out of this house, they already knew she knew him. She stopped in the dining room and looked at the boarded window. It was special glass put in by the alarm people, and in order to get to it, the men had ripped the special conductive screen over it.

Jane picked up the telephone in the living room and dialed the alarm company's number. She had perfected the nervous-young-woman-who-lives-alone voice, so the man on the other end was eager to send a technician to replace the window in the morning.

Then she called Cliff.

"Janie, Janie," he said. "You do the weirdest things to my cars."

"Is it broken?"

"No."

"I didn't paint it, did I?"

"No."

"I didn't keep it too long."

"No, you just parked it out in the boonies."

"Cliff, I'll make you a deal."

"You'll wash and wax it, and I won't charge the wear-and-tear fee and the pickup fee and the reshelving fee? Gee, I don't know . . ."

"No," she said. "You'll forget your fees, and I'll forget my refund."

There was a shocked silence. "Jane, you okay?"

"Why?"

"You don't seem . . . normal."

"You know a lot of normal people, Cliff? You have a lot of them come by to rent a car?"

"Well, no, but—"

"I'm just tired. I'll try to screw you out of some money next time. Thanks for handling things."

"Sure, Janie."

The next morning when she went out to get her mail, the man from the alarm company pulled into the driveway. It took him twenty minutes to fix the window, and then Jane said, "Can you wire the vent in the peak under the roof for me too?" She said it with a sad look in her eyes, so he didn't argue. "We'll just put it on your next bill," he said, and hurried to get his ladder off the roof of his truck.

For the next three days, she went out only at night and in the early morning to run on the long grassy strip along the river. She was too agitated and impatient to read, so she cleaned her house, then invented chores that would make it cleaner, and kept moving all of her furniture into new relationships. When she had finally settled on an arrangement that placed all of the furniture along the walls so that her living room was a vast open space, she did stretching exercises and Tai Chi in the middle of it. In the evening of the fourth day, she acknowledged that it was time to go out and face Jake.

He had been spending all of his time watching. He had painted the whole side of his house that faced hers, planted geraniums, mowed his lawn, and dug out every nascent dandelion. Finally, in desperation, he had altered the habits of his long lifetime and taken to reading his newspapers and magazines in his yard.

Jane walked across her back yard and into his and sat down on the grass beside his lawn chair. After a minute he said, "Am I imagining it or are people getting dumber?"

"I don't know."

"Hardly a day goes by when I don't read about somebody doing himself some real harm when if he'd just called up and asked me, I could have told him what to do."

"Who is it this time?"

"Take your pick. Today it's Washington, but there's never a shortage of the mentally needy. I ought to hang out a shingle."

"You've done everything else."

"What?"

"You've painted that wall on my side maybe three times."

"It's the weather side. Takes special care."

"Jake, I've decided we'd better talk some more before you fall off a ladder peering in my window and hurt yourself."

"Very thoughtful," he said.

She chose her words carefully. "Those four men weren't looking for me. They were looking for a friend of mine. He was the guy you saw knocking on my door. I helped him to go away."

"I'm not supposed to ask questions, I take it?"

"I'm telling you the things you have a right to know," she said. "He's safe because they can't find him. We're safe because they'll know he's not coming back here." She stood up and smiled. "The end."

He nodded, his lips pursed in thought. "Why did you change your mind about telling me?"

"A lot of reasons. One is that I don't want you to decide one day to have a talk with your friend Chief Dormont; you can't be expected to keep a secret unless you know it's a secret. Another is that if he or someone like him comes to my door some night, I don't want you to think I'm in danger and haul out the old twelve-gauge and blow his head off."

"You've done this before, haven't you?"

She didn't answer.

"You said 'someone like him.' That's it, isn't it?" he said. "The secret isn't him, it's you."

"Telling would hurt me," she agreed. "It would hurt me a lot." She stared into his eyes for a moment, until she had seen whatever she was looking for, and then she released him. "I've got some shopping to do. You need anything?"

"No," he said. "No thanks." He watched her go. The long brown legs and the strong, erect back made her seem taller than she was, but not tall enough for this.

Jake set the newspaper on his lap and stared off at the big trees along Franklin Street. The little girl next door hadn't grown up to do something as normal as having a little outlaw sex. She was—well, hell—she was Jigon-sasee. How could she think he wouldn't know? Did she expect him to live for sixty years in a town called Deganawida and never bother to find out why they had chosen a name nobody could even spell? They used to teach it to kids in the grammar schools, although God knew what the hell they were teaching them now.

Maybe she was crazy. White people went crazy and thought they were Jesus Christ or Napoleon, but those two would strike an Indian woman as having no more to do with her than a couple of Australian marsupials. Besides, whatever sex was really about, one of the things it did was determine the way people thought about themselves. He had never heard of an adult woman who identified with a man.

Jigonsasee would make sense to her, he thought. Sometime in the distant past, a woman lives in a bark lodge all by herself on the trail that runs east and west below Lake Ontario a few miles from here. She feeds the warriors who pass by on their way to murder each other. One day, off the lake comes a canoe with a lone Huron in it who has paddled all the way across from the Canadian side. He's a fugitive, a man in exile from his tribe up there. He's been skirting the land, looking for the smoke of somebody's fire so he can bring them his message. The message doesn't seem like much, since all it really amounts to is that peace is better than war. His name is Deganawida.

The first fire he sees belongs to the woman. She takes in the wandering stranger and feeds him, and she is the one to whom he tells his message. And he calls her Jigonsasee, which means "New Face." So the solitary woman and the tribeless man meet up with a warrior driven crazy by the murders of his two daughters. His name is Hiawatha, and he has become a wanderer too and a cannibal, and together they convince all five tribes to stop slaughtering each other. The crazy cannibal combs the snakes out of the hair of the worst of the warlords. The visionary outcast foreigner tells the tribes in detail how to bind themselves together into one alliance and how to run it. And the Iroquois confederacy never changes at all after that. What Deganawida said to do is followed precisely by each generation.

Maybe three or four hundred years pass, and the two smartest men of another generation, another race—Benjamin Franklin and Thomas Jefferson—get stuck with the assignment of putting together a structure for a new society. Only all they have in the world to imitate is a lot of theoretical treatises written by dead Frenchmen and one working model of a confederacy of states called the Iroquois. By then the solitary woman and the visionary exile and the cannibal madman who invented the league are so long gone that nobody even knows the century when they did it. But the Iroquois, who are very much alive, have passed down exactly what these three said and what they did.

The one who would matter to Jane was Jigonsasee, a woman part Betsy Ross and part Joan of Arc, but mostly Mary Magdalene, still called the Mother of Nations and the Great Peace Woman, because she was the one who decided it was better to save two fugitives than to keep endlessly feeding the warriors who came along the trail on the way to butcher people just like themselves.

Jake sat in the lawn chair with the sunset bathing his face and warming his joints and the distant, tall trees waving slowly in the May breeze, all bright green with their new leaves. Jane's secret was not the saddest thing he had ever heard. He was an old man now, and he had been to war and watched the wife he had loved and prized close her eyes and die. But it was sad enough. He admired heroes as much as anybody did, but he had no desire to see anybody he cared about taking risks just to be more like some dead person.

A girl like Jane, who was as quick and full of life as the squirrels in those trees, with so much promise—it seemed like such a waste. Saying it that way made him admit that what could promise be except an expectation that she was made to do something special, even risky? If you wasted something that was good enough, it wasn't called waste, it was sacrifice.

And Jane Whitefield didn't seem crazy, not even a little bit. Probably, she didn't even know that she was trying to live the life of a thousand-year-old Indian woman, any more than his own daughter thought that when she was teaching high school she was Socrates. It was just that when she wanted to do a good job, this was the first way that occurred to her, an impulse she thought was instinctive because it had been emulated over so many generations that it didn't even take conscious thought.

It was dark when Jane left her groceries on the back seat of her car and walked out of the parking lot and across the street to the newsstand. It was a little open shanty made of boards with peeling white paint and a green metal awning that Raymond Illia covered up each night at sundown. Raymond was busy rearranging the bricks he put on top of the stacks of newspapers to keep the wind from blowing them away. He glanced up and grinned. "Hey, Jane. Want to play cowboys and Indians?"

"No, Raymond," she said. "The Indian always has to talk funny."

"You can tie me up."

"You've been reading your own magazines again, haven't you? The ones you keep face-down."

"Caught me!" he said, way too loud. Raymond was Jane's age, but for some reason his mind had stopped growing at about the time they were in eighth grade. Everybody knew it, and now it was long past the time when people had mentioned it in whispers and clicked their tongues, which was what they did when there was a tragedy. Deganawida was too small to ignore people. Instead, some subtle shift had occurred to accommodate Raymond, and life had gone on. Raymond got some sort of disability payment from the state, but he could read and make change, and it seemed to suit him to stand around outdoors, greet people and chatter and be important.

Jane stepped to the stacks of newspapers and picked up *The Buffalo News, The New York Times*, the *Chicago Tribune*, and the *Los Angeles Times*. She gave Raymond the coins, and he happily slipped them into the coin changer that hung from his belt. "Take care, Raymond," she said.

She walked back into the supermarket parking lot, got into her car, and tossed the papers on the seat beside her. As she started the engine, she glanced around to see if the aisle was clear, and her eye passed across the top newspaper on the pile, the *Los Angeles Times:* MYSTERY MAN SLAIN IN SANTA BARBARA. She picked up the newspaper.

SANTA BARBARA—A man found murdered in his apartment on a quiet street in this quiet seaside community has been identified as Harry Kemple . . .

Jane closed her eyes and sat clenching the wheel with one hand and holding the newspaper in the other. She opened her eyes after a few seconds and forced herself to find the name again.

. . . Harry Kemple, a gambler who was wanted by the Chicago police for questioning in the death of a Mafia chieftain in a card game five years ago. Police sources say Kemple had been living under the assumed name Harry Shaw, but when police took the deceased's fingerprints, a routine procedure in cases of violent death, they were surprised to discover his true identity. A spokesman for the Justice Department denied that Kemple had been in any witness relocation program ...

Heat seemed to travel in a wave up Jane's spine to her neck and temples. Her breaths sounded strange to her, coming in little gasps, and then she realized she was crying. Harry was dead. Somebody had made a mistake. Harry had stayed under for too long to get caught any other way.

Jane tried to collect her thoughts. She had to call Lew Feng. She turned the engine off and realized her hands were shaking. She took the keys and hurried to the line of pay telephones on the wall of the supermarket.

She put a quarter into the slot and dialed the number of Westminster Stationers in Vancouver. The operator said, "Please deposit two dollars and fifty cents." Jane fished quarters out of her purse and pushed them into the slot. Finally, there was a ring. There were two clicks, and then the machine. "Due to the recent death of the proprietor, Westminster Stationers will be closed until further notice." It was the voice of Charlie Feng, Lew's son. The machine disconnected, and Jane began to feel dizzy. They had killed Lew Feng.

She looked into her purse. There wasn't enough change left. She couldn't charge this to her home number. She half walked and half ran to Raymond's stand. "Raymond," she said. "Can you give me change for a ten?"

"Sure," he answered, and started to count out bills.

"No," Jane said. "Real change. Quarters."

He started pumping quarters out of the coin changer and whispering to himself, but he only got as far as five dollars before the coins stopped coming. "I guess I don't have it," he said. "Maybe the supermarket—"

"Give me what you have," she interrupted, handed him the ten-dollar bill, and then ran back to the telephone.

This time she dialed the other number. It was the one in Feng's back room, the one he gave clients in the name trade. This one rang four times before the machine kicked in. This was Charlie Feng's voice too. "Due to a recent death in the family, we will be closing our mail-order business. Please do not send us your change-of-address forms because we are discontinuing our mailing list." It was a warning. Somebody had the list of new names. Charlie's voice changed pitch and said something long in Chinese and then the recording ended.

Jane had not memorized the telephone number in Medford, Oregon, because having it in her mind would be an irritant, a constant, inescapable reminder that all she had to do was pick up a telephone. She looked in front of the phone book for the area code, then dialed information.

"What city, please?" said a young man's voice.

"Medford."

"Go ahead."

"Do you have a listing for John D. Young? It's a new number."

She heard keys clicking. "I'm sorry. We don't have a John D. Young."

Jane closed her eyes and tried to keep calm. "I know the phone was ordered, and there was a number. He just got there a couple of days ago. Four at the outside."

"I'm sorry," he said. "Maybe he hasn't activated his account yet."

"Is there a way to find out?"

"Not really. The business office puts the information in after the phone is in service."

"Look," she said. "This is really important. He lives at 4350 Islington, Apartment B. Can you ring Apartment A or Apartment C and let me talk to them? They can find out what's wrong."

"I'm sorry. I can't do that."

"I know you have these things on your computer. Can't you just call up an address?"

"I'm not allowed to do that unless the police or fire department asks me to. Is there any other number I can get for you?"

Jane thought for a second. "Yes. Western Union."

The operator went away, and the universal recording of a woman's voice said, "The . . . number . . . is 555-6297. Once again . . . 555-6297."

Jane dialed and a man answered, "Western Union."

Jane said, "Never mind." She controlled her frustration. "Thanks anyway." She hung up. Telegrams always had the name and address of the sender printed across the top automatically. If it didn't get handed right to him, it would tell somebody the only place he had left to run to.

She leaned on the wall and thought. It had to be something that was open nights. She dialed the information number again. This time it was a woman's voice. "What city, please?"

"Medford."

"Go ahead."

"I need the number of a message service. One that delivers messages in person."

"Any particular one?"

"No. If you know Medford, please pick one that's close to Islington Street."

The operator went off, and the female computer came on and gave Jane another number. She dialed.

A woman answered. "Valentine Party Girls."

"Excuse me?" said Jane.

"Valentine Girls."

Jane's head was pounding. "Can I order a message delivered and pay over the phone with a credit card?"

"Sure. Tell me what day you'd like it delivered."

"Today. As soon as I hang up."

"Tonight? That could be tough. We have to arrange for the right person, and . . ."

"No you don't," said Jane. "I don't care who it is, just so it's right away. It's not a fun thing. It's urgent."

"All right. Give me your credit card number."

Jane pulled out her Visa and read off the number.

"What's the address for the message?"

"It's for John Young, 4350 Islington, Apartment B as in boy."

"That in Medford?"

"Yes."

"Message?"

Jane hesitated. She hadn't had time to think it through. "Say, 'Harry died. Come home. Mom.' Make that, 'Love, Mom.' " She listened while the woman repeated it in a monotone.

"That's right."

"Okay, now we come to the tricky part."

"What's that?"

"If you want this delivered tonight, the only person I have is a male stripper. He's getting ready for a bachelorette party in an hour. I'm afraid he gets a hundred dollars. It's not his fault that—"

"That's okay," said Jane. "It's important."

"Just so you understand."

"And, please, write it down. Make sure the stripper knows that if Mr. Young is not home he should slip it under the door. Not in the mailbox or something— under the door."

"We'll do it."

Jane thought for a second. What else was there? "And if you don't mind, could it be on a plain piece of paper? Not your regular stationery or something?"

"Don't worry," the woman said. "I've already got it that way. Nobody wants this kind of message on a valentine."

"Great," said Jane. She leaned against the supermarket wall again. "Wonderful."

"And I'm sorry about Harry," said the woman.

"Thanks." She hung up and took three deep breaths. What now? Could she wait until she got home to call the airlines? Yes. She had to go home anyway, and it would be quicker because she could pack while she was talking. She hurried to her car, started it, and drove. The ripe cantaloupe in the back seat smelled like garbage, so strong it made her feel queasy. She rolled down her window and drove faster.

She pulled into her driveway too fast and heard a bag fall over and some cans rolling around on the floor. She ran into the house, took the steps three at a time to the second floor, and looked at the answering machine. The message light wasn't blinking, and the counter still said zero.

Quickly, she looked up the airlines section of the Yellow Pages and started at the top, with American Airlines. "When is the first flight out of Buffalo that will get me to Medford, Oregon?" There was a flight to Chicago, then Portland, with a hop down to Medford/Jackson County airport that would take until 7:00 A.M. Pacific time.

As she accepted her reservation, she heard the doorbell ringing downstairs. She nearly screamed in frustration, but clenched her teeth, read off her credit card number, and waited until she had heard the woman distinctly say, "You're confirmed," before she relinquished the telephone.

She ran down the stairs and flung the door open. It was Jake. "Sorry, Jake, but I've got to leave in a minute."

"That's why I'm here," he said. He stepped in, and

she had to fight an impulse to give him a hard push in the chest and slam the door.

Instead, she pivoted and hurried up the stairs. "I've got to pack." She was already thinking about what to take. There was no good way to bring a firearm aboard an airplane. It would have to be the matching manicure kit and jewelry box and makeup kit. There was a thick, heavy gold chain in the jewelry box that clasped to two screw-on handles of the hairbrushes, and those screwed into two lead-filled lipstick tubes. When the parts were assembled that way she had two long, weighted handles connected by a chain, and that made a very ugly set of nunchaku. There was also a big nail file with an ivory handle and a blade that was stainless steel and sharpened like a razor.

She was vaguely aware that Jake was following her upstairs. "I saw you roar in, so I figured you planned to leave right away. He's not safe after all, is he?"

"Right," she snapped, and wondered instantly why she had let that out. The frustration was driving her to madness.

"Have you warned him?"

"I tried, but I don't know if he got the message or—" Saying it out loud was not what she wanted to do, so she didn't. "I've got to go there."

"I'll go with you," he said. "I'll be ready before you are."

"No."

"I saw those men. Did you?"

"Yes." Then she admitted, "Not close."

"I did. I'd know them anywhere. And if they followed you to where he is, they must have seen you. They didn't see me."

"Look," she said. "This is crazy. Why am I arguing with you? It's none of your business. I'm going, you're not."

He said, "I know you're wishing I'd fall in a hole.

But I can see them coming and you can't. I can even report them to the police and you can't, or you would
have already. They don't know me, but they know you,
and no matter how good you are or how smart or how
young, you can't be in two places at the same time and
watch your own back. If you're going because you
think you have to save that fellow's life, then you ought
to think in practical terms and take the help that's available. You think about that, and I'll be waiting for you."

He walked off down the stairs and Jane kept packing.
It was awful. Why she had ever admitted it, told this
old man her secret, she couldn't imagine now. But as
she worked, she knew she was denying things she had
no right to dismiss. There was no getting around the
fact that Jake was the only one who could recognize
the four men.

She closed the suitcase and ran downstairs. She
started to activate the alarm system, then changed her
mind and turned it off. If John came here, he would try
to break in again.

She hurried to the car, and there was Jake sitting in
the passenger seat with a sportcoat on and his suitcase
lying on the back seat. She got in beside him. "Please
listen," she said. "This isn't the Rowland boys throwing
Dave Dormont into Ellicott Creek. John and I both
knew a nice, gentle man named Harry. He and John
helped each other at different times. I took them both to
another nice man named Lewis Feng, who helped them
to hide. Today Lew Feng is dead. Harry is dead. John
may be dead. If those men think you're a problem,
you'll be dead."

"I'm old," he said, "but I'm not feebleminded. I
know what I'm doing. I'm just waiting to see if you
do."

She started the engine and backed out of the driveway. "Just don't talk," she said quietly. "I've got to
think."

J ane Whitefield sat in the airplane seat and stared out the double pane of glass into the darkness. She had killed Harry. She just had not made the right connections. When she forced herself to look at John Felker objectively, he was a nobody, just an ex-policeman, no different from thousands of others, content doing some dull job because he'd had enough excitement to last the rest of his life.

He had assumed that somebody had chosen him because he had once been a cop. Every cop has a lot of enemies who are criminals, and they don't retire just because he does. And being an ex-cop who went to night school instead of getting a Harvard M.B.A. made him the sort of outsider who could easily be made to take a fall in a big accounting firm. Either explanation had sounded plausible, and she had accepted his assumption without really examining it.

What made John special enough to be worth some gigantic paranoid's nightmare of a conspiracy? She had been stupid. John could be excused for assuming that his enemies were his own, because no human being could be expected to imagine that when his life was destroyed, that wasn't the main event. Jane couldn't be excused. She stated it to herself: Jane is presented with an ordinary guy who tells her that one day, without warning, enormous resources have been brought into play by extremely cunning enemies he can't even identify, all designed to destroy his ordinary life, and the one who warns him is one of the most wanted fugitives in the world. Who are these people really after? Just the mention of Harry's name should have been enough to make it obvious to her.

She had even said it that night. Why would they spread the word all over the prison system so just about everybody in the whole country who wasn't eligible for jury duty would know? That was no way to kill an ex-cop. It was a way to be sure he heard he was in a kind of danger he couldn't hope to fight off. They had wanted to get him running.

Then the four men had followed John's bus all the way from St. Louis to Buffalo. If they had wanted to kill him, surely they could have found some way before he got to Deganawida. They hadn't wanted to kill him. They just wanted to see where he went.

Later that night, when they had come upon the abandoned car on Ridge Road, they had pulled their guns. What were they trying to do—kill him? No. If they had wanted to do that, they could have stood around the car and fired through the doors. They were trying to capture him. When she had seen that they weren't going to shoot, for an instant she had thought they might even be cops.

John had made one mistake, but it hadn't been the one he thought. It was that one night, years ago, he had decided that the three men arrested with Harry had not been after him because of Cappadocia. That had to be the mistake, because nobody but those three men would have known that he had ever met Harry. Why had he assumed that a man who was running from one problem had gotten attacked for something unrelated? Because that was what Harry had told him. If only he had known Harry better, things would be different now.

Poor little Harry. After five quiet years in Santa Barbara, he would have heard a knock on the door and answered it without having that preliminary twinge of fear. He would never have forgotten the sickening sight of the men in his card game, all of them shot four or five times in the head and chest, but by now he would have convinced himself that he was safe, not because of the elaborate precautions but because he was Harry, and Harry had raised optimism to the level of the mystical.

Most of the people who were called gamblers weren't that at all, because they never bet on anything. Harry had been a player. Even his only attempt to move up in the world and be the one who owned the table and took the rake had been manic optimism: He had actually expected he would be the first man in history to run a high-stakes poker game in a place like Chicago without meeting somebody like Jerry Cappadocia.

People who read in the newspapers that Harry was a gambler probably would assume that he had become one because he was good at it. Gambling wasn't the name of a profession; it was the name of a delusion. When he had come to her in the night, he had been in possession of ten thousand dollars, all in hundreds, and one suit with shiny spots on the pants where he sat down. Now he was dead. Whether it was Cappadocia's friends who got him because they thought he had set up the murders or it was the murderers making sure he never talked didn't matter to anybody except Jane.

If it was Cappadocia's friends, they would have tried to make him talk before they killed him. If he had told them what they needed to know, then maybe they'd let John . . . She stopped herself, sick and ashamed. She also knew better. Whoever had forced John to run to her, and followed them both to Lew Feng, then killed him to get Harry's address, had constructed a big, wide trap to do it. They would close it now. John Felker dead would be slightly less troubling to them than John Felker alive, and killing him would be so easy.

It wasn't until the plane had landed in Chicago and

she had changed airplanes for the flight to Portland that she found herself sitting next to Jake. He sat in silence, not even looking at her, until she said, "You can talk, you know. I didn't say you had to turn into a stone."

"Didn't want to be a bother," said Jake.

"The flying part is safe, Jake. You don't have to be afraid yet."

"That doesn't mean I have to sit here like a moron and be impressed by it. It's always been my belief that the greatest human achievement is swimming. A few clever monkeylike fellows have figured out how to make a machine that will lift people into the air at some speed, but this isn't flying. It's riding. Swimming isn't a cheat like that. It's a fundamental extension of human powers."

She looked at him with suspicion. "Do you think a lot about dying?"

"That's a hell of a thing to ask a man my age," he said. "I don't actively think about it. Besides, I seem to have exhausted my sources of information—for the moment, anyway."

"Go on. You've been thinking about it since we left home."

"I wasn't thinking about falling out of the sky," he said. "I was thinking about the dead, the people who were around when I was doing most of my living— Margaret, your parents, my sister Ellen ... there's a long list."

"Does that make you afraid?"

"When I was young it did. I remember when I was thirty or thirty-five I used to still hate to go to sleep at night because I didn't want to miss anything—like a child. That was how I thought about death, too; I dreaded having my curiosity frustrated. But I guess you can only flinch so many times before the punch gets familiar. You've already felt it hit so many times in your imagination that it loses interest."

"Do you think other people get that way—soldiers, people who have to think about it a lot, cops?"

"I don't know," he said. "Do you?"

"People always find some way to do what they have to do, don't they? Pretend the plane that crashes isn't going to be theirs."

"Yes," he said. He looked at her closely, his sharp old eyes studying her.

She opened her purse and took out the article she had torn from the Los Angeles newspaper. She had read it three times on the way to Chicago, but she read it again, keeping her eyes down where Jake couldn't see them.

After they landed in Portland, she walked to the airport shop and bought a Vancouver newspaper. She had no trouble finding an article about the murder of Lewis Feng. There was a photograph of the policemen standing in front of the stationery shop while two of the coroner's men wheeled a body bag to the curb. When she got to the part of the article that described what had happened to Feng, she put it down. He had been tortured. Of course, they would have had to do that. He would never have given them his client list unless they had first brought him to the point where the future didn't matter as much as getting through the present. He would have to be willing to trade anything to make the pain stop. He had suffered for her mistake. She had done that to him.

The flight down to Medford was short, but she was aware of each second as she breathed in and out in an agonizing mechanical count. As they drew nearer, she concentrated on preparing herself for the most likely possibility. John had driven the five hundred miles down from Vancouver, gone to the apartment, opened the door, and found the four men waiting for him.

The article had said Harry was taken without a struggle in his apartment, his throat cut silently. He could have let somebody in and turned his back for a moment. But John wasn't Harry Kemple. John was big and strong and alert. For him it would have to be something different, and more horrible—maybe three of them to hold him down and his eyes would bulge when he saw the knife come out and he'd push off with his feet to keep his neck away from the blade. She caught herself actually shaking her head to get the image out of her mind.

She glanced at Jake. She knew he had seen it, but he pretended he hadn't. He stared straight ahead, stiff and erect. There was a kind of integrity to him, a separateness from the airplane, a refusal to slump in the seat and give up his will to the machine.

This time when the plane touched and bounced and then rattled along the runway to taxi to the terminal, Jane was one of the people who were incapable of waiting. She was unbuckled and ready. They had not checked their bags on the final leg of the trip because she had known that she would go mad waiting for them to come rumbling down into the baggage area. They walked into the terminal, put their suitcases into storage lockers, and stepped outside.

When the cab pulled up on the 4300 block of Islington, Jane picked the place out at once. It was the sort of building the Fengs would have chosen. It was a sprawling new apartment complex of the sort where people didn't pay much attention to their neighbors because there were so many of them, and each wing would have a few moving out at the end of each month and new people coming in to replace them. But it was also the sort of place where you could murder a tenant without anyone noticing unless you did it with a bomb.

She walked along the sidewalk in front of the complex and saw that it was divided into sections that had their own numbers: 4380, 4370, 4360. When she reached 4350, she looked for the parking space in the carport at the side of the building. She found B, but the Honda wasn't in it.

"Not home," said Jake, and she remembered his presence.

"Time for you to go for your evening walk," she said.

"Right." Jake started off on his stroll. He walked along the long row of parking spaces looked for all of the signs that Jane had told him about: a car with a man sitting in it, maybe pretending to wait for somebody while he read a newspaper. He scanned the windows for faces and then searched the surrounding block for a gray Honda Accord; a man who thought he might have unwelcome visitors might not park his car in a space with his apartment number on it.

Inside the hallway, Jane read the letters on the doors. They started with F. She worked backward until she found B. She heard someone across the hall in Apartment A walk close to the door, probably to look at her through the glass peephole. She tensed her legs and prepared to move quickly. After a moment there was a creak and she could hear the person moving off.

She turned to Apartment B and rang the bell. She could hear it jangling beyond the door. She knocked, then rang again, but there was no sound that she hadn't made. She turned and knocked on the door of Apartment A.

A woman about her age, wearing a sweatshirt that had a stain on it Jane identified as baby formula, opened the door and stared at her with a resigned look. "What can I do for you?"

"I'm sorry to bother you," said Jane, and she could tell the woman was thinking, Not as sorry as I am, "but I've been trying to reach my friend, who just moved into Apartment B. His phone isn't working, and—"

"Oh," said the woman. She brushed a long strand of corkscrew-curled hair out of her left eye, and it bounced back perversely. "They haven't moved in yet."

Jane felt the tension beginning to grip her. "Are you sure?"

"Believe me, in this place I'd know it. People carrying furniture around sounds like an earthquake."

"Is there a manager?"

"Yeah. In the next building. Apartment A." Jane heard the first faint sounds of a baby waking up, amplified by an electric monitor. "Oh," said the woman vaguely, and the harried look returned to her face.

"Thanks," Jane said, and turned away so the woman could close the door. It didn't prove anything. John Young didn't have any furniture yet.

She went outside the building and walked around the corner to the window of Apartment B. The window looked into the living room. It was just four bare walls enclosing a shiny imitation-parquet floor. The bedroom door was open, and there was nothing in there, either. Even the closet doors were open, something that the people who gave apartments their gang-cleaning between tenants did to air them out.

The next thing Jane saw made her turn away. It was a small piece of white paper on the floor that had been slipped in under the door. She was starting to walk when she saw Jake coming around the building toward her. She pointed to the window, and he looked inside.

"That's my note on the floor," she said. "He never made it."

"Are you sure?"

"I'm going to check with the manager, but it looks that way."

"I'll do that," said Jake.

In a few minutes Jake returned. "No. He would have had to check in to get his power and water turned on. He hasn't been here."

They walked out of the apartment complex, down Islington Street, with no destination. She hadn't thought of this—not that he wouldn't be in his apartment now, but that he had never been here at all. Even if the four men had found Harry's and John's addresses on the same list, how could they have stopped John so quickly? He would have had a good head start. They could have made it to the apartment before he did, but how could they catch him on the road?

Jake cleared his throat, and she knew she had to ask, so she said, "What is it?"

"Well," he said. "Is there any chance that he didn't entirely trust you?"

She was stung. "No chance," she said. Was there? Could he possibly think that she had some ulterior motive for everything she had done? "No."

"I see," said Jake. "So he knew you really well."

"Yes, we had an affair," she said, "since that's the bush you're beating around. But I'm being logical. He ran into trouble, but he knows the reason he got out was because I risked my life for him. He was carrying a lot of money, and some people would get suspicious of anybody who knew it. But I didn't even let him spend any of it. I put up all the expenses. And he came to me; I didn't look for him."

"What do you want to do?"

"How can I know?"

Jake walked along, looking around him instead of at her. "There are only a couple of really strong possibilities. One is, they found him and killed him before he got here." She caught him watching her for a reaction. "In that case, there wouldn't be much to do, would there? They'd be long gone."

"I hope your other possibility beats that one."

"You said he used to be a policeman?"

"Yes," she said. "Eight years."

"Is it possible that he hasn't quite gotten over it? Bear with me now. Suppose he stopped and picked up a paper and read about this fellow getting killed, just like you did. This Harry was some kind of friend, right? Or at least somebody who had done him a favor . . ."

"Jake!" she gasped. She stopped and gave him a quick hug. "You did it. That's right. It's true. I talked to him for hours, endlessly. I was trying to tell him that he couldn't afford to act like a cop anymore, figuring things out and then going off to do something about it. Even while I was saying it, I could see there was something in the back of his eyes, some door back there that closed. He was protecting something. And now I know. He didn't have any other way to see things."

"So he just might have gone on south to Santa Barbara."

"Might have? I'm telling you, I'm sure that's exactly what he would do. He's thinking like a cop. He never stopped thinking that way, because he didn't know how. He read, or heard on the radio, that Harry was murdered in Santa Barbara. He owed his life to Harry, and the people who killed Harry are also after him. He's down at the scene of the crime trying to figure out who they are."

"Unless something happened on the way here."

"But that's what's been bothering me all along. The four men killed Lewis Feng and deciphered his list. Then what did they do? They went right away to Santa Barbara and killed Harry. That's not a guess. We know they did because Harry's dead. Meanwhile, John was driving from Vancouver to Medford. How could they find him unless they were actually following him? They couldn't and they weren't following him."

"How do we know that?"

"Because John left right after I did. First they had to break in at Lew Feng's, kill him, and find his list. Harry was obviously the priority because they got him. Even if they found both names and addresses right away and split up, two to get Harry and two to get John, he would have at the very least an hour's head start—fifty miles.

He would be in one of thousands of little cars driving the five hundred miles down the coast, so they couldn't have gotten him on the road."

"Some other way? It must be a nine- or ten-hour drive. A motel?"

"It's the same problem. They would have to stop at every hotel or motel for five hundred miles and look for a car they'd never seen before. They never could have found him. They could have murdered Harry in Santa Barbara and still have flown here in time to surprise John, but they didn't. John hasn't been here, but neither has anyone else."

"How do you know that?"

"The lady across the hall has a baby, so she's here during working hours and would have heard them. She heard me walking up the hall—one woman, not four two-hundred-pound men. Everybody else in the complex is here at night. When those men tried to sneak into my house, they had to break a window to do it, didn't they?"

"Yeah," he said. "I guess they did."

"Well, they didn't break any windows here or jimmy a door or anything else."

"No, they didn't." He waited and watched her.

She avoided his eyes and craned her neck to look up and down the street. "Did you happen to see a pay phone on your rambles? This doesn't look like a street where cabs cruise for passengers."

20

As the plane turned to come in over the Santa Barbara airport, Jane looked down and tried to imagine Harry living here. She had been here once before, when she had left a client in Los Angeles and wanted to spend a few days out of sight. It was a beautiful, quiet place, but there was something about it that had never seemed quite right to her—like a graveyard with flowers that grew in too lush and luxuriant not to be a sign of a haunting.

It was a place where lots of people had died for no reason at all. Father Junipero Serra stopped here in the 1780s and founded a mission for the Chumash Indians. The Chumash had lived along the coast and done a little fishing in the kelp beds and a lot of gathering in the tidal pools, and hunted in the hills that ran along the coast a couple of miles inland. It had been an easy, unchanging life, and they hadn't prepared themselves for the arrival of the Europeans by generations of fighting as the Iroquois had. They were easily enslaved, and forced to build stone buildings and aqueducts and work in the fields for the priests. She had seen virtually all that was left of the Chumash years ago: a cave in the hills painted with mystical figures and a few intricate baskets behind glass in the little museum up the road from the mission. The coast of California was a sad place for Indians: Chumash, Gabrieleno, Cupeño, Tataviam, Luiseño, Costanoan, Miwok, Ipa, Salinan,

Esselen—all either exterminated by 1900 or down to 1 percent of the 300,000 people the priests had counted when they took their first inventory of souls.

Jane had brought Harry to Lew Feng, walked out of the shop, and taken the next flight out of Vancouver. She had insisted that she never be told where Lew Feng sent him. She had not wanted to have that piece of information in her mind, waiting to come out as soon as somebody inflicted enough pain. But Santa Barbara should have been a shrewd place for Lew Feng to put Harry. If she had known, she would have agreed with it. There were lots of people in their fifties and sixties wandering around town doing nothing. They played golf, walked on the beaches, and sauntered around State Street looking in store windows. It was the sort of town where all you needed was the money to pay the rent and a dull, plausible story that would explain why you had chosen to pay it there. To the sort of people who were looking for Harry, Santa Barbara would have been invisible, just another cluster of exits on the freeway up the coast.

Jake noticed the change in Jane as they walked to the car-rental desk at the airport. Until now she had been held in a rigid immobility by the simple fact that airplanes traveled faster than girls did, but now she was eager, ready to move. She was very good at standing there, the young woman waiting for old grandpops to rent the car, but her eyes were always in motion, never settling on anything for more than a second or two.

As soon as he had the keys, she picked up her bag and set off. She took the keys out of his hand without speaking and got in on the driver's side. She maneuvered the car along Sandspit Road to the freeway and took it through the town to the Salinas Street exit, then swung up the first street. "Why is it called Ocean View?" Jake asked. All he could see was tall apartment buildings and long, skinny palm trees.

"It's California real estate language," she said. "If it's called a view or vista of something, it means it's not near it."

"But *view* means you can see it. I can't see it."

"You could if you were eighty feet tall. They're not responsible for your shortcomings. Ninety-two. That must be it up there. The big white building on the left."

"What do we do?"

"I go in, you stay inconspicuous and watch."

"What am I watching for? Your friend?"

"John isn't likely to come in daylight. If you do see him, whatever you do, don't let him get away. Talk to him. Ask directions or something. And remember, he's got a lot to be scared of. Until he sees me, he's as dangerous as the others."

She closed the door, slipped her shoulder into her purse strap, and walked across the street to the apartment buildings. Jake couldn't see anybody to watch, so he watched the buildings. He had considered coming to a place like this to wait out his last few years. It was pretty, a lot of palm trees and stucco buildings you couldn't see the ocean from, but it was just the front door of a nursing home, really, and those weren't much different anywhere. At least in Deganawida there was a chance that somebody might visit.

Jane came back smiling and sat in the driver's seat. "We're in luck. I rented the apartment next door to Harry's. We move in before dark."

"It just happened to be vacant?"

"There was a murder. People always move out in droves. But next door is better than I had hoped."

Jake wondered how a person came to know things like that, but she seemed to know a lot of them. She started the car and drove back down the street, turned right, then left, and went down a long, straight residential street with houses that looked like cottages.

"Where are we going?"

Jane seemed to be pulled back reluctantly from whatever she had been thinking. "There are homicide detectives in there right now. They never work nights except the first one, when the body's on the ground and they still have some hope of catching somebody. The fact that they're still in there after a couple of days is great news."

"It is?"

"It means they still have it sealed, and John probably hasn't come in yet."

"Are you sure that's what he'll do?"

"No," she said. "I'm guessing. But he'll feel the way I do, which is that we killed Harry. He and I did. He might not find anything by looking at the apartment, but he has nothing else to look at. And if he's thinking like a cop, then seeing what the other cops looked at might tell him a lot."

"So where are we going now?"

"You're going to drop me off downtown. Then you're going to pick up a few essentials."

"Such as?"

"Food that we can eat without a lot of cooking. There's a refrigerator in there, so get whatever you want. Two shotguns, short-barrel—something like a Winchester Defender or a Remington 840. One box of double-ought buckshot—make that the little boxes that hold five each. Get six. Two blankets, a pillow if you need one. An electric baby monitor. There are lots of kinds, but Fisher-Price makes a good one. No, two of those, and batteries for them. And a roll of electrical tape."

"What are you going to be doing?"

"I'm going to the library to see if there was anything in the local papers that the wire services didn't pick up. Then to the police station to see if John is hanging around trying to strike up a conversation. That kind of thing."

She pulled over on Figueroa Street. "Can you remember all that stuff?"

"Sure," he said. "When do you want me to pick you up?"

"I don't. See you later."

The supplies didn't take much thought. It seemed to Jake that the differences between places had virtually disappeared during his lifetime. If you blindfolded somebody, put him on a plane, and set him loose on the main drag of any decent-size town in the country, he would be hard-pressed to say where he was. If there were palm trees or snow, all he'd really know was a list of places where he wasn't. The supermarkets just had different names.

The shotguns took some thought. He kept himself from ruminating on the implications of them by concentrating on composing some small talk that would carry him through if there was some custom out here that required him to answer any questions. He decided he had no choice but to be Jake, the retired codger from Deganawida, since he suspected you couldn't make this kind of transaction without showing somebody some identification. He decided that buying double-ought in May was highly suspicious, since as far as he knew, deer season anywhere on earth had to be in the fall, to give the does and fawns a fighting chance. He finally hit on the idea that he was buying the guns as a gift for a friend who had a ranch up near—he studied the map—New Cuyama. He suspected the peculiarity of buying two at once was actually an advantage, since nobody who needed a shotgun to commit suicide or rob somebody would need two.

When he went into the store, he was almost disappointed that he didn't need to say anything to the clerk except that he was paying cash. He supposed that having a story to tell had made him look self-assured. He bought a cleaning kit while he was at it because they always test-fired the damn things at the factory and left them dirty.

The sun was getting low by the time he finished. He took a turn and drove toward the sunset for a few blocks. He figured he should at least see the Pacific if he was this close to it. The street came out on a winding road through a kind of suburb, but still the ocean didn't turn up. Finally, he accepted his failure and checked the map. Sure enough, around here the coastline wasn't to the west at all but to the south, which was damned inconvenient for visitors who were accustomed to thinking of the relationship of the sun and the continent and the ocean as pretty well stabilized.

He turned left, found the ocean immediately, and was glad. He stood on a broad lawn under some fifty-foot palm trees and stared past the white sand at the endless blue that extended out past the slow rolling waves, and across the world. It made the air smell different and dropped the temperature ten degrees. What he was looking at seemed as infinite as the sky. The word *infinite* was full of frustration; it was just another word for "so far you can't see it." There was something that made him want to see beyond the horizon.

As he walked back to the car, Jake tried to formulate his complaint. If seeing was detecting light, and light could curve, then under certain circumstances a person ought to be able to follow the surface of the ocean past the horizon, around the whole world. Then he realized that what he would see at the end of it was himself, from behind. If infinity was looking at his own ass, he supposed he could pass it up. He felt satisfied with his decision not to give up on the Pacific, and relieved that he hadn't been unable to find the biggest thing on earth.

When he made it back to the apartment building again, Jane was there to help him unload. When they had everything inside, she closed the door and locked it, and he set about unboxing the two shotguns on the kitchen table. She picked one up and sighted it, then pumped the action and clicked the trigger a couple of times and looked into the chamber. After that she let Jake sit at the table to clean and oil them while she went into the bedroom with the baby monitors.

Jane watched the street through the bedroom window as she put the batteries into the monitors and put tape over the little glowing ON lights. It was dark before she saw the last of the police cars drive off. She went out the door, walked around the side of the building, put one of the baby-monitor transmitters into an empty flowerpot, and set it in the bushes beside the building. Then she walked until she found the bathroom window. She had noticed that the bathroom window in the apartment she had rented had louvered slats that could be cranked open. She examined the bathroom window of Harry's apartment, found that it was the same and that the glass slats didn't fit any better than hers did. She was able to push one of them up out of its holder just enough to fit the second transmitter in and set it on the sink. Then she went back to her own apartment, set the two receivers on the kitchen counter, and turned them on.

When Jake was satisfied that neither shotgun would blow up in his face if he had occasion to pull the trigger, he put them inside the hall closet. He saw that Jane had made the only bed and put the other blanket on the couch. She came out of the kitchen, picked up the shotguns, and pushed four shells into each one. He approved of her not putting a shell in the chamber. She also had enough sense to lay them flat on the floor by the door instead of propping them up. Then she went back into the kitchen to cook two frozen dinners of steaks and mashed potatoes and broccoli, and he approved of this even more, so he left her alone. By now Jane had virtually disappeared; she was living entirely inside her head.

After dinner they washed the two dishes he had bought, and Jake sat on the couch. He had expected Jane to sit down with him, but she brought the two little baby monitors into the living room, got down on the floor, and started doing stretching exercises like dancers did while she listened to the static. As he watched her, he thought about how odd it was to watch children grow up. Miraculously, the little seven-pound animals that looked like hairless monkeys changed into something that looked like this, and what was in their heads at the end of the process seemed to get farther and farther away from what you would expect.

He couldn't keep silent any longer. "I had a funny thing happen today," he said. "I couldn't find the Pacific Ocean."

"Remind me not to let you navigate." He could see her move her lips, returning to her counting.

"I found it eventually, through sheer persistence. But it reminded me of the Herndons. Did any Herndons come up with you?"

"There were two. Betty was my age—valedictorian of my class, I think—and she had an older brother. He had a streak of gray when he was about fifteen, and everybody thought he was handsome and mysterious. Actually, I guess he looked like a skunk."

"Paul, that was. He's an engineer or something way out west. Maybe around here."

"Is that why the Pacific Ocean reminded you of the Herndons?"

"No. The part about being mysterious did. The one I was thinking of would be Paul's grandfather's sister. Amanda was her name. People always said the money came from some Herndon who invented something in the 1800s, but you'd never hear it from them. There used to be rumors about them when I was a kid."

"What kind of rumors?"

"Well, there was never a dumb Herndon. Some people used to say that the good Lord chose to have every Herndon born with a complete knowledge of the principles He uses to make the universe work."

"Come on," said Jane. She stopped doing push-ups and looked at him.

"The secret would have been safe with them. They were, every last one of them, too inert to do anything about it and too secretive to tell anybody who wasn't another Herndon."

Jane sat up, laughing. "You know, that's true."

"Of course it is. And things always seemed to go just fine. They bought railroad stock, and the railroads went up. They were the sort of people who would have their lawn infested by sables."

"I still don't see what this has to do with the ocean."

"I was talking about Amanda. She was a grown woman by the time I remember her. But when she was little, maybe two years old, she was swinging on a swing in the front yard. The sun was right in her eyes, and one of the neighbors heard her say, 'Daddy! Move the sun!' And he smiled at her and stood there and stared up at the sun for a long time, and that was that."

"That was what?"

"Well, you have to think about it. What was he doing?"

"What *was* he doing?"

"People said later that he did it. He moved the sun about an hour forward. They say the city people didn't seem to notice it, since the position of the sun didn't mean much to them. That evening they just looked at their watches one extra time to be sure the hand was on the number that said, 'Go to bed,' and that was that. The story goes that the scientists with their equipment sure did, but they hushed it up because they couldn't explain it. The farm folks talked about it for some time, but there wasn't much they could do about it except add Herndons to the list of things they couldn't control, like rain and frost."

"That's the silliest thing I've ever heard."

"Well, you know how these things get going. Little Amanda also told several reliable and veracious children that there were two moons, not one. But people remained divided on that issue since it could have been her idea of a joke, and she never said it again after she reached the age of discretion."

"You made all that up, didn't you?" she asked. "Admit it."

"Not at all. Myself, I've always thought the story had to do with daylight savings time. Once you reached the point when the president of the United States could tell you what time it was, as though the sun, the moon, and the rotation of the earth were mere distractions, people realized that anything could happen. There was no limit, or any reason to have one."

She smiled. "Do you really think that's what it's about?"

"Maybe," Jake said. "But maybe it's only about love."

"And maybe it's about talk." Now she began to do her sit-ups.

"Well, I'm at the stage of life where I'm examining the things I've picked up along the way and trying to distribute them where they'll do some good. This is how I got them, so I talk."

"You always talked too much," she said. "You can't pull that deathbed-legacy stuff on me."

"I didn't say the story was going to change your life," he said. "But we live by picking up the belongings of the dead as they fall. The first few things you learn tend to be the most important—the mental equivalent of a pocket full of money or a serviceable revolver. After you're a little older—"

She said, "Wait . . ." She picked up one of the monitors and listened, then put it down and held the other near her ear. "Did you hear that?"

21

Jane slipped out the door of the laundry room, stepped along the side of the apartment building quietly, then sat down beside a bush against the corner of the building. The scent of the yellow night-blooming wisteria and jasmine and what else—the jacaranda trees, probably—was overpowering. She had seen the petals falling on the ground like purple snow. It must be the jacaranda because the bright explosions of cerise and orange bougainvillea climbing up the walls didn't smell at all.

She made herself small, hugging her knees and keeping her head down to listen. There was a faint noise of slow, careful footsteps beside the building. It sounded like the walk of a man who was in good shape—he held his body in tension, then eased to the next foot, but he wasn't very good at this. She kept listening, but she didn't hear another set of feet. It could be John.

She let the man reach the window of Harry's apartment and listened to his breathing. He was taking in breaths through his open mouth and blowing them out quietly to keep himself calm. She judged the level, and felt the disappointment. He was only about six feet, a little taller than she was. Not John, then.

Maybe it was a policeman checking the window. Jane waited, holding her crouch. It was too late to slip away now. He was too close. She waited for the flashlight. She could make it over the fence to the next building in a couple of seconds, while he was still saying "Stop or I'll shoot," but she decided not to. There was no such thing as one policeman: It was like one ant. She could survive what he would do if he saw her. She had rented the apartment, so this would just be a loss of anonymity.

Then she heard the man fiddling with something in his pocket, rattling keys or change or something, and then a click. Next there was a scraping noise, and she decided to look. The man was wide at the shoulders, wearing a sportcoat the way a cop would to cover a weapon, but he was prying out the window screen. When he had set it on the ground, he slipped his knife blade in farther, and she heard a metallic scrape and a clank.

He was breaking in. He was one of them. What was he doing here? Harry was already dead. The man slowly slid the window to the side, then reached in, grasped something solid, and pulled himself up. She was glad she had seen that. She would stay away from those arms.

His upper body was inside. Keeping his legs from working and scuffing the wall, he pulled himself in like a snake. She stood and moved along the wall toward him. This would be the time to attack, incapacitate the legs somehow, but she hesitated. She had to find out what he was doing here. If he was back because he had left some evidence, she would need to know what it was.

She waited for a moment beside the window, then she saw him pull down the shade and close the curtain. She stepped to the next window, where the kitchen was, and tried to hear him moving around, but the glass muffled the sounds. He pulled that curtain too. In a moment a light came on, and Jane moved back to the first window, slowly raised her head to the corner, and lifted the shade a quarter inch.

She could see him on his knees in the middle of the

room. He had put a towel along the bottom of the door.
Was that it? No, he had done that to keep light from
shining under it into the hallway, and now he was looking at something on the floor.

She moved the shade aside a little and stood higher to
see it. Blood. There was a huge reddish brown stain in
the middle of the dirty shag carpet. She ducked down
again and felt sick. Harry must have lain there dying for
a long time.

She was staring away from the window at the cinder-
block fence when there was a bright flash of light that
made the porous texture of the wall visible for an instant, then left it in darkness again. She cringed for a
second, heard the click and whirr before she identified
it—not a gun, a camera. She moved to the window
again and listened. There was another flash, then the
same click-whirr. She looked while he was still holding
the camera to his eye. It was a Polaroid that unfolded
with a bellows. He aimed the camera away from her at
the door, down by the latch where the black fingerprint
powder was thick, and it flashed again.

She had been comfortable with the theory that he had
forgotten something when he had killed Harry, but taking pictures didn't make sense. That was what cops did.
If he was a cop, why break in at night? Was he a re-
porter or something? Even they didn't have to break in
to take pictures, and it was hard to imagine a paper
printing pictures that didn't have a body in them. She
ducked and slipped back along the wall of the building,
picked up the transmitter in the flower pot, slowly slid
the louver of the bathroom window up and reached in to
find the one on the sink, then hurried across the patio to
the other side.

She could see Jake through the window, not sitting on
the couch where she had left him, but standing by the
door with one of the shotguns in his hands. She hoped
what she was about to do wouldn't give the old man a

heart attack or, worse, make him whirl and open up on her. She reached up and knocked on the window. He turned, the shotgun ready, but something must have told him that nobody raps on a window if what they really intend is to shoot through it.

He held the muzzle upward and hurried to slide the window open. "You scared me," he whispered.

"Not as much as you scared me," said Jane. "Bring me the car keys."

He reached into his pocket and produced them, then unlatched the screen to slip them through. "I think there's somebody across the hall."

"There is." She handed Jake the two transmitters. "I'll be back when I know who it is."

"Wait for me," he said.

"You can't go out the door. He'll hear."

Jake handed her the shotgun. "Take this," he said, then handed her the other one, and picked up his coat. He put one leg through the window, then the other, turned onto his belly, and lowered himself to the ground. He had done it very well, but he seemed a little stiff as he followed her down the walk. They stopped under the thick bower of wisteria at the front corner of the building and looked out into the street.

They could see the man's car at the curb. Sitting behind the wheel was a second man.

"Can you see his face?"

"You mean you can?"

"Come on," she said. She pulled him around the edge of the fence to the next apartment building and waited.

"I still can't see his face," he whispered.

"The guy in the apartment building will come out and get into the car with his buddy. The second they're around the corner, we sprint for our car. If they go to the police station, we forget it."

"If I have to sprint, we can forget it now. What if they go somewhere else?"

"We'll see." Jane was preoccupied. If the killers were still here, they must be waiting for John, and that meant he was alive. It occurred to her that the pattern was to frame John for everything they could think of. Maybe the man had planted something that had belonged to John in the apartment. But why would he take pictures? And how could he expect to plant something after the police had already spent days going over everything? Nothing she thought of made sense.

Then she saw the man. She touched Jake's shoulder. The man walked casually, his arms swinging and his head up, almost skipping down the three steps from the building to the sidewalk. He stepped across the lawn to the car. Jane whispered, "When he opens the door."

When the man grasped the handle and pulled, the dome light came on. It took three full seconds for him to swing it open, sit down in the passenger seat, and swing it shut again. They were both in their mid-thirties, dark-haired.

"It's them," said Jake.

The car moved ahead slowly a hundred feet before the headlights came on. At the corner it turned right. "Let's go," she said, and they hurried down the steps to their car.

Jake held both shotguns across his lap while Jane wheeled the car around and went after them. At the first block, she glanced down the long street on her left and saw nothing, and then the next, and the next. On the fourth street she saw a set of taillights a block away, so she followed them. "I hope it's the right car."

"I think so," said Jake. "It's green like the other one."

The car pulled straight across Milpas to the freeway entrance ramp, and then the light changed and Jane couldn't follow. She kept moving, turned right onto Milpas to the next intersection, extended a left turn into a U to come back at the light, turned right, and came up the ramp.

The green car was far ahead now, and Jane pushed the rented car up to seventy until she could see the two dark heads in the back window, then dropped back and let a station wagon pass her. She went along behind it for a while and then let a big shiny steel tanker truck slip in front of her, too. "I can't see him anymore," said Jake.

"And he can't see us," she answered. "Just watch the exit ramps to the right."

Most of the familiar parts of town had slipped past them when the car suddenly moved to the right and coasted up the ramp at Sueño Street. Jane kept her direction for as long as she could before she too peeled out of the traffic and coasted up the ramp. What caught her eye now was the big blue sign at the end of the ramp that said SHERIFF. Maybe she had just stumbled on to something that had nothing to do with anybody, the local cops spying on each other. But the green car kept going past the lighted one-story sheriff's complex, and past a taller building with a sign that said COUNTY AD-MINISTRATION and an older, bigger one that said HOSPI-TAL, and then turned around in the street and came back at them. Jane said, "Get ready," speeded up, and flashed past the car as it came down the road back toward Santa Barbara. She took her foot off the gas pedal and kept going slowly, watching the car in her mirror.

It moved along a road parallel to the freeway, then turned to get back onto it. "Do you think they were try-ing to lose us or to see us?" asked Jake.

"I don't know," she said. She turned around quickly and speeded up the road after it. "I think it was just a precaution."

The car kept going back through town and left the freeway at the Cabrillo Boulevard exit. Jane followed it, keeping the distance as great as she could without los-ing it. But instead of staying on the winding road past the bird sanctuary and on to the beaches and the harbor, it turned left toward Montecito.

Jane watched it until it moved up one of the little streets below the freeway. She pulled the car to the side of the road and turned out the lights.

"This doesn't feel right," she said.

"You think they know we're following them?"

"You're sure those are the men who tried to break into my house?"

"Positive."

"The last time I saw them, they did something like this. They went ahead on a dark country road and waited for us." Jake was silent, so she took a deep breath. "Okay. Then we're at crazy time now."

"What's that?"

"I can't just let them go away this time. They killed Harry. If they go now, chances are they'll get John, too, sooner or later. Do you understand?"

"You're saying you're going to follow two killers up a dark road that's probably a dead end," he said. "Sounds perfectly sensible to me."

"No, I'm saying it's time for you to get out."

"You know anybody who does what you tell them to?"

"Lots of them."

"Oh," he said. "Should have brought them."

She drove ahead and pulled over on the gravel shoulder at the end of the street where the car had disappeared. Jake wrapped the two shotguns in his coat and got out of the car.

They hurried away from the roadside, into the darkness, where headlights wouldn't reach them. Jane knew that walking along the road, even twenty feet from it, was probably what the men wanted them to do. There was a low fence beside her, with thick shrubs and vines entangled above it. She pushed some of the plants aside and stepped over, then held them so Jake could climb

over too. When she looked around her, the land she saw
didn't seem to have the silhouette of a house on it.
There was a long, curved plot of open grass. She moved
along the fence in the direction the car had gone.

As they walked she began to feel more sure. They
would be up ahead somewhere, waiting just out of sight
of the road. When she had walked along the fence for
a hundred feet, she saw the green car. It was on the
other side of the field, just below the elevated hill that
carried the freeway, parked behind a big grove of trees,
its lights off, just about where it would be if the men
were waiting for someone to drive up the dark street
outside the fence into an ambush. She crossed the lawn
above it and looked down.

"What is this?" asked Jake.

"I don't know. A park or golf course or something,"
she said. She reached out and tapped the bundle Jake
had wrapped in his coat.

He handed her one of the shotguns and put his coat on.

"Last chance," she said.

"No talking," he whispered.

Suddenly, there was a rattle of a car starting, but it
came from the wrong place. Jane pulled Jake to the
ground and aimed her shotgun toward the sound. There
was a second car. This one was white. It was up along
the hedge at the edge of the field, and now it was
slowly moving along toward them. She pushed the
safety off with her trigger finger and then put her hand
on Jake's sleeve. "Not yet."

The car moved closer and closer to them. She waited
for the lights to come on, the window to come down.
As it drifted past them, she kept her hand on Jake's
arm. She could hear the soft swish of its tires on the
grass. She looked up and saw there was someone in the
passenger seat beside the driver. On the bumper there
was some kind of rental sticker, and then the car was

going on into the darkness. There had to be a gate somewhere in that direction. In a moment she saw it coming back up outside the fence. She ducked down before the lights went on, and then it was gone.

She took her hand off Jake's arm and started to make her way toward the green car, with Jake at her side. They moved onto the grass and approached the car from the side, keeping low along the hedge at the edge of the lawn. Jane touched Jake and put her mouth close to his ear. "Get down and get ready. If somebody shoots, take your time. You're invisible until you pull the trigger."

"I'll save a shell for the radiator," he whispered. "Nobody's going to kill me and ride away from it in comfort." He eased himself to the ground and lay prone with the shotgun aimed at the car. Jane began to crawl on her belly, closer and closer to the dark shape. She had gone twenty feet when she touched something hard and cold. It felt like a piece of metal, set into the ground. A drain? She ran her fingertips across it and felt raised letters. I . . . N . . . M . . . E . . . M . . . O . . . a cemetery. It was a grave marker.

She heard a snick-chuff sound, coming from the other side of the car. Somebody was digging. She could hear the clods of earth landing on the pile, some granules rolling back down, and then snick-chuff again. So that was why the other two had left. They were working in shifts. It was a lot of work to dig a grave, but not much room.

She crawled closer until she was beside the car. The trunk was open, but there was no light inside the lid. She knew she had to look inside, and that when she did, the sight she was going to see was John. They were in a town they didn't know any better than she did, and they had decided to use the old, reliable way of disposing of the body: finding a fresh grave, digging it up, and burying the new one with the legitimate resident.

She forced her breaths to come more deeply. The air

seemed to seep into her lungs and lie there, and then she would have to think to force it out and let in more. She tasted her dry tongue and made her way to the back of the car. She put her hand on the rear bumper and experienced a sensation like the one she had felt when standing on a high diving board as a little girl, those few seconds when it still seemed possible to turn and go back down.

She found herself counting silently: one ... two ... three, and then popped her head up and saw ... nothing. The trunk was empty except for a flashlight. The way it was lying there on the center of the flat, empty surface was almost like an instruction from somewhere to pick it up.

She grasped it and took a few breaths to calm herself. She could hear the shovel noise again, and now she could tell it wasn't one shovel. They were both digging. She began to crawl toward the sound. She couldn't see a silhouette or a shadow, but then she reached the place and she knew. They were already too deep in the hole, over their heads with piles of dirt on both sides. She moved to the nearest pile of dirt, feeling her way for John's body.

She grasped the slide of the shotgun and stood up just as the flash came. She saw all of it at once. The two men were standing over the casket and they had the top half of it open, and the one from the apartment was taking another flash picture. Down in the coffin was Harry Kemple. The darkness closed on all of them instantly, there was the familiar whirr, then the man aimed again and the flash came with a click, and then darkness.

Jane shone the flashlight into the open grave and shouted, "Police officers. Freeze." She hoped Jake could hear her and not just see the light and shoot it.

The two men in the pit below her stood still, straddling the casket. They seemed unsure of what to do, but certain that they weren't going to be able to find adequate footing in the narrow hole to turn around and face her, let alone draw a gun and shoot her. They raised their hands.

"Turn around," she said.

They slowly, carefully tried to free their feet from one side of the casket, turn about to step across it, and face in the other direction, but neither was able to do it with his hands in the air. Each had to lean across the casket and hold the opposite wall to do it. Then they raised their hands again and tried to stare past the beam of the flashlight to see her.

"It's not what it looks like," said one of them. She recognized his thick arms and broad shoulders. He was the one who had climbed in Harry's window, and he looked down so she could see the camera at his feet. "It's just a camera, see?"

The other, a taller, thin man with a permanent look of distaste holding the muscles around his lips rigid, said, "She don't think we killed him, for Chrissake." To Jane he said, "I know this looks strange. Weird, even."

"Save it," she said gruffly. "First I want to see you slowly take your guns out and toss them up over the pile of dirt, one at a time. And give a lot of thought to how you look while you're doing it. If I get startled, you're dead. First you, the tall one."

The tall man hesitated for a second, and she added, "We know you're armed. Just having a gun on you means I can shoot now and never have to answer any questions." Looking at them, she decided that they had certainly been arrested more times than she had, and they were beginning to sense that this wasn't normal. She pumped the shotgun. There was already a shell in the chamber, and she ejected it onto the ground, but the sound had its desired effect. The tall man bent over, took a gun out of an ankle holster, and threw it over the mound of dirt to the grass. The second man took a gun out of the waistband of his pants at the small of his back and did the same.

"Now turn and put your hands on the side of the pit."

This seemed to comfort the two men, who executed the movement with an assurance that could only have come from practice. They had their legs apart and their arms out from their bodies, and leaned across the casket to look down at the poker-faced Harry.

"Now, tell me your names."

The tall one said, "Samuel Michko."

The wide one said, "Ronald Silla."

She said, "All right, Sam and Ron. Tell me what you're doing here."

Sam and Ron strained to look under their outstretched arms at each other. "She's not a cop," said Sam. He turned toward the light. "You're not a cop."

"No," she said. "Bad luck for you. I'm the woman you've been chasing all over the continent."

"Uh," said Ron, as though he had been kicked. Sam was silent.

"Why did you dig up Harry?" she asked.

"To take his picture," said Ron, pointing at the camera again with his foot.

"What do you want his picture for?"

"You don't know how Mr. Cappadocia's mind works," said Sam. "He's from the old school. You tell him there's a duck, you better be able to show him some feathers."

Jane's mind silently exclaimed: Cappadocia? They work for Jerry Cappadocia's father? They should have wanted to talk to Harry, not kill him. She needed to think. She said, "It's a lot of work."

Sam turned a little to squint up at the light. "Jerry was important. Usually, somebody important gets popped, and sooner or later there's no big mystery. Somebody else ends up with whatever he had. But Jerry

Cappadocia dies, and that's it. Nothing happens. So Harry gets to be important."

"You mean Mr. Cappadocia wouldn't believe Harry was dead?"

"He figured it was just possible that Harry got cornered and went to the cops to make a deal."

"What kind of deal?"

"The only kind that's worth anything. They'd stage his death, and he'd tell them whatever he saw that night. You think they wouldn't do that?"

"I've heard of it."

"Harry was the perfect candidate. He's been gone for five, six years, and nobody has stopped looking. And all the cops wanted him for was questioning. He didn't do anything except see Jerry die."

"Why didn't you take pictures right away?"

"What do you mean, right away?" asked Ron. "How the hell were we supposed to do that?"

"When you killed him."

"Killed him?" snapped Sam. "What are you talking about killed him? Martin killed him. Mr. C. read it in the papers and sent us out to make sure."

She sensed that if she didn't say exactly the right thing now, she was going to reveal her real ignorance and they would know she couldn't catch them in a lie. They had said Martin. She had to find out who Martin was.

"That's all we're doing," said Ron eagerly. "We're not bothering anybody. It's over. We're just taking pictures."

"Tell me what you know about Martin."

"Nothing a lot of other people don't know," snapped Sam. "When Mr. C. heard Martin was out, he called everybody in and told us to make sure he didn't drop out of sight. So some guys watched him. That's all."

"That isn't all, is it?" She tried to make it sound ominous.

"It was the money," said Ron.

"Martin don't need lessons from you," said Sam. He looked up at Jane again. "Obviously."

Jake suddenly appeared at Jane's elbow. She was startled and shone the flashlight on him, then remembered and turned it back to the pit. Both men had moved fast, but they had only gotten to the piles of dirt at the edge of the pit. They slowly slid back, taking little showers of loose dirt with them, and assumed the position again.

"Don't make me kill you," she said.

"No argument there," said Ron.

"Where was I?" said Sam, resigned. "Next thing we hear, he's got a lot of money. This does not look good in a man like Martin after eight years."

Without knowing when it had happened, Jane realized who they were talking about. Eight years. Of course. An ex-policeman who suddenly had a lot of cash and was ready to run. They thought he knew where Harry was, and he was going to hide in the same place. But why did they call him Martin? Had he used a false name to get to Buffalo? She had to be sure. "Eight years? As a cop?"

"Cop? What cop? Martin did eight of a five-to-ten for a concealed weapon. Harry did, like, two of a three-to-five for fraud or something, years ago. Martin being what he was, which was what got him the hard time for a small bust, they—"

"What he was? What was he?" Her head was pounding now, building up a pressure behind her eyes.

"Jesus," said Ron. "She doesn't know."

"Know what?" said Sam, annoyed.

"Anything. Anything about him."

Sam squinted up into the beam of the flashlight. "He's right, isn't he?"

She tried to think of an answer, but all she kept running into was the truth. "Yes," she said.

Sam rolled his eyes and shook his head in frustration.

"Martin is a guy you hire when you want somebody to be dead. He was kind of on the edge of being famous at one time, which was probably why the cops felt it was worth searching him one night. They found a gun—"

"They probably planted it on him," said Ron.

Sam said icily, "You want to tell this?"

"No," said Ron. "I was just saying he wasn't dumb enough to let them find a . . ." He shrugged and let it trail off.

"Anyway," said Sam. "He got ten years, because they couldn't prove he had done anybody with it, but they knew damned well that was what paid the rent. So he did eight of the ten, which is a world record for recent times unless you kill somebody while you're in the joint—"

"Which he did," said Ron. "That's what I heard. They just couldn't prove it was him." He looked up at Jane. "So many suspects, you know? In a maximum security prison it seems like half the population is there for dusting somebody."

"Shut up, will you?" hissed Sam.

"Why, you in a hurry to finish the story so she can drop the hammer on you?"

"I'm trying to save your ass. I sense that there's a misunderstanding here. If she didn't know he was a killer, maybe we got something to talk about. Now I lost where I was."

"Jail," said Jane. Her voice was hollow.

"Jail. Right. Martin was Harry's cellmate in Marion. A guy like Harry, he just can't defend himself. His only hope is if there's somebody around like Martin, who likes him but not too much, if you know what I mean. That's the way it was. So Mr. C. figures it's just possible that when Martin gets out, he's going to look up his old cellmate, Harry. Who else has he got after eight years?"

"And then somebody found out he had money?" asked Jane.

"The money," said Ron eagerly. "He gets out after eight years of unemployment, and he's got a lot of money. He is walking up to every bank in Chicago, and the tellers are coming up with, like, wads of it. Sometimes the manager has to come and match his signature and stuff."

Sam said, "So where's this money coming from? Who is going to give this guy who has only one skill all this money? And who's the mark that's worth that much? The guy that nobody else has been able to find for five years."

"So you followed him from St. Louis?"

"Hell, no," said Sam. "We followed him all the way from Chicago. We were all set to hang around St. Louis. We figured if he was there, that was where Harry must be. We got a room, changed cars so Martin wouldn't notice there's this car with Illinois plates. With four guys to switch off, we figured we could probably keep going long enough to see where Harry was, and keep Martin from killing him."

"Then he gets on a bus," said Ron, outraged at the memory of it. "What the hell is a guy with a suitcase full of money doing getting on a bus? We didn't have any choice but to drop everything, pile into one car, and follow the bus."

"All the way to Buffalo," said Sam. "We lost him after he hooked up with you." He gave a sour little nod. "As you know."

"And he got to Harry," said Ron.

For the first time Jake spoke. "Where is he now?"

"That *is* the question, isn't it?" sneered Sam.

Jane said, "Did he kill Jerry Cappadocia?"

"No," said Ron. "I told you he was in jail. He just got out."

She stared at them for a moment. "What is his full name?"

"James Michael Martin."

Jake was touching Jane's elbow. After a moment she glanced at him. He whispered, "What do you want to do with them?"

She could see that the two men in the pit knew exactly what she and Jake were whispering about. They exchanged anxious looks, as though each one was trying to get the other to agree on what desperate effort they should try. She said to them, "Before you leave, cover up poor Harry."

She turned and walked across the open lawn. Jake hurried after her. "Shouldn't we call the police or something? They'll come after us."

"No, they won't," she said. "They know I don't know anything. Never did." She walked on. Now and then her foot would light on a flat metal marker, but she paid no attention. If the dead could feel anything, it wouldn't be anger at a foolish girl far from home, stumbling in the darkness.

22

Later that night, Jane didn't agree to Jake's proposal to move out of Harry's apartment building. She just didn't resist. She didn't seem to care where her body was, just so there was no distraction while she stared at the opaque surfaces of walls and at the reflections in darkened windows. He picked out a small, cheap motel on Cabrillo Boulevard across the street from the ocean that he had discovered earlier that day. He parked the car and went inside while she sat motionless in the passenger seat. She walked into the room he rented, lay down on the bed, and closed her eyes. The next afternoon when Jake went out alone, she might have noticed that he had taken both of the shotguns with him, locked in the trunk of the car, but she didn't show any interest in what he did or where he went.

When he came back and knocked on the door after the sun had set, she let him in. She didn't ask where he had been. When she saw that he had brought dinner from a take-out fish restaurant, she sat down at the little table across from him and ate. When they were finished eating, as Jake stood up to take their two plates out to the trash bin in the parking lot, she looked up at him with a curious alertness.

"How good a friend is Dave Dormont?"

Jake was surprised to hear her voice after so many hours, and relieved to have a chance to talk to her, to be able to look at her and see her eyes. "A good friend," he said. "I've known him for close to sixty years."

"I want you to call him."

Jake felt a little uneasy, an intuition that her voice didn't sound right. She didn't sound like a young woman who knew she had gotten in too deep and was ready to turn the whole thing over to the police. Her eyes glittered as though there were something hot behind them. "I think that's a good idea."

"It is," she said. "Call him at home. Tonight."

Jake smiled. "There are times when you have to step back and turn things over to the people who get paid for doing it." He waited for her to agree.

She didn't appear to be listening. "Those men said he had been in jail. If he was, there would be a file. I want you to get it."

"A file? What kind of file?"

"Police have a system for sharing information about criminals. The federal government gives them money for a network called the N.C.I.C. Some of it is computerized, but that's not what I want. I want a copy of his file from the prison at Marion, Illinois." She glanced over at the telephone expectantly.

Jake sat down at the table and studied her. "If Dave Dormont could get something like that, it would be privileged information. Why would he give it to me?"

"Because you pulled him out of Ellicott Creek fifty years ago," said Jane. She wasn't smiling. "And you've spent the next fifty telling everybody in Deganawida what a great guy he is, and paid your tickets instead of asking him to fix them."

"What do you want to do with it?" said Jake.

She looked at him, and her eyes had not changed. They were still sharp and clear and unblinking. "I want to know who he really was—who did this to Harry and to a man you don't know in Vancouver and to me. I have a right to know."

"I can't argue with that," said Jake, warily. He looked up at her again. "It just doesn't feel right." Then he added, "So I can't ask Dave to do it."

"Okay," she said. She picked up the paper plates and plastic spoons, pushed them back into the bag, and headed for the door.

Jake could see the wall coming down between them. "I managed to get a full refund on those two shotguns," he said, watching her face.

She didn't flinch. "I should think so," she said. "They've never been fired."

"And wait until you see the deal I got on the plane tickets back to Buffalo."

She seemed completely normal now. "How much?"

"Three twenty-two."

"Great," she said. She set down the plates, picked up her purse, sat down and wrote rapidly, then tore the check out of her wallet and handed it to him. "Thanks, Jake. Thanks for everything."

"You didn't have to pay me back now," he said, staring at the check.

"It's the best way to do things," she said as she stuffed the wallet back into her purse. "If I forgot, you'd get all uncomfortable about reminding me, wouldn't you?"

"I don't know," he admitted.

She walked to the door with the plates and garbage. "And don't feel bad about the file. I'm not mad about it."

She stepped out the door and closed it behind her. Jake sat at the table and thought about it. He tried to tell himself it was right. Hell, he knew it was right. You didn't leave a loaded shotgun lying around in the same room with a woman who had just learned that the man she thought she loved was using her so he could kill somebody. The file was the same thing as the shotguns. Whatever she had planned to do with that fellow's file, it wasn't something that was good for her. He was lost in thought for a long time, and then it occurred to him that there was no rational reason for a woman not to have put down her purse before she took the plates out to the trash bin. He stood up and hurried to the door, but before he opened it he knew that she was gone.

Jane walked without hurrying. There were a lot of pedestrians out at this time of night in Santa Barbara, coming and going from the restaurants and movie theaters. She bought a copy of *The Santa Barbara News-Press* from a vending machine on State Street near the art museum and sat on the steps to read it in the light of the streetlamps. She could see after only a few minutes that there wasn't much action in a town this size, but there were enough cases on the calendar to work.

She walked along State Street and turned right on Anapamu. The big white building on the right with its gigantic green lawns and patches of brilliant flowers had been a place that she had liked when she was here before, until she had learned that it was a courthouse. She climbed one of the outer staircases that ran along the wall and stepped into the second-floor hallway. The scuffed, uneven Mexican tiles and antique furniture along the walls outside the courtrooms made it all seem benevolent and pretty. She walked along the hall past the closed doors of the courtrooms and turned down the next hall. She read the names on the doors. Judge Joseph Gonzales, Judge David Rittenour, Judge Karen Susskind. She found a pay telephone at the end of the hall near the restrooms and looked up the number in the telephone book beneath it.

"Police department," said a male voice.

"This is Judge Karen Susskind," she said. "I'd like to speak to the watch commander, please."

"Yes, ma'am."

In a moment there was another voice. "Yes, Judge."

"I need some assistance right away."

"What can we do for you?"

She glanced at the newspaper. "I'm supposed to pass sentence on a gentleman named Richard Winton tomorrow morning at nine."

"Yes," he said. "I remember the case."

"Well, I've received some information that I need to have checked out as soon as possible. Nothing in this building is open, and I can't reach the district attorney. All he could do is ask you, so I thought I'd ask you directly."

"You're still at the courthouse?"

"Yes," she said in mild frustration. "I'm still studying the case."

"What sort of information do you need?"

"I just received an anonymous phone call here in my chambers. The person said that Mr. Winton isn't who he claims to be. The person said his real name is James Michael Martin, and he's not a first offender. This James Michael Martin was supposedly just released from the prison in Marion, Illinois, and he has a long record."

"Well, that's something we can check," said the watch commander. "We can run Winton's prints through the F.B.I., but it'll take some time . . ."

"I would appreciate it if you would make the request right away. But we can't wait for the outcome. Find out if there is a file on this James Michael Martin in the prison, and get it faxed to you tonight. If it's the same man, I'll know it in a second, and I'll have the information I need for the sentence."

"I'll get on it right away," he said. "Do you want it delivered to your home?"

"Home?" she laughed. "I don't expect to be home for hours. How long will it take?"

"Give us one hour," he said.

"All right. If I'm away from my desk for a minute, my assistant will be there. And if there are any delays, call me. I'll give you the number of the private line in my chambers." She read him the number off the pay telephone, then hung up.

It took forty-two minutes before she heard the sound of a large man with heavy shoes and a lot of jangling metal on his belt come up the tiled staircase, taking the steps two at a time. She stood with her back to the big wooden door of the judge's office so that the thick old-fashioned door frame would hide her, until she was sure he would see. She stepped forward into the hallway and saw the policeman coming. He was a motorcycle cop with high boots and a helmet under one arm. In his other hand he carried a thick manila envelope with a string tie to keep it shut.

She stepped back to the door and put her hand on the handle, then leaned forward as though she were opening the door a crack. "It's here, Judge," she called, then trotted ahead to meet the policeman.

She pointed at the envelope. "Is that the Martin file?"

The cop said, "Yes, it is."

She snatched it out from under his arm. "Oh, thank you so much. Maybe I'll get to go home tonight after all."

He grinned at her. "Glad to help." He turned and started to walk off as she hurried back toward the door of the judge's office. While she walked, she listened for the click of the man's boots to recede down the hallway. She made sure she didn't reach the door until she heard them on the staircase.

A minute later, she heard the motorcycle start and then the whine of the engine as it sped down the block toward the station. There was only one more thing that had to happen. She considered not waiting for it, but she decided that a little patience was worth it. The pay telephone on the wall rang once and she snatched it up. "Judge Susskind."

It was the watch commander's voice. "This is Lieutenant Garner at the Police Department, Judge. I was—"

"It's not the same man," said Jane.

"So you don't want Winton picked up and held for the fingerprint check?"

"Definitely not," she said. "It must have been some kind of practical joke. Whether it was on me or Mr. Winton, I couldn't guess, but someone wanted me to delay sentencing." She added, "Thanks to you, we won't have to do that. Goodbye."

She used the pay telephone one more time to call for a taxi, then walked down the outer staircase into the dark garden, past the beds of flowers that had closed their petals for the night and up the empty sidewalk toward the art museum to wait for it.

A few hours later, Jane sat in her room in the big hotel beside the Los Angeles airport and stared at the photographs in the file. There was John Felker staring into her eyes, only this time there was a black placard under his chin that had numbers on it. Then there was the one of his profile, the one she had lain next to in bed and studied in the light of the moon, thinking it looked like the head on a Roman coin, or the way Roman coins should have looked. Here it was, labeled with the same number on the same placard.

For a whole night in Santa Barbara she had considered all the ways it could be another mistake. The two men standing in the grave would have said anything to get out of it. Maybe the story made sense because they had anticipated that they would need to have a story to tell. As soon as she had formulated this idea, she had known it couldn't be true, because the story they had told wouldn't have done them any good at all with anyone in the world except Jane Whitefield.

The file had ended that. He was not John Felker. He was James Michael Martin, age thirty-eight, 7757213. He killed people for a living. The file was thick. There were all sorts of documents, from his arrest and trial record through his eight years in Marion. There was a note stating that he had a mechanical aptitude, but the prison counselor felt that vocational training was not an avenue worth exploring with this prisoner. He had gotten two fillings from the prison dentist, marked with a pencil on a diagram of numbered teeth. He had taken a class in bookkeeping and one in computer programming. He had been to the prison infirmary once—no, twice—for upper respiratory congestion, and received non-narcotic cold medicines. His general health was, each time, assessed as "excellent."

She set these sheets aside on the bed and pushed back farther in the file to the older entries. There was a summary of his record, provided at his entrance so that the prison officials would know whom they were dealing with. Five arrests, beginning at age eighteen, which could mean there had been more while he was a minor. Aggravated assault in Chicago; charges dropped twice. Manslaughter in Chicago; charges dropped. Suspicion of murder in St. Louis; released for lack of evidence.

Her eye caught something that made her stop because she wondered if she had imagined it. She went back and looked at it: arresting officer, John Felker. That was how he had known what to call himself. Martin had probably thought a lot about the man who had arrested him that time. He had known when the real Felker had retired from the police force, even learned his real Social Security number. This must have been the arrest that had made Martin seem important enough to watch, because the next arrest was the final one, for an illegal concealed weapon, something a cop wouldn't know about unless he searched him. As Ron the gravedigger had said, it was something he probably would have gotten six months for unless the judge knew a lot about him and knew he had to swing hard because this was the last chance before somebody else died.

The Social Security number worried her. Martin probably hadn't obtained it just to fool her. He might have gotten it because, of all the codes and serial numbers that a person collected in his life, it was the best one to have if you wanted to find him. It never changed, and it got attached to other things: credit cards, bank accounts, licenses. She wondered whether she should try to call the real John Felker to warn him. She looked at the telephone on the nightstand beside the bed, but she didn't reach for it. She decided to wait. Martin might have learned what he could about Felker in order to harm him, but he wouldn't be able to devote himself to that right now.

She moved to the back of the file. Born April 23. It gave her a special kind of twinge that she knew she wasn't supposed to be feeling. They had been together on the Grand River reservation on his birthday. Somehow that made it more horrible, increasing the distance he had placed between them. She was ashamed of feeling that way, still. It was one thing to be surprised if somebody hit you in the dark; it was another to keep feeling surprised, over and over, as the blows kept coming.

Then she noticed his place of birth. Why had she assumed it would be St. Louis? She recognized that the trouble came from her clinging unconsciously to a wish that at least something he had said to her be true. She wanted to detect some point where he had wavered, maybe forgotten himself and actually talked to her without calculation. She wanted to believe that they had been, if only for one minute, nothing but a man and a woman lying in the dark, telling each other things. Everything he knew about St. Louis he had probably learned while earning that suspicion-of-murder arrest.

The place of birth was, somehow, even worse than the birthday. He was from Lake Placid, New York.

She stood up and walked all the way to the door and then back to the wall, over and over as she explored the stinging sensation. Not only was everything he had said a lie, but he must have been listening to what she said and secretly thinking she was stupid, making her tell him where they were now and where they were going, and listening always without wanting to hear what she was saying but, instead, to be sure that she was still fooled. He had asked questions, made her talk about what she felt and about her family and her people, not because he was even morbidly curious, but because everyone knew that the best way to lie to someone was to make her do the talking.

She pushed aside the memories of Felker and forced herself to think about Martin. He had killed Harry over a week ago. He had just gotten out of prison after eight years, so any friends he might have had would not have been the sort he could trust. If he had gone to any of them, Cappadocia's men would have seen it because they were following him. He could not have prepared an escape to the Caribbean or somewhere while he was sitting in a cell. It took papers even he couldn't have collected in there without having somebody find out. What had he done? He had gotten out of jail and collected the money. Was that the whole payment in advance or just earnest money? It didn't matter, because he was too cunning to expect that he could kill Harry and then go back to Chicago for the rest. Nobody could be certain if Harry ever knew who had killed Jerry C., but if John had gotten a pile of money from them, then he knew. He would be smart enough to see that once he killed Harry, he would be taking Harry's place. Not Chicago, then. The partial payment was all he could expect to make on the deal.

She corrected herself. Even that was a wrong assumption. He had let her see money, and she was assuming that he had shown her all of it. All she could be sure of was that he would not go anywhere that she could figure out, in order to get more.

She walked to the window and stared out at the lights along the San Diego Freeway far below her. He wasn't infallible. He had gotten caught a few times. She went back to the bed and studied the arrest summary again. Stopped for questioning by a surveillance team. Okay, you watch, then you arrest. So what? Maybe this meant something to the cops who were supposed to read it that it didn't mean to her. But farther down the page was the reason the surveillance had been mentioned. He had been arrested in the company of Jerry Cappadocia. He hadn't been under surveillance at all. Jerry Cappadocia had been. John . . . James Michael Martin had been just a bodyguard or something. That was in the file to show what kind of connections he had. They didn't want the judge to think he was just some ordinary jerk. He was a special jerk, with organized-crime buddies.

Jane stared across the room at the window and listened to a big plane rumbling down the runway. No, the story didn't make sense. Cappadocia's friends had been, even now, looking for Harry to make him talk, and to do that, they had to keep him alive as long as that kind of conversation took. But John Felker-slash-James Martin had been looking for him to kill him. And the guys in the grave, who worked for the Cappadocia family, didn't talk about James Martin as a member of the team. He was just a guy you hired to kill people.

Then the thin surface she had been walking on, the one that assumed anything anybody said was true unless it was disproven, seemed to give way. She was suddenly on the other side of it in her mind, looking at it in reverse.

The police had assumed Martin was some kind of employee of Jerry Cappadocia. Certainly, he had known him. But there was more than one reason to be near Jerry Cappadocia with a gun.

It was like reversing a puzzle piece; suddenly, it fit. If Jerry Cappadocia had been in danger, he might hire a killer like Martin to protect him. If he did, was that all he would do? No. He would carry a gun too, or he would have some of his own people do it for him. The surveillance was on Jerry Cappadocia, so he was the one the police wanted, but they didn't find a way to arrest him or any of his men, which meant that none of them was armed. Jerry Cappadocia hadn't been in danger that night. Or he hadn't thought he was. But maybe the one thing that had kept him alive was the police surveillance. Even though he must have seen Martin searched and the gun pulled out of his belt or pantleg or somewhere, Jerry still would not have suspected. To him, it must have been like watching the police discover that his dentist owned drill.

For the first time after all these years, she understood Harry. He had always claimed he had never seen anything at the poker game the night Jerry Cappadocia was murdered. But he had run anyway. He seemed to think nobody would ever believe he hadn't seen anything, and maybe nobody would have. But that wasn't the reason he had run. He had run because he *had* seen something and couldn't tell anybody. And the only thing that made sense, that fit his sucker personality, was if what he saw convinced him that the one who had ordered the killing was his friend, the man who had kept him alive in prison.

When she thought about it that way, she even knew what Harry had seen. He had recognized the men that Martin had hired to kill Cappadocia. He had recognized them when nobody else had. They were strangers, outsiders. But Harry had seen them before. He had probably met them where Martin had met them—in prison. Martin was still inside, where nobody would suspect

him. Nobody suspected him even now, after he had
killed Harry.

When her eyes focused again she was looking at the
bureau, where her purse lay open in front of the mirror.
The money. Even that had been misinterpreted. He got
out of prison and wandered around collecting money
from banks, so everyone suspected some clients had deposited money in his name. Maybe that was where it
had come from to begin with, but he had had it for eight
years, long before he met Harry. In fact, there was probably less of it now, because he had paid his subcontrac-
tors to kill Cappadocia for him. Then, without warning,
the rest of it came to her: Martin had put up the money,
but he couldn't have given it to them himself, because
he was in jail.

Martin would have cooked up some convincing reason why good old Harry should go to some safe-deposit
box or bank account or dig up a hole to get the money
and give it to the two men. It would be compelling, and
Harry would believe it, just as she would have. Then
Harry saw the men one last time, kneeling over Cappadocia's body to search the bloody clothes for poker
money.

Now Jane knew the reason why Martin could kill
Harry and not be afraid of the people who had paid him
to do it: There were no such people. All anybody had
paid him for was the death of Jerry Cappadocia. He had
done it by farming out the contract. And the ones he
had hired could never talk, because they had actually
pulled the triggers and nothing they could say would
ever keep them alive. He had nothing to fear from anyone except Harry.

So he had fooled the person who could lead him to
Harry, made her take him on the same trip that Harry
had taken. Maybe he had even let those four men see
him in St. Louis, brought them along behind him as evidence to convince her that he was a victim. He had

known they wouldn't try to kill him until he had led them to Harry. She didn't let herself turn away from any of the anguish of it now. She had insisted that his new name be John because she had known it would make him feel less strange and disoriented, and that would keep him from making mistakes. But he had been watching everything she did, and that had been the last bit of information he had needed from her. It told him that no matter what last name Harry had on Lew Feng's list, he would still be called Harry. Even if all he could get from Lew Feng under torture was the list, he could still find Harry Kemple. He had cut Harry's throat quietly, without a struggle, and let him bleed to death on that dirty shag carpet in the apartment in Santa Barbara.

Jane started to pace again. Another big plane took off on the nearest runway and she could feel a faint vibration under her feet, but she didn't let it distract her. As she concentrated on the facts she had accumulated, she knew that they were beginning to assume their proper order at last. She tried to reconstruct the story in a logical sequence this time, to be sure she had the truth. The truth mattered. It had started with Harry. No, it had started nearly ten years ago, when she had met Alfred Strongbear on the reservation in Wyoming. That was the real beginning, because it happened first and it was what made everything else possible, even probable. Once she had saved someone like Alfred Strongbear, it was inevitable that she would meet someone like Harry. Alfred might not have had a heart attack on a cruise ship, but something someday would make him give a man like Harry her name and address.

Harry had remembered it the way he remembered the names of underrated racehorses that might one day make him some money. He had gotten caught at something a couple of years later. One of the two gravediggers had said it was fraud, but that didn't really tell her anything, because most of the things Harry did could have been called fraud. In any case, he hadn't run to her to avoid the arrest, so it must have come quickly and without warning. Then she realized that this might not be the reason why Harry hadn't tried to hide. Harry was an optimist. Right up until the guards put his watch and wallet into the envelope and marched him off to get fitted for a uniform, he had been perfectly capable of believing he would get off somehow.

He was put into a maximum-security prison, not because he was dangerous, but because his accretion of minor arrests must have made him look worse than he was. His cellmate was a man named James Michael Martin. Harry was very lucky to draw a man like Martin as a cellmate in a violent place like that. The soft little gambler might as well have had VICTIM stenciled on the back of his shirt above the number, but Martin was a killer. Martin saved Harry's life. He probably saved it daily, just by being there and letting other prisoners judge that he would rather have Harry to talk to than see his body hauled off in a bag. So Harry, who had no other way to thank Martin, had told him the story of the old man on the cruise ship and the name and address of Jane Whitefield, the woman who made people disappear. Coming from one career criminal to another, it probably had made a nice gift. She caught a glimpse of herself as she passed the mirror on the bureau, and the expression of intense anger startled her. She walked back to the bed and lay on her back to stare up at the ceiling.

After two years, Harry had gotten out of prison about as reformed as most prisoners. He had started his floating high-stakes poker game, sure that in another few years he would be a one-man portable Las Vegas. Harry had been so elated that he had gone to visit his old friend in Marion to tell him all about it. When Harry had run into trouble, with Jerry Cappadocia showing signs of moving in on the game, he had told Martin that, too.

She sensed that she was missing something important. Her muscles tensed and she sat up. What she was forgetting was Martin's relationship with Jerry Cappadocia. Martin had been with Jerry C. the night of his arrest. They were acquaintances. He would have known that Cappadocia would be interested in Harry's card game, so he made sure that he heard about it. She went over it again. Could even Martin have been capable of that much premeditation? Was he that good? As she questioned it, she felt a chill. Yes, he was. She had seen his work. He nurtured relationships with people and remained detached. He watched and waited and listened to them for as long as necessary, until he heard something that he could use.

Martin made sure that Jerry C. heard about the game, and then got himself into it. Now Martin had to find the proper instruments for killing him. He selected two prisoners he and Harry knew in Marion. Maybe they weren't killers yet, but in Marion it wasn't hard to find two men with faces that hadn't been seen in Chicago and who were willing to learn to pull a trigger. They were about to get out. Maybe they already were out and he had recruited them earlier and told them to wait until he could arrange the right opportunity. It was impossible for her to know which it was, and she was concentrating on coaxing out tidbits she could be sure about. She was sure Martin would need to pay the two killers in advance.

Martin still had five years to go on his sentence. He couldn't ask his two men to kill an important gangster and then wait five years until payday. He could easily have time added to his sentence, or even die before they saw a dime. They had recently gotten out of prison themselves, so they had no money. They would need some to disappear as soon as they had killed Jerry

Cappadocia, and that could only mean that they would have to be paid in advance. Martin was in prison, so he needed a bag man on the outside.

It had to be someone he could trust to go and get some of the money wherever Martin had hidden it and give it to the two men. It also had to be someone who was not going to be around after Jerry Cappadocia was killed. The only possible choice was Harry. Martin probably told Harry that he was giving the two former prisoners money to invest in some criminal scheme— loan-sharking, bookmaking—some crime, anyway, or even Harry would have sensed an odd smell wafting past his nostrils. It didn't matter what story Martin told him. It had been good enough. Harry gave the money to the two men he and Martin had met in prison.

Martin had the money for Harry to give them, because he too had been paid in advance. When the client had come to Martin two years earlier and hired him to kill Jerry Cappadocia, that had put Martin in the same position the two men were in now: He needed his whole payment in advance. The day after a man like Jerry C. was killed would not have been a good time for the killer to go to his client to get a pile of money. If the smallest detail went wrong, he would have to be running. Even if everything went perfectly, Jerry's father still had a big organization that remained intact, and all of it would be diverted to finding out who was meeting with whom and who had any money he hadn't had before.

So Harry got the money, gave it to the two men for his friend Martin, and went back to his floating poker game business. A week or so later, when Harry was inside the bathroom of the motel staring through the vent above the door, he recognized the two killers. If he recognized them, he would know that what they were doing was what he had paid them for, and come to the inescapable conclusion that Martin had intended them to kill him along with the others.

Harry had considered his options—telling the police or Jerry Cappadocia's father, or even going back to Marion to tell his friend Martin that he would never talk—and decided that any of them would eventually get him killed. But he still had one more option hidden in his memory, and he used it. He ran to Deganawida, New York, and knocked on Jane Whitefield's door.

She had hidden him for a time and then taken him across the continent to buy him a new identity from Lew Feng. Poor Lew Feng. Martin had tortured him for his list of names. Maybe Martin hadn't been able to find the place in the shop where Feng kept it without doing that. She was reasonably sure that she could have. That he hadn't even tried made him seem inhuman, completely devoid of emotion. But what seemed worse at the moment was that the torture had served a second purpose, and she suspected that that too had been taken into account. Even if Martin could have simply broken in, found the list on his own, deciphered it, and chosen the right Harry on it, he probably would not have done it that way. He was anticipating that it would have occurred to someone that the one who had taken the list was likely to be a person who had been to the shop before—a person who had known about the list because he was on it. Leaving Lew Feng's body lying in the shop mutilated was a way of misleading everyone. The mind immediately fell into the assumption that the only person who would have needed to torture Feng for information was someone who had no other way to get it. The mind began conjuring up shadowy strangers to suspect—ones who had traced some fugitive to Feng's door. Felker remained just another potential victim, like everyone else on the list.

She couldn't hold her body still anymore. She stood up and walked to the window again to stare down at the endless stream of cars moving in both directions—white headlights on one side of the freeway, red taillights on the other. There were still a few blank spaces in the picture she had constructed. Martin had been paid in advance to kill Jerry Cappadocia. He had gotten himself arrested while he was stalking Jerry and gone to prison. He had waited over two years to hire a pair of substitutes to do it for him. Was Martin, then, an honorable murderer? Once he had accepted the contract and taken the money, did he feel he had to deliver? Maybe he did. Certainly, a professional killer who took money in advance and never fulfilled the contract would have a hard time getting work in the future from any potential customer who had heard about it.

She recognized that the important information was in the last words: *who had heard about it.* The person who hired Martin to kill Jerry Cappadocia was somebody who could tell other potential customers. Then she made it more specific, and when she did, it felt even more likely. The client was somebody in the underworld, who not only could tell others but could signal his displeasure in a more vivid way than gossip. He was somebody who might get Martin killed. He had to be another gangster type, or Martin could have kept the money and forgotten about Jerry C. If the client hadn't been somebody like that, why would he care about Jerry Cappadocia, and how would he have known that Martin was the one to hire to kill him? People like Martin didn't advertise.

But if all of that was true, why hadn't this underworld rival surfaced by now, five years after Jerry had been killed? He should have done what Mr. Cappadocia's men had been expecting, what even Harry had predicted. He should have tried to take over.

She stepped back to the bed and bent over to look through the file again, page by page, until she found the list of people who had visited Martin in prison. The first visitor had come right after he had begun serving his sentence. It was Jerry Cappadocia. That must have been Jerry's condolence visit. The second was Martin's defense attorney, Alvin Berbin. There were three visits from him in the first few months, probably about an appeal of the conviction. Then, almost three years later, Harry Kemple came back to visit his old cellmate. She had not guessed wrong about that. He made four visits on successive weekends, just about a month before he showed up at her door. There were no more visitors in the next five years.

She straightened and tossed the file to the foot of the bed. She had been hoping for too much. The client wouldn't be foolish enough to visit his hired killer in prison. There was nothing in the file to give her any way of finding out who had hired Martin to kill Cappadocia.

She concentrated on Martin again. Martin had served the five years that remained of his sentence, secure in the knowledge that most of his money was in the bank, Jerry was dead, his two stand-in killers were long gone, and nobody—not the police, not Mr. Cappadocia—had ever suspected him of being involved in Jerry's murder. There was only one minor difficulty. His two shooters had carelessly left Harry Kemple alive.

She wondered if Harry had even remembered that he had told Martin in prison that the best way to start searching for him would be to visit a woman named Jane Whitefield. Of course he had remembered, but he also had remembered that it would be five years before Martin could come after him, and he had the police and Mr. Cappadocia to worry about that night. He certainly must have thought about Martin now and then during the five years in Santa Barbara. But at the end of them, he must have been confident that his troubles were behind him. Martin would have a hard time finding him, and why should he try? Harry had remained silent for five years. Harry, being Harry, must have decided that five years would be enough to convince James Martin that he would never talk.

Martin had not forgotten about Harry. He had collected the rest of his money and gone to her, and she took him to Lewis Feng, who pointed him to Harry in Santa Barbara, and that was the end of Harry. But what then? Martin wouldn't have taken a plane out of Santa Barbara. That would have put him on a shortlist of people who had left the small town while Harry's body was still warm. And if he left the Honda she had bought him in town, the police would begin to look for John Young.

He would drive out, and the place where he would go was a place he would know but that nobody in Chicago would. After a year in jail, that might be anywhere. After eight in jail and a fresh murder, he would go home.

She put the file into her flight bag and walked down the stairs to catch the shuttle to the airport. She didn't mind waiting in the terminal for a flight to Syracuse. She could use the time to buy the next batch of newspapers and read.

23

Jane checked into a motel near the airport in Syracuse and read newspapers. She started each day by finding more of them. When she had read all the ones she could buy, she spent the afternoon in a branch of the public library that subscribed to even more.

The car had about 530 miles on its odometer when he had gotten it from Lewis Feng. Jane guessed he had then driven it five hundred miles to Medford, six hundred to Santa Barbara, one hundred down to the big east-west routes that started in Los Angeles, and almost three thousand to Upstate New York. Make it five thousand miles, then. Jane searched the newspapers for the dealers' ads. There was a nearly new Honda Accord in a dealer's lot in Watertown, but it had a standard transmission. A lot in Ogdensburg had a Honda Accord and it was even gray, but seventeen thousand was too many miles. There was nothing in Massena.

As she moved outward, the odds got worse. Syracuse, Rome, Utica, Troy, Albany all had lots of used-car dealers, and she wasn't sure anymore whether she was seeing all of their ads. Her best hope was that it was the sort of car they could clean up in half an hour and then use as bait to draw people onto the lot. John Young would have taken their second offer, right after the ridiculous low-ball one they always tried. As soon as they could get the Oregon plates off it, they would have it in the front row, all shined up and looking seductive.

It would have to be a dealer. He couldn't abandon it, because leaving a new car would set off a search for John Young. He couldn't sell it himself, because that meant staying in one place, having an address and, probably, a phone number in the papers for a few days. And by now there probably wasn't anybody alive who would buy a barely driven new car from a stranger who didn't advertise it and couldn't wait a day for a decision, without checking to see if it was stolen. It had to be a dealer. He would be relying on the fact that in a few days it would be in the hands of a new owner with a set of New York plates on it.

Then, after three days of staring at identical advertisements for identical cars in newspapers from all over the state and calling dealers on the telephone who wouldn't tell her no until they had offered her everything they had, she found it. The ad was small but effective. "Almost new! Less than five K mi.! Dave's Honda-Subaru in Saranac Lake." When she called, she talked to Dave himself.

Jane rented a car in Syracuse, drove to Saranac Lake, and saw the car. It was sitting in the front row, right under the line of colored pennants, gleaming in the sunlight. She found a motel and checked in, spent a few minutes dressing in a modest schoolteacher's spring dress, then strolled back to the lot. She walked into the showroom and let Dave find her.

"Hi there!" said Dave. He was tall and blond, with eyes so blue that they seemed to be clouded somehow. There was another man with a tie in the showroom, sitting at a desk with a telephone on it, but from the look of the place, he was just there so Dave would have someone to talk to. "What can I show you today?"

"That Honda out there," said Jane. "Is that the one in the paper?"

"That's it," said Dave gleefully. "You don't often see a used one that new. Want to drive it?"

Jane thought for a moment, then glanced at her watch. "I guess so." They hated that. The whole game was taking as much time as possible, talking to you, making friends, and getting you to accept what they thought about cars and money. If they were really good at it, at the end they could get you to feel ashamed of using up so much time and then quibbling over a few hundred dollars.

She followed Dave out to the lot and stood by the door while he dropped the key chain into her hand. Then he said diffidently, "Mind if I come along? I can answer any questions you might have."

"If you want to," said Jane. "But I don't want to take up too much of your time."

He slipped into the passenger seat and buckled his seat belt. "No problem," he said. "I got Bob in there to mind the store, and to tell you the truth, it's a real treat to get out." He looked like a dog going with the family on a picnic, gazing around him happily and pushing his muzzle toward the half-open window. "You from around here?"

"No," she said. "I just came up on vacation and I saw your ad."

"That's pretty much what happened to me. That was twelve years ago. Somehow I had the idea it would be fishing in the spring and summer, hunting in the fall, skiing in the winter. But I seem to spend just as much time on this lot as I did in Jersey."

She drove south on Route 3 toward Tupper Lake. It was a good road, and in the spring it was cold and clear at this altitude. The green pine forests on the sides of the mountains looked sparse, turning thick and wet where they merged into the leafy trees halfway down, and below them the lake started so abruptly that it looked like the mountains went down into it.

"See that?" asked Dave.

"See what?"

"The miles. Less than five thousand."

"Are you sure the one who sold it to you didn't turn it back?"

Dave laughed. "You're just like my wife. Suspicious. No. The cable's untouched, and I checked the labels on the doors. It only cleared customs from Japan two months ago. The guy drove it here from Oregon. Those are all good miles."

"Good miles?"

"Yeah. He broke it in right. He didn't beat it to death in city traffic, just drove the long, easy straightaways across the country."

"It's a nice car," she conceded. "What made him get rid of it?"

"If you'd seen him, you wouldn't have to ask. He was a big, tall fellow. I'll bet he was six-foot-six. This is a fine piece of machinery, but for a man that size driving it four thousand miles—well, it was pretty hard on him. The Japanese don't design a car for a man that size. It would be stupid: They don't have any."

"You'd think he would know how tall he was when he bought it."

Dave was stumped for a moment. "You would, wouldn't you?" He recovered quickly. "He fit in okay, but I guess a long trip like that makes little problems seem like big problems."

Jane pulled the car onto the shoulder, then hooked into the far lane to drive back to Saranac Lake. Dave didn't like the look of that. "This is a real steal. I don't know if you read the papers, but the dollar has gone way down against the yen since this baby was built. You try to buy one of these right off the boat, it's going to cost you an extra three thousand dollars."

"Is that right?" She had read so many newspapers in the past three days that she could have quoted the figures. The small papers always printed the car ads at the end of the business section. She turned into the lot and drove the car into its space with its nose to the sidewalk.

As they got out, Dave said eagerly, "Well, what do you think?"

"I just don't know," she answered, her eyes fixed wistfully on the car. "I like it, but . . ."

"But what?" he asked.

"I just keep wondering why the last owner got rid of a new car."

"I told you why."

"What did he buy when he traded it in?"

"Nothing. He said he made one mistake by being too hasty and that he wanted to look around some more first."

Jane was beginning to feel a hope. It was too early to let it grow. Of course he wouldn't buy another car from the same lot; it would be too easy to trace. But if he had no car at all, maybe he was still in the area. "I wonder . . . I know this is kind of unusual, but I can't afford to buy a car and go buy another one next month like he did. Do you think I could talk to him?"

Dave's face was beginning to show the strain. "I don't know. Talking to him isn't going to do you much good. The car is what it is, no matter what he says. Take the car to your own mechanic. Have him look it over."

"I just drove in today. I don't have a mechanic."

"I can recommend a couple."

She just looked at him sadly, and he saw the problem. The town was just too small, and anybody she picked could be a friend of his. "I'll go look at the papers and see if we can get him on the phone."

She followed Dave inside and watched him finger through the drawers in his single filing cabinet. At last he pulled out a manila envelope and shook it out over the desk in front of Bob. Whatever Bob's function was, it didn't include moving or even looking down. He never took his eyes off Jane.

There were an owner's manual, a couple of slips of white paper with seals and computer printing on them, a pink slip, and a yellow bill of sale. He snatched it up and stared at it for a moment. "There," he said. "Annabel Cabins in Lake Placid. Let's give them a call." He was pursuing this with stoical determination now. She had made him decide he was going to prove there was nothing hidden by his sheer persistence in uncovering it. He dialed the number he read off the paper.

"Hello," he said. "This is Dave Rabel down at Dave's Cars in Saranac Lake. How are you this afternoon?" He listened for a second, then said, "No, I'm not trying to sell you anything. I just wanted to get in touch with a fellow who's staying there. His name is John Young. He still with you?" There was a long pause while wrinkles appeared on Dave's forehead. "You sure? Well, thanks for your time." He hung up, shrugged, and looked at her.

"He's not there?"

He shook his head. "I'm sorry. Well, we tried."

She decided she could take the risk of not letting go. "He checked out, or he's never been there?"

Dave looked indecisive, but he sensed that he wasn't going to be able to get past it. "I remember he said that was where he was going, but I guess they didn't have a vacancy or something." She could tell he was wondering why John Young had been able to give him the phone number but hadn't used it to call for reservations.

"What if it's stolen?"

Dave smiled. "No, there are built-in safeguards. His name was on the pink slip, and I saw his license and it had the same name. Besides, when you register a sale, they run the I.D. number of the car on the computer."

Jane backed away from the desk. "Well, I'm sorry to put you to so much trouble."

"You mean you're giving up?"

"I just wouldn't be able to feel comfortable unless I knew more about the car's history."

Dave was fighting his frustration now. "It doesn't have any history. It's brand-new. Anybody can see that."

"I'm sorry," she said. "But that's the thing that's worrying me. I know it's probably silly, but . . . Well, thanks for trying."

She headed for the door, but Dave couldn't bear it. "Wait," he said. She turned and looked at him. Her shamefaced expression wasn't forced. She hated putting this nice man through hell for nothing.

He said, "Maybe we can dig him up. He wouldn't have driven across the country just to sell me a car. He's got to be staying around here."

"But how could I find him?"

"Let me make a few calls. If he's looking for a car, there aren't that many places to look. Give me your phone number and I'll call you if I have any luck."

She said, "I'm at the Holiday Inn down the road. My name is Janet Foley."

He grinned. "But you've already checked in, right? You're not going to disappear like he did?"

"No," she said. "Room two forty-three."

She had lunch in a small restaurant on the way back to the hotel, then walked back to her room. The telephone was ringing when she opened the door.

"Janet?" he said. "It's Dave Rabel. It's pretty much what I was trying to tell you. John Young bought a used Ford Bronco up at Taylor's Used Cars in Lake Placid. He must have decided he needed a big, roomy car."

"Did they have his address?"

"I got his hotel from them, but he checked out three days ago."

"I give up," said Jane.

"You mean you'll buy the car?"

"No," said Jane. "I mean I can't. I appreciate your trying so hard, but I'll just have to wait until I see a car I'm sure about."

He sighed. "You're passing up the best used-car deal in the north country." He waited for her answer and nothing came, so he decided to end it on a friendly note. "But I guess you get hurt less by being too careful than not careful enough."

"Thanks," she said. "I knew you'd understand," and hung up. She said aloud, "Where were you when I met John Felker, Dave?"

She kept her key but picked up the suitcase she hadn't unpacked, went downstairs, and then drove to Lake Placid. She parked the car and began to walk from store to store in the small downtown section. She knew exactly what clothes he had because she had bought them. His suit and sportcoat would be useless here, because they would make him stand out. He had a couple of pairs of jeans and some shirts, but he would need a warm jacket for spring in the Adirondacks. James Michael Martin would not have bought one on the way here. He would have waited so he could choose something that local people were wearing, and buy it where they had bought theirs.

At the first store, Jane showed the young man at the cash register the picture of Felker she had taken. The clerk was in his thirties, wearing shorts like the ones she could see on the rack near the door and a T-shirt that said LAKE PLACID. He barely glanced at the picture, so she had to force out a few tears. "He's my boyfriend and we had a fight and . . ." The clerk was alarmed enough to reassure her. "No. Honest. I'd remember. He hasn't been in here."

At the second store an older woman said, "Are you a policewoman?" When Jane tried the tears, the woman seemed to harden. "I don't think chasing a man around is any basis for a relationship. If I *had* seen him, I'd be doing you a favor to keep it to myself." Jane could tell that she hadn't.

The part about the policewoman gave her an idea. She went back to the car to dig out the prison file. At the third store, she showed the mug shots. "Have you seen this man?" The clerk looked closely, and said, "No, ma'am," very quickly.

The fifth establishment was a big sporting-goods store. As soon as she produced the picture, she knew she had crossed his trail. The girl at the cash register looked as though she was in high school, and at the sight of the mug shots she turned pale. "What did he do?"

Jane pressed her. "Have you seen him?"

"Well, yes. He bought some things. About three, four days ago."

The manager was thin and alert, not many years older than the girl at the register. He had been labeling stock in the back of the store when he realized something out of the ordinary was happening. He hurried to the front. "Darlene," he said officiously. "I'll handle this." But when he saw the picture, he looked worse than the girl had. "Oh yeah. What did he do?"

Jane was stern. "Did he buy anything?"

"Yes," said the manager. "Lots of things."

Jane said, "He would have paid cash. Large denominations, probably hundreds."

"He did," said the manager. Jane could tell that his mind was running quickly through the list of crimes that hundred-dollar bills proved without a doubt.

"Do you, by any chance, have any of the money on hand?"

"No," he said helplessly. "It went to the bank."

"What bank?"

"Winslow Federal." His mind tripped over the conclusion she had placed in front of him. "Is it counterfeit?"

"If it is, we'll let you know." She hurried to bury the "we" in the middle of the conversation. "What did he buy?"

"Oh, God," he said. "You confiscate it, don't you? If it's not real you just take it."

Jane felt sorry for the man; he seemed to be sure he was going to have it taken out of his pay for the next six months. "If you took it to the bank, it's not your problem anymore," she said gently. "It's like a hot potato. Nobody gets burned except the one who's holding it." This seemed to make him feel better. When she could see the blood rising back into his face, she said, "Now, I'll need a copy of the receipt for what he bought."

"Sure," said the manager, who, looking about fifteen years old now, ran to the back of the store. He returned with a carbon copy of the receipt. Jane took it and slipped it into her file without looking at it. She said, "Now, is there anything he said or did that would help us find him?"

"His car," said the manager. "I helped him carry all this stuff out. It was black. Big—"

"A Ford Bronco?" she asked.

"Yes!" he said, looking astounded. "Big wheels."

"Do you remember any of the license number?"

He looked ashamed. "No. I'm sorry. I didn't think—"

Jane decided it was time to get out. "I didn't expect you to," she said kindly. "You've both been a big help. Thank you very much." She was already at the door by the time she finished the sentence.

When Jane was back in her car, she took out the receipt and studied it. As she read it, her mind was tracking him: a pair of hiking boots, a sleeping bag, a tent, a fishing rod and reel, lures, a hatchet, a down-filled nylon jacket, a compass. He wasn't going to a hotel in Saranac or Lake Placid. He was on his way into the mountains.

24

Martin was on his way into the back country, into the vast, empty spaces. The Adirondacks were enormous: almost eleven thousand square miles, some of it public park land, some private property, and dozens of towns. In that space, there were only eleven hundred miles of highways. Once he was off the paved roads, he could be anywhere in the six million acres that the federal government had decreed in 1894 would be "forever wild." She studied the map she had picked up at the hotel gift shop.

He had a fresh car with New York plates on it. He wouldn't drive any farther east into Vermont or north into Canada over the St. Lawrence River, where he would be a foreigner again. He certainly wasn't going south, where the country flattened out and the population centers began, and he wasn't staying in the eastern part of the mountains, where most of the millions of visitors would start arriving as soon as the weather warmed up a little. He would backtrack now, go west on Route 3, the way he had come in, and back through Saranac toward Tupper Lake. From there he could go southwest for eighty miles without ever being closer to a settlement than twenty miles. Looking at the map, she was almost certain of it.

Before she left Lake Placid, she drove to Taylor Ford and spent ten minutes looking at a new Bronco. She paid very close attention to the oversize tires. Then she drove back along Route 3 toward Tupper Lake. There she spent a few hours wandering from one store to another, as she had in Lake Placid. This time she used the photograph she had taken of him instead of the mug shots. He had bought lots of groceries at Winwood's Grocery Store, but the girl at the checkout counter didn't remember much about them except that they were the sort of things men bought. Jane wasn't sure what this meant until she had watched a few men come into the store. There were a lot of preserved foods, not many fresh vegetables or much perishable meat. They were provisions for people who didn't want to come back to town for a long time.

It was nearly dark when she learned about the canoe. She walked into a boating store that called itself a marina, showed the picture, and the man at the counter recognized him instantly. Martin had been very particular about the canoe. It was fourteen feet long, built to be light "the way the Indians made 'em," with a very shallow draft. He had insisted on lifting the canoe and carrying it around in the parking lot before he would pay for it. That, the man told her, had been a sight, because it had been more canoe than he personally would have been happy carrying any distance on his head, but this guy could handle it and hold a horse under his left arm at the same time. He had set it up on the roof of the Bronco, strapped it down, and then paid cash.

Jane spent the rest of the day selecting her own provisions without returning to any of the stores she had visited. She bought her own canoe at a fancy outdoorsman's store in Saranac Lake. It was only eight feet long and weighed forty pounds. She bought an axe, a survival knife with fishing gear in the hollow handle, and a backpack at a hardware store in Wawbeek. She bought the rifle in Veterans Camp. When this was done, she had reached her weight limit. There was no way to carry a sleeping bag or tent, so she picked up a light nylon tarp. That afternoon when she went back to her room in Saranac Lake, she opened the prison file again.

She read through the file searching for any piece of information that might help. She studied his medical records closely. There were no allergies, no old injuries that had left him with a weakness, no medicines he had to take, no deficiencies in his vision or hearing that would give her an edge. Ron the gravedigger had said something about his having killed another prisoner in Marion, but if it was true, there was nothing in his record about the fruitless investigation that must have followed, so she had no indication of how he had chosen to do it.

She turned to the report of his final arrest. He had been working when they had spotted him in the surveillance of Jerry Cappadocia, so maybe the report would give her a sense of how he behaved when he was planning to kill somebody. The place of the surveillance was 9949 Madison Street. He had been picked up outside a building called Dennaway's. What was that? It sounded like a bar, or maybe a restaurant. She picked up the telephone and called long-distance information, then dialed the number they gave her.

"Dennaway's," said a female voice.

"Hello," said Jane, forcing her voice into the cheerful, businesslike tone she had learned years before when she worked as a skip-tracer. "I'm calling from the Better Business Bureau, and I find we have a blank in our descriptive listing for Dennaway's. Can you help?"

The woman hesitated. "Well, we have a little of everything, from Versace to Donna Karan."

It was a women's clothing store. Martin had been planning to kill Jerry Cappadocia at a women's clothing store. "I'm just drawing from memory here," said Jane, "but didn't you have a men's department at one time?"

"No, we've always been exclusively a ladies' couturier."

Jerry Cappadocia must have been shopping for the girl, buying her presents. What was her name? Lenore Sanders. "I'll make sure that we get it right. Thank you for your help."

"It's a pleasure," crooned the woman. "Is there anything else I can tell you?"

Jane decided there was no reason not to push it as far as she could. Any bit of information she could change from a speculation into a fact was worth having. She made her voice go soft and confidential. "Well, if you're not too busy, maybe we can clear this up right now. Do you have a regular customer named Lenore Sanders?" Unless Jerry Cappadocia was stupid, he would have tried to buy Lenore the clothes she might have chosen. He would go to the stores where she shopped.

"Let me look in the computer," said the woman. Jane didn't feel hopeful. Five years was a long time. But after some audible clicking of keys and a pause, the woman said, "Oh, here she is. But I can't imagine why she'd be writing to the Better Business Bureau about us. She hasn't bought anything here lately."

"Oh?" said Jane with a hint of suspicion. "I can't imagine that it isn't the same person. It's such a distinctive name. Do you have an address for her?"

"Oh," said the woman triumphantly. "I see the reason. She lives in St. Louis now. Lenore Sanders Cotton. Mrs. Robert Cotton, 5353 Dibbleton Way in St. Louis."

"That's the one," said Jane. "But you say she hasn't bought anything lately?"

"Not in almost a year. I guess she must stop in whenever she's in town."

"Yes," said Jane. "That's got to be right. She said she mailed something back to you that was damaged, and it wasn't credited. What is your return policy?"

The woman sighed. "I'm afraid I know just what happened. The person who used to handle returns was ... Well, she's no longer with us. So we're undoubtedly guilty. What was the item?"

Jane took a guess. "It looks like a sweater."

The woman scanned the computer. "Yes. I see it. We'll just send her another one."

"That sounds like a good idea. And I'll tell you what. Since it was just one of those things and you're going to the expense of fixing it, why don't you just tell her it was a mistake you discovered yourself without talking to us? It'll seem like a happy coincidence."

"Thank you so much," said the woman.

"You're welcome," said Jane. "Goodbye."

She sat on the bed and thought about it. Lenore Sanders had managed to bounce back from the death of Jerry Cappadocia. She had left town and married somebody named Robert Cotton. Jane felt a strong curiosity about her that she couldn't think of a way to justify. She certainly wasn't going to find out anything about James Michael Martin from Lenore. The girlfriend hadn't been present during the surveillance or she would have been mentioned in the report. She certainly wasn't at the poker game the night Jerry was murdered.

Jane leafed through the pile of newspapers she had collected over the past few days, until she found the *St. Louis Post-Dispatch*. It was a morning paper, so they would be very busy right now. She scanned the bylines for a name that fit. It had to be somebody in one of the distant offices. She dialed the number she found on the editorial page.

"This is Ginny Surchow at the Washington bureau," she told the operator. "Can you connect me to research?"

There was only a second of delay before a woman answered, "Research."

"Hi," said Jane. "This is Ginny Surchow. I was wondering if you had anything for Mrs. Robert Cotton."

"*Mrs.* Robert Cotton? Yeah, some advice on choosing a husband."

Jane chuckled, not sure how funny that was. "Maybe I'd better start with him. Got a lot?"

"What haven't we got? Come on down and take a look. We'll be here until they put the paper to bed."

"I can't come down. I'm in Washington. Just give me a quickie."

"All right," said the woman. "Give me a minute." After the minute was up, the woman returned. "I have an article here that has him being investigated for money laundering in 'seventy-nine, another one for receiving stolen goods in 'eighty-two. He owned the warehouse and he owned the truck, but the guys on the scene said they were moving the TV sets on their own. In 'eighty-five it was drugs, but he was nowhere near them and there was something wrong with the evidence, so the charge went away. By 'eighty-nine, we start running articles describing other people as 'having connections' with Cotton."

"Anything really solid?" asked Jane.

"No recent convictions that I can see. So he's described in the late ones as 'alleged organized crime figure.' No, this last one has him promoted to 'suspected gang kingpin.' "

"I get the picture," said Jane. "Thanks."

She hung up before the woman had a chance to ask her any questions. The whole exercise had been pointless. All she was doing now was filling in blank spaces in the story that didn't need to be filled. Lenore Sanders had drifted out of the story entirely. She had gone off to another city and found herself a man who probably wasn't noticeably different from Jerry Cappadocia. Jane knew all she was going to know about James Michael Martin.

She picked up the telephone again and called Jake Reinert.

"Janie?" he said. "Where are you?"

"I'm sorry I had to leave without you, Jake," she said. "I just wanted to spend some time alone. You understand."

"Where are you spending time alone?"

"The beach. It's very restful here, and I was having such a good time that I started to feel guilty about you."

"Janie? Maybe you ought to come home."

She rapped on the table beside her bed. "Oh." She called over her shoulder, "I'll be right there," then said, "I've got to go. It's dinner time here. And no, it's not a date, worse luck. It's just another woman I met on the beach. 'Bye."

She turned in her key and left before dawn, driving along the perimeter of Tupper Lake slowly, stopping now and then to scan the shore. She drove up seven old logging roads before the sun came up without finding one that went farther than a few hundred yards. She knew it would be one of the old roads. From the time the Adirondacks had been surveyed, in the 1830s, until the government had decided to protect what was left of them, in the 1890s, logging had gone on unimpeded. After that it had been controlled in most of the park, but the roads were still visible in lots of places, even some of the old narrow-gauge railroad spurs that had been built to get the logs out. James Michael Martin had been born here, and he might even have picked out the one he would use while he was still sitting in his cell in Illinois.

It was after ten when Jane saw the tire tracks on the old road above the lake. The road was now only a set of ruts that started in the marshy land along the lake and turned up into the forest immediately. Down in the flats, the tracks from his new tires were deep, with black mud mushroomed out of the lozenge-shaped depressions even after three days. As the trail swung up and away they faded, soon only an impression of a big weight that had crushed the growth of thistle and milk-weed and goldenrod that had healed the ancient ruts. As the trail went higher, the ground was hard, with rocks close to the surface and a network of roots where the big trees on both sides intertwined. There were places here and there where the thick plastering of last fall's leaves had been rotted black by standing water or washed away by spring rains, and then she could see the tire treads again. There was still the chance that even this early in the year, when the deep drifts of snow had barely melted from the high peaks above the lake, this might only be innocent fishermen trying to get to the fish while they were still eager and hungry.

The treads were the right pattern, but there might be hundreds of exact duplicates on pickups and jeeps all over the mountains. She drove on, bouncing her rented car over exposed roots and dipping into trenches where rain rivulets had rushed across the path toward the lake below.

At eleven she saw the first glint of light. It was sharp and piercing, a flash as though a chunk of the sun had fallen into the brush to the right of the road. She stopped the car, took her rifle, and walked the rest of the way off the path, stalking quietly along the carpet of wet leaves on the forest floor. When she was still thirty feet away, she stood still and stared at it.

The big black Bronco had been pulled off the path through some bushes and into a thicket of low thorny trees that formed a bower over the roof. She moved her head and saw the flash again and, this time, identified it. The rear window wasn't curved like the rear window of a car, but broad and flat, and it caught the sun like a mirror.

She cautiously moved sideways until she could be sure that the cab was empty and the door locks pushed down. She walked up and touched the hood. It was warm, but the warmth was uniform from the baking of the sun, not a hot spot in the center because the engine had been running.

She peeked in the back window and saw that the truck was empty. James Michael Martin had not left anything at all inside. The food was gone, the clothes, the tent. The canoe was gone, and he hadn't even left the straps he had used to tie it to the roof. It was odd that he had used the name John Young to buy the car. He had money, and he must have had some kind of identification that she hadn't provided that said James Michael Martin. But then it occurred to her that after eight years in jail he didn't have a valid driver's license.

Jane went back to her rented car, slid her canoe off the roof, loaded all her gear into it, and dragged it into the deepest brush at the other side of the trail, then came back the same way, carefully pushing the plants upright and tossing leaves over the keel marks.

She had to back up nearly a quarter mile to find a place where she could turn her car around. She did it clumsily deliberately, breaking a lot of brush. If anyone later came this far, they would believe this was where she had stopped and gone back.

When she reached the road, she drove all the way back to Saranac Lake to turn the car in at the Hertz lot. Now she was on foot and unencumbered. It took three hours for the bus to get her back to the town of Tupper Lake and three more hours to walk around the lake and back along the logging road to the place where she had found the Bronco. As soon as she had made it off the road and taken the first two turns, the woods closed around her and no sound of civilization reached her ears.

People who lived in this part of the country didn't use the word *Adirondacks* much; they called it the North Woods. It was just as well. The surveyor who had put the word on his maps had thought it was the name of a vanished tribe. What it really was was an Iroquois word meaning "bark eaters," the name they called the Algonquin. It meant hunters who couldn't kill enough to eat.

This hadn't been anybody's territory in the old days. Huron, Algonquin, and Montagnais had come across the St. Lawrence to hunt big game here, and the Abnaki and Mahican had come across the Hudson and Lake Champlain. Mixed bands of all of the Hodenosaunee, including her own people, had also come up along the chain of lakes at the spine of the mountains to hunt. The Hodenosaunee, the People of the Longhouse, had never built their longhouses here. This country had been wilderness even to them, a place to hunt in parties of five or ten. They had built small temporary huts of bark and saplings, found the game, and then gone home to the south. Here the rocky peaks and high altitudes were too harsh for growing corn and beans and squash. Sometimes the snow in the winter was twenty feet deep.

Jane walked among the trees fifty feet from the path all the way into the forest, not so much to hide her trail as to foreclose the remote possibility of meeting Martin alone and unarmed. The trees here were all second growth, sprouted since the lumber had been cut away in the old days, and it had grown in thick. The trees that would ultimately grow tall and form a canopy were not yet old enough to shade the others and make them die out.

The sun was just beginning to move behind the tops of the mountains to the west when she found the Bronco again. She could see that she had been lucky to find it the first time. He had hidden it well, but he must have done it in the afternoon, when the sun would have fallen on the convex windshield and been dispersed and not on the flat tailgate window.

Jane stood and studied the Bronco. It still bothered her that he had bought it as John Young. The Department of Motor Vehicles had a record of the sale, so it was public information. She thought about Martin, not

John Felker, because he had never been, or about John Young, because he had just been her version of the same person. Martin hadn't come up here to stay. He had come back to the mountains to wait. He had killed Harry, and now Jerry Cappadocia's father would be sending people out to look for him.

He had very little to worry about. He had killed Lew Feng, the person who had constructed John Young. He would be waiting for the news about Harry to come out and circulate to all of the people who might care and then to get stale. Jane supposed he had thought she would never figure out that he had killed Harry; she would assume that the four men had killed Lew Feng, gotten the list, and killed Harry. Now nobody had a way to find out about John Young because Lew Feng was dead.

She thought about the last night in Vancouver, and the truth settled on her slowly. She had thought he was upset because she had parted with him so abruptly. By the time he had known she was going, she was already on her way to the airport. But what he had really been upset about was that she had left him no safe way to kill her. She had slipped away. Now he was here waiting to see whether she had stayed fooled. If she had, there was no way for anyone to find him. But what if she hadn't?

She looked at the Bronco closely. There was nothing visible. She went to the ground, slithered between the big wheels, and looked up at the undercarriage. There was nothing out of place that she could see. She slowly pulled herself toward the front of the car looking for wires, or maybe a pipe that didn't look as though it belonged. When she saw the two plastic water bottles, she eased herself closer. There was duct tape around the tops. She touched one of them and brought the smell of gasoline away on her finger. The two bottles were tied against the exhaust manifold. She could have hot-wired

the car and driven it a mile or two up the trail before
the plastic melted and dumped a couple of gallons of
gasoline all over the engine compartment.

If she had gotten out before the fire burned along the
freshly greased underside and reached the gas tank,
people in town would have seen the smoke and come to
find her running away from John Young's car. He had
known that in order to find the car at all, she would
need to ask a lot of people if they had seen John Young.
When John Young didn't come out of the woods after
weeks, they might not be able to prove that she had
killed him, but they would certainly suspect it.

Either way, she couldn't win and he couldn't lose. If
the car burned, there would be nothing left of her or the
two plastic one-gallon bottles. John Young would go
back to being James Michael Martin. If it didn't burn,
then it would mean he could be John Young forever, because she hadn't come for him. She might not have
been able to imagine that John Felker could have killed
Harry, or she might have gone to Medford and found
that he had never made it there, and believe for the rest
of her life that the four men had caught him. She rolled
out from under the vehicle and sat beside it. She could
feel the malevolence exuding from it now. A person
would have to feel a vast distance between himself and
anyone he planned to burn to death.

She wasn't looking at the work of someone who was
scared, a panicky person trying desperately to throw
barriers between himself and retribution. He had gone
over entirely. No, that was wrong; before she had even
met him he had been enlisted on the other side. He had
come to her for one reason only, pretending to be an innocent victim so that he could find a man who thought
he was a friend and cut his throat. She stared at the big
black vehicle to let it burn the last of her feelings for
John Felker away. As the sun disappeared over the top

of the mountains, the Bronco seemed to grow like a shadow.

Jane rolled back under it. She had only a half hour of light left after sunset and a lot to do. She opened the hood of the Bronco by reaching up from underneath to pull the cable to release the latch. She left the two bottles undisturbed. Instead, she unhooked the two battery cables and buried them at the foot of a bush ten paces away.

Then she found her canoe, dragged it to the edge of the water, and knelt beside it to check her equipment. She spent some time getting used to the rifle. The first one she had found that was suitable was a Winchester 70 XTR Standard 30-06 bolt action. It held five shots, and the receiver was tapped for scope mounts. It was heavy, seven and a half pounds without the Weaver K4 scope. The man at the store had told her that her husband would be very pleased.

She loaded the magazine and set the rifle on top of the nylon tarp in the hull in front of her seat and wrapped it once to keep it from catching drops from her paddle blade when she changed sides. Then she distributed the weight of the rest of her possessions as evenly as possible. She spent a few minutes staring out across big Tupper Lake to memorize the shape and took compass readings to help her find the outlet at the other end.

When the lake was obsidian-black and glassy, Jane pushed her little canoe into the shallows among the reeds, settled her weight into it, and began to paddle. She moved the canoe steadily along the quiet, calm water. She set the compass down on the hull in front of her and moved out from the shore to where she could see any flicker of light in the woods above it. The darkness was comforting now because she knew that somewhere deep in the forest, a man who had embraced the left-handed twin, the Evil-minded, was waiting for her.

25

J ane paddled steadily but quietly. She judged the distance from her starting point at Martin's hidden vehicle to the southern tip of big Tupper Lake to be ten or twelve miles. She planned to take three hours to get there, so she would reach the head of the lake about the time the moon rose. As the afterglow of the sunset disappeared, the swallows that had been skimming the surface of the lake for mosquitoes returned to their nests and she was alone.

She glanced down at her compass now and then as she got used to the little canoe. Six strokes on one side, then six on the other seemed to hold the canoe's course straight and to keep her arms from feeling the strain. The simplicity of the act of paddling and the quiet swish of the light craft gliding on the still water soothed her. She let her senses explore the world around her. Route 30 ran along the far side of the lake, so once in a while she would see a tiny glow of light from a cabin or a fishing camp across the water. The west side, where she paddled, was dark.

The chill of the evening had begun to settle on the mountains, a still, frosty mist that made the air that entered her lungs burn a little. After she made the bend in the lake and passed the distant lights of the little town of Moody, she saw nothing to mark the far shore. At this time of year there probably weren't many tourists, and the locals were locked in their houses recovering from the skiers, so the highway was already deserted.

She knew that he had come down this side of the lake, and she could visualize his passing if she allowed herself to reconstruct it. He had the kind of concentrated premeditation that seemed possible only to those who had given themselves over entirely to scheming. If he had parked the Bronco in the afternoon, he too probably had made this stretch of the journey at night. He was entering the last part of his trail that went near the places where even a sprinkling of people lived, where any roads had ever been.

She could hear the night whisper of the trees now that she had moved away from the roads. He had been born here. The North Woods could never represent safety to anyone who had been born here. He wasn't running to safety. He was running because he knew he could go farther and deeper into a dangerous place than the ones who were chasing him. It was like a taunt, not meant to discourage pursuers but to lead them farther and farther out until they were in a place where he was stronger than they were. It was a place where shots could be fired without falling on a human ear, where any number of people could die without their bodies ever being found.

Her grandfather had told her old Nundawaono stories. Sometimes the people they happened to had names, but usually they were just the Hunter or the Woman, and they always seemed to end up alone in the forest, as she was now, and the forest was alive with frightening beings. There were flying heads with long streaming hair that sailed through the air, always searching the ground for something to feed their voracious craving for flesh. She couldn't help feeling the hair on the back of her neck start to stand as she thought about the way she must look from above right now, alone in the middle of the empty lake, but she refused to turn her head and look over her shoulder.

Then there were the stone giants. When she looked to either side, she could almost see them stepping forward to free themselves from the camouflage of the bare rocky peaks of the dark mountains that surrounded her now, coming down to hunt her, their skin made of rock so she could not shoot them, and with such enormous strides that she could not outrun them. They were all supposed to have been killed off at Onondaga, a hundred miles south of here, except one, who still roamed the woods. That was the way the stories went: There was always one left, and it was the one her imagination could construct out of the shapes in the rocks above her right now.

The creature that had always struck her as especially horrible was the Naked Bear, because it had come too close to revealing overtly the secret of the stories. The secret was that the stories weren't true, but they weren't exactly imaginary, either. This was a bear, a creature whose nature was to kill people, but it wasn't just a bear. It was hairless, made to look like a human being, and it talked: "Ongwe ias"—I am the one who eats you.

The surface of the big lake was almost invisible. She paddled on, going faster now because the slight sweat she had raised by paddling helped to keep her cool and her arms felt limber and strong after an hour of the rhythmic sameness. Her strokes had lengthened and become sure. It had been a couple of years since she had been in a canoe, but now everything had come back, because even when the mind forgot, the synapses in the brain that controlled physical movement had been altered to hold the pattern forever.

The moon came up an hour later, but she still could not see the end of the lake. The paddling had already become unconscious, and she spent the time making herself firmer and stronger. Her grandfather's stories were cautionary tales: The lone hunter the woods devoured had made some mistake out here. A turned ankle or a case of dysentery or even a failure to see signs on a trail thirty miles from a road might as well be a bullet through the head. The thought made her afraid, but it was the right kind of fear, so she nurtured and studied it. The fear made her alert and cautious, aware of every sound. She felt the irises of her eyes opening wider, letting in more of the light from the moon that the black water reflected up at her. The people in the stories never survived by strength, only by cleverness. A human being was a small, fragile animal with skin that could be punctured and bones that broke. The only way to stay alive was to think clearly.

She stayed a couple of hundred feet from shore, where the tiny, almost imperceptible swish of the paddle would be difficult to hear and the shape of the canoe would be hard to separate from the shimmer of the surface of the lake. She studied every foot of the shoreline as she went, watching ahead for a faint glow, sniffing the air for the smell of smoke.

It was after midnight when she reached the southern tip of big Tupper Lake. The end was just a sense that the darkness had thickened in front of her. She paddled toward the shore through the standing reeds in the shallows that scraped quietly against the hull of her canoe, and passed along the shore until she found the inlet. It had been marked on the maps, but in the dark it was only a sensation that sounds were coming from farther back, not muffled, but open and alive. She had planned to camp here and wait for first light, but now that she had made it, she did not want to stop.

The river was slow and the banks thick with low trees and bushes. He had a three-day start on her. She tried to feel his presence ahead, but it seemed wrong. He wouldn't paddle this far, down to the tip of the big lake, and then stop a mile up the river. He would go on, farther from policemen, electric lights, and roads.

If she guessed wrong and he had stopped along the little river, then it would be better to come on him in the dark, when he might be asleep, than to swing around a bend in bright sunlight and find him waiting. She paddled on up the little river into the dark forest. The river was swollen with water from the melted snows above, but she could make slow headway by paddling hard and not letting the canoe glide. She threw herself into the work, watching the trees along the banks for signs and the water ahead for obstacles.

At three in the morning, she was stopped by a big old tree that had fallen into the water across the channel. She let the current carry her a few yards backward and then headed her canoe into the opposite bank. She pulled the craft up on the mud into the weeds and found a flat place in the trees to lay out her nylon tarp. She wrapped herself in her down jacket, rested her head on her backpack, and went to sleep with her hand touching the stock of the rifle.

Dawn came three hours later, with the chirping of chickadees and the rap of a woodpecker back in the woods. It was still blue half-light in the forest, but she found that objects around her were beginning to have clear edges. She sat by the side of the water to eat her packaged breakfast of dried beef and eggs. She had brought nothing that she couldn't eat uncooked, but she would have liked a fire now for the warmth. In the night she had kept up a sweat, but during the three hours of sleep she had stiffened and the cold and damp had settled on her.

When she had finished eating, she loaded her canoe and dragged it around the fallen tree, staring at the ground. There were no keel marks, no footprints. She launched her canoe and paddled to the opposite bank, then stepped ashore again. She walked to the place where the roots of the tree had lifted a piece of the bank and found no signs there, either. She widened her search until she found one. He had pulled his canoe up onto the bank at least a hundred feet downstream from the fallen tree trunk. He had caved in the bank a little to destroy his keel mark. Then he could only have walked into the forest. It took her a few more minutes before she found his footprint in the dirt: the ripple-soled hiking boots he had bought in Lake Placid. She moved ahead in the direction the toe was pointing, but she lost him again.

She walked back to the place where she had found the print. It was a single mark, a misstep maybe, but it was disturbing. There were no tracks going back: He had made only one trip. He had managed to pack all the gear and supplies he had bought onto his back, lift the canoe, and walk through the woods around the barrier. It made her feel small and weak and alone. He was so much bigger and stronger, and he wasn't using his size to make mistakes but to be more careful. He had started to walk long before a tracker would look for footprints, and gone into the woods instead of staying on the bank. The only reason she had found any mark at all was because she had known there had to be one.

She walked back to her canoe and stepped in. This time she didn't wrap the rifle in the tarp but kept it beside her as she pushed out into the stream and began to paddle. It was after 10:00 A.M. when she reached the mouth of the stream at Round Lake. As soon as she recognized what it was, she went back down the river a hundred yards, pulled her canoe up into the woods, and brought the rifle back with her. She hid in some bushes near the edge of the lake and scanned the shoreline through the rifle scope.

There was no smoke, no canoe, no sign of human life anywhere along the margin of the lake. She opened her map and studied it. There was a small circular road

marked 421 that went west at the other end of Round
Lake, leading to a little town called Sabattis and back.
After that, there was nothing. The logic of it said he
wasn't waiting for her here. He had started out in the
tourist spots, where strangers were a common sight, and
he had laboriously made his way down here. He wasn't
going to stop until he had left even that road behind
him.

Jane went back to her canoe and put it into the water
again. She spent the afternoon going across the lake and
down the stream to the bridge where the road crossed it.
She searched the area around the bridge for a half hour
but found no sign that he had been here, or that anyone
else had, either. She made it to the edge of Little Tupper
Lake in late afternoon and stopped to eat dinner and
watch the water. The lake was oblong like big Tupper,
formed by glaciers moving south and scraping the
mountains. She used the rifle scope to look for the usual
signs of life, and she began to feel a foreboding.

She had been paddling deeper and deeper into the
western reaches of the forest, away from the dramatic,
scenic peaks and the resort hotels built below them and,
finally, away from even the smallest roads. Now she
was at the edge of a five-mile lake, and it looked enormous, with thick forests beyond and jagged mountains
as a backdrop. The quiet was overwhelming. In the
night the quiet had seemed like a cloak to her, protecting her, but now in the clear, bright late afternoon it
seemed like an emptiness waiting for something to fill
it. She could hear birds in the forest and a buzzing
blackfly that kept making spirals in the air behind her
ear. Beyond those constant, unchanging noises there
was no sound. When she moved, the crunch of a twig
made her spine stiffen.

When she had come up here as a child with her parents, they had stayed on Cranberry Lake in a cabin and
fished and gone east to hike up Mount Marcy because

that was what tourists were supposed to do. But they had never left the marked trails. In those days the rangers used to tell people the Adirondacks were the oldest mountains on earth. Since then, the scientists had learned that they were young and still growing.

Today the part about growing made them seem alive, capable of at least that much intention and therefore almost sentient, but with a brutal kind of sentience: the blind, brainless reflex of monstrous stomach-turning sea creatures that lived in the dark and rose toward sounds so they could eat. She knew that what she was feeling was a form of agoraphobia. If she didn't shake it off, she was going to end up cowering somewhere, trembling and unable to take care of herself.

She waited for the blackfly to settle, then slapped at it but missed, and this only seemed to wake others. She pushed her canoe into the water and headed for the middle of the lake. She told herself she was doing it to stay out where the blackflies weren't swarming, but it was actually to stay in the open, away from the banks.

She camped for the night at the tip of Little Tupper. She forced herself to do what she knew she had to do. She picked out a package of dried food, read on the label that it was designed for a hearty meal, and ate all of it. She walked knee-deep into the icy water to bathe and wash her clothes, then hung them on a low limb to dry. At the end of it, she was exhausted. She made her tarp into a lean-to and fell into a deep sleep beneath it.

She was in dark emptiness for an hour, and then her mind began to work again. In her dream it was still night, but she became aware that there was a splash and then another and then a dripping sound. The splashes were footsteps. She sat up to reach for her rifle, but it wasn't there. She turned and looked at the lake. A man was coming up out of it, walking toward her, the water dripping off his clothes as he sloshed to shore. He walked up onto the bank and stood across the campfire

from her. For a moment she was angry at herself for
having built a fire, but then she remembered that she
hadn't. It had just come. Then she recognized the man:
He was Harry Kemple. He leaned down and warmed
his hands at the fire, and she could see steam rising
from the shoulders of his dripping suit.

"Harry!" she said. He didn't seem to pay any attention to her, so she yelled, "Harry! It's me!"

Harry looked up at her and then back down at the
fire. "What—you think this is some kind of coincidence? Like I'm going to be surprised to see you?"

"I'm sorry," she said.

He held up his hand and nodded wearily, the way he
used to. "No harm done." He bent closer to the fire.
"Jesus, it's cold out here."

"I'm sorry he killed you."

He shrugged and pointed to the place where the un-
dertaker had stitched up his throat. The sewing was
thick and crude, like the laces of a shoe. "It only took
about a minute."

"It was my fault," she said. He seemed to oscillate, as
though she was seeing him through water, and then she
realized it was her tears.

"Yeah," he said. "But it doesn't matter."

"What doesn't matter?"

"None of it. People are born and they die. What any
of them do in between doesn't look like much from a
distance. Viruses and rusty nails and people like Martin,
they're working all the time on the same side. Always
were, always will be. If they didn't exist, we'd die anyway." He scratched at his stitches gingerly, then looked
back down at the fire and rubbed his hands together.

Jane could sense that some new rule was in place.
Harry was waiting for her to ask the right question.
"Did Martin kill Jerry Cappadocia, too?"

He turned his head to look to the right and the left,

then at her. "Am I talking to myself, or what? I'm trying to tell you nobody gives a shit."

Maybe he needed to tell her something that nobody else could. A dead person wouldn't come if a living one could give the same answer. "Do you know who hired Martin to do it?"

Harry seemed angry. "Of course I do. You still don't get it, do you? What's it going to get you if I tell you the name of one more criminal you never met and will never see?"

"I'll get to know. That's what the mind is for. It has to know."

Harry rolled his eyes and sighed. "Jerry was a scumbag. I told you that years ago. Another scumbag just like him paid some money so he could take his place with some girl."

Jane gasped. "Lenore Sanders. The one who hired Martin was Robert Cotton. Of course. The reason nobody figured it out was that it never occurred to them that it wasn't about money and power. Cotton got the girl and nobody noticed."

"It doesn't matter," said Harry. "Nothing happened. Hanegoategeh, the left-handed twin, took Jerry off the count and Hawenneyu, the right-handed, replaced him. The Creator creates, the Destroyer destroys, and it goes on like that. It was a harvest. Bobby Cotton is ripening too."

Jane said, "What you're telling me is that it's just good and evil in this constant fight and that there's no outcome."

"Right. It's a wash. You're out here to get revenge, punish Martin. I'm telling you not to bother. I stopped caring when he got me. I'm just a dream." He looked up from the fire. "It's you I feel sorry for."

Jane began to feel afraid. "Why?"

Harry pointed off into the woods toward the next lake. "He's the real thing. Every time he kills somebody, it makes him stronger. He gets better at it—a little faster, a little less easy to surprise. He watches what we do to get away, how we try to fight back. Once he's seen anything, he knows how to beat it; and every time he gets somebody, that's one person who could have stopped him who can't anymore. I'm telling you, he's a monster. Killing me fed him."

"How can I turn a monster loose?"

Harry tugged at the laces on his throat. "Nice of you to think of that now, kid."

She stepped forward through the fire, but it didn't burn her. She put her arms around Harry. He was cold and hard, like a side of beef in a freezer, and she could feel the water squeezing out of his suit and soaking into her clothes.

Harry sighed, then said grudgingly, "He's going way back into the woods, as far as he can go. Make sure you see him before he sees you. Don't feed him again."

Then her arms closed, because there was nothing between them. Harry was at the shore already, walking back into the water, up to his knees, his waist, his chest, and then she could just see the top of his head for a moment before it disappeared, leaving a little ripple.

26

She awoke feeling cold and wet, just as the day was
beginning. She knew all of it now. Harry had told
her the answer to the question that the police and half
of the no-neck population of the Midwest had been asking for five years. She already had traced the conspiracy
all the way back to its source, but the words had not
come to her until she had imagined Harry saying them.
A criminal with a name she had never heard until a
couple of days ago had wanted Jerry Cappadocia's
girlfriend.

Harry had told her the first time he mentioned Lenore
Sanders, five years ago, that Jerry had a rival. Jane had
never considered what that meant, and she was not the
only one. Everyone who had heard the story of the mas-
sacre at the poker game had known immediately that
whoever had paid for Jerry's murder had to be another
criminal. He was a criminal by definition: A man who
hired killers to kill his enemy was a killer. It had not occurred to any of the others that the motive could be
anything except taking over Jerry's territory, because
that was what criminals did. But Bobby Cotton was a
criminal who lived in St. Louis. He had no practical
way of taking Jerry Cappadocia's holdings in Chicago,
so he never tried and never revealed himself. All he
had wanted was the girl.

Jane had been given all of the information she had
needed, but it had lain in a jumble in the back of her

mind until the dream. She should have wondered why St. Louis kept coming up. When Martin wanted to fool her, he had told her he was a cop from St. Louis. Why had he chosen St. Louis? It was because he knew the city and knew a lot of details about the cop who had arrested him there. But why had he been arrested in St. Louis in the first place? He had been there on business, killing somebody there. She should have known instantly that it was unlikely that anybody in St. Louis had been enough of an annoyance to Martin's usual customers in Chicago to make them send him down there. Martin may very well have been working for Cotton that time; he had at least come to Cotton's attention.

Harry had told Jane so much about the girl that she should have wondered what had happened to her. It was ironic that nobody had spent any time thinking about the girl in five years—probably since she showed up at the funeral wearing a black dress she had bought at Dennaway's. Most murders weren't about money. They were about love. Whenever the cops found a body, the first thing they did was go out to look for the wife or the husband or the lover. She opened her eyes, looked up at the sky, and held the story in her mind to determine whether it felt like the truth. Yes, she had put the issue to rest. She was satisfied that she knew what had happened five years ago. As Harry had warned her, it did her no good at all.

She looked out at the surface of the lake before she stood up. At first she thought she was just looking to be sure that Harry had only been a dream, but then she sensed that she had wanted to ask him something. It was something she had thought of after he was gone. There was something she had figured out after what Harry had said. She opened the map and looked at it, and it was as though her mind had been wandering across it as she slept. She looked at the string of lakes and was sure. She folded the map and set to work.

When she loaded her possessions and paddled up the next stream to Big Rock Lake, she knew he wouldn't be there. She knew that he wouldn't paddle on up the next stream to Bottle Lake, either. It was too small.

Martin had told her what he was going to do, if she just had the sense to read it. He had made a big deal out of lifting the canoe and walking around the parking lot with it before he would buy it. He was going to portage. Nothing else made sense. He wasn't going to take the easy way up the whole string of lakes. He was going to stop at Big Rock Lake, lift his canoe and all the provisions and gear he had bought, and walk through the woods with them to the next chain of lakes. He had put the roads far behind him, and now he was going to leave the water, too.

He was going to a place where there was no easy way, where his strength and his stamina would separate him from any likely challenger. He had passed here three days ahead of her—maybe four now—and he hadn't needed to go cautiously. He was wearing out his pursuers, so that when he met them he would have had four days to rest, hide his camp, and survey every inch of the surrounding country. Anybody who came after him would arrive with a canoe on his back that he had carried for miles, and would probably be in a state of exhaustion—fly-bitten, scratched, and half dead.

She looked at her map as she paddled. He would go west from Big Rock Lake to Charley Pond, then down into Lake Lila or even Lake Nehasane, and there he would stop and wait. He had come so far already that it was highly unlikely that anyone at all would follow. It was May, and the weather from now on would be tolerable, if not balmy. He had enough food to last for a long time, maybe into the summer if he was any good with the fishing gear he had bought in Lake Placid.

Jane Whitefield had spent ten years of her life hiding people. If a chaser was coming, usually he came hard

and fast. If you could disappear without leaving any
trail and stay hidden for two or three months, the
chance of ever being found dropped close to zero.
James Michael Martin had nothing to worry about from
the police. They didn't know he had killed Harry, and
weren't looking. He had little to fear from the friends of
Jerry Cappadocia, who wouldn't have any way to know
that he would come to the mountains. The only possibility he had to fear was that Jane Whitefield would
overcome her self-deception and be able to track him
this far.

She spent an hour looking for his trail up from Big
Rock Lake. She never found it. She tried to match his
premeditation. It was mid-afternoon. If she could make
the portage today and camp at the head of the chain, she
could start the day fresh and maybe even find him before he expected her to arrive. She considered hiding
the canoe in the woods and taking only the rifle and
pack, but another look at the map made her reject the
idea. The next chain of lakes was longer than the last,
and the woods here were old and thick. She would lose
time, and time meant exhausting her provisions and her
strength.

The portage was about ten miles on the map, but
there was no telling how long it would be on a winding
trail. She took an approximate compass heading, packed
her gear tightly, lifted the prow of her canoe, walked
under it until she could lift it, and set off up the bank
of Big Rock Lake to the west.

The canoe was light, and she had decided to travel
with only the gear that she could carry strapped to her
back. But the weight of it all together was seventy or
eighty pounds. She walked westward for an hour, then
set all of it down and lay on the forest floor, staring up
at the dappling of the sunlight far above on the translu-
cent leaves. At the end of fifteen minutes she slowly
raised her body, set the burden on her shoulders again,

and strained to lift the canoe. By the end of the second hour, she was staggering under the weight, her arms aching and her breaths labored and hoarse. She kept from looking at her watch while she rested, not wanting the rest to end.

Martin had been right. A person couldn't come four days into the forest without carrying four days' food, some fresh water, a canoe, and enough clothing to stave off hypothermia; and if she did, she had to carry it all on this portage. Some thug from Chicago would probably be lost by now, and begin to think about himself, not Martin.

Her footsteps converged with the deer run at four in the afternoon. It was narrow and went through glades and up hills, but it was clear. The hoofprints were usually obscured by the leaves, but the weeds were trampled down, and so it was easy to follow. She stopped now and then to glance at her compass, but it was difficult to tell on the winding trail whether most of the straight stretches tended to the west or the south. Finally, she put the compass into her pocket and trusted the deer. They would know how to get to water.

She had been on the deer run for a long time when she saw the second track. The deer path went down a little hill and crossed a small muddy patch, where their hoofs sunk two inches into it and a trickle of a stream ran. But among the marks of delicate cloven hoofs was the wide, deep imprint of the ripple-soled boot. He had found the deer run, too. Maybe he had known about it from the time when he was a teenager, and remembered.

She set down her gear and studied the print. It was difficult to tell how fresh it was because the constant flow of the little rivulet kept the mud damp all the time. She had a small feeling of dread that began to grow. If she followed the trail the rest of the way to the lake, there was a risk of coming on him somewhere ahead.

He would have seen the tracks too, and he might even be still-hunting, sitting in the brush with his rifle ready, waiting for the deer to come along this path that they had trampled with long use.

She dropped a leaf into the little stream and watched it float down to her left. She lifted her canoe and followed it. She kept her steps up along the crest of the hill, where she wouldn't leave a print in the mud, but kept the trickle in view. The going was harder because the constant supply of water had coaxed the brush to grow into almost impenetrable thickets wherever the ground was flat, but she managed to get around them and find the stream again and again. After a few hundred yards, the stream joined another and grew. It still wasn't big enough to float her canoe, but it was heading somewhere.

At last, as she was beginning to lose the sunlight, the stream emerged from the woods where she had hoped it would, where it had to, in the place where streams emptied: the nearest lake. She eased the canoe to the ground, slipped off her pack, and sat staring at the water. Somebody had named it Charley Pond, but there was no telling when or who Charley had been.

She stayed back in the trees and kept low to take in what she could see of the pond. He had been here. The track proved it. He had led her along a chain of four lakes, and now he might think he had gone far enough. From here on, he could be anywhere.

She had done all of her tracking with her mind. He had bought a canoe, so he must plan to travel by water. He had hidden the Bronco at the edge of big Tupper Lake, so she had followed. He had chosen a canoe that was light enough to carry, so he must plan to portage to the next chain of lakes. From now on she would not be able to do it by reasoning; she was going to have to rely on her eyes and ears.

Jane made her camp in a deep thicket a hundred

yards back from the lake. She finished just as the sun went down. Without artificial light or even a fire, she had now taken on the rhythm of the forest, and she lay down with the sun.

This time when she awoke it was late, nearly midnight. She lay still, but slowly touched the smooth stock of her rifle. She used the next two minutes to listen for the sound that had awakened her. There was a wind in the treetops, millions of leaves fluttering softly, but it felt cold. In another minute, she heard the first raindrops. She had chosen the thicket in the little hollow so she couldn't be seen, but it was a terrible place to be in a downpour. In the darkness she quickly hauled her gear up the slope to a spot under some tall trees, overturned the canoe, put the pack and rifle under it, stretched the nylon tarp from the canoe's gunwale to the lowest branch of the closest tree, and used the sling from the rifle to lash it there.

She curled up with the canoe over her like a shell as far from the open side as she could go. The rain came harder now, pelting down steadily. In the distance she heard the rumble of thunder. She lay there for a long time, not exactly comfortable, but not wet, and then she fell asleep.

Sometime in the night she woke up to loud thunderclaps and then she could see the next flash, lighting up the forest around her for a second, and then the crash came, shaking the earth. The storm kept on until three in the morning, until the rain slowed and then stopped. She rolled out from under her canoe, crawled out of the lean-to, and stood up. She had not caught much of the rain, but the moisture had leached up from the ground into her clothes and she was wet and cold.

When she saw the moon, she knew it was time to move. It took her only a few minutes to stow her gear, and then she lifted the canoe once again. She slipped and slid as she carried it down the slope, but then she reached the water. Once she was launched and paddling on the dark pond, she felt strong again.

27

Jane had paddled across Charley Pond and Lake Lila by five in the morning, and she was still paddling. Her clothes had dried and the old feeling of competence had returned. She began to look for a place to head in as soon as she entered Lake Nehasane. It was still dark, the lake overshadowed by thick forests that ran up a mountainside to the east, and the sky clouded over.

She began to search in earnest after a couple of hundred feet. While she looked for shelter, she didn't stop watching for the enemy. The rain had been hard enough to wash away any marks he had made in the woods, but it had also been hard enough to make him take some measures that he wouldn't have taken in clear weather. He might hang clothes or a bedroll out to dry, and it was cold enough now to make anyone want to build a fire.

She kept her rifle propped on the seat beside her, muzzle upward. The big hunting knife with the hollow handle was in her belt. Before long, she saw the place to pull the canoe out of the water. It was a low bank with big rocks on both sides. She was almost certain that Lake Nehasane was where he would be. It was a big oval with lots of depths and a complicated shoreline, and it was fed on the upper end by the outlet of Lake Lila and emptied on the other into the Stillwater Reservoir. It was big enough to have plenty of fish. The lures he had bought were for lake fishing—flatfish and poppers for bass and northern pike and sinkers for bait-casting in deep water.

She would go ashore and hide her gear in thick cover and wait. Sooner or later he would be visible somewhere along the shore or on the lake. After a few more minutes, she realized that she had misjudged the time a little. She could see that dawn was coming, so she paddled harder. She took a shortcut across open water and began to paddle with determination. As she reached and held her top speed, the silence exploded in her ears. The bullet hit the canoe with such velocity that she felt it swat the craft a few degrees to the side.

Jane ducked low, and the next shot gave a whip-crack sound before she heard the deep, echoing report of the rifle. As she reached out with her paddle to pull the canoe along, she looked down and saw the entry and exit holes of the first bullet, just below the waterline. The canoe was filling up.

The next shot shattered the left strut beside her leg. The canoe seemed to buckle and founder, and then she was sideways and going down. The canoe just listed to the side and scooped itself under. In an instant she was in water so cold it seemed to clap the breath out of her lungs. She gasped, and her legs kicked in a reflex to try to lift her body out of the water. The fourth shot hit ahead of her, smacked into the water and threw up a splash so close she could feel droplets on her face.

She ducked again, putting her head under, and saw the canoe sinking far down below, looking yellowish, then green, then brown as it slowly drifted into black depths. She held her breath and swam under the surface, her hands scooping the water and her legs pulling her wet boots in a clumsy frog kick.

She saw the next bullet from under the water. It shattered the mirror surface ahead of her, not there at all one second, and then a bright silver streak made of bubbles and speed, and then lost. She came up and broke into a freestyle, swimming as hard as she could, and then her hand hit rock. She hoisted herself out, and when her feet touched, she was running. The trees started six feet back from the rocks, and then she was among them, sprinting into the woods.

She ran hard, through brambles and thickets and across glades blanketed with ankle-high plants that could have been poison sumac or ivy, scrambling higher up the side of the hill. After a time she found herself far above the lake. She lay face-down on a big rock and looked back down the way she had come, but she could see no movement in the forest below her. Then she saw the canoe.

He must have been shooting from across the lake. He had gotten into his canoe and paddled to the place where she had run into the woods. He was drifting off-shore, scanning the woods and hills. Then she heard his voice. It made something in her reverberate. It was the voice she had listened to at Grand River and tried to make herself remember afterward, but now the familiarity of it made her feel sick.

"Jane!" he called. "It's me!"

She pressed her face against the rock, trying to disappear into it.

"I found your pack in the water. I didn't know it was you. Don't be afraid!"

She pushed herself backward on her belly and down behind some stunted pine trees, then looked down cautiously. His head was turned up toward the woods around the lake, looking for movement or color. She couldn't see her pack in his canoe, and she couldn't imagine how it could have floated back up, but she did see the binoculars. He lifted them off the floor of the canoe and began to search the hillside. She dropped to her belly again and slithered away from the rocks into the trees.

In a moment he would land and come for her on foot.

She stood and ran again. The ground was slippery from the rain and every step was uphill. There was no doubt that he would follow, and she knew she was leaving tracks. She had to go for distance now, just paces that she could put between them. The trees and brush seemed to grab at her and hold her back, and at every clear space she could almost feel the crosshairs settling between her shoulder blades.

It must have been an hour later when she stopped to catch her breath. She lay down with a stitch in her side and limbs that felt like stone. She was too tired to think, but she listened and stared into the woods she had come from, trying to gasp for air without making noise.

Then the voice reached out to her again. "Jane!" he called. "You're making a mistake!"

She held her breath and then realized that she had to go on, and she needed to keep breathing hard to do it. Hiding would just give him time to catch her. "You're alone, with no food or water!"

She sprang to her feet and ran on, higher into the woods. At noon she was at the peak of the mountain. It was bare rock, nearly at the tree line, with only scraggly pines to hide her. She moved along the ridge, trying to see him coming. If only she could find a hiding place, a cave or something. But there was nothing up here that would hide a rabbit. She started down the far slope, then rested again when she reached the heavy growth of leafy trees below.

Then she saw him. He was up on the summit exactly where she had stood, and he was combing the valley below with the binoculars. Above his shoulder she could see the barrel of the rifle and the sling across his chest.

She moved down lower on the mountainside. For once, he wasn't lying. She had already pushed herself to exhaustion, and she hadn't eaten or had water since midnight. In about four or five hours the mountain air would turn cold, and she was dressed in wet clothes. Even if he didn't find her, she was going to be in trouble.

But he was carrying a pack and rifle and ammo and binoculars. All she had left to weigh her down was the knife in her belt. She could take advantage of her loss and try to outrun him. They had both been moving fast through the woods for hours now, up a fair-size mountain. If she was this tired, he must at least be feeling the strain.

Jane slipped deeper down into the forest, controlling her breathing now, stretching her legs, and shaking her arms to loosen the tightness in her back and chest as she broke into a trot. The going was easier now, all downhill, so she ran harder, trying to keep her momentum from building out of control and making her turn an ankle. She took no care to hide or stay quiet, only to build up her speed. She ran for fifteen minutes and then came to a rocky, clear streambed. She could tell it had filled up in the rain the night before because the banks were muddy, but now it was shallow again. She sloshed into it, and then realized it could help her. She rushed upstream thirty feet and took a dive up the bank to the right, a belly flop into the mud. Then she pulled her knees in and got to her feet and walked down backward into the streambed.

She looked at her work. It wasn't bad. It looked as though she had gone up the bank, slipped, and gone on to the east. She cupped her hands and drank deeply from the stream, then hurried on downstream a hundred feet before she found a place where there were three stones she could use as steps, back up into the woods to the west.

She concentrated on picking up the pace again, her eyes always searching the forest ahead for the next twenty yards that would afford a foothold and her legs lengthening her strides to take them as quickly as possible.

She ran on for two hours before she found a rocky outcropping, like a shelf near the top of the next mountain. She gained it, chose north, and picked up her speed again. This was the place to lose him, while darkness was coming and there was nothing to retain her tracks. After half a mile, the rock and the sunlight both ran out. She kept going into the dusk until she found a huge thicket of thorny bushes in a hollow.

As night fell, she went down on her belly and crawled into the thicket below the level of the thorns and foliage. When she was fifteen feet into the middle of it, the bushes were taller and older, the spaces between them wider, and she could make better progress. She crawled another thirty feet before she found a patch of weeds. She rolled over and over on them until they were flat, then curled up, consciously relaxed each aching, strained muscle, and lay there for a moment with her eyes open. It made her feel dizzy and light to lie there staring into the darkness, as though she were floating.

The dream started as soon as she closed her eyes. She still couldn't see anything, but she could feel that she was being held. She was in her mother's lap, lying against her breast, her face on the soft silk, where she could smell the perfume. She could feel the smooth, strong hands gently stroking her back. "Mama?" she said.

"Shush," came the whisper. "Go to sleep, Janie. You need your rest." Her mother's voice began to hum to her softly, tunelessly.

Jane whispered, "How did you come?"

"I'm not out there anymore, Jane. I'm inside you now, and my mother is inside me, and her mother is inside her, all the way back. We're all here, just like those Russian dolls, one inside the other."

"What am I going to do, Mama?" Jane could hear her own voice, and it was the voice of a child.

Her mother treated it like the question of a child. She held her, rocked her, and said distantly, "Whatever you can, dear." Then the voice came from farther away, as though her mother were holding her out to look at her. "Are you hungry?"

"Yes," said Jane.

"You should eat," said her mother. "In the morning. But now you need to sleep."

"He's coming for me."

"Yes, he is," her mother said. "That's why you have to lie still now."

Her mother's arms held her and rocked her back and forth, back and forth. "You'll always be my baby girl." She began to hum again, the low, breathy sound that had always put Jane to sleep.

28

It was after midnight when she heard him on the rock shelf above her. He walked without trying to muffle his footsteps, and then he stopped and shouted, "Jane! I know you can hear me!"

She sat up, her heart pounding. She had forgotten where she was and a thorn jabbed into her back. She winced and slowly bent down again. She could feel the thorn slipping out, and then her shirt was wet in the back.

"Jane!" he called from up the mountainside. "You're not going to lose me. I was born up here. I can track you longer than you can run." He waited, probably listening to hear her breaking from a hiding place and running, then called, "I don't want to hurt you." There was another pause, and now he said, "You've got to understand. I can't let somebody who hates me run around loose in the woods where I can't see her." She could hear him walking along the ledge now. Whether he was just shouting into the woods and was trying to send his voice in every direction or had seen her and was trying to get a better angle for a shot, she had no way to tell. "All you have to do is come in, and you can have food, water, everything. I'll only tie your hands when I'm asleep."

Jane felt the heat well up from her belly and move up her spine to her throat. She wanted to scream out at him, but that was what he wanted, too. She clenched her teeth and stayed still. It was like a hot iron pressed against her skin. She had taken him into hiding out of pity. He had used her, and done so with a cold, efficient detachment because he could—because she had let him. Now he didn't even have to make up a nice lie anymore.

She was cold, wet, dirty, and hungry in a place where those conditions weren't just discomforts but could kill her. He offered what?—to make her his slave in exchange for scraps of food and a chance to lie by the fire? It occurred to her he might not even be lying. It might appeal to him to keep her alive for a time, maybe for the whole summer, while he waited.

Then, some evening in September the sky would turn iron-gray and there would be frost on the ground in the morning. It might be a quick bullet in the head while she was still sleeping—tied up to sleep, he had said. More likely it would be a knife across her throat, the way he had done Harry. Winter would be coming and he would have to leave the mountains. Maybe he would explain it to her first: You have to understand. I don't want to do this, but I can't set a woman who hates me loose in the world.

Then she saw the beam of his flashlight stab into the darkness. It was incredibly bright, racing quickly across the expanse of forest. Wherever it passed, the trees lit up and threw huge shadows behind them that moved. She ducked down again and pressed her face into the dirt.

In a moment the beam passed and went out. She kept down, not daring to move. After a long time she heard his voice again, this time from farther away along the rock shelf. "Jane! I know you can hear me! I don't want to hurt you ..."

Slowly, she crawled to the edge of the thicket, slithered out on her belly, and rose to a crouch. There was no way she could run through these woods in the darkness, so she began to walk. She had lost her compass, but now and then she could see the sky through the trees, and at some point the clouds would clear and she would be able to find the north star. She walked through the woods, not sure of the direction she had been going, not planning now, just covering ground. She knew that he would not give up. He had no reason to stop looking until he found her body. He could keep tracking her for weeks. She could be dead in two or three days.

The clouds didn't clear. Instead, the cold wind penetrated her light shirt, bringing with it big icy drops that slapped the leaves and exploded into mist. After that, the body of the storm arrived overhead. The rain came down in an avalanche of water, plastering her wet clothes to her skin and making the trail muddy and the stones slippery.

She walked into the wind because it usually came from the west or the northwest, and because she knew that this was one thing that would be as hard for him as it was for her. She went on for hours. She was shivering, and her hands began to feel numb. At last, when she climbed onto a flat place in the middle of a grove of tall, thick trees, her foot slipped out from under her and she fell.

The ground was wet and spongy, but it didn't feel cold anymore. She rolled over onto her back and lay there. It felt good. She hadn't known how good it was going to feel. She knew she was going to have to get up, but not now.

This time when she dreamed, she felt her mother's lap again. She wanted to stay there on the soft, smooth fabric, feeling the hands petting her to sleep. But then she heard something. It was a voice, harsh and hoarse. She looked up and saw, far above her in the sky, the tiny shape of a man falling. He was hundreds of feet above her, turning over and over as he fell, and he was screaming. She said, "No. No, not this." She closed her eyes tightly, but it didn't make any difference. Her eye-lids were clear.

Her father was plummeting downward at incredible speed, but the distance was so great that he just kept falling, minute after minute. She watched him, trying to will him to stop, to make the air under him thicken and hold him, but it didn't work. It never worked. She was as terrified as he was, looking down at the ground and feeling his sensation of falling. She held her breath as he came faster and faster.

Now she could see him clearly. He was the way he always had been, dressed in a soft, worn red cotton shirt and a pair of washed-out blue jeans. He was coming head-first, his arms outstretched and his mouth wide open. He seemed to be looking into her eyes as he fell. Jane went rigid, pressed her fingers over her eyes, and braced herself for the impact.

She could hear the wind now, hissing past him and making his clothes flutter and flap. Something strong forced her hands apart as it always did, to make her see him die. Just as he was about to knife into the weedy plateau where she lay, the sound of fluttering seemed to increase, and he swung upward again, so close to her that she could feel the wind in her face.

He soared up into the sky, and she could see that he was changing. His arms were outward from his shoulders, and they were black and had long feathers. He flapped them, and it made the same wind sound, and he shot upward as quickly as he had fallen. He rose higher and higher until she couldn't see the red shirt and the jeans anymore. He was just a black shape against the bright sky. He gave a loud cry, not a word but a shout, as though he were calling to her.

She heard another voice answer him. It was harsh and hoarse like his, and it seemed to be coming from over-head. She opened her eyes, and it was daytime, and her father was gone. She looked up at the crow. He was big, perched on a limb near the top of the tree maybe sixt feet above her head, riding on the leafy end of a branch as it bobbed up and down in the morning sunlight. He called, "Gaw," and another crow flew in, his wingspan at least two and a half feet. The sun shone on their feathers so they looked as though they had been combed with a viscous oil that put blue-purple-yellow highlights over the coal-black. She must have heard them in her sleep and invented a dream to incorporate the noise.

The crows looked friendly to her, benign. She watched them without moving until she could tell them apart. She sat up slowly and glanced around her at the other trees, and saw more crows above and streaks of white crow shit on some of the tree trunks. There were bits of wet, downy feather here and there in the weeds. She had managed to stumble into the middle of a rookery in the night. They had found her there and decided she was not a threat.

Crows posted sentries higher up than she could climb, with eyes so sharp they could see a leaf move from a thousand yards off. That was what her two friends were doing up there. If the killer came anywhere nearer than that, the cry would go up. She stood up slowly and quietly, so the sentries would not be alarmed by the prone figure popping up.

She said quietly, "Thanks, Daddy," to the crows, not because they would magically know what she meant, but because it would help them get used to the fact that she would be making sounds and moving around.

Jane now saw things with a mad clarity. So much came into her mind that she could only acknowledge that it was there, and not go over it step by step. She had been trying to fight against the enemy and the woods at the same time. She had accepted his terms of battle: that they would go deep into the wilderness and bring with them the equipment of civilization—guns, tents, boats, and compasses. Whoever brought the most and the best had the advantage. He was bigger, stronger, faster. He had all the food and the warm clothes. He had let the journey use up everything she could carry, and let the chase wear her down to nothing.

The crows had reminded her. She didn't have to think like a frightened, half-starved white girl lost in the woods. She didn't have to invent a way to escape, or invent anything at all.

She spent a few minutes under the tall trees collecting a handful of coal-black wing feathers, ten inches long, that had fallen to the ground from the limbs above. Then she went for a walk, looking around her for the right kind of tree. She found one at the edge of the next clearing. It had that special smooth, grayish bark that had always reminded her of an elephant's legs. When she touched the trunk it was hard and cold like granite. It was definitely genus Carpinus: ironwood. She stepped back and stared up at the limbs. She found the right one in a few minutes. It was ten or twelve feet up, and the wind had broken it off at the joint and the knot had come with it. The limb was at least four inches thick and fifteen feet long. She looked around for a way up, but there was none.

Jane remembered a night in Los Angeles years ago. She had been driving along a freeway at two o'clock in the morning, and she had seen a boy climbing up a metal signpost beside the pavement so he could spray graffiti on the exit sign. He had put his belt around the pole, held both ends in his hands, and walked up. Jane took off her belt, slung it around the smooth trunk, and tried it. She was up in a few seconds, touching the limb. She got her hands around it and walked herself along it, hand over hand, until she had bent it to the ground. Then she patiently pushed and pulled and walked with it until it tore off and fell at her feet.

It took her half an hour just to carve through the limb

with her knife. The wood was incredibly heavy, close-grained and hard. But as she worked she got better at it, and learned to split off long strips at a time from the handle of her ga-je-wa. The knot at the end she carved into a lump about four inches in diameter, and she had curved the handle in toward it a little, tapering the handle slightly and flattening it like a blade.

After two hours of carving, it was a little over two feet long and looked like a slightly cruder version of a war club she had seen in the New York State Museum in Albany. She tested it by thumping the ground a few times, then practiced swinging it. The shape gave it a kind of hammer force, and it was rock-hard and heavy. She stuck it in the back of her belt as the Nundawa warriors used to carry theirs. The ga-je-wa would not make her Martin's equal, but it would make close combat a different kind of experience for him.

She resumed her walk, listening to the birds for the right kind of call. The one she needed was different from the deep-woods birds'. Those all made some metallic, low-register *thunk* or *vit* or *whit*. She walked and listened for a warble. When she heard it she walked toward it, and came out into a mountain meadow. The thrushes, birds like the robins at home, might eat a lot of things, but right now they would be looking for the first berries. She walked the margin of the meadow until she found them. There were wild strawberry plants growing in a patch on the east side of the meadow, where the sun was the strongest. It took her some time to find enough that had turned red, but she ate the green ones too. They were hard and tart, but they wouldn't kill her. She found rain water collected in some of the lower parts of the meadow and drank from the puddles.

As she crossed the meadow to look at some bushes that might be blackberry plants, she almost stepped on the antler in the weeds. It was big—what hunters called an eight-point rack—but this was only half of it. When she picked it up, she could imagine the scene. The snow was probably still on the ground when mating season started. Two bucks had fought here until one of them had broken this antler. The other had gotten the does, and this one had gone off to sulk and grow a new one. She stuck it into her belt with the war club.

The blackberry bushes were something else she couldn't identify, and whatever they were, they didn't have berries, but beyond them she found the stand of hickory and maple trees. She took a great deal of care looking for saplings of the right size. She needed ones that had grown straight because they were out in the sun and not stunted or interfered with by their overarching parents.

When she found some, she took out her knife and began to cut, strip, and shape them into ga-no. They needed to be three feet long and so perfectly round and straight that she could roll them between the palms of her hands without detecting a shimmy in the tip. When she had prepared fifteen of them, she set them aside and went to work on the wa-a-no. It was a hickory sapling an inch and a half thick, with a slight natural bend. She made it four feet long and carved bits of it off until she could just bend it with all of her weight. Then she started to work on the bowstring.

Inside the handle of the survival knife were some fishhooks and two hundred feet of monofilament line. She cut three lengths of the fine, transparent fishing line, tied them to a standing sapling, and braided them the way she braided her hair, because it was the only way she knew. When she had braided three strands of three, she braided those three braids, ending up with a nine-threaded string that had a little thickness and body. It took all of her strength to string her bow.

She stopped to listen to the crows in the rookery, and after a time she was satisfied that Martin was not close enough to hear her work on the antler. She found two heavy rocks and used one as a hammer and the other as an anvil to break it. Then she found that by using the knife as a chisel and the war club as a hammer, she could chip pieces from the base that were sharp and roughly triangular, then carve an indentation on each edge. If she split the tips of the arrows a little, she could slide the arrowheads in and tie them in place with the fishing line.

She took the crow feathers and cut them along the quill so the wider side came off in one piece. She feathered her arrows in the Seneca fashion, two lengths of feather tied on with a spiral twist, so they would spin in flight. The trick was to glue both sides in place with a little sticky pine sap so they would stay put while she tied them with the fishing line.

Jane stood up, nocked the first of her arrows, pulled back the string of the bow, and let it fly at a big maple across the meadow. It revolved in flight like a rifle bullet and sank deep into the bark. When she was in college, she had thought how odd it was to give young women physical-education credit for practicing the way Stone Age men had killed bears. Now it seemed odd to her that she had not really known how to use a bow until a Japanese-born instructor had taught her. She had told people she had chosen archery because the only other class that fit her schedule was golf. Now she admitted to herself she had known that it was because the bow reminded her of her father, making her little arrows and letting her play in the back yard with them when she was about ten. She had missed him all the time in college, and it had helped her to feel close to him.

Jane walked to the tree and tried to tug her arrow out, but she found it was in deeper than she had expected. She took her knife and dug it out, then went back to put a new bone tip on it. She was a lot better at this than she had imagined. The old wa-a-no had been made with such a strong pull that most European men who met the

Iroquois couldn't bend them without practice, and probably no woman at all could have done it. But she had made hers a foot longer and more supple than the old ones in the museums.

She took the knife, cut the legs off her jeans, tied one at the bottom, and made it into a quiver to carry her fifteen arrows. Part of the other leg she made into a strap to hold the quiver on her back, and the rest she tied around her waist as a sash to hold her war club, the way the old warriors had done.

She cut five more saplings to length for extra arrows and shoved the remaining pieces of the deer antler into the bottom of her quiver to hold it open. She looked about her for a place to preserve the last five long crow feathers. She found that the only place where they wouldn't get bent was in the band that held her hair in a ponytail, so she stuck them in and let them hang downward at her back. She stopped and looked up at the sun. It was late afternoon now. She had spent the whole day remembering and making while the crows kept watch.

When she walked away from the mountain meadow, she found that the forest had changed; she could see in it now. The foliage wasn't just a green wall anymore. It was complex and comprehensible. This was the last remnant of the great forest that had covered all of the land of the Hodenosaunee and beyond. Maybe it made sense to walk in it now, to see that it was still intact, holding the seeds of the same plants that could spread and sprout again after she was gone.

In the old times, the men had come out here prepared with a song about how they weren't afraid. It was for when they were being tortured, to spit their last breath at the enemy so he would fear the ones who came after: "I am brave and intrepid. I do not fear death or any kind of torture. Those who fear them are cowards. They are less than women . . ."

It was as though this had been meant for her, and it made her feel light and small and weak. Killing was what men did, but she was the only Seneca in the forest and she would have to be the one.

29

S he moved deeper into the forest below the meadow, where the glaring evening sun hit the foliage at a low angle to make leaves glow and sink shadows into near darkness. This stand of trees was old, not replanted with one species. Each kind took its small niche and grew there. The collar of pine trees at the top of the mountain merged into the birch, maple, hemlock, slippery elm, and hickory down lower. Where the dirt beneath was deep and the thousands of years of rotting leaves and the mineral water runoff from the peaks had gathered, the trees grew tall and the taproots sunk deep. This group of maples was old and thick, this elm grove had taken hold late, the seeds maybe blown here in a storm twenty years ago, maybe carried here in a deer's belly and dropped undigested in the right place.

The world she had lived in before, the cement, houses, and roads, wasn't any different from this. It was wilderness, too. The planet Earth was a place where the lone hunter made his way through the wild country. There was something out there that wanted the hunter dead, and he had to defeat it or be killed by it.

The hunter's name never changed. In the language that Jane knew best, the hunter's name was "I." As she stalked through the forest, doing her best to slip between the trees without moving a branch, to step on the damp, soft forest floor where dry twigs would not crack, she became the hunter. She could not see herself, turn her eyes around and be frightened by the fact that she was only a slender girl walking alone on the deer run. She could only see where she was. What she was doing made her who she was. Her eyes, watchful, cautious, and alert, saw the trail ahead and the sky above.

As her mind projected more and more of its will and attention outward into the hunt, she obliterated Jane Whitefield. The hunter was tall, with long, naked brownish legs made strong and quick by years of running. The hunter's eyes had sharp, clear vision that could detect movement beside the path ahead and ears sensitive, after so many days in the forest, to any sound that wasn't exactly as it should be. The hunter was shrewd and had fought many times against opponents who were bigger and stronger in other parts of the wild country that didn't look like this.

Now the lone hunter slipped quietly through the North Woods, doubling back in a path parallel to last night's run. Lake Nehasane was five or six hours away, and the hunter accepted the distance and traveled patiently, always thinking. The simple tactic of coming on the enemy in the woods and beating him in a hand-to-hand fight was not possible this time. The enemy had more upper-body strength than the hunter had, and a longer reach. Approaching the enemy across an open space would mean quick death because the enemy had the only rifle in the world right now.

She thought about the ways of using the forest. The Hodenosaunee had come here to hunt bears in the winter. They had come up on snowshoes, sometimes chasing the bear, sometimes goading it into chasing them. They moved quickly on top of the deep drifts while the bear floundered along, sinking in deep and finally exhausting its enormous strength. The old hunters had sometimes built V-shaped fences in the forest and driven herds of deer in toward the center to the narrow tip, to be slaughtered. They had also perfected a deer trap, using a bent sapling and a rope, so the deer would be hoisted in the air with the rope around its hind legs. None of those ways would work on an enemy like this one.

She walked all night, accepting the fact that there was no food. This time the warrior had a slight advantage from inhabiting a female body. The body was smaller and lighter and needed fewer calories just to move around, and had more reservoirs of stored fat among the muscles and sinews, because it was built to endure, to bear and feed children even when food was scarce. She found more berries in secluded copses in the woods, and chewed the leaves plucked from trees along the trail to stave off hunger pains, and drank from the streams. The warrior's body had been inured to fasting by the discipline of years of fitting a size-twelve body into a succession of size-ten dresses.

When it got to be too dark to travel, she lay down near the path and slept until dawn. She stood up and walked on, always quiet, alert, and careful. She walked for the whole day, and as she did, she sometimes saw the places where she had fought her way through thick bushes, breaking branches and leaving tracks.

It was early evening when she made her way around the shoulder of the last mountain and looked down on Lake Nehasane. In the woods she painted her skin and stained her clothes with a green solution of ground moss, making stripes on her legs and arms like camouflage. When she came upon the residue of the enemy's campfire on the rock shelf where she had once cowered at hearing his voice, she took some charcoal and streaked her face.

She looked down on the enemy's camp on the opposite shore of the lake and studied it. The murderer had moved his tent to a stretch of shore in the center of an open space where there were no trees or brush to afford a stalking ground. The canoe was far up on the shore with the tent, where he could protect it.

Then she saw him. He emerged from a path near his camp, walked to his fire pit, and dropped an armload of wood. He carried his rifle in his other hand and a hatchet in his belt. He set the rifle aside and knelt down to build his fire, banking the wood to last the night, but she could see from the attitude of his head that he wasn't even looking at it. He was watching and listening for her. He was at least eight feet from the rifle. He was tempting her. He had known that she would come back, because she was tired and cold and hungry. He was trying to make her come in and sprint for the gun. He knew exactly how a desperate, frightened person thought. He didn't know because he had been one himself, but because he had made a living out of tracking and killing them. She turned away into the sheltered leaves of the forest and started to make her way around the lake toward him.

The sun was behind the western mountain when she found the place in the forest that she had been looking for. She had imagined it while she was walking and had kept going through the woods until she found it.

She used the knife and the deer antler as scrapers and dug the hole five feet wide and as deep as she could before she hit bedrock. She used her five spare arrow shafts as the frame to hold the branches and matting of grass to cover the hole. She attached the fishing line to the eight hooks and hung them carefully six inches apart from the overhanging limb of the hemlock tree. She tested the height again and again. It had to be perfect.

Then she walked back thirty feet along the trail, bent a sapling almost double, and tossed some leaves over the path beside it to make it look like a deer trap. She judged that thirty feet would give him the time to think, even running at full speed. She calculated where to leave her bow. When she had finished her work, she went through the forest making V marks with her knife in the bark of the biggest trees to mark the trail.

In the darkness just before dawn, she climbed to the side of the mountain to take another look at the camp. When she was satisfied that he was asleep, she took one last look up at the sky, where the stars were already beginning to fade. Life was good and precious, and she was glad that she had never needed to be told that it was. Many Seneca warriors had died alone in the wilderness like this. There were probably some lying unburied all around her now.

She made her way to his camp, floating like a wisp of smoke through the forest without moving a leaf or dislodging a stone. At the dark edge of the camp a few feet from the tent, she lay on her belly and watched, a shadow inside a shadow.

She listened for the sound of his breathing. She had heard it, lain awake beside him listening to it, watching over him and hoping he would survive. Now, as she listened, she heard it again, but it wasn't right. It wasn't coming from the tent. She slowly turned her head to follow the sound. He was sleeping in the woods behind the canoe, waiting for her to try to kill him in the tent. He would have some kind of alarm to wake him when she tried so he could come out of hiding and shoot her.

She considered for a moment. He had to see her, and when he did, she would have to be doing something he understood, or he might react unpredictably. She crawled to the front of the tent, took the last of her fishing line, and tied it to the zipper on the door flap. Then she crawled back to the edge of the woods, almost at the start of the trail she had blazed.

She gave a strong tug on the line and the zipper moved and started to come down when there was a deafening *Barroom!* and the front of the tent blew outward, with a three-inch hole in it. Jane leaped into the air at the sound. It was a spring gun. He had another gun! She took a step toward the tent, but her mind settled again. Either a spring gun worked when it was set off or it didn't. You wouldn't load the shotgun with more than one shell.

She whirled and saw him. He was coming to his feet, his hair tousled the way it had been in the mornings at Grand River, and she almost called out to him. But the rifle was in his hand and was coming up. His eyes were cold and dead and certain.

She pivoted on her toes and dashed through the space in the bushes just as the rifle cracked. The shot hit somewhere behind her. She had laid out the path carefully to wind through the thickest part of the woods, so there would be no second shot. She had sighted along the trail and made sure there was no straight stretch that was long enough to allow him to stop, aim, and shoot before she turned again and placed a rock or a tree between them.

She ran hard now, sprinting from one marked tree to the next, digging the balls of her feet into the dirt and pumping her arms. She could hear him on the trail behind her, running as hard as she was, his feet hitting harder and louder than hers, determined to get her this time. As she listened, she began to be afraid. She could tell that she had underestimated his speed; he was gaining on her.

She tried to go faster, making her strides longer to pass each mark and take the next turn. At the big sycamore she couldn't take the turn without falling, so she went into a slide on her side to push off the root with her foot and dash up the next corridor toward the rocky outcropping ahead.

At last she was on the path, running up the little incline between the jagged slabs of stone, then into the chute that the two long rock shelves formed. There was another shot, which went over her head, but she was in the stretch now. She could see the bent sapling. When she reached it, she took a jump and ran on.

Thirty feet farther on, she glanced over her shoulder and saw him appear between the stone outcroppings. She took two steps, put her head down, and leaped over the covered pit. She hit the path hard and let her momentum push her to the right into the brush.

She rolled behind the rock, picked up her bow and the arrow that she had left fitted to the string, turned, and cautiously looked above the rock through the leaves of the bush.

He was coming hard, charging toward her, the gun in both hands across his chest. She could tell from the look on his face that he had seen the bent sapling. He was sure he had spotted a trap and stepped over it without breaking stride. But the confident, almost amused look wasn't for the sapling. He had seen her leap over the spot where the pit was dug. His eyes were on the path. He was going to jump over the pit.

She pulled the bowstring back, straining to hold it steady. She listened for his footsteps: louder and louder and then a stutter-step. He was timing his approach to push off into the air. Through the leaves she saw the enemy's eyes. They were on the narrow path, down on the matting covering the pit. With his size and his strength, the jump was going to be easy. He kept his eyes on the pit as he launched himself into the air, higher than he needed to.

As he reached the top of his arc, the hooks caught him. Jane saw the upper part of his torso abruptly jerk backward and a look of horror contort his features. His momentum made five of the fishing lines go taut, and the bough of the tree above him bent, then tugged back, pulling him upright. His breath was sucked in with a whistle.

Her right hand released the bowstring. The arrow streaked through the air and made a *thunk* as it struck

him. He gave a harsh, loud shriek of pain. She nocked
another arrow and pulled the string back. She had time
to see the black feather of the first arrow sticking out of
his shoulder as she released the second.

He was straddling the shallow pit, holding himself
upright to keep the hooks from going deeper into his
face and chest and trying to claw at the arrow shaft
when the second arrow struck his right leg.

The wounded enemy grunted in rage, swatting the arrows out of his shoulder and thigh, where they had penetrated the fabric of his clothes. He dropped his rifle,
pulled his knife from his belt, and slashed wildly at the
fishing lines. She aimed her third arrow for his chest. It
flew straight, but he ducked down just as it came so that
it glanced off his back and sailed into the forest.

She dropped to the ground and began to crawl when
the enemy grasped his rifle. The woods echoed with
shots. He fired wildly, shooting into bushes in her direction as rapidly as he could. Two shots, three more, four
this time. She lost count as a bullet bit into the bark of
the tree a foot above her head. There was silence again,
and she used the time to retreat quietly up the trail a
few paces, then slip off into the deep brush. She was in
trouble. The arrows weren't getting through the thick
down jacket. It was like armor. She kept going silently,
trying to move farther into the brush.

He was enraged now, and he was free. The arrows
weren't doing enough damage, and the fishhooks had
only nettled him. He could still kill her, and the pain
would make him desperate to do it this time.

Then she heard the scraping sound and stopped. He
was climbing up on the stone outcropping that had been
meant to keep him in. He was a little hurt but not at all
incapacitated. In a moment he would be on top, and he
would see her and the rifle bullet would explode
through her body. She slipped behind a tree trunk. She
couldn't wait here, hiding until he found her. Jane's

hand trembled as she fitted the arrow onto the string and leaned against the tree. The bow wasn't powerful enough. She hadn't been strong enough to use one that could penetrate that padded jacket. "They are less than women." She felt anger rising in her chest. She was going to die; she had been doomed from the moment he had heard her name from poor Harry. The injustice of it stung her, and her chest tightened with hatred as she decided how to deny it. She stepped out from behind the tree into the open and held her bow downward, the arrow ready. She turned to the side as though she didn't know he was up there and was waiting for him to come up the path. She gave him a profile to aim at.

Out of the corner of her eye she saw him reach the peak of the ten-foot boulder. She saw his face turn toward her. Then, quietly, he stood up and the rifle started its steady rise to his good shoulder.

She was already half turned, and she raised the bow quickly. In her anger she pulled the arrow back until the bone tip touched her knuckle. She stared back into his eyes. In a second the right eye would reach the rifle sight. The left eye was already beginning to close, and next the gun would roar. Her fingers loosed the arrow.

It flew upward with a hiss, the feathers spinning. When it hit, she heard a *chuck*. The rifle fell, the hands shot upward and gripped the place where the arrow had gone in, just where the zipper sides came together below his neck. He sat down on top of the rock and his balance seemed to leave him.

He began to slide, reaching ahead of him for the rifle. She pushed off and ran toward him. It was at least twenty paces, but she was charging now, dashing along through the calf-high vegetation to get there before he could pick up the gun. She didn't know when her hand went behind her to grip the handle of the heavy war club. When she got there his hand was on the rifle and it was coming up again. She swung the war club with all her might into the back of his skull. She heard the crack of bone and saw his head slump forward. When she swung the club into his skull again, she felt it hit soft tissue. She had done it. He was dead.

Jane drew a deep breath and threw her head back so far that the feathers in her hair brushed her spine and her painted face glared up through the leaves at the sky. Then she let out a piercing whoop of triumph and gladness.

30

Jane staggered a few feet, fell to the ground, and began to cry. She cried in gratitude that she was alive, in relief that the killer was finally dead. She wept in mourning for the little gambler Harry, who had felt a knife brought across his throat by a man he had thought was his friend, and she keened for her lost, dead lover.

Then, as the sun rose higher into the tops of the trees, her tears stopped coming. She stood up, looked around her, and knew what she was going to do. She walked back to the enemy's camp and collected the tools she would need, then followed the path to the little stream of water that she had drunk from in the night. She rolled an old, rotten log down the bank into the stream to divert it from its course and then began to dig in the bed. The first few inches were small pebbles and gravel, and below them was mud. She packed the stones and mud against the log to make it into a dam. After an hour of digging, she was hip deep, and hit rock.

She couldn't bear to touch his hands, so she brought up his sleeping bag, rolled him over onto it with her foot, and dragged him down to the streambed. When she had covered the body and pushed the three feet of mud and stones over him, she pushed the log away and let the stream return to its course, first washing over the grave in a little flood and then in a muddy, cloudy stream. In a few minutes the water was clear again, as though it had never been disturbed since the mountains

315

first rose up from the earth. Then she walked back up the trail she had made for him, cut down the rest of the monofilament fishing line and the three hooks that hadn't caught his flesh, untied the bent sapling, and filled in the hole she had dug.

She walked back to the camp, ate his food, and drank water beside the beautiful black lake. Then she tossed the paddle, the car keys, and four days' worth of dried food into his canoe and pushed it to the edge of the lake to wait for her.

She found matches in his pack and collected all of the firewood he had gathered and built a big fire on a flat stone shelf above the water. She burned first his clothes, the wallet she had bought him with the identification that said he was John Young, then the rest of his packaged food, the tent, and the sleeping bag. She unloaded the rifle he had carried into the woods and pumped the shotgun he had used as a booby-trap to verify that it was empty, and placed them on the fire to burn off the wooden stocks and forepieces, then added the fishing pole to burn the cork handle and line and melt the fiberglass. Everything he had brought into the forest she took apart or cut into pieces and put into the fire.

When all of his possessions had burned, she brought more wood, built the fire bigger, and watched it burn to embers. She threw her bow, her arrows, and her war club into the fire too and watched them flare up and burn, then lay down to sleep on the bare ground twenty feet away.

When she woke up she saw that it was the middle of the afternoon. She walked to the edge of the lake and looked down into the water. She could see the reflection of her face, still streaked with green and black, and the black crow's feathers in her hair. She dived into the icy water, plunging into silence and darkness, then gave a kick and an armstroke and shot up through the surface.

She scrubbed herself and let the feathers float away, then climbed out and dried off in the warm sun on the rocks.

She walked to her fire and found that it had cooled. She scraped the embers off into the water with the canoe paddle, then collected the bits of metal and fire-altered plastic and put them into her quiver. As she made her last walk around the campsite to look for anything she had missed, she remembered the money. Whatever else James Michael Martin had done, he would not have been able to bring himself to leave the money. She searched the area again, then remembered that he would have hidden it before he had moved his camp, probably in the first hour after he had arrived at the lake.

She walked to his old campsite and searched in the places that fit his mind. It was not tied to a rope and put in a watertight container weighted with rocks to hang under the surface of the lake. It was not high in any of the trees close enough for him to keep an eye on it. Then she noticed that his old campfire looked different from the one in his new camp.

He had built the new one in a pit. The charred wood and ashes of this one were on a level spot near the place where his tent had been. She pushed the charcoal debris aside and dug down an inch, where she found a thick bundle sealed in a moisture-proof plastic bag. Inside the bag was the pack she had given him the night they had run to Olcott, and inside the pack was the money. The remains of a fire had been moved here and placed on top of the buried money. If something happened to him, the ones who had come for him would probably spend some time looking for the money. When they didn't find it, they would camp and build a fire. The place they would probably choose was the site of his old fire: just add some new wood and set a match to it. After an hour or so, the money would be gone. She reached into the pack, picked up one of the green stacks, and read the white band the bank had put around it. The print said, "ten thousand dollars." There were thirty-five identical stacks of hundreds. He had been confident enough to hide all of it in one place.

Jane carried the bag of money to his canoe, pushed off, and began to paddle out of the wilderness. As she moved the canoe back up the chain of lakes, she stopped every hour or two, put down her paddle, and dropped something into the deepest places: the rifle barrel and action into Lake Lila, the shotgun barrel into Round Lake, the melted fishing pole and loose eyelets into Little Tupper, each fragment miles from the last one.

At the portage she had to drag the canoe for part of the way, because it was too heavy for her to carry. When she felt tired, she rested. It took her almost four days to emerge from the forest onto big Tupper Lake.

She had no way to get rid of the canoe, so she paddled to the Bronco, dug up the battery cables, took the plastic bottles of gasoline off the exhaust manifold and poured them into the tank, loaded the canoe onto the roof, and drove out of the mountains. She reached Lake George after dark and left the canoe at the edge of the water there.

She used the cash from John Young's wallet to buy gas in Glens Falls, clothes in Saratoga Springs, and a gigantic meal of pancakes and eggs on the outskirts of Albany. The coffee tasted so good that she bought a sixteen-ounce cup of it to drink in the car.

A few hours later, she carefully wiped the Bronco clean inside and out while she washed it at a coin-operated car wash in Yonkers. Then she left it parked on the street with the keys in the ignition in Queens near La Guardia. It wasn't a neighborhood where she could be certain the Bronco would be stolen and disappear forever into the world of chop shops, but it might, and if the police noticed it before the thieves, it wouldn't matter. It led only to a person who had never existed. If the police started making a list of other people who might have left it there, they would begin with ones who had taken flights out of La Guardia. She walked to the waiting area outside the terminal, took a cab from La Guardia to Kennedy, and bought a ticket for the next plane to Rochester.

It was after three in the morning when she parked the rental car on the quiet street and walked across the thick grass to the railing. She looked down into the deep chasm at the place where the longhouses had once stood, all running east to west beside the winding stream of the Genesee. She listened, and this time the city was so quiet that she could hear the water down there, running into the rocks and curving around at the far bank to head north to Lake Ontario.

In the old days the people would have been asleep in the longhouses. Probably, on a cool night like this one she would have been able to smell a little smoke coming up from the coals of the fires. Up here in the cornfields the ground would be bare. Very soon it would be time for Ayentwata, the planting festival, so the women would have begun to turn the ground with digging sticks to prepare it for seeding.

She heard a dog in a yard a block away give a low bark, and then another dog joined him in a pained, crooning howl. "It's only me," she whispered. A few seconds later, the low wail of a fire engine's siren moving past on St. Paul Boulevard reached the range of human hearing and then diminished.

She walked on along the railing to the place above the rocks. She opened her pack and took out the two big pouches of Captain Black's pipe tobacco that she had bought in the shop at the airport. She opened the first and held it out over the cliff, then shook it to let the shreds pour down into the chasm and spread in their long fall to the rocks where the Jo-Ge-Oh lived. "This isn't the stuff you're used to, little guys," she whispered, "but it must be good because my father used to smoke it." She opened the second package and poured it down to them. "He was Henry Whitefield."

Then she picked up the knapsack and unzipped the top. She held it out over the railing. "Thank you for my life." She turned the knapsack upside down. In the moonlight, she could see the hundreds of pieces of paper money fall, turn, flutter like butterflies, and drift down toward the dark water below.

She carried the knapsack as far as the trash barrel at the edge of the park and left it there. Then she got into the rental car and drove back down the street toward Mt. Read Boulevard. At this time of night she expected she could make it most of the way to the Thruway entrance without running into any traffic.

Jane Whitefield came up the sidewalk in Deganawida in the early morning, wearing the new outfit she had bought in Saratoga Springs. She saw that Jake Reinert was watching her from the old wooden swing on his porch. She walked up the steps and sat down beside him.

"Glad to see you, Janie," he said. "You might even say relieved."

"Me too."

He looked off into the distance at the big old trees planted along Franklin Street, swaying a little in the breeze and fluttering their thousands of leaves. "The fellows we met in California never came to see you."

"I didn't think they would." She patted his arm and stood up to go to her own house, but he stood up too, looking a little nervous.

"The person who did come was a fellow a bit older than you. He came in the middle of the night, like they always do. He had a little boy with him, looked to be about six or seven. He was scared . . ." Jane looked at Jake, waiting for the rest of it. "They're back in my kitchen now, eating some breakfast."

1

The tall, slim woman hastily tied her long, dark hair into a knot behind her head, planted her feet in the center of the long courthouse corridor, and waited. A few litigants and their attorneys passed her, some of them secretly studying her, more because she was attractive than because she was standing motionless, forcing them to step around her on their way to the courtrooms. Her chest rose and fell in deep breaths as though she had been running, and her eyes looked past them, having already dismissed them before they approached as she stared into the middle distance.

She heard the chime sound above the elevator thirty feet away. Before the doors had fully parted, three large men in sportcoats slipped out between them and spun their heads to stare up the hallway. All three seemed to see her within an instant, their eyes widening, then narrowing to focus, and then becoming watchful and predatory, losing any hint of introspection as they began to move toward her, one beside each wall and one in the middle, increasing their pace with each step.

Several bystanders averted their eyes and sidestepped to avoid them, but the woman never moved. She hiked up the skirt of her navy blue business suit so it was out of her way, took two more deep breaths, then swung her shoulder bag hard at the first man's face.

The man's eyes shone with triumph and eagerness as he snatched the purse out of the air. The triumph turned

to shock as the woman slipped the strap around his
forearm and used the momentum of his charge to haul
him into the second man, sending them both against the
wall to her right. As they caromed off it, she delivered
a kick to one and a chop to the other to put them on the
floor. This bought her a few heartbeats to devote to the
third man, who was moving along the left wall to get
behind her.

She leaned back and swung one leg high. The man
read her intention, stopped, and held up his hands to
clutch her ankle, but her back foot left the ground and
she hurled her weight into him. As her foot caught him
at thigh level and propelled him into the wall, there was
the sickening crack of his knee popping. He crumpled
to the floor and began to gasp and clutch at his crippled
leg as the woman rolled to the side and sprang up.

The first two men were rising to their feet. Her fist
jabbed out at the nearest one and she rocked him back,
pivoted to throw an elbow into the bridge of his nose,
and brought a knee into the second man's face.

There was a loud slapping sound and the woman's
head jerked nearly to her left shoulder as a big fist
swung into her cheekbone. Strong arms snaked around
her from behind, lifted her off her feet to stretch her
erect, and she saw the rest as motion and flashes. The
first two men rushed at her in rage, aiming hard round-
house punches at her head and face, gleeful in the cer-
tainty that she saw the blows coming but could do
nothing to block them or even turn to divert their
force.

Two loud, deep voices overlapped, barking for dom-
inance. "Police officers! Freeze!" "Step away from
her!" When her opponents released her and stepped
away, she dropped to her knees and covered her face
with her hands. In a moment, several bystanders who
had stood paralyzed with alarm seemed to awaken.
They were drawn closer by some impulse to be of use,

but they only hovered helplessly nearby without touching her or speaking.

The judge's chambers were in shadow except for a few horizontal slices of late-afternoon sunlight that shone through the blinds on the wood-paneled wall. Judge Kramer sat in his old oak swivel chair with his robe unzipped but with the yoke still resting on his shoulders. He loosened his tie and leaned back, making the chair's springs creak, then pressed the PLAY button on the tape recorder.

There were sounds of chairs scraping, papers shuffling, and a garble of murmured conversation, so that the judge's empty chamber seemed to be crowded with invisible people. A female voice came from somewhere too close to the microphone. "This deposition is to be taken before Julia R. Kinnock, court stenographer at 501 North Spring Street, Los Angeles, California, at ten ... seventeen A.M. on November third. The court's instructions were that if there is an objection to the use of a tape recorder, it will be turned off." There was silence. "Will the others in the room please identify themselves."

"David M. Schoenfeld, court-appointed counsel to Timothy Phillips." Schoenfeld's voice was smooth, and each syllable took too long to come out. Judge Kramer could almost see him leaning into the microphone to croon.

"Nina Coffey, Department of Children's Services, Los Angeles County, in the capacity of guardian for a minor person." Kramer had read her name on a number of official papers, but he had never heard her voice before. It was clear and unapologetic, the words quick and clipped, as though she were trying to guard against some kind of vulnerability.

"Kyle Ambrose, Assistant District Attorney, Los Angeles." As usual, the prosecutor sounded vaguely confused, a pose that had irritated Kramer through six or seven long trials.

Then came the low, monotone voices that were at once self-effacing and weighty, voices of men who had spent a lot of time talking over radios. They started quietly and grew louder, because the last part of each name was the important part.

"Lieutenant James E. Bates, Los Angeles Police Department."

"Agent Joseph Gould, Federal Bureau of Investigation."

There was some more shuffling of papers and then Julia Kinnock said, "Mr. Ambrose, do you wish to begin?"

Ambrose's parched, uncertain voice came in a beat late. "Will you state your name for the record, please?"

There was some throat clearing, and then the high, reedy voice of a young boy. "Tim ... Timothy John Phillips."

Schoenfeld's courtroom voice intoned, "Perhaps it would be a good idea to ask that the record show that Lieutenant Bates and Agent Gould here present have verified that the deponent's fingerprints match those of Timothy John Phillips, taken prior to his disappearance."

The two voices muttered, "So verified," in the tone of a response in a church. Amen, thought Kramer. Schoenfeld had managed to sidestep onto the record with the one essential fact to be established in the case from Schoenfeld's point of view.

Ambrose's voice became slow and clear as he spoke to the boy. "You are to answer of your own accord. You are not to feel that you are in any way obligated to tell us things you don't want to." Judge Kramer could imagine Ambrose's dark eyes flicking to the faces of Schoenfeld, the lawyer, and Nina Coffey, the social worker. It was a confidence game, as Ambrose's legal work always was. The kid would have to answer all of the questions at some point, but Ambrose was trying to put the watchdogs to sleep. "Mr. Schoenfeld is here as your lawyer, so if you have any doubts, just ask him. And Mrs. Coffey will take you home if you're too tired. Do you understand?"

The small, high-pitched voice said, "Yes."

"How old are you?"

"Eight."

"Can you tell me, please, your earliest recollections?" Judge Kramer clenched his teeth.

"You mean, ever?"

"Yes."

"I remember . . . I guess I remember a lot of things. Christmas. Birthdays. I remember moving into our house in Washington."

"When was that?"

"I don't know."

A male voice interjected, "The lease on the Georgetown house began four years ago on January first. That was established during the murder investigation. He would have been four." The voice would be that of the F.B.I. agent, thought the judge.

"Do you remember anything before that, in another house?"

"No, I don't think so."

"When you moved in, was Miss Mona Turley already with you?"

"I don't know. I guess so."

"Who lived there?"

"My parents, me, Mona."

"Did you have relatives besides your parents? Cousins or uncles?"

"No, just my grandma."

"Did you ever see her?"

"Not that I remember. She lived far away. We used to send her a Christmas card every year."

"Did you?" There was the confusion again, as though Ambrose were hearing it for the first time and trying to fathom the implications.

"Yeah. I remember, because my daddy would put my handprint on it. He would write something, and then he would squish my hand onto a stamp pad and press it on the card, because I couldn't write yet."

Ambrose hesitated, then said gently, "Do you remember anybody else? Any other grown-ups that you were with?"

"You mean Mr. and Mrs. Phillips?"

"Yes."

"I know about them. I don't think I ever saw them."

"So when you say your 'parents' you mean Raymond and Emily Decker?"

"They were my mother and father."

Judge Kramer's brows knitted in distaste. This was typical of Ambrose. Get on with it, he thought. An eight-year-old's distant recollections weren't going to get Ambrose anything in a criminal investigation. Such meticulous, redundant questioning had bought him an inflated reputation as a prosecutor—laying the groundwork for an unshakable, brick-hard case. It looked like magic to juries, but to Judge Kramer and the opposing attorneys who knew where he was going, it was like watching an ant carrying single crumbs until he had a hero sandwich.

"So you lived in Washington from the time you were four until . . . ? We'll get back to that. Tell me what it was like in Washington. Did you like it?"

"It was okay."

"Were your parents . . . nice to you?"

There was a hint of shock in the boy's voice. "Sure."

"How about discipline? Rules. Were there rules?"

"Yeah."

"Can you tell me some?"

"Ummm . . . Pick up the toys. Brush your teeth. My

father always brushed his teeth when I did, and then he'd show me his fillings and tell me I'd need some if I didn't brush the ones in the back."

"What happened when you didn't follow the rules?" Ambrose was casual. "Did they hit you?"

Now the little voice was scandalized. "No."

"Did you go to school?"

"Sure. The Morningside School. It wasn't far, so sometimes we walked."

"So life was pretty good in Washington?"

"Yeah."

"What did you do when you weren't in school?"

"I don't know. Mona used to take me to the park when I was little, and then later sometimes I'd go with my friends. She would sit in the car and wait for me."

Ambrose paused and seemed to be thinking for a long time, but then Judge Kramer recognized the sound of someone whispering. After a second exchange it sounded angry. He knew it was Nina Coffey. The lawyer Schoenfeld said, "I must point out that this is not an adversarial proceeding, and this part of the story adds no new information to any of the investigations in progress. Miss Coffey has consented to this questioning because she was assured its purpose was for the safety and future welfare of the child. She has a right to withdraw the consent of the Department of Children's Services if she feels this is unnecessarily traumatic. The child has been over this ground several times with the psychologist and the juvenile officers already. Perhaps we could depart from our regular habits of thoroughness and skip to the recent past."

Ambrose sounded defensive. "Then would one of you care to help us in that regard to make the record comprehensible?"

Nina Coffey said, "Timmy, tell me if anything I say isn't true."

"Okay."

"Timmy was raised from the time of his earliest rec-ollections until the age of six by Raymond and Emily Decker. They hired Miss Mona Turley as a nanny when they came to Washington, D.C. He has no direct knowl-edge of earlier events. He was told he was Timmy Decker. From every assessment, he had a normal early childhood. It was a loving home. Miss Turley was a British citizen and a trained nanny, a legal resident alien. There are no signs of physical or psychological abuse, or of developmental difficulties that would indi-cate deprivation of any kind." She said pointedly, "This is all covered in the caseworker's report, so it already is part of the record."

Judge Kramer felt like applauding. His finger had been hovering over the FAST FWD button, but he knew that he wouldn't have let it strike. Either you listened to all of it or you were just another politician in a costume.

Ambrose went on. "All right. Now, Timmy, we have to talk about some unpleasant things, and I'll try to keep it short. What happened on the afternoon of July twenty-third two years ago?"

"I don't know."

Schoenfeld prompted. "That was the day when they died."

"Oh," said Timmy. "Mona and I went to the shoe store after school. Usually we came home at three, but that day we didn't. After we bought the shoes we walked in and everything had changed. I remember Mona opened the door, and then she stopped and went, 'Uh!' Like that. Then she made me wait outside while she went in alone. She was inside a long time. I thought it was a surprise, and she was telling my parents I was there so they could hide. So I went around to the side of the house and looked in the window. And I saw them." His voice cracked, and the judge could hear that he was trying to keep the sob from coming out of his throat in front of all these strange adults, so it just stayed there, with the muscles clamping it in place. Judge Kramer had heard a lot of testimony that had to be forced out through that kind of throat, so he had become expert.

"They were covered with blood. I never knew so much blood came out of a person. It was everywhere. The walls, the floor. I could see Mona was in the next room on the telephone. Then she hung up and walked into my bedroom. I ran around to that window, and it was broken. All my stuff was gone."

"What do you mean 'stuff'?"

"My toys, my clothes, my books, everything. They stole my stuff. She kept looking around my room and frowning."

"What then?"

"She looked up and saw me. She ran out of the house and grabbed me. She took me to the car and we drove away."

"What did she say about it?"

"She started to say that my parents were called away, but I told her I saw them."

"What did she say then?"

"She said that awful things sometimes happen, and a bunch of stuff about how they wanted me to be safe more than anything. I didn't hear a lot of it because I was crying and wasn't really listening."

"Where did she take you?"

"She had a friend. A man. He used to come to the house to pick her up sometimes. She said he was a lawyer. She took me to his house."

"For the record, do you know his name?"

"Dennis."

"Was his last name Morgan?"

"Yes."

"Do you know the name of the street?"

"No. It wasn't anyplace I ever was before. We drove

a long time on a big road, and then at the end there were a lot of turns. By then it was night."

"What happened there?"

"She put me to sleep on the couch, but I could hear them talking in the kitchen."

"What did they say?"

"She told him about my parents. She said it looked like an abuttar."

Abattoir, the judge translated. No wonder Nina Coffey was all over Ambrose. This kid had looked in his own window and seen his parents—or the ones he knew as parents—lying on the floor butchered, and Ambrose was asking him about spankings and dental hygiene. The man was a dangerous idiot.

"What did he say?"

"He said she did the right thing to call the police, and the wrong thing to leave. Then she said a lot of things. She said it looked as though whoever came in wasn't even looking for them. They were looking for me."

"What made her say that?"

"They broke into my room at a time when I was usually home and my parents weren't. She said it looked like they tried to make my parents tell them something. And then the only things they took were my stuff, and all the pictures."

"What pictures were those?"

"My father used to take a lot of pictures. Like when we were at the beach ..." Here it comes, thought the judge. The sob forced its way out, and there was a squealing sound, and then the tears came in volume.

"Come on, Timmy," said Nina Coffey. "Let's go take a break."

Amid the sounds of chairs scraping and feet hitting the floor, Ambrose said redundantly, "Let the record show that we recessed at this point."

There was another click, and the recording began

again. "We will continue now. It is six minutes after eleven," said the stenographer.

Ambrose said, "Timmy, I'm sorry to ask so many sad questions."

"It's okay," said the little voice. There was no conviction behind it.

"You were at the lawyer's house. They didn't agree, right?"

"He told her to go to the police. Mona said they would just make me stay in a place where I wouldn't be safe. They talked for a long time, and I fell asleep."

"What happened when you woke up?"

"The lawyer—Dennis—he was talking on the telephone. I couldn't hear what he was saying. When he hung up, he and Mona talked some more. He gave her some money. He had a lot of money inside of books on the bookshelf, and some in his pocket. He gave her that too."

"Then what?"

"The phone rang and Dennis answered it, and talked to somebody else. Then we all got in the car and Dennis drove. This time we drove all night and all the next day, almost. Then we got to Jane's house."

"What is Jane's full name?"

"I don't know."

"Where does she live?"

"I don't know."

"Tell me about her."

"We went to her house. She put us in a room upstairs, and we went to sleep. When I woke up, she made us breakfast. Mona was already awake."

"I mean about Jane. What was she like?"

"I was afraid of her at first."

"Why?"

"She was tall and skinny and had long black hair, and she seemed to listen to people with her eyes."

Ambrose paused. "I see. What did she do?"

"She and Mona talked for a long time. Then I heard her say she would make us disappear."

"Is that why you thought she was scary?"

"No . . . maybe."

"How long did you stay with Jane?"

"A long time. I think Mona said it was three weeks, but it seemed like a year. Then we all got in Jane's car and she drove us to Chicago."

"What did she do then?"

"She stayed for a day or two, and then one morning I woke up and she was gone."

"Was Mona surprised?"

"No. Mona acted like it was normal, and didn't talk about her again. Mona and I lived in Chicago after that. Mona was Diana Johnson, and I was her son. She wanted me to be Andrew, but I didn't like it, so I got to stay Tim."

"How did you live?"

"Like people do."

"I mean, did Mona have a job—did she go to work?"

"Yes. While I was in school."

"They called you Tim Johnson at school?"

"Yes."

"When did you start—what grade?"

"Kindergarten. I had already been in kindergarten, so it was the second time."

"And you're in the second grade now?"

"Yes."

"Were you afraid in Chicago?"

"At first I was. It was different. I was afraid the bad people would get Mona, and then I would be all alone. But after a while I made some friends, and got used to it, and I didn't think about that part much anymore. I was sad sometimes."

"And Mona pretended to be your mother for over two years?"

"I guess so."

"What else did she do? Did she still see anybody you knew from Washington?"

"No. She used to talk on the phone a lot."

"To whom? Jane?"

"No. Dennis."

"Did you ever hear what she said?"

"Once in a while, but it wasn't really okay. She would go in her bedroom and talk to him. Sometimes she would tell me what she said."

"Then a little over a week ago something changed, didn't it?"

"Yes. Everything."

"You found out who you were, didn't you?"

"Yes."

"Excuse me, Mr. Ambrose." It was Schoenfeld's resonant voice again. "Maybe we should let Timmy tell us exactly what happened in his own words from here on. I believe you've done an admirable job in laying the groundwork, but now we're in new territory, and I have no objection to letting Mr. Phillips speak freely and tell us whatever he can that will aid in the possible prosecutions." Of course not, thought the judge. Schoenfeld could be magnanimous. He had already established that Timmy was Mr. Phillips, and nothing else that anyone said or did from there on was of any consequence for Schoenfeld.

"Thank you," said Ambrose. "Timmy, tell us what happened."

"I came home from school, and Mona was there, and so was Dennis the lawyer, and so was Jane. Dennis said he had spent two years trying to figure out why anyone would want to hurt my parents and me, and now he knew."

"This was in Chicago?"

"Yeah," said Timmy. "He told me that when my mother died they had special doctors look at her, and that she had never been to the hospital to have a baby.

He said he got to look at a copy of the birth certificate they had at my school, and it wasn't real. He said I wasn't adopted. They just drew a picture of a birth certificate and said it was mine. He said that the reason they did that was because they loved me very much and had always wanted a little boy."

Judge Kramer stopped the tape and backed it up to listen to the last exchange again. It was a hell of a way to explain a kidnapping. In spite of everything, he had to admire Dennis Morgan. After what he had seen, this little boy was going to be an annuity for the psychiatrists for the next fifty years. There was no reason to make it worse.

The tape kept running. "Then he told you about your other parents?"

"Yes. Mr. and Mrs. Phillips. They died when I was one."

"And your grandma?"

"I knew about her already, but I didn't know she had died like all my parents. She had been dead for three years."

"Did Mr. Morgan tell you that she had left you some money?"

"Yeah. He said that when Mr. and Mrs. Phillips died she put all the family money in a big pot and said it could only go to me. And when I was gone she hired a company to take care of the money and keep looking for me forever."

"Did she say what they were called?"

"Trusty."

Judge Kramer prayed that Ambrose wasn't about to drag an eight-year-old on a field trip through a morass of legal terminology. What could the child possibly know about trustees and executors?

"What happened last week to change that? Did he tell you?"

"He said that the Trusty had gotten tired of looking

and waiting, and they were going to say I wasn't alive anymore. So he called Jane again."

"I'm very curious about this Jane. I understand about Mona. She was your nanny, and she loved you. The lawyer, Mr. Morgan, was a very close friend of Mona's, right?"

"Yeah. They were going to get married when the people came and got my parents. Then they couldn't because we'd get caught. That was why he looked so hard to find out where I was really supposed to be—so Mona could go back to being Mona and marry him."

"But why was Jane doing it? Did she know your parents?"

"No. Mona had to tell her about them that time when we went to her house. Mona thought they worked for the government, so the people who hurt them must be spies. It took Jane a long time to find out that my parents didn't work for the government."

"Then Jane was Mona's friend?"

"I don't think so. Dennis was the one who called her."

Judge Kramer could image the F.B.I. agent. He was going to make his career sorting all this out. Not the least interesting question was why a prominent Washington defense attorney had the telephone number of a woman who made people disappear. They would be going over the record of Morgan's former clients right now to see if there were any on their Most Wanted List.

Even Ambrose seemed to sense that he had crossed the trail of an unfamiliar creature. "The lawyer knew her?" he repeated. "Did he pay her?"

"No. Dennis said he tried, but she had decided that so many people loved me that I must be a fine boy."

"Hmmmm . . ."

Judge Kramer had a vision of Ambrose's raised eyebrows, as he had seen them during cross-examinations.

"Did anybody say anything else about her?"

"Dennis. He said that from then on we had to do everything that Jane said, exactly. It didn't matter what anybody else said, we should listen to her."

"So she was the boss."

"He said that he had done everything he could to find out things, but the only way to solve this was to walk into court and surprise everybody and say who I was. He said the bad people knew I must be alive, so they would be expecting me to come. Jane was the one who knew how to get us past them."

"So you all took an airplane to California?"

"No. Jane said we had to drive all the way or the bad people might see us. Every day we got a new car. She would go to a place where they rented them, and then drive all day and then leave it and rent another one. Then we were in California."

"What then? Did you stay in a hotel?"

"No. Jane said that if people were after me, they would be watching hotels near the courthouse, because they would be expecting us to do that. So we went to the courthouse right away."

"What time was it?"

"About dinnertime. Jane opened the lock on an office and we stayed there all night. I fell asleep on a couch."

"What happened when you woke up?"

"I heard Dennis come into the office. He had been out in the building by himself. He said they had pulled a trick on us, and now we had to go to a different building. So we ran out and got into our car and drove again. Jane said on the way that it didn't feel right."

"Did she say anything else?"

"She asked Dennis if there was any way of doing this besides actually showing up in court. Could we call and ask for a delay or something. He said that he didn't know who was honest and who wasn't. A phone call wouldn't stop the case for sure, but it would tell the bad guys I was coming for sure. Then he said if they fooled

the judge they could do something that day, right away.
I don't know what. Jane drove for a long time without
saying anything. Then she said, 'Is there any way to
know what's in the building?' "

"What did she mean by that?"

"She said, 'We want to fade in. If Timmy's the only
boy in the crowd, we're in trouble.' She said something
about adoption and custody."

"I see," said Ambrose. "Did Mr. Morgan know the
answer?"

"We stopped at a phone booth and he looked in
the book and made a call. He came back and got into
the car and made Jane scoot over, so he could drive. He
said he and Mona would be getting a divorce before
they got married, and Jane would carry his briefcase
like she was their lawyer. But we would go to Courtroom 22 on the fifth floor instead."

"Did Jane agree?"

"At first. But then we got near the courthouse, and
Jane said two men in a car were following us. They
kept coming faster and faster, and then they tried to get
in front of us, and they bumped the car."

"What did Mr. Morgan do?"

"He got all nervous, and kept trying to go fast and
keep the car straight. Jane said to him, 'Well? What's it
going to be?' and he said, 'I can't get them into the
building. It's got to be me.' He was scared. He looked
pale and sick and sweaty."

"And Jane?"

"She was quiet. He drove to the parking lot and
stopped. Mona kissed him, and Jane yanked me out the
door and we started running."

"Did you see what Mr. Morgan did after you were
out of the car?"

"I heard this loud bang, and I turned around and it
looked like what he had done was go backwards into
the other car. One of the men jumped out and started

hitting him. He tried to fight but he wasn't good at it. And the other man got out of the car and ran after us, so Dennis tried to tackle him, but the man kicked him, and the first one grabbed him around the neck. I didn't see any more because Jane and Mona and I were running and I tripped, but Jane held my hand and kept me from falling. We ran up the steps."

"Did anyone try to stop you?"

"There was a man on the other side of the glass door, and he saw us and put his foot against it so it wouldn't open. Jane didn't stop. She let go of me and hit it with her shoulder and stuck her purse in it when it opened a little. The man put his arm there to push the purse out, but as soon as his arm was in there she jerked the purse out by the strap and shut the door on his arm. When he pulled the handle to get his arm out, she pushed the door into his face and we ran on."

"Anybody else?"

"There were men right by the elevator, and they started coming toward us. We ran up the stairs. I counted four flights, but there was a door and it only had a two on it. We ran through it, and when we passed the elevator Jane pushed the button and ran to another staircase, and we got up to the third floor. We got to the fourth floor, and we heard a door below us slam open against the wall, and some men were running up after us. Mona was breathing hard and then she was crying too. She touched my arm at the top of the next landing and said, 'This is my stop. Keep going. I love you, Timmy.' "

"What did Jane say?"

"Nothing. She just looked at her, and then we ran up to the fifth floor. Just when we got to the top, I looked back and saw Mona on the stairs. She was holding on to both railings and kicking at these men. I saw one of them reaching out like he was trying to hug her. But right then, the door that said five swung open right in front of us. It was one of the men that was by the elevator. He looked surprised, and Jane just punched him and kept going."

"She hit him in the jaw?" The judge could sense Ambrose's raised eyebrow again.

"No. In the neck. Then we were on the fifth floor, and we ran down this long hallway. When we got to the corner I could see 'TWENTY TO THIRTY' painted on the wall with an arrow pointing to the left, but the door we had used to get there opened up again and three big men were running after us. Jane jerked me around the corner and said, 'Run to the room that says twenty-two. Don't stop for anybody until you're right in the front where the judge sits, and yell, "I'm Timothy Phillips." ' I tried to say something, but she said, 'Don't talk, just run.' "

Judge Kramer pushed the STOP button and sat in his dark office. He had been on the bench when the little boy had burst through the doors and run up the aisle screaming. The bailiff had made a reasonably competent attempt to head him off, but he had actually touched the bench and yelled, "I'm Tim Phillips." What had happened in the hallway Judge Kramer had heard from one of the policemen who had piled out of the adjoining courtrooms to quell the disturbance.

Judge Kramer pressed the intercom button on his telephone.

"Yes, Judge?" came his assistant's voice.

"Where are they holding this 'Jane' woman?"

"I think they took her for medical treatment to County-USC. I'll find out if she's in the jail ward and let you know."

"No," Kramer said. "Just call the precinct and tell them I want to see her."

"Would you like a conference room at the jail?"

"Have them bring her here."

* * *

The male police officer was tall and rangy, and the female was short and blond with her hair drawn up in the back and cinched in that way they all knew how to do. The department never had all-male teams transport a female prisoner anymore, so the judge should have been used to it, but the pairs still seemed to him like married couples from a planet where people wore uniforms. They ushered the prisoner into his chambers. When her face came into the light he felt his breath suck in. He had never gotten used to seeing a young woman's face with bruises and cuts and blackened eyes. He tried to see past them.

She was not quite what he had heard described on the tape. She was tall, as tall as he was if he stood up, and this realization made him intuit that it was better not to, so he stayed down behind his big desk. Her hair was black and hung loose to a place below her shoulder blades, but that probably wasn't the way she wore it; they had combed it out because they always searched women's hair. He could see that Timmy's description was not wrong, just uninformed. This woman had the strange, angular beauty he associated with fashion models: it was striking, but geometric and cold. The judge's taste ran more to women like his late wife and the little policewoman, who looked round and soft and warm. The woman's hands were cuffed in front of her instead of behind, which meant they weren't taking all the precautions, but the police officers were wary: the policewoman kept a hand at her left elbow, and the man was a step behind and to her right, leaving just enough room to swing his club.

Judge Kramer said, "Thank you very much, officers. We've got some coffee in the outer office, and I keep soft drinks in the little refrigerator under the water cooler. I'll be finished with the prisoner in about fifteen minutes."

The policewoman said, "Your Honor, we should mention—"

He interrupted, "I know. I spoke with the arresting officer. Has she hurt anyone since she's been in custody?"

"No."

"Then I'll chance it."

The prisoner held out her hands, and the male officer unlocked the cuffs, took them off, and said to no one in particular, "We'll be right outside."

When they had closed the door, Judge Kramer said to her, "Sit down, please."

The woman sat in the chair in front of the desk.

Judge Kramer probed for a way to break the silence. "I hear you're one of those people who could kill me with a pencil."

She said simply, "If I am, then I wouldn't need a pencil." She looked at the tape recorder on his desk. "Is that running?"

He said, "I want to assure you that no record will be made of this conversation. I just listened to a deposition of Timothy Phillips, and I decided that the only person left who can answer the questions I have is you. Mona Turley and Dennis Morgan are dead."

She nodded silently and watched him.

"What do you know about the child's situation?"

"Who are you? Why are you the one who has questions?"

His eyes widened involuntarily, as though someone had thrown a glass of water in his face. "I'm sorry," he said. "When you've been a judge for a few years, you're used to being the only one in the room everyone takes at face value. My name is John Kramer. I'm the judge who was presiding in Courtroom 22. We hadn't gotten to the petition to declare Timothy Phillips legally dead when he ran in and disrupted my court. For the

moment, the matter is still undecided, and I've left it
that way."

"Why?"

"First I had to recess while the officers took you
away. Then I had to adjourn for a few days to give time
to the authorities who can verify Timothy's claim. In a
day or so, oddly enough, I have to set a date to give the
petitioners the opportunity to refute the claim—
fingerprints, blood tests, and all. Then I have to rule on
it."

"Will you be the one who decides what happens to
him after that?"

He shook his head. "Not directly. At the moment he's
in the care of a very protective woman from Children's
Services named Nina Coffey. After a time there will be
criminal cases—probably several of them. There will
be a family court case to decide who is granted guard-
ianship of Timmy. There will be some sort of civil action to settle the disposition of the trust. I can influence
the direction some of those cases take if I find out the
truth and get it on the record so it can't be ignored. I'm
asking what you know because I don't have much time
and I need to know where to begin. Once I rule on the
petition that's before me, it's out of my hands."

"Is any of this legal?"

"What I'm doing is so contrary to legal procedure
that it has no name."

She sat erect in the chair and met his gaze steadily
while she decided. "He was a ward of his grandmother
because his parents were killed in a car crash. She was
old at the time—about eighty. Whoever she hired to
watch him didn't. Along came Raymond and Emily
Decker, and he disappeared. I have no way of knowing
what was going on in their minds at the time. They may
have been kidnappers who stalked him from birth, or
they may have been one of those half-crazy couples
who create their own little world that doesn't need to

incorporate all of the facts in front of their eyes. If you read the old newspaper reports, it sounds as though maybe they just found him wandering around alone in a remote area of a county park, picked him up, and then convinced themselves that he was better off with them than with anybody who let a two-year-old get that lost. I've tried to find out, and so did Mona and Dennis, but what we learned was full of contradictions."

"What sorts of contradictions?"

"Timmy says they sent pictures of him to his grand-mother, sometimes holding a newspaper, sometimes with his fingerprints. He doesn't know what the letters said. If the Deckers knew where to send the letters, then they knew who he was. But I can't tell whether it was a straight ransom demand or they were trying to keep him officially alive so he could claim his inheritance when he grew up, or whether they were just being kind to an old lady by letting her know her grandson was okay."

"What do you know about the grandmother?"

"From what Dennis Morgan said, the police stopped looking. That means they never saw the letters. Grandma kept looking, so maybe she got them. She must have believed he would turn up eventually, be-cause she tied up all the family money in a living trust for him and made a business-management firm named Hoffen-Bayne the trustee. She died a few years ago."

"Before or after Raymond and Emily Decker?"

"Before. But I'm not the best source for dates and ad-dresses. I'm sure if you don't have it in the papers on your desk yet, it'll be in the next batch. Anyway, I don't think she hired somebody to kill them for kidnapping her grandson."

"You're the only source of information I have right now. Who did kill them?"

"I don't know."

"Who do you *think* did it?"

"When someone killed the Deckers, they also stole all of Timmy's belongings, every picture of him, and a lot of paper. If you're looking for somebody, you would want the photographs. But they took his toys, clothes, everything. That's a lot of work. The only reason I can think of for doing that is to hide the fact that he was alive—that a little boy lived there. Maybe they did such a good job of wiping off their own prints that they got all of his too, as a matter of course. I doubt it."

"Who would want to accomplish that?"

She hesitated, and he could tell she was preparing to be disbelieved. "What I'm telling you is not from personal knowledge. It's what Dennis Morgan told me. This company, Hoffen-Bayne, got to administer a fortune of something like a hundred million dollars. They would get a commission of at least two percent a year, or two million, for that. They also got to invest the money any way they pleased, and that gave them power. There are some fair-sized companies you can control for that kind of investment. As long as Timmy was lost, the trust would continue. You're a judge. You tell me what would happen if Timmy turned up in California."

"The court would—will—appoint a guardian, and probably in this case, a conservator, if you're right about the size of the inheritance."

"That wouldn't be Hoffen-Bayne?"

"We don't appoint business-management companies to raise children, or to audit themselves."

"Then the power and money would be in jeopardy."

"Certainly they would have to at least share the control."

"And they did try to have him declared dead."

"That's a legal convenience. It relieves them of responsibility to search for him, and also protects them if someone were to ask later why they're administering a trust for a client who hasn't been seen for seven years."

"Then it would have been even more convenient if he were really dead. They wouldn't have had to go to court at all."

"Filing a motion is a little different from hiring assassins to hunt down a six-year-old and kill him."

"Maybe. I think filing the motion was a trap. I think Dennis Morgan was poking around, and somebody noticed it. It's not all that hard to find out what you want about people; the trick is to keep them from knowing you're doing it. Dennis was a respected lawyer, but investigating wasn't his field; lawyers hire people to do that. I think they sensed that if a Washington attorney was interested, then Timmy was going to turn up sometime soon."

"And you—all of you—got caught in the trap?"

"Yes." She stood up. "You asked me what I think, so you would know where to begin. I've told you. Dennis couldn't find anybody but Hoffen-Bayne who would benefit from Timmy's death—no competing claims to the money or angry relatives, for instance. Nobody tried to break the will during all the years while Timmy was missing. But I don't know what Dennis got right and what he got wrong, and I can't prove any of it. I only saw the police putting handcuffs on four of the men in the courthouse, and there won't be anything on paper that connects them with Hoffen-Bayne or anybody else. I know I never saw them before, so I can't have been the one they recognized. They saw Timmy." She took a step toward the door. "Keep him safe."

The judge said, "Then there's you." He watched her stop and face him. "Who are you?"

"Jane Whitefield."

"I mean what's your interest in this?"

"Dennis Morgan asked me to keep Timmy alive. I did that. We all did that."

"What are you? A private detective, a bodyguard?"

"I'm a guide."

"What kind of guide?"

"I show people how to go from places where some-one is trying to kill them to other places where nobody is."

"What sort of pay do you get for this?"

"Sometimes they give me presents. I declare the pres-ents on my income taxes. There's a line for that."

"Did somebody give you a present for this job?"

"If you fail, there's nobody around to be grateful. My clients are dead." After a second she added, "I don't take money from kids, even rich kids."

"Have you served in your capacity as 'guide' for Dennis Morgan before?"

"Never met him until he called. He was a friend of a friend."

"You—all three of you—went into this knowing that whoever was near this little boy might be murdered."

She looked at him as though she were trying to de-cide whether he was intelligent or not. Finally, she said, "An innocent little boy is going to die. You're either somebody who will help him or somebody who won't. For the rest of your life you'll be somebody who did help him or somebody who didn't."

The judge stared down at his desk for a few seconds, his face obscured by the deep shadows. When he looked up, his jaw was tight. "You are a criminal. The system hates people like you. It has special teeth de-signed to grind you up."

As she watched him, she could see his face begin to set like a death mask. He pressed his intercom button. "Tell the officers to come in." He began to write, filling in lines on a form on his desk.

The two police officers swung the door open quickly and walked inside. The man had his right hand resting comfortably on the handle of the club in his belt.

The judge said, "I've finally straightened this out. Her real name is Mahoney. Colleen Anne Mahoney. She was attacked by those suspects on the way into the courthouse. Apparently it was a case of mistaken identity, because she had no connection with the Phillips case. I'm giving you a release order now, and I want all records—prints, photographs, and so on—sealed . . . no, destroyed. Call me when it's been done." He handed the female officer the paper. "I want to avoid any possibility of reprisals."

"Will do, Judge," said the policewoman. Kramer's instinct about her was confirmed. She had a cute little smile.

The policeman opened the door for Jane Whitefield, but this time nobody touched her. She didn't move. "You should have those teeth checked."

He shrugged. "The system was never meant to rule on every human action. Some things slip through."

She stared at him for a second, then said simply and without irony, "Thank you, Your Honor," turned, and walked out of his office.

DANCE FOR THE DEAD
is available in bookstores everywhere.

SHE WILL HELP YOU DISAPPEAR,
IF IT HELPS YOU STAY ALIVE . . .

The Jane Whitefield Novels

by

Thomas Perry

Published by Ivy Books.
Available in bookstores everywhere.

Jane Whitefield is a name to be whispered like a prayer. A shadow woman who rescues the helpless and the hunted when their enemies leave them no place to hide. Now, using the bone-deep cunning of her Native American forebears, she arranges a vanishing act for Pete Hatcher, a Las Vegas gambling executive.

SHADOW WOMAN

It should be a piece of cake, but she doesn't yet know about Earl and Linda—two professional destroyers who will cash in if Hatcher dies, killers who love to kill . . . slowly.

SHADOW WOMAN
by Thomas Perry

Jane Whitefield, legendary half-Indian shadow guide who spirits hunted people away from certain death, has never had a client like Dr. Richard Dahlman. A famous plastic surgeon who has dedicated his life to healing, the good doctor hasn't a clue why stalkers are out for his blood. But he knows Jane Whitefield's name—and that she is his only hope.

THE FACE-CHANGERS

Once again Jane performs her magic, leading Dahlman in a nightmare flight across America, only a heartbeat ahead of pursuers whose leader is a dead ringer for Jane: a raven-haired beauty who has stolen her name, reputation, and techniques—not to save lives, but to destroy them. . . .

THE FACE-CHANGERS
by Thomas Perry

Available April 1999 in bookstores everywhere.
Published by Ivy Books.